THE RAVEN'S HEAD

KAREN MAITLAND

headline
review

First published in Great Britain in 2015
by HEADLINE REVIEW
An imprint of HEADLINE PUBLISHING GROUP

1

Cataloguing in Publication Data is available from the British Library

ISBN 978 1 4722 1505 5 (Hardback)
ISBN 978 1 4722 1506 2 (Trade paperback)

Typeset in Adobe Garamond by Palimpsest Book Production Ltd, Falkirk, Stirlingshire

Printed and bound in Great Britain by Clays Ltd, St Ives plc

HEADLINE PUBLISHING GROUP
An Hachette UK Company
338 Euston Road
London NW1 3BH

www.headline.co.uk
www.hachette.co.uk

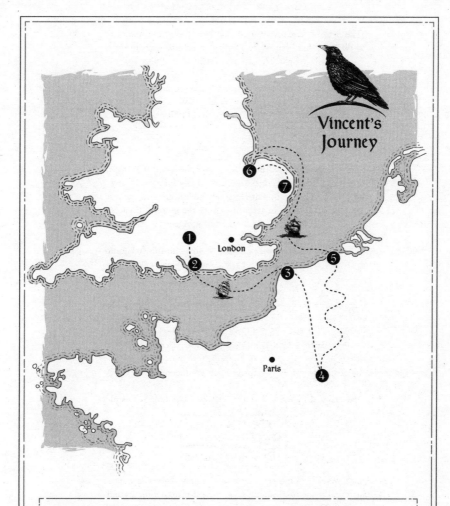

Vincent's Journey

Vincent's childhood journey

❶ ♂ Winchester
❷ ♄ Portsmouth
❸ ♃ Calais
❹ ☿ Châteaux Ricey-Bas

Vincent's adult journey

❺ ♀ Port of Hondsdamme (Damme)
❻ ☽ Bishop's Lynn (King's Lynn)
❼ ☉ Langley near river Yare

London

Paris

And know that the head of the art is the raven who flies without wings in the darkness and in the brightness of the day: in the bitterness that is in its throat the nigredo, the blackest of black, will be found.

From *Artis aurif,* 1610 edition

Take some 'stone'. Divide it into four parts – air, fire, earth and water. I am unable to discover that it can be done in any way other than the following. A human being lives, dies, and depends upon blood. Likewise the stone. Consequently they say that this stone is a living stone, and therefore because there is no higher soul than a human being, they take the stone of a human.

Avicenna, a Persian physician, (AD 980–1037)

One for sorrow
Two for mirth
Three for a funeral
Four for a birth
Five for heaven
Six for hell
The seventh takes your soul for the Devil to sell.

One of several versions of a traditional rhyme
for counting magpies, known as witch birds

Cast of Characters

England

Hudde – an under-forester
Meggy – Hudde's wife
Wilky – their five-year-old son
Jankin – one of Wilky's older brothers
Pouk – the dog

France

Vincent – seventeen-year-old apprentice to Gaspard
Gaspard – aged scribe and librarian in the household of Philippe
Philippe, Le Comte de Lingones – wealthy nobleman in the French court of King Louis VIII
Amée, La Comtesse de Lingones – Philippe's daughter
Estienne – Philippe's deceased great-grandfather
Hélène – Philippe's deceased great-grandmother
Charles – distant cousin of Philippe
Albertus – friend of Philippe who lives in Ricey

Langley Town, Norfolk

Gisa – fifteen-year-old niece and ward of an apothecary
Uncle Thomas – the apothecary, who owns a shop in Langley
Aunt Ebba – the apothecary's bed-ridden wife

Langley Abbey

Father Arthmael – abbot and leader of the Premonstratensians (White Canons)
Father John – brother in charge of the boys at the abbey
Felix – eleven years old and eldest of the boys being educated at the abbey
Mighel and Peter – youngest and smallest of the boys at the abbey
Father Madron – young Premonstratensian

Langley Manor

Lord Sylvain – baron and lord of the manor
Odo – Sylvain's manservant
Pipkin – Sylvain's cook
Isolda – Sylvain's daughter
Hamon – Isolda's lover

All of the quotations that head the chapters in the novel are taken from the writings of early Christian and Islamic alchemists.

Prologue

There is a secret stone, hidden in a deep well, worthless and rejected, concealed in dung and filth.

Only the long-eared owl watches in the forest tonight. And only the owl hears the hoofs of the two horses as they draw ever closer. It swivels its head to stare at the white-robed riders. Its great eyes blink. Then it launches itself on silent wings and is gone.

An angry wind rattles the branches of the trees, muffling the creak of leather and the crunch of iron shoes as the horses pad through the dried leaves. The cottage hunkers down, invisible among the twisted trunks. But even these ancient trees cannot conceal the tiny croft from the horsemen who are threading their way towards it. For it is whispered that the white riders can see as clearly at night as ordinary men can see by day, and little wonder, for the riders are masters of the blackest of the black.

In the cottage, the rush lights have long been extinguished and the fire damped down for the night. Behind the warped shutters, the family lie curled up around each other, sleeping. Only the dog lying by the hearth hears the approach of the two riders. It scrambles to its feet, the fur between its shoulder-blades raised. It sniffs at the crack beneath the door, then throws back its head and howls in fear.

'Quiet, Pouk,' Hudde mutters gruffly, sinking almost at once back into sleep.

But Meggy elbows her husband in the ribs. 'There's something out there.'

'Pigs come rootling for mast, is all,' Hudde says, without opening his eyes. He turns over as best he can in the narrow bed, and pulls the rough blanket over his head, trying to shut out his wife and the whining hound.

Outside, the two white riders swing themselves from their saddles, tether their horses a little way from the cottage and glide towards it, wading through a puddle of cold moonlight, their sandalled feet making no more sound in the dead leaves than the paws of wolves hunting.

Inside the cottage the dog runs anxiously back and forth. Then, as if it senses the staff being raised on the other side of the door, it backs into the far corner and crouches there, shivering.

The thump of the staff against the wood brings Hudde tumbling from his bed. He's on his feet before the echo dies away. Meggy, too, scrambles up, gathering her brood of children in her arms and hushing them. They cling to her and to each other in the dark room.

Their mother has often warned them that if they make a sound after they've been put to bed the lantern-man will come for them, reaching in through the window with his long arms to drag them out and carry them back to the marshes to drown them. They can only escape if they are quiet, for then he will not know there are children in the house and will pass on by. The children squeeze each other into silence, burying their faces in each other's arms for fear that the lantern-man will hear them breathe. But the white riders are not to be fooled as easily as the lantern-man and once more a staff hammers on the door.

2

Hudde snatches up his own stout stave.

'Who is it comes calling in the dead of night?' He sounds defiant, challenging, but Meggy knows him well enough to hear the apprehension concealed beneath the brave words. No human creature, save poachers or outlaws, would venture into the forest at this hour.

'Peace be upon this house,' a voice answers soothingly. 'Pray let us in, Master Hudde, it is a bitter night.' The man's tone is gentle, noble even.

Hudde relaxes slightly. He recognises the voice. The man has come here before. Perhaps he brings a message from Hudde's master, though a message that cannot wait till morning must be grave news indeed. Hudde drags on a pair of breeches and, with a taper touched to the embers of the fire, he lights the lantern that hangs ready trimmed by the door. Meggy fusses anxiously about her children, scrubbing at sleep-drooled mouths with the corner of a blanket, as if God Himself has come calling and she is ashamed to show her children to him unwashed.

No sooner has Hudde lifted the brace from the door than the two white-hooded figures step into the room, pressing the door closed behind them. The hound leaps forward with a growl, but the older of the two men merely turns and fixes the yellow eyes of the dog with an unblinking stare, holding out his hand flat above its head. The dog whimpers and, as if the man is pressing a great weight down onto it, sinks to its belly and shuffles back into the corner.

Both men stand quite still, their hands folded into the white sleeves of their robes, the hoods of their cloaks drawn over their heads. The younger man is scarcely more than a youth, though he has already learned to keep his body composed, save for a twitch at the corner of his left eye that

3

betrays a nervous excitement. The older man's chin is frosted with white stubble beneath a purple-veined nose. His expression betrays nothing of his thoughts, but his eyes quarter every inch of the tiny cottage, as if he is determined to examine all and forget nothing.

Hudde shuffles anxiously, wondering why the men don't announce their business at once. Perhaps they're expecting some meat or drink to be offered.

'We have only small ale, sirs, and some bread . . . we have bread and cheese . . .' He glances uncertainly at his wife, hoping that there is still some left from supper.

The man bows his head, acknowledging the proffered hospitality. 'My thanks to you, Master Hudde, but we require no refreshment. We have merely come for the boy. Make him ready to travel and we shall be on our way.'

His gaze sweeps over the huddled children and settles, heavy as a millstone, upon a small boy, whose shaggy locks blaze flame-red against the duller amber and rust-browns of his siblings.

Meggy's arm shoots out to pull the child to her side, grasping him so tightly that he squeals. She glances at her husband, silently urging him to say something, but he's just standing there dumbly, like one of his trees, so it's left to Meggy to protest.

'You've not come for him yet, surely.' She tenderly brushes a tangle of hair out of the boy's eyes.

'The child was promised to us,' the older man says. 'Your husband came to us on St Stephen's Day begging for more time to pay what he owed us for the grain we sold to him. The boy was offered in settlement. And, as agreed, you will receive food and coin every quarter day for the next seven years – that is,' he adds carefully, 'unless the boy dies.'

4

Hudde winces. The shame of that day still burns in him. It had cost him every scrap of pride he had left to admit that he couldn't pay what he owed. But he'd lost two months' wages after that poacher had put an arrow through his shoulder. The wound had turned foul and his body had burned with a fever, which had left him weak as a nestling. He'd tried to explain his misfortune to this man, but he'd only stared at Hudde with cold, dead eyes as if he was no better than an averer, faking sickness to steal alms.

Hudde had been certain his plea would be refused, but then a miracle had happened. The man's gaze had alighted on little Wilky clinging to his father's breeches. Ignoring Wilky's brothers, he'd reached out an arm and drawn the child close, his fingers probing the boy's head, limbs and body, as if he was inspecting a puppy for the potential to become a good hunting hound. With a deep sigh, he'd released Wilky, but he could barely tear his eyes from the boy.

'In settlement of your debt, we will take the boy and educate him,' the man announced curtly. 'In addition, you will receive a modest sum until the boy is twelve, for you doubtless have other debts to pay.'

Hudde was so bemused he thought at first they were asking him for money. The father pays the master to teach his son – that is always the way of it. It wasn't until the coins were thrust into his hand and his fist was guided to make a clumsy X on the parchment that he realised they were paying him!

He'd returned home giddy with relief and gratitude that they had cancelled the debt. But for days after he had brooded over the matter. He could not fathom why any man should give him money for the privilege of teaching his son.

5

Eventually, unable to make any sense of it, Hudde had stopped trying to reason it out, just as a man abandons a tangle of cord that is so badly knotted it can never be undone.

But now Hudde is finally goaded into speech. 'Aye, I did promise him right enough. But . . . see, our Wilky's nowt but five summers old. I thought he'd be with us another two years at least, maybe more.'

'And what would be the point of that?' the man says. 'Can you afford to keep seven children through another hard winter? Suppose another accident should befall you. Safe in our care, the boy will be fed and clothed, and will be taught his letters. The sooner he begins, the faster he will learn.'

'But he's so young, so small,' Meggy protests. 'He needs me. Just another year, I beg you. Give me time to get him used to the idea. We'll bring him to you ourselves, when he's ready.'

'The parting will not get any easier, however long you delay it,' the white rider said impassively. 'And all the signs tell us it will be a bitter winter. There will be much starvation and sickness. By spring the boy may be dead. Which would you rather, woman, that *we* take the child or death does?'

Wilky starts to sob. He understands little of what they are saying. No one has told him of this bargain, but he understands the word *death*. He's gone to sleep next to a living child and woken to find him cold as a frog. In his short life, he's been forced to watch two of his little brothers wrapped tightly in winding sheets and laid in the frozen earth. Now at night he dreams of them tying a bandage around his own jaw so he cannot cry out, of the hard clods

6

of dirt falling on him, pinning him down, of no one coming to help.

The white rider stares curiously at the child, then shrugs and turns towards the door, as if to make it plain he intends to waste no more time on this. 'If you are regretting your decision, Master Hudde, you can always return the money you were given and settle your debt, and we will trouble you no more.'

Hudde and Meggy gaze helplessly at one another. Both know they can no more return the money than they can send the rain back up into the clouds. The money is gone, spent, finished. Meggy sees the expression on Hudde's face and knows he is going to give them her son.

She wants to seize the stave and drive the men from her house. She wants to scream that they will never have her children, not a single one of them, that she would rather they all starved together than be parted from each other. But she says none of these things. She knows the pain of burying her children. She knows the bitter finality of that parting. Better to think of the boy living, warm, well fed and happy than think of him lying out there alone in the dark forest and hearing the sobs of his ghost on the howling wind.

Hudde lifts his son onto the horse and seats him in front of the younger of the two riders. The man wraps his heavy woollen cloak around them both, holding the boy firmly in the crook of his arm. The man's clothes have an unfamiliar, bitter perfume, like a mixture of woodsmoke and crushed cow parsley, but it is neither of those. The boy begins to struggle again, but the arm around his waist tightens painfully.

'Sit still, you little fool, else you'll fall and break your neck.'

Wilky has never sat on a horse before and it is a dizzyingly long way to the ground. The tears that wet his cheeks burn in the wind. As the horse is kicked into a trot he clutches at the man's arm, and twists his head to look back at his parents, brothers and sisters all crowded in the doorway. It is too dark to see their faces, but he hears the crack in his mother's voice as she calls out, 'Be a good boy, Wilky, and do whatever you're told. We'll come to see you soon . . . very soon . . . if you're good.'

The boy clings desperately to that promise as the riders canter away into the darkness.

But Meggy should have trusted a mother's instincts, for there are evils in this world far worse than death. If she had known, if she could have even imagined, she would have cut her own son's throat before their very eyes, sooner than let the white riders take him.

Chapter 1

**Under the Astrological House of Libra, the Scales,
in the year of Our Lord, 1224.
Near Ricey-Bas, France**

*If you would understand what birds are saying, steal
crows' eggs from the nest, boil them, then return them
to the nest. The crow will fly to the Red Sea to find a
stone, which she will touch to the eggs and they will
become raw again and, in time, hatch. If you then place
this stone in your mouth you will understand the
language of every bird.*

'What foul mischief are you up to now, *petit bâtard?*'

I hadn't heard old Gaspard creeping up on me and I was
so startled that the arrow in my bow shot out through the
slit window and landed with a thwack in the chamomile
bank far below, just inches from where Charles was standing.
He squawked, like a startled goose, and started to run, falling
over his own feet as he twisted round, trying to see where
the arrow had been fired from. I flung myself off the wooden
box I'd been standing on and crouched on the dusty floorboards of the turret room, hoping he hadn't seen me.

'Did you hit someone?' Gaspard demanded.

He dragged himself up onto the wooden box and peered

down through the slit window, trying to see what damage I'd done. If I had killed someone, it would certainly have come as no surprise to him, since he was always telling me I'd end my days on the gallows. Satisfied that no one lay bleeding below the tower, he fetched me a hefty blow across my shoulders with his staff. Fortunately, his joints had swollen again in the wet weather, so he couldn't balance long enough without his stick to hit me again, though I knew he was itching to do it.

Leaning on his staff, he limped heavily over to the small brazier and, perching himself on a stool, swayed back and forth, like a tattered rook in the wind, warming his twisted hands. 'So, what were you doing, *garçon*?'

'Killing crows,' I said.

'In other words idling your time away, when you should have been working.'

Actually, I had not been idling my time away. I had in fact been wondering whether I could murder Charles and get away with it. Not even wondering, really, just fantasising about it, picturing the insipid little slug lying in his coffin and Amée burying her beautiful face in my shoulder as she sobbed her heart out, convinced that only I could comfort her in her grief. The reality was, of course, that if Amée was going to sob on anyone's shoulder it would be one of the *jongleurs* that she was always flirting with, or the languid young men who hung around her father, like ticks on the arse of a sheep, hoping that now Philippe was rising in favour at the new king's court, he'd drag them up with him.

'Have you finished copying that deed? Let me see it.' Gaspard thumped his stick on the wooden floorboards, sending up a small puff of dust. 'If you've time to waste chasing crows . . .'

10

I gathered up the three sheets of parchment from the sloping writing table and thrust them into his misshapen fingers.

'Light, *petit bâtard*, light! You couldn't see a white cat in this gloom.'

He had a point. There were slit windows at intervals all the way round the turret room, but they were so narrow the only thing they let in was the cold. It was a wonder to me that a colony of bats hadn't taken up residence in the chamber long ago. They'd certainly have found it dismal enough for their tastes. Even the swineherds who worked for Philippe had better dwellings than we did. I kept reminding Gaspard that the rest of the château was stuffed with fine tapestries, thick hangings and sumptuous cushions, not to mention fine wines and good food. He should ask Philippe to send a few trifles our way.

But Gaspard only waggled his grey beard. 'The master pays our wages and feeds us,' he croaked. 'If he thought we were in need of anything he would send it.'

'But he's never going to know if you don't tell him,' I said. 'He never sets foot up here, much less sees the arse-rags we call blankets, or tastes that vinegar the scullion fetches up as wine.'

'And where would we put these fine things, if he did send them?' Gaspard asked. 'There's barely room enough to work as it is.'

He was right about that, of course. Apart from our two writing desks and a piss pail, every inch of the walls and floor was crammed with teetering piles of books and boxes of documents. If they fell down it would take them a week to dig us out of the drift of parchment and vellum.

Sometimes I feared I'd turn into a bat myself, stuck up

there night and day, scratching away. Gaspard rarely left the turret room even for meals for he complained the noise and music of the Great Hall gave him a headache. I'd have been only too glad to leave him to his icy chamber and descend to enjoy the chatter and dancing. Then the raddled old bird could have had all the peace and quiet his withered heart desired. But, no, I was ordered to eat in the tower with him, in case he wanted something fetching. Then he'd send me to my straw pallet in the corner, where I was forced to lie awake half the night listening to him flick through the pages in some old ledger, making that irritating, dry little cough of his and humming tunelessly to himself.

When Gaspard did finally retire to bed, he'd toss and turn, grunting like a farrowing pig, until he finally fell asleep, and that was when the snoring began. It was a mark of just how saintly I was that I hadn't smothered him to death long ago. Was this how I was going to end my days, withering away in a dusty turret until I was as desiccated as him, finally croaking out my last sour breath without having kissed a girl, never mind bedded one?

Gaspard was running his crooked thumb down the deeds I'd copied. I learned from painful experience to stay well out of range of his stick whenever he read any of my work. After years of scratching away on parchments and peering at documents, his eyes had grown dim, though he'd sooner have gouged them out of his head than admit as much. But he could still manage to spot a mistake at fifty paces, as if the violated words leaped up at him from the page, screeching like ravished maidens.

'Five errors on the first page alone,' he barked, flinging his stick at my head.

I dodged it, which I knew wouldn't improve his temper.

He made a grasping motion, like a disgruntled baby, indicating he wanted his stick fetching for him, but I pretended not to notice. If the old bird thought I was going to hand him a weapon—

There was the sound of someone climbing the stairs and, without so much as a knock, the door was flung open. Gaspard didn't look up from the parchment, but his frown deepened. 'Did you drop your manners on the way up? Wait outside till I bid you enter.'

'I trust that remark was not intended for me,' a voice said gravely.

The expression on old Gaspard's face was of a man who'd inadvertently swallowed a live ferret, and little wonder, for none other than our master, Monsieur le Comte, was standing in the doorway.

I'd been apprentice to the old scribe since I was ten and, throughout those seven interminable years since I'd moved into Gaspard's turret, I'd never once known Philippe to visit it. I'd often suspected he didn't even know the place existed.

Gaspard flapped wildly at me and I handed him his stick. He tottered forward, looking as dazed as if he'd just been whacked on the head with it.

'Monsieur le Comte! What . . . what an honour. I trust there is nothing amiss?'

Between bowing repeatedly, like a bird pecking crumbs, the old scribe groped for the roll of parchment and the quills that were always kept ready in case Philippe wanted to dictate a message or letter. The mood had been known to seize our master even at the dead of night and he thought nothing of sending for us to come to his hall in the early hours of the morning, seeming amazed that we'd been sleeping. It was as if we were pieces of parchment ourselves and Philippe imagined we were simply filed away among the books on the shelves, waiting until he wanted to use us.

'A chair for Monsieur le Comte,' Gaspard demanded. 'Quickly, *garçon*,'

But there wasn't a chair, only the two high stools we used at our desks. I scrubbed at the top of one of them with my sleeve and pushed it into the tiny space in the centre of the room.

Philippe made no move to sit, but gazed at the stacks of books and wooden cylinders as if he was searching for something. He was a tall, lean man, with a prominent square jaw. His tawny hair had been curled at the nape of his neck to match the curl of his fringe on his brow. He was already clad for dinner in a dark blue tunic. A long, sleeveless white tabard flowed over it, decorated with a rich panel of scarlet and gold embroidery at the neck. He looked what he was, a man ascending rapidly in the service of the new king, Louis VIII, who even as Crown Prince had been dubbed Le Lion.

Gaspard's trembling hand hovered over the jug of vinegary white wine, but he seemed to realise it was hardly suitable to offer to Philippe.

Philippe appeared to recognise the old man's dilemma. 'Fetch us some wine, *garçon*. And take your time. I would speak with your master alone.'

On any other occasion I would have been as eager to escape from the tower as a hound released from its kennel, but I found myself resentful at being excluded. I'd copied Philippe's documents and contracts, read his letters and written secret love notes for half of the men and women in his service – which, I might add, was the only time any woman in that manor deigned to look at me – and in all that time I'd never once divulged a single confidence, not that I'd had much opportunity. Who did I ever get to talk to except old Gaspard and the birds? But that aside, you would have thought I could have been trusted with whatever message he wanted to dictate to Gaspard. Besides, I'd get to know about it sooner or later, anyway. They were bound to want it copied, and though Gaspard told me repeatedly that a good scribe must learn to copy without reading or remembering, I always ensured I remembered everything.

But I bowed my head respectfully and closed the door behind me. I made sure that I clattered enough on the stairs for them to be satisfied I'd retreated, then tiptoed back up and, sitting on the steps, pressed my ear to the gap beneath the door.

'. . . disturbing news today from a *friend.'* Philippe stressed the word as if the source of this news mattered. 'There are certain rumours being whispered about me at Court. I had these past weeks suspected something of the sort – odd looks, men who were once affable now growing cold. But I couldn't discover the cause until today.'

'The king shows you great favour,' Gaspard said. 'And there will always be those about him who are jealous of that. The old king's advisers are always cast off when a new king takes the crown.'

The old crow's voice had a wary, sycophantic tone. Was he afraid Philippe was accusing him of spreading rumours? Surely not. Even if he hadn't been the most loyal servant in Philippe's employ, Gaspard had no more chance of spreading gossip than I did, stuck up there.

'It was the same when the king's late father came to the throne,' Gaspard continued. 'Out went the old and in came the new. A king always likes to surround himself with his

15

own men. But you needn't fear the jealousy of others, Monsieur le Comte. It is plain to see from his letters that our lion puts much trust in you.'

'Not for much longer, if this rumour reaches his ears,' Philippe said grimly. 'The king needs strong men around him if he is to consolidate the lands he's gained from the English Crown. Le Comte de Champagne is bitterly opposed to the banning of Jews from lending money, he makes a good income from taxing them, and the king will find it hard to stand against him. Louis cannot afford to have any weak spot in his armour that his enemies can use to pierce him.'

'But, Monsieur le Comte, why should you be that weak spot?' Gaspard said.

I pressed closer to the door – this I did not want to miss. The floorboards creaked and I heard footsteps crossing the room. I hurtled down the spiral steps, as the door opened. Philippe was evidently taking no chances. I stood, pressing myself against the cold stone walls, praying he would not venture onto the staircase, for I dared not retreat any further down for fear he would hear me moving.

But he seemed satisfied they were not overheard and the door closed above me. I knew it was foolish to risk going back, but I couldn't help myself. I had to learn the rest of this tale.

'. . . but I must have proof,' Philippe was saying. 'If it should be challenged, I would lose not only the king's favour, but my titles and lands too. Even my own villeins would own more than I. My daughter would be fortunate to find any man more favoured than a butcher to wed her. There must be something – a record, a letter – that would banish all doubt. You must have come across some document, Gaspard.'

'I am certain the proof is here, Monsieur le Comte.'

Gaspard sounded even more agitated than our master. 'I cannot lay my hands on it immediately, but that is only because I've had no cause to look for such a thing. But I swear nothing, not even an order to buy meat for the hounds, has been thrown away since I came here nigh on fifty years ago, that I can promise you. And the librarian before me was just as diligent. If you can but give me a little time to search . . .'

'Search thoroughly, Gaspard. Come to me day or night as soon as you discover anything, anything at all. All our futures depend on you. You must find it!'

Chapter 2

Norfolk, England

*Visitabis interiora terra, rectificando, invenies occultum
lapidem – VITRIOL.*

*Visit the interior of the earth and by rectifying, you
will find the hidden stone.*

Wilky's eyes water in the stinging wind and, though his
body is enveloped in the cloak of the white rider, his nose
is numb with cold. The boy pulls the edge of the cloak over
his face to shield it. His teeth rattle as the horse's hoofs
thunder over the stones. He's sure they are flying as fast as
a dragon. He keeps glancing up at the man who grips him
so tightly, fearing that he might have turned into a demon
or the lantern-man, not that Wilky really knows what the
lantern-man looks like, though he must be monstrous. But
in the darkness the boy can see little of the rider's face,
except a pair of glittering eyes fixed on the track ahead.

The rhythm of the beast gradually lulls the child into a
stupor. He cannot keep his eyes open. Slowly his head droops
down into the soft wool of the cloak. This is just a dream.
He will wake and find himself back in his bed, curled like a
puppy around his heap of brothers and sisters, warm and safe.

The rhythm changes. Wilky jerks awake. He is not in his

own cottage, but clattering through an archway into a courtyard that seems, at first, to be on fire. Yellow and orange
flames from blazing torches lick across the stones. All around
him, the giant shadows of men and of sweating horses twist
over the high walls. The heavy wooden door in the archway
shudders closed behind the riders and men come running
to take the reins.

Wilky is lifted down and set on the cobbles. His thin
legs are so cold and numb, he staggers. He gazes longingly
at the brazier by the high gate, desperate to steal a little
handful of warmth, but he's afraid to move.

A huge stone building with slit windows towers above
him on one side, and a cluster of smaller buildings face him.
The other two sides of the courtyard are sealed by walls so
high not even his eldest brother could climb them, and he
can climb the tallest oak in the forest. The boy is trapped.

He squeals in fear as a heavy hand suddenly grasps his
shoulder. 'This way, Regulus.'

He stares up at the man, recognising the frosty chin of
the older of the two white riders.

'I'm not Re-lus,' he says stoutly. 'I'm Wilky.'

'You are Regulus now. You will answer to that name, do
you understand? There is no boy called Wilky.'

'But *I*'m Wilky. It's me,' the boy says.

Perhaps the man doesn't know who he is. Maybe he took
him from the cottage mistaking him for some other boy. If
Wilky tells him, if he explains he is not this other boy, then
they will take him home. He tries desperately to make them
understand, but no one is listening to him.

As Regulus is pushed towards the great building, a low
door near the end opens silently and the younger of the
two white riders hurries out.

'I've told him we have the boy. You're to take him straight down.'

'The child has just been removed from his home. He's exhausted and confused. He won't understand what's being asked of him. Can't Arthmael use one of the others tonight?'

The young man snorts as if the question surpasses stupid. 'If he could, he would not have waited for this boy. I wouldn't try his patience any longer.'

Regulus jerks as the fingers gripping his shoulder dig sharply into his flesh. 'Have a care how you address me, Madron. I have flogged boys scarcely younger than you. I know how you ingratiate yourself, but you are not Arthmael's successor yet. Remember, I supply what he needs, not you.'

Regulus, still protesting that he is Wilky, is propelled forward into a small chamber, but all things are relative and to Regulus the room is as big as his whole cottage, bigger even, for it has a vaulted ceiling. On the opposite side of the empty chamber is another door.

When it is opened, the boy expects to see a byre or a forest on the other side. Where else do doors lead? But instead there is a set of stone steps spiralling downwards into the darkness. An eerie red glow flickers across the wall. A rush of damp, stale air carries snatches of an acrid stench, but the smell is not of any animal or herb the child recognises. In a panic he turns, trying to flee back across the chamber, but the grip on his shoulder is too fierce and he is hauled back.

'Your mother instructed you to be a good boy and do exactly as you are told,' the white rider whispers into his ear. 'Your father wanted you to come here. He gave you to us. Your parents would never send you into harm, would they? Go down, Regulus, just a few steps, that's all. One day you will learn there is far more to be afraid of in this world than what lies beneath here. Then you will truly understand fear.'

Chapter 3

The slab was like an open book, exhibited to all who entered that they should look at it . . . And now I shall make known to you what the wise man has hidden.

I scattered a few crumbs of bread and some fragments of mutton in the slit window and waited for the magpie to pay its morning call. I had this notion that if I could tame the bird I could coax it down in the gardens in front of Amée and show her the bird feeding from my hand. In one of the hundreds of books stored in the turret, I'd read about a poor woodsman who'd won the love of a noble lady by training a wolf to eat from his fingers. She was so enchanted by his gentleness and skill in taming the savage creature that she instantly fell in love with him.

If you ask me, that woodsman was lucky he had the time to go taming wolves. I couldn't escape from work long enough to train a rabbit, never mind track down a wolf. The only wolves I'd ever encountered were the dead ones the hunters brought into the courtyard, swinging upside down from a stave. But surely any woman would be impressed by a man who could call the wild birds to him.

I thought I'd start with an easy one. Magpies are thieving little vermin anyway, so bold they will fly in a woman's face and try to snatch her necklace. On second thoughts, perhaps a magpie wasn't the best bird to show off to Amée.

I brushed the crumbs from the ledge just as the door opened and Gaspard staggered in, a tower of ledgers and documents clamped to his chest, held there by pressing his chin down on top.

'This mess, this mess!' he screeched at me. 'How am I to find anything?'

He was right about the mess. Anyone visiting the chamber on that day would have sworn that our little turret room had been plundered by English soldiers. Chests lay open. Cylindrical boxes had been pulled apart, their lids scattered and the scrolls they'd contained strewn over the dusty boards. Books and parchments had been heaped on desks, stools and boxes, only to slide off in great avalanches to the floor. You couldn't take a step without crunching a roll of parchment underfoot or tripping over a leather-bound book.

One moment Gaspard was yelling at me to tidy up and the next demanding that I leave that and search for another box. He would be halfway through rummaging in a chest when it would suddenly occur to him that whatever he was looking for might be in another place entirely, so he'd abandon what he was doing and totter off on a new quest.

He'd even made me clamber up through the trapdoor into the eaves. I hadn't known there were boxes up there. They were smothered in dust and bird dung. The rolls of parchments inside were mildewed and crumbled away even as they were unrolled, those that the mice hadn't already gnawed. I imagined the generations of mouse-pups that had been whelped on those words and suckled among all those sentences. How many stories had they shat on and royal proclamations had they pissed on through the decades?

I had asked Gaspard a dozen times what we were looking for, trying to convince the old fool that it was pointless for me to go searching through documents when I didn't know what I was trying to find. I could easily have what he was looking for in my hand and cast it aside without recognising it.

I reminded Gaspard of the story of a boy who is sent to capture an elephant. They tell him to look for a creature with large ears. But since he's never seen an elephant, he brings back a bat, for that has large ears. So they tell him to look for a beast with a long nose and he returns with a shrew, for that has a long nose. Then they tell him an elephant has a bare, skinny tail and he returns with a mouse, for that has a bare, skinny tail. No one has told him that the creature he seeks is bigger than a house.

'And if the elephant was in that chest, you still wouldn't find it,' Gaspard snapped, cuffing me round the head. 'I told you already you're to bring me anything, anything at all, that mentions Monsieur le Comte's grandparents. And don't ask impertinent questions.'

The days passed and the nights, too, for we continued to search by candlelight and when, finally, I couldn't keep my eyes open any longer, I was invariably woken by Gaspard still scrabbling away, like a squirrel digging for his buried nuts. The pile of papers concerning Philippe's grandparents grew into a bale and then a haystack. Gaspard had been right: neither he nor the librarian who'd occupied this chamber before him had ever thrown away the smallest scrap of writing, from the bill of sale for a hound to an order for a lady's gown. I was beginning to think that we'd discover the bones of the old librarian himself tucked away on one of the shelves, bound in ribbon and sealed with a lump of wax.

But nothing we found satisfied Gaspard. The old man

grew more frantic by the hour, tossing books and scrolls aside before he'd read more than a few lines, then frantically trying to find them again in case he'd missed something. If he wasn't making himself sick from lack of sleep, he was certainly making me ill.

Then at dawn one morning, after I felt I'd only just fallen asleep, he shook me awake. 'I need you to go to the still room and fetch all the goat-leaf seeds they have.'

'All, Master Gaspard?'

'Yes, every last seed, and if it isn't enough you'll have to get more.'

'But the still-room maid will never give me all she has. What do you want them for, anyway?'

'Tell her . . . tell her I need to purge myself. Something I've eaten has disagreed with me.'

That was news to me. I'd not seen him eat anything these past few days, save for the few morsels of bread he chewed while searching through yet another ledger.

'She has purges already made up, Master Gaspard, in case of poison.'

'I don't want one of her purges,' the old crow said, flapping his hands impatiently. 'I want the seeds. Steal them if she'll not give them to you. I *must* have them.'

I'd suspected for a long time that Gaspard was losing his wits. Now I was certain. Days and nights of searching for this wretched document had sent him scurrying into his dotage.

'Tell no one else what I've sent you for, *bâtard*. No one. Do you hear?'

The old man grasped my ear, as if I was some kitchen scullion, and dragged me to the door, pressing an old leather bag into my hand. I think he would have booted me down

25

the stairs, if he could have done it without falling flat on his scrawny arse.

Yawning, I groped my way down the spiral stone steps. The sun was only just beginning to rise and no light yet penetrated the narrow slits in the walls. The icy morning chill painfully reminded me that the first frosts couldn't be far off. I didn't know which was worse in that turret room, the stifling heat of summer, or winter, when even the ink came close to freezing.

Even at this hour, the Great Hall was already bustling with maids and scullions falling over one another as they fetched perfumed water to fill the lavers and laid the tables for the first meal of the day. I winked at one of the younger maids, but she stalked past me with a face as sour as last week's milk.

I knew Philippe's daughter, the adorable Amée, would still be sleeping soundly, as I wished I was, but even so, I found myself repeatedly glancing towards the door to the family chambers in the impossible hope she would glide into the hall. Not that she would have noticed me if she had. Even the lowliest of kitchen maids looked through me as if I was nothing but a chewed bone to be kicked into the rushes.

But that didn't stop me dreaming, and often as I lay awake at night, while Gaspard scratched away at his books or his balls, I imagined Amée stumbling as she crossed the hall and me being there to catch her, or her favourite brooch being lost and me finding it. But since the closest I ever got to her was looking down on her when she walked below in the gardens, unless I learned to fly, I'd have as much chance of getting her to notice me as of persuading old Gaspard to take up jousting.

I suddenly spotted Charles by the great fire and hastily slipped out in case he should still be brooding about the arrow that had only just missed him. The sight of me might remind him of who occupied the turret room.

The torches had long since burned away in the courtyard, but the grey dawn light didn't yet have strength enough to penetrate the corners. The stone still room was in darkness. I knocked at the stout door, but there was no answer. The old woman who had charge of it would probably still be sleeping, or out gathering herbs, for many had to be plucked at dawn with dew upon them or in moonlight when their potency was at its height.

I tried the handle and found to my great relief it was not locked. Once inside, though, there was only the dim red glow from the damped-down fire to light the chamber and that wasn't enough to be able to distinguish a mummified cat from a monkey's paw, never mind one jar of seeds from another. I had no choice but to risk lighting a candle.

It took me some time to search the shelves, even though all the pots and containers were labelled with crude drawings of the plants so that those who couldn't read could identify the contents. But eventually I found a small pot containing goat-leaf seeds and hastily tipped the whole lot into the leather bag that Gaspard had thrust at me. The still-room maid was sure to miss them, for she'd never let any pot run empty, but with luck she wouldn't discover the theft for a few days.

I had just replaced the empty container on the shelf when the door creaked open behind me. As I whirled round, both I and the woman in the doorway gave a squeak of surprise. It was Amée! My face burned as hot as a baker's oven. The early-morning light cast a halo round her loose flaxen curls.

27

I'd never been so close to her before and, in spite of praying ceaselessly for a moment like this, now that it had happened I found myself gawping at her like the village mooncalf.

'I saw the candle,' she said. 'I thought Meli was in here. Who are you?'

I bowed low, knocking several pots with my bag as I did so. I lunged wildly at them to steady them before they crashed to the floor. Amée giggled and I knew even my ears had turned scarlet. This was not how I had pictured our meeting. My first and possibly my only chance ever to impress her, and here I was, floundering around like a cow on ice.

I took a step forward and bowed again, taking care not to knock against anything else.

'Vincent, Comtesse, apprentice to Gaspard the scribe.'

She was trying unsuccessfully to suppress a grin and I suddenly realised how dishevelled I must look, having been dragged from my bed without time even to wash my face or comb my hair.

'So what is an apprentice scribe doing in a still room?' she asked.

'I, too, came looking for Meli. I need physic for my master, Gaspard.'

At once her face was all concern. 'He's not sick, is he? My father is depending on him. Perhaps I should come and see.'

'No, Comtesse. It's . . . it's only a touch of indigestion. He's been working late, missing meals.'

'For my father, I know,' she said, frowning. 'I'll see that good meat is sent up to tempt his appetite and you must see that he eats it. He mustn't make himself ill. We desperately need his services. My mother is fretting so much, it has brought on one of her dreadful headaches. She's sent

28

me to ask Meli to prepare an unguent to rub on her temples. But I know the only thing that will really help is for this terrible anxiety to be lifted. Has Gaspard discovered anything yet?'

I hesitated. I knew he hadn't – at least, I was pretty sure he hadn't. But I couldn't tell Amée that. I wanted to be her hero and I'd hardly be that if I brought her bad news.

'I think he might have found something, Comtesse,' I said. 'But please don't tell Monsieur le Comte yet, in case it proves false.'

Her face broke into such a glorious smile, it made my groin throb and my knee tremble. She was a beauty.

'Does he seem encouraged, though?' she asked eagerly.

Gaspard seemed completely moon-crazed, that's what he seemed, but I wasn't about to say that.

If only I could find the lost document, whatever it was, before he did . . . I pictured Amée flinging her soft little arms about my neck in gratitude and planting a dozen kisses on my mouth, her father insisting on bestowing his daughter's hand on me in abject gratitude.

Yes, all right, I knew that was never going to happen! Even if I single-handedly rescued Amée from the jaws of a slavering lion or slew a fire-breathing dragon to save her, she'd still end up married to some wealthy nobleman, and I'd be lucky to be tossed a gold ducat for my pains, but if there was any justice in this world . . .

'This document is very important to Monsieur le Comte,' I began, hoping she'd assume I knew all about it and innocently tell me what Gaspard would not.

But back then I knew nothing about how to draw a man or woman into revealing their secrets. I didn't know how to form the questions that would make them tell me more or how to read the subtle signs that would reveal a lie – a downward glance, a twitching hand, a rubbing of an ear. I hadn't learned to utter the ambiguous phrases that would lead them to confide all, believing I knew all. Those skills I had yet to learn, for though I didn't know it then, my whole future was to be constructed from those velvet lies and pretty deceptions.

As it was, Amée merely smiled sadly. 'That document is important to all of us. Our whole future rests upon its discovery.' She turned. 'If you see Meli, tell her she is to attend my mother at once. And the moment Gaspard is certain he has found what my father needs, you must bring us word immediately.'

I opened my mouth, trying desperately to think of something to detain her, but the space where she had been standing was empty and only the cold dawn light filled the doorway.

Up in the turret, Gaspard was waiting for me with the impatience of a ravenous baby demanding the breast. God's arse, what a revolting thought! Had some poor woman once been forced to give suck to a creature like Gaspard? Although, looking at the dried-up old crab apple, I should think his mother's breast must have been the last one he ever got to lay his hands on.

But it was plain the old man was agitated. His eyes were red from dust and lack of sleep, but there was a wild excitement in them that was almost frightening. Though I often joked about him being mad, for the first time I began to fear he really had become crazed or even possessed. He tore the leather bag from my hand and limped across to the table, clutching it fiercely like a miser protecting a bag of gold.

He started to pour out the seeds, then seemed to remember I was still standing there.

30

'What are you doing hanging around in here, *petit bâtard*?' He gazed wildly around the room, then snatched up the blankets in which he wrapped himself at night. 'They're filthy, stinking. Why haven't you washed them?'

He threw them at my head. A cloud of dust flew out, making me cough.

'There, see? Is it any wonder my chest wheezes, sleeping in such filth? Take them to the wash house and see you get every mote of dust out of them, and yours too.'

'I'll get one of the maids—'

'No, you won't, you lazy brat. I'll not have the master think we make work for others while you stand idle. Besides, it will do you good to get out in the fresh air. A lad of your age hanging around dusty old books all the time, it's not natural. I thought you'd be only too eager to spend the morning bantering with the linen maids. Don't think I haven't seen you making sheep's eyes at them from the turret.'

I gaped at him. In all the time I'd worked for him, he'd never once been concerned that I needed fresh air. If he'd had his way, I'd have been chained to the desk with leg-irons. First the goat-leaf seeds, now a sudden desire for clean blankets, the old crow was definitely up to something. I reckoned he'd found the document or thought he was close to it and was inventing reasons to get me out of the way. But for the moment there was nothing I could do except lumber down the stairs under the heap of smelly blankets.

I lugged them across the courtyard to the big washing pool near the drying green, where three maids were already pounding linens. Two of the girls were as broad and shapeless as milch cows in summer, with low-swinging udders to match. Their great hams wobbled as they bent over the

31

washing. The other was a thin, scrawny little thing with pustules spattered over her pale face.

Even had I been vaguely attracted to any of them, flirting, as Gaspard had urged, was out of the question. They giggled when they saw me and laughed even harder as they watched my clumsy attempts to clean the blankets. That was when they weren't giving exaggerated gasps of horror and pinching their noses when they saw how black the water turned. I'd no doubt the tale would be all over the château by nightfall.

I spread the blankets, only slightly cleaner, on the drying green and contemplated what to do next. It was clear Gaspard would be delighted if I stayed away all day. Part of me longed to do just that for I might not get the chance of another day's freedom to enjoy myself until the ancient one was mouldering in his grave.

On the other hand, curiosity was eating me up, and curiosity is a demon who will not relinquish its hold on you until its voracious appetite has been satisfied. I'd have no peace until I discovered what Gaspard was trying to hide. So, I turned my back on freedom, crept back up the spiral staircase and, as silently as I could, I lifted the door latch.

Chapter 4

Norfolk, England

And the air of the four quarters of the world must occupy three parts of the room that the death song of the swan may be distinctly heard.

Gisa is sitting in the narrow beam of sunlight that penetrates the dark interior of her uncle's apothecary's shop, grinding a root of black hellebore. She does not need to see her hands in order to do her work. She has pounded roots, dried herbs and minerals for her uncle so often that her fingers can feel just when the texture is right. But she is grateful for the warmth of the sun, hungry for it, for she seldom has the time to feel its touch on her cheek.

A shadow falls across Gisa's lap. The girl glances up, frowning. A man is standing outside the shop, but she cannot see his face because the sunlight is behind him. Sighing, she lays aside the pestle and mortar and crosses the narrow room towards him. The shutters on the small shop have been lowered from the window to form a counter, which protrudes like a tongue into the street beyond.

Most customers are served through this window. They are admitted to the shop only when her uncle needs to inspect a wound or examine a bloodshot eye. Otherwise the door is kept barred for fear that curious children will sneak in or would-be murderers: on these shelves are stored more ways to dispatch a man into the next life than can be found in King Henry's arsenal. Some of the potions and powders would kill a man gently with an endless sleep. Others would make him suffer all the agonies of Hell long before he descended into Satan's realm.

The man at the window says nothing, asks for nothing, but as soon as the girl recognises the bulbous, pitted nose and the sharp green eyes, a cold stone rises up in her throat. She wants to call for her uncle, vanish until they have concluded their business, but she dare not keep him waiting outside. Reluctantly, she unfastens the door and the man sweeps through. The heavy folds of his black tunic almost catch in the door as Gisa hastens to close it behind him. He gazes down at her. A faint stench of urine hangs about him. He stands too close, always too close, and she wants to move away, but the edge of the table is pressing into her back, trapping her.

The light from the window flashes on the silver embroidery at the neck of his black tunic and around his black hat. 'Osle' – the townspeople call him, though never within his hearing – *the great black bird*. It is an old name from the elder faith, for the Christian saints are powerless to protect them from those ancient fears that cannot be caged by the words of the Church. The goodwives cover their children's eyes as Osle passes, spitting on their fingers to deflect the malice of his gaze. They hurriedly cross the square to avoid being grazed by his shadow, though they are seldom put to this trouble, for he rarely comes to the town except to visit the apothecary's shop and that in itself unnerves them.

'My uncle is in the courtyard, Lord Sylvain,' Gisa mutters. 'I'll fetch him.' She tries to edge away, but he blocks her in.

'Today is your birthday, is it not? Fifteen, a young lady now.'

She blushes, wondering how he could possibly know that. Her aunt and uncle have not remembered. Secretly she thinks herself a woman, but his words have turned her into an awkward child again. He stands too close. His gaze is too intense. There is nowhere safe for her to look, without turning her head away from him. She's seen women do that when they are feigning indifference, but are really trying to seduce a man. She's frightened he will think she is playing that game. She stares down at the black leather tassels on the purse that dangles from his belt. Each thong ends in a silver bauble in the form of a snake's head. The merest twitch of his body makes them writhe. To her embarrassment, he follows her gaze and reaches for his purse, as if he thinks she is a street urchin begging for a coin.

'I have a gift for you,' he says.

He pulls out a small package wrapped in shining white silk.

Since she makes no attempt to reach for it, he lifts her hand and places the gift in her palm, closing her thin fingers around it. She feels the magical softness of the silk, but at once it grows sticky in her sweating hand.

He commands her to unwrap it and she does, though she doesn't want to. She doesn't want this gift, whatever it may be, but she dare not offend him.

The white silk lies open, covering her hand. In the centre of the cloth is a brooch in the form of a white enamelled swan with a snaking arched neck. Its beak, which is fashioned from gold, is opened wide as if the bird cries out in agony.

'The mute swan sings only as it dies. Did you know that, Gisa? The most pure, the most sublime beauty can only be achieved through death. But then,' he sweeps his hand about the room, indicating the stacks of jars and boxes cramming the shelves, 'who knows better than you and your uncle that perfect healing is to be found in the deadliest of poisons?'

Without asking for her permission, he takes the swan and pins it to her kirtle directly over her thudding heart.

Chapter 5

*For true whiteness is hidden under blackness and is
taken forth from its belly.*

I jerked awake on my pallet as Gaspard's head hit the wooden
desk. He cursed, pushing himself upright again. He must
have nodded off where he sat. It was hardly surprising. He
was exhausted, only his obsession keeping him going. I once
read about a hermit who was so devoted he drove thorns
into his knees and rolled naked in the snow to keep himself
awake during his vigils, and when that failed he even cut
off his own eyelids so that they wouldn't thwart his resolve.
I reckoned it was only a matter of time before Gaspard
started slicing away.

The flames of the hanging oil lamp, swaying in the
draught from the window, sent shadows and tiny lights
flickering about the dark walls. For a few minutes more,
Gaspard studied the book in front of him. Then, with a
great sigh, he closed it and staggered over to the straw
pallet I'd rolled out for him. Without even removing his
shoes, he lowered himself with a groan and fell instantly
asleep. I waited until I heard the steady rhythm of his
wheezes. Then I tiptoed across the room and pulled a
blanket over the old man's thin body, tucking it in beneath
his grey beard. He didn't stir.

For the past two days, every time I'd returned from the

latest spurious errand Gaspard had sent me on, I'd heard him scratching away with his quill behind the door. But always when I entered he'd hastily shift the book in which he was writing to the far side of the desk, barking some nonsense to distract me until he'd had time to dry the last few words with sand and close the page, then shove it under a sheaf of documents. The book was an old one, judging from what I could see of the cover. The leather bindings were torn and worn thin in places, revealing patches of the bare wood beneath, and most of the gold leaf on the winged ox that decorated the front was rubbed away, leaving only the outline of the beast impressed in the leather.

'So have you given up the search, then?' I'd asked him, the first time I'd caught him scribbling.

'Certainly not,' he'd snapped. 'I'm not like you young ones, abandoning a task because it's too difficult. If something is lost, I keep searching until it is found. Though how I am expected to find anything in this mess is beyond me. Look at it! Books and papers thrown around as if you were scattering manure on a field. It's a disgrace.'

'It was you who dragged everything out,' I'd protested, then wished I'd held my tongue as his staff cracked across my ear.

'I wouldn't have to tear the place apart looking for things if you'd put them in the right order in the first place. You're useless, *bâtard*, useless. I should have taken a pig as my apprentice. You don't realise how grateful you should be . . .'

It was a speech I'd heard many times before – the bastard child of an English nun should consider himself the luckiest soul alive to have been taken into a noble French household and accorded the singular honour of becoming a scribe's apprentice. Most nuns' brats were buried alive in the nunnery crypt within the hour of their birth or else raised on scraps until they were old enough to tread dog shit in a tanner's yard.

Of course, I had only Gaspard's word that I was the child of a nun for I don't remember ever having had a mother. My earliest memories were of crawling through straw to nestle among the puppies of a wolfhound and snuggling into the warm hairy belly of the dog as it lay in the corner of the stables. I remember sucking the ear of one of the puppies while another licked my toes. Maybe I was suckled by the wolfhound or even a wolf, like one of those wild children they sometimes found in the forest.

I'd been born far away from France, across the sea, in an English city called Winchester. I'd pretty much fended for myself for as far back as I could remember, stealing food or begging for it, always hungry, until the day the French army marched on Winchester when Prince Louis came to seize the English throne. I must have been eight or nine years old then. I saw my chance and made myself useful fetching and carrying for the French, for which they paid me by sharing their food and giving me a place at their fire. Gaspard made the most use of me, for Philippe had brought him as his scribe and the old man needed an agile boy to climb the trees and gather oak apples for ink or find fresh feathers for quills. I made sure he always had plenty of both.

But the good times lasted barely a year. Then the French were driven out and sailed home. I didn't want to go back to my old life sleeping rough and stealing scraps from the midden heaps. At least the French fed me well. No one noticed I'd crept on board with them until we were well out at sea and by then it was too late to send me back.

I was too small and skinny to be of much use in Philippe's kitchens or stables, but by then I could speak French as fluently as my mother's tongue. Gaspard persuaded Philippe I'd learn Latin and my letters just as quickly, so I was hauled up to the turret to become the old man's slave. But if I'd known I was going to spend the rest of my life caged up with that raddled crow I'd have stayed in England and starved.

I watched Gaspard for a few minutes, just to make sure he really was asleep. Then I edged over to the desk and quietly opened the book I'd seen him writing in, taking care to support the heavy cover, so that it wouldn't thud against the desk. Not that the old man would have heard it if it had: he was so exhausted the turret could have collapsed and he'd still have been found sleeping peacefully in the rubble.

I was certain that this book must contain some great secret, if Gaspard had tried so hard to conceal the contents from me. But it seemed nothing more inflammatory than the mundane records of the Church of St Luke's written in several different hands. Judging by the dates, the entries had been made around a century before. There were lists of candles, vestments, chalices and other costly objects given to the church by Philippe's ancestors as penance for sins or as thank offerings for members of the family returned safely from war. There were colourful accounts of storms, droughts, fires, fevers and famines that God in His mercy had sent to ravage the countryside and chastise the sinful parishioners. And between them were the tedious life stories of virtuous priests or faithful deacons deemed worthy of being remembered after their deaths.

Occasionally notes, written in a different hand, had been added in the margins, a pernickety correction of some minor

40

error in the record or a detail the scribe must have thought a glaring omission from his predecessor's account. But the ink of the additions was as faded as that of the original entries.

Yet I was sure that this was the book I'd seen Gaspard writing in, and not just once but many times. Glancing down at the slumbering old man, I continued turning page after page, looking for anything he might have added, but could see nothing. Finally I came to the last entry in the book. It was written in smaller letters than the rest and little wonder: there was much to cram into the few pages remaining, as if the scribe had been determined not to begin on a new book until the very bottom of the very last page had been used up.

A Faithful Account of the Great Virtue of Hélène and of the Wickedness of Her Sister, Lisette.

I had half closed the book, intending to search among the other papers on Gaspard's desk, but I found myself opening it again. The ink of this last entry was just as old and faded as it was in all the others, but the title piqued my curiosity. Just what mischief had this wicked sister got up to? It sounded a great deal more interesting than the pious acts of some village priest.

Estienne, Le Comte de Lingones, was a virtuous and well-favoured man.

The opening line was not promising, yet another tediously worthy saint, but I read on, hoping the juicy scandal of the naughty sister would quickly emerge.

41

He was betrothed from infancy to Lisette, the eldest daughter of Le Marquis des Roches, though as is the custom, the pair had not laid eyes upon one another since they were children. But when Estienne had returned from the wars, having proved his valour on the battlefield, it was thought high time the couple should wed.

So our saint was to marry the wicked sister. What dreadful sin had she committed? Adultery, was that it? Did she prove to be a whore? I hoped there'd be plenty of detail.

Estienne was invited to des Roches's château to spend the weeks there in preparation for his nuptial feast. He rode in at the head of a fine procession, bringing gifts for his bride, including a dainty honey-coloured palfrey decked out in the finest scarlet bridle and saddle. On the afternoon he was to arrive, the marquis's daughters were up in the solar dressing in their finest clothes. Lisette and her sisters tried on jewel after jewel and had their maids bind their hair first one way then another to make art endow them with what nature had failed to bestow.

All that is, except little Hélène, youngest and fairest of des Roches's daughters. She had been quickly elbowed out of the way and had had her own jewels snatched from her neck by one of the sisters who fancied they would suit her far better. But Hélène made no complaint. She was a gentle, innocent girl, but her elder sisters were jealous of her, for when Hélène came into the hall, their charms paled in the eyes of all those around them, as the light of the moon fades in the brilliance of the sun.

Hélène saw no reason to primp and preen, for she

modestly believed that no one would even glance her way. Besides, she thought it much more pleasant to be out in the warm sunshine than trapped in a dark room with her squabbling sisters. She threw on a simple gown and ran outside to gather flowers instead.

So it was that when Estienne's procession galloped into the château grounds, the first woman he saw was Hélène, her soft cheeks flushed as pink as the roses in her arms, the sunlight glinting from her flaxen hair and her warm, welcoming smile. It did not occur to Estienne that this was any other than his betrothed, and without even asking her name, he dismounted, swept her up in his arms and, seating her on the palfrey, led her into her father's court-yard with his own hand.

When Lisette, his bride-to-be, heard the clatter of the hoofs below she scurried excitedly to the casement. But her joy turned to rage when she saw her youngest sister seated upon the bridal horse and Estienne smiling at her as he reached up to grasp her waist and swing her down.

As soon as the marquis hurried out to meet his future son-in-law and present his daughters, Estienne realised his mistake. But it was too late. The damage was done. He had fallen hopelessly in love with Hélène and, by comparison, Lisette seemed insipid. She was rendered all the plainer by the furious scowls she was directing at her youngest sister.

Over the weeks that followed, Estienne gallantly paid court to his betrothed, but neither she nor anyone at the château could fail to notice that his gaze strayed constantly towards Hélène whenever she was nearby, and his eyes searched for her when she was absent. And they also observed how Hélène repeatedly turned towards the sound of

Estienne's voice, as if she could not help herself. It was plain she, too, was in love.

When Estienne pleaded with the marquis to grant him his youngest daughter's hand in marriage instead of the elder's, the marquis not unnaturally refused. But finally after both Hélène and Estienne entreated him on their knees, he could see that if he was not to lose this wealthy suitor entirely, he had no choice but to agree. But he declared that Hélène could not marry until her elder sister was safely wed to another for fear of shaming Lisette, and further that the youngest daughter would come with but half the dowry of the elder, for the marquis was a shrewd man and realised that, if Estienne was so determined to have the girl, he would not be obliged to part with nearly as much to sweeten the bargain.

A match was quickly arranged for Lisette with an old widower who was far wealthier even than Estienne. But her new husband's riches did nothing to assuage Lisette's fury and bitterness. She brooded constantly about what her sister had stolen from her and was determined to have her revenge. On the night before Hélène's marriage, she covered herself with a cloak belonging to one of her maids and stole away to consult the wise woman who lived on an island in the lake. Lisette sought death for her sister, but the woman refused to grant her wish, fearing that she would be accused of the murder.

Instead she persuaded Lisette that revenge would taste far sweeter if she watched her sister's marriage grow sour, and what better way to turn a man against his wife than if she failed to bear him heirs? The wise woman gave Lisette a charm to hide in the marriage bed to curse it, so that any child conceived in that bed would be stillborn. And so it came to pass that Hélène bore three sons, but not one drew breath.

Hélène, fearing that her husband would indeed try to put her away and take another to his bed, summoned a wise woman who lived on the edge of the forest to help her. This woman was cousin to the one Lisette had consulted and the forest woman recognised the evidence of her cousin's handiwork. She knew at once how Hélène had been cursed.

She told Hélène that she must never again lie in her husband's bed. Instead she must persuade her husband to lie with her in secret, deep in the forest beneath a cleaved oak that bore mistletoe, and when the child was born she must give birth beneath that same tree, for only that could protect the babe from the curse. She warned Hélène that on no account must she tell anyone of this for fear that word would reach Lisette, who would do the child harm. Then she gave Hélène a tame white dove, telling her to release it if she needed to summon her.

Each day Hélène rode out of the château alone on her palfrey, searching the forest until at length she found the oak the old woman had described. With her own hands she built a little bower beneath it. When all was ready, she persuaded her husband to come to meet her alone, telling him she had a great treasure to show him. She led him to the bower decorated with flowers and laid ready with wine, fruit and meat. Soothed by the wine and intoxicated by the perfume of the flowers, Estienne succumbed to his wife's tender words and gentle caresses and made love to her. At once Hélène felt her womb quicken with child.

But as the weeks passed and the maids noticed their mistress's swelling belly, rumours began to fly about the château that the babe was none of her husband's getting, for both maids and manservants knew she had not been once to his bed these many months. They remembered seeing her repeatedly slipping out alone to the forest around the time the child had been conceived and concluded that she had gone to meet her lover. They laughed and whispered in corners, wondering how Estienne could be so blind as not to realise he had been cuckolded.

When Hélène felt the birth pangs coming upon her, she again slipped out alone and went to the little bower beneath the oak. She released the dove, which flew straight to the wise woman, and she hastened to help Hélène in her travail. When the babe was born the wise woman bit through the cord with her teeth for she would not use iron to sever the bond between infant and mother. Hélène was too afraid even to look at the child, fearing that, like her other sons before, this boy would not draw breath. But the wise woman rubbed his little chest and chafed his tiny hands and feet, and soon Hélène heard the sweetest sound in the whole world, the cry of her own living child.

After seven days she returned home and placed the baby in the crib with her husband's own coat of arms carved into the headboard. Estienne brought the boy to the church to be baptised and stood for the child, declaring him to be his true son, and he named the infant Tristan. Then the proclamation went out that Monsieur le Comte at last had an heir for his lands and titles.

There were those who still claimed that the child was a bastard, but whenever such rumours reached Estienne's ears, the gossipmonger who spread such tales found himself lashed to the blacksmith's anvil where his tongue was ripped out with red-hot pincers. And thereafter whatever any man's private thoughts might have been regarding the paternity of the child, he quickly learned to keep them to himself. For Estienne knew that his wife's honour was above reproach and her virtue shone brighter than the north star. He loved Hélène more with each day that passed for all she had endured to give him his precious son.

Here the strange tale ended, but the scribe had added something more:

This is a true and faithful account as told to me by Estienne, Le Comte de Lingones himself, on the day of the marriage of his own beloved son Tristan, upon whose life he swore a solemn oath before God.

It was signed *Father Vitalis, priest of this parish of St Luke's, anno Domini, 1141.*

I quickly scrolled back to some of the earlier records, flipping back and forth between this signature and other entries by Father Vitalis. They were all written in the same hand using the same type of ink, the black having a slightly greenish tinge as is common when old inks fade over time.

So that was it. I had searched through the book from cover to cover and there wasn't a single word that had been freshly added to these ancient texts. No pages seemed to have been torn out. This simply could not have been the book my master had been writing in.

I closed the covers and was about to examine some of the others on the desk when the old crow gave a great trumping snort and rolled over to face me. Thankfully his eyes were still closed, but I wasn't about to take any more risks that night. Besides, staring at those old dusty pages had made me as sleepy as a bear in winter. I tiptoed back to my pallet but, though I was aching with tiredness, I could not sleep. I was sure the ancient one had been writing something of great importance, but what on earth was it? Had he found the document Philippe wanted after all and was copying it for him? I should get up and search again, but in the morning . . . the morning would be time enough.

Chapter 6

A weakling babe, a greybeard old,
Surnamed the dragon: me they hold,
In darkest dungeon languishing
That I may be reborn a king.

Regulus stumbles down the last step of the spiral staircase and through a door at the bottom, which is as stout as the door of his own parish church. It closes behind him with a thud that echoes from the stone walls. The white rider's hand still grasps his shoulder, but if it is to prevent the child darting forward, the restraint is not needed, for the boy's only thought is to retreat. But even in his fear he knows that is impossible. His gaze ranges frantically around the great chamber, like a trapped fly.

The long cellar is divided into three by the arches that support the vaulted ceiling. There are no windows. How could there be, so far beneath the earth? But torches gutter on the soot-blackened walls and here and there on the many tables fat candles burn, adding their acrid fumes to the room. Beneath the middle arch is a furnace shaped like a giant egg. Bellows and long pincers lie beside it on stacks of wood. The ruby glow of the fire spreads out into the room, staining the stone flags on the floor as if they are wet with fresh blood. In the far corner, a great vat rests on six short pillars. But even the firelight cannot penetrate the black hole beneath it.

There are pestles and mortars, boxes and jars, charts and books. There are round tubs, big enough for a woman to bathe in up to her neck, and wicker cages on four legs, large enough to contain a boy. Regulus's gaze darts over all these things, but he has no names for these objects and doesn't understand what they are for, so they simply blur into a tangle of shapes in his mind.

His attention is captured by the great glass flasks with bellies round and swollen as his mother's when she is heavy with child. Some are suspended over candles or tiny brass braziers. The vessels are full of rising steam that turns to beads of liquid at the top of the flasks, dripping back down onto whatever blackened mess lies within. Other flasks sit in nests of stinking horse shit, belching into each other through long glass tubes, which, to Regulus, look like birds pecking each other's chests with long sharp beaks.

Something flies across the room. The boy ducks and cringes as the long feathers of its tail brush his head. A black-and-white magpie gives a harsh croak and perches on a shelf on the far side, glaring down, its head cocked. *One for sorrow,* the rhyme pops into the child's head and he finds himself anxiously searching for a second bird – *two for mirth* – but he cannot see one.

'I have brought you the boy, Father Arthmael,' the white rider says.

A tall, gaunt man steps from behind one of the archways into the glow of the furnace. The skirts of his white robes turn as red as the burning wood. Tiny reflected flames glitter in his eyes as if a fire is burning inside his skull, but his fingers, when he caresses the boy's face, are cold. He touches the boy's red curls.

'Rubedo, the red death,' he murmurs, 'the slayer and the

slain.' He glances up sharply at the white rider. 'His youth, his colouring are right. But can we be sure?'

'His father brought him to us on St Stephen's Day and see on his right index finger – the snake.'

Father Arthmael seizes the boy's wrist and pulls it closer to the furnace. The boy struggles, afraid of the heat. He has had a terror of fire ever since, as an infant, he was bouncing on his father's outstretched leg playing horses and slipped off, his fingers plunging into the glowing embers of the hearth fire. His father had snatched him up straightaway, but he had sobbed for hours from the shock and pain of the burn. He still bears a raised scar encircling one finger like a jagged ring, and it is this scar that Father Arthmael examines.

'Ouroboros.' He exhales the word as a deep sigh. 'Yes, that is what you saw. Yet if we look at the space contained within the line and not the line itself, it is *sol*, the sun, the egg of life itself. A blink of the eye, and the empty space becomes the solid object. Behind the shadow is the light, but that light in turn hides another shadow. You must learn to see deeper.'

'This *is* Regulus,' the white rider snaps. 'I know it.' The irritation in his voice makes the boy glance up. When his mother's voice crackles like that, it is time to hide.

'Regulus,' Father Arthmael repeats slowly, as if chewing the letters. 'Our little wren. Do you know, Regulus, that a man who seeks wisdom and the divine must first seek the wren? If he can find a bird so small and invisible in a great forest, he will find the *elixir vitae*. And that I will find, little wren.'

The boy has seen hundreds of wrens. He knows they are not invisible. They come to feed near the cottage. His parents, his sisters and brothers are asleep in that cottage tonight. In spite of the heat of the room, he shivers with misery. When can he go home? When will his father come for him and take him home?

Father Arthmael lifts an empty glass flask from the shelf and places it on the flags. It is not as big as those bubbling on the tables, but it is as big as the boy's head. The lights from the flames catch this, too, and wriggle across its shiny throat. They are inquisitive children, determined to touch everything.

Father Arthmael comes closer and the boy backs away until he is pressing into the leg of the white rider behind him. He is afraid of them both, but more afraid of the tall one.

'Urinate into this,' Father Arthmael says.

The white rider lowers his head to the boy's ear and whispers, 'Piss into the flask, child.'

Regulus shakes his head. 'Don't want to.'

The man regards him with a frown. 'Do you mean that you have no urge to urinate at this time, or are you refusing to obey?'

'The boy is exhausted,' the white rider says. 'In the morning—'

'I intended to begin tonight,' Father Arthmael says, his voice sharp with anger and exasperation. He sighs. 'Patience, diligence and perseverance,' he breathes, as if he is reciting a prayer. 'They are the servants and the masters of the royal art.' He nods towards the boy. 'Very well, but see that he's kept separate from the others for now and fed only on herbs and the flesh of birds until he passes water. I must have it. It is the seed, the primal matter.'

The white rider turns the child and leads him back through

the door, but they only retrace their steps halfway up the stairs. There he pauses before another door, which Regulus had not noticed on the way down. The man turns the key, which is already in the lock, and reaches inside for a candle, which he lights from one of the torches on the staircase.

The room is tiny, narrow, though it does not seem so to the boy, for he has known only a single-roomed cottage crammed with a press of children and animals. A narrow bed occupies most of the room, with just enough space for a rough wooden table. The white rider sets the candle on a spike on the wall above it. A flat disc of brass stands on the table, engraved with concentric circles and letters, though to the boy they look like the casts of worms or the trails of a snail.

The man shows Regulus two pots set side by side on the floor.

'This glass one is for pissing into. This clay one is for shitting into. You must not shit into the glass piss pot. You will be punished if you forget. Do you understand?'

The boy understands nothing. At home he simply wanders outside to a hole his father digs, which the whole family uses. Everything that is to be thrown away goes into the hole, piss and shit, withered apple cores and bloody pigeon guts. When it is full, his father simply digs another.

The white rider makes him point to the glass pot and the clay pot in turn, reciting which each is to be used for over and over until he is sure the boy has memorised it.

'I will come again in the morning with food.'

He makes to snuff out the candle, then looks at the hunched, shivering little figure and smiles gently. 'I will leave the light for you. Sleep now.'

But the boy, all alone in the locked room, cannot sleep.

He has never slept by himself in a bed before. He has never slept without hearing the sound of the wind in the trees and the murmur of his parents' voices or the snorts and snuffles of his brothers and sisters. He lies on the bed and pulls the blanket over his head. He is cold. He is afraid and now, at last, he desperately wants to piss, but is too afraid of that pot.

Chapter 7

Purify the lead by special washing, extract the blackness and the darkness from it and its whiteness will appear.

At first I couldn't tell if the sound was real or part of my dream. I forced my eyes open. Thin blades of silvery morning light pierced the narrow slit windows. I heard the sound again and realised it was the ancient one, tip-tapping towards the door on his staff. His beard was freshly combed and he had a book clamped under one arm. As he shifted it to lift the latch, I glimpsed the winged ox on the cover and knew it was the one I had leafed through the night before.

On any other day, as soon as Gaspard was awake, he'd have thrown something at my head to rouse me and set about issuing orders before I'd had a chance to untangle myself from my blanket. But that morning he was moving quietly, as if anxious not to waken me at all. I knew the old crow better than to believe he'd suddenly decided I should be allowed to rest after all my work. So what was he sneaking out to do?

I quickly shut my eyes, giving what I fancy was a pretty convincing snore. It fooled him anyway, for I heard the latch drop back into place as he closed the door behind him. As his stick clacked away down the stone steps, I sprang up and rushed to the slit window directly above the door where I knew he'd emerge from the turret.

I had to wait for so long I began to fear he'd changed his mind and was coming back up, but at last I saw the figure limp from the door and vanish into the early-morning mist. He was heading not towards the Great Hall or the gate, but towards Philippe's private solar in the tower that stood alone, separate from the main building. I waited at the window, my stomach growling ever more fiercely. I considered whether to go down to the kitchens in search of food, but they lay in the opposite direction to the solar and I feared I might miss Gaspard's return. In the end I scrabbled in the basket containing the remains of last night's supper and found a pork bone with some meat left on it. I took it back to the window and gnawed on it as I kept watch.

It was a long time before I saw Gaspard emerge from the mist and pick his way back towards the turret. I ducked in case he glanced up, but the old crow hobbled along, leaning on his stick, his head bent down against the chill air. I folded away his blankets and pulled the straw pallet to one side. I was just dragging my own on top of it when the door opened.

'Only just risen, you lazy squab?' Gaspard said.

But for once he didn't accompany these words with a thwack from his stick, or even a sharp prod. He looked remarkably cheerful. I was so unaccustomed to seeing a smile on his face that for a moment I thought he was having some sort of fit. 'You're out early, Master.'

'There's much to be done,' he said. He rapped a pile of document cases, which promptly tumbled to the floor with a clatter. 'There's all these to be put away, and tidily, too. You can start by taking the old books up to the roof space. But I want them stored neatly, mind, and in order. Don't just fling them up there.'

I'd been so startled by his buoyant humour that it wasn't

56

until he mentioned books that I registered his hands were empty, save his staff. He had not brought the church records back with him.

'Did you find what Monsieur le Comte wanted, then?'

He smiled again, showing a row of crooked brown teeth. 'Indeed I did, and the master was most gratified. That is the art of being a good librarian. You must always be able to lay hands on anything your master requires. Keep everything, *chiot*, throw away nothing, however insignificant or old. You never know when it might be needed. "The cornerstone which the builders rejected", that is what an ancient book is, Vincent, a cornerstone. Many might consider it worthless, but one day it may prove to be the very stone upon which the whole house stands. Words, Vincent, always hoard the written words as if they were royal jewels.'

Gaspard so seldom called me by my name that I often thought he'd forgotten I'd ever had one, but to hear it uttered twice made me think it was I whose wits were wandering. But the old man's fit of affability could not last long, and with his very next breath he was back to his usual curmudgeonly self.

'Up that ladder with you, *petit bâtard*,' he said, banging his staff on the wooden boards. 'Do you expect me to go climbing through trapdoors at my age?'

I pushed the rickety ladder into position and, seizing as many books as I could carry in one arm without turning the ladder over, pushed my way up into the dusty space beneath the eaves. It was only when I got in there that I realised I had forgotten to bring a candle – the feeble grey light wandering up through the trapdoor was not enough to distinguish a bat from a rat, never mind to try to set the books in any kind of order.

I knelt and poked my head down through the trapdoor. Given the ancient one's unaccustomed good humour, I hoped for once he would pass me a candle instead of making me climb down to fetch it. But as I peered down, I saw Gaspard pulling a money bag from under his robe. He lifted the lid on the small chest where he kept his few possessions and slid the purse right to the very bottom beneath his summer robe, locking it with a key he took from around his neck. I hadn't even known he had a key for that chest, for there had certainly been nothing worth locking into it before and, believe me, I'd checked. The one thing I did know was that the money bag looked extremely heavy. Philippe must have been more than gratified by whatever the old crow had discovered for him.

For once, I was not bored witless by carrying the endless stacks of books and documents up that ladder and setting them in some kind of order. Not that I bothered much with the latter: I knew the old man could never climb into the loft to inspect my work. But pretending to sort the books gave me ample time to think.

What did I actually know? Well, first, someone was threatening to expose Philippe and ruin him. Philippe had said he needed proof that would silence them, but proof of what exactly? Gaspard had clearly found whatever he was looking for in those church records, but most of the entries had concerned the day-to-day affairs of the church and the parish. Save the lists of gifts to the church, there was little mention of Philippe's ancestors until that last entry – the story of Estienne's courtship and marriage. And not just his marriage, but the birth of his heir, Tristan, which, if I remembered correctly, just happened to be the name of Philippe's grandfather.

I began to smile as the truth slowly took shape in my head. Gaspard hadn't found that entry. He'd written it. That was why the story was crammed into such a small space. Yet the ink on the page was ancient, faded. If he'd written it only the evening before, it would have been a deep black. I should know. It was one of my many irksome tasks to spend hours and hours hunting for oak apples and collecting them before the insects emerged, in order to turn them into dried slabs of iron-gall ink ready for Gaspard to wet and use. Fresh iron-gall ink was as black as Beelzebub's beard.

Unless . . . I turned to the pile of books beside me. I was sure in my searching I had seen something . . . I riffled through the books and scrolls, cursing myself for not having put them in order after all. It took me a long time to find what I was looking for, but finally I had it in my hand – *Diverse and useful recipes*.

I thumbed through the pages, which covered everything a man would ever wish to know and quite a few things he wouldn't, from how to make pastes that would clean stained leather to physic for horses with colic. There it was! I kissed the crumbling binding. What was it the ancient one had said? *Keep everything, chiot, throw away nothing, however insignificant or old.*

I hugged the book to me, rocking back and forth. It was all I could do not to let out a whoop of delight. If Philippe would pay handsomely for the forgery Gaspard had created for him, then what might he pay to someone who had the knowledge to expose that fake?

Chapter 8

Then the swan roasted will become food for the king.

Gisa's uncle holds the swan brooch close to the candle and examines it from all sides. The light from the flame undulates over the golden beak so that it looks as if it is opening and closing in a silent and desperate plea for mercy.

'It's a costly gift, my child,' her uncle says at last. 'Lord Sylvain thinks highly of you.'

'It has nothing to do with the girl,' his wife says.

Aunt Ebba lies propped on a mountain of pillows in the bed, which she seldom leaves and which Uncle Thomas never enters, unlike the fat ginger cat that lolls on the bed beside his mistress. Strangers, when they learn that the apothecary's wife has not left her chamber for five years, remark that her husband cannot be much good at his trade if he can't find a cure for his own wife. Neighbours are more charitable, at least towards Master Thomas, for they remember that, in the beginning, Ebba had taken to her bed with a head cold, but found being waited on so pleasant that she is more than content to have her husband and niece dance daily attendance on her and on that indolent cat.

'The baron plainly intended the brooch as a token of the esteem in which he holds you, Thomas,' Aunt Ebba says. 'Who would give such a jewel to a child?'

'A child no longer,' Thomas reminds her. 'Gisa is fifteen

now, my dear, and by my reckoning Lord Sylvain has been a widower these twenty-five years, maybe more.'

Ebba snorts. 'A man of his wealth and position is hardly going to pay court to an apothecary's niece, especially a girl who's as plain as a kitchen mouse and whose father . . .'

Aunt Ebba folds her lips tightly in case the words should defy her and escape. They do not talk about Gisa's father. They never mention his name. It is one of the many rules the girl has been forced to learn since her uncle and aunt have, of their great Christian charity, taken her into their home. Something for which, as Aunt Ebba daily reminds her, she should be eternally grateful.

And at this moment, Gisa *is* grateful to the great white sow as, in her more shameful moments, she dubs her aunt, though always under her breath. Yesterday she believed herself miserable here, but now she knows she'd rather spend the rest of her life emptying her aunt's piss pot and rubbing her sweaty yellow feet than one night under Sylvain's roof.

Ebba makes a grasping movement with her sausage fingers and Thomas hands her the brooch, which she examines with as much care as he did. The cat stirs itself and sits up. It has never in its life bothered to hunt a real bird, but now its green eyes fasten on the white swan. It leans forward and sniffs. Then, with a yowl as if it has been pecked on the nose, it shoots off the bed, its tail bushed, and flees to the door, scratching frantically to be let out.

'Did I prick you, Apricot, did I?' Ebba is distraught. 'I'm so sorry. Here, my poor sweeting, here. See what I have for you.'

She dangles a strip of dried mutton from the jar she keeps by the bed in case Apricot should require a treat, but the cat continues to wail and scratch until Gisa is forced to open the door and release it.

Ebba turns the brooch over. The golden pin on the back is covered with a little leather sheath to prevent just such an accident. She cannot imagine what could have hurt her poor baby.

Thomas takes the brooch from his wife and returns it to Gisa. 'You'd best wear this on your cloak when you take the delivery up to Lord Sylvain.'

Gisa jerks as if she has been struck. 'I can't go, Uncle. Please, send the boy.'

A young lad comes daily to the shop to run errands and deliver physic to wealthier customers.

Aunt Ebba leans forward. 'She certainly can't go. I need her here and, besides, who will mind the shop?'

'He specifically asked that Gisa deliver it,' Thomas said. 'The ingredients are costly and fragile. He doesn't trust the boy.'

'It isn't seemly for a young woman to go alone to a man's house,' Aunt Ebba says primly, quite forgetting that, only moments before, she had declared Gisa to be a mere child. But, then, Ebba has never known a moment's embarrassment about contradicting herself when it suits her purpose. 'Besides, Mistress Anne said she was coming back after dark the other night and saw a ball of blue light crackling over the roof of that tower of his. Like the flames of Hell, she said it was. Goodness knows what he gets up to at the dead of night all alone there.'

'I believe the fires of Hell are red, my dear,' Thomas says mildly. 'At least, they appear so in the wall-paintings in the church.'

Aunt Ebba looks mutinous. She hates to be corrected. 'What has the baron ordered anyway that's so special?' she snaps.

Thomas hesitates. He finds it difficult to refuse to answer

a direct question from his wife. If she is thwarted in any way, she will have one of her attacks, which only adds to his sense of guilt and failure.

'Quicksilver and sulphur as always, also monkshood . . . and dragon's blood. That is what will take me time to obtain for him.'

'Dragon's blood?' Ebba squawks. 'I hope he's paid you in advance. The merchants won't wait for their money and we can't afford to buy—'

Thomas holds up his hand in an effort to dam the torrent of objections. 'I know it, but he has already paid me half, the rest on delivery if the quality is good.'

'Then you must be sure it is, Thomas. You're too soft with these foreign merchants, too trusting. You must inspect and test every bag they offer before you part with a penny. What does he need it for anyway?'

Thomas shrugs. 'Perhaps he has the flux or ulcers of the mouth.'

Gisa frowns. 'But we have better herbs to treat those in the shop, Uncle Thomas, much cheaper too, and he could have them at once.' She blurts out the words and instantly regrets them.

'And what do you know about treating flux, girl?' Ebba snaps. 'Do you imagine you are an apothecary now?'

Gisa flushes and stares at her fingers. She wants to say that, after years of preparing ointments and simples on her uncle's instructions, listening to folk describe their ailments and hearing what Thomas recommends, she can hardly have failed to learn as much as any apprentice in the trade. But Aunt Ebba, too, served in the shop when she first married and she still can't tell mouse-ear from mugwort, let alone remember what they cure.

'Cheaper,' her aunt mutters, with contempt, shrugging up the pillow, like a hen fluffing its feathers. 'I trust you are not saying that to our customers. We're not here to sell *cheaper*. We are here to sell them the most expensive that we can persuade them to buy. How else are we to make a profit? Just you remember who puts a roof over your head, girl, and food in your stomach. If the baron is fool enough to pay for dragon's blood, then let him. And if he wants you to deliver it, you will go and tell him it is the finest and most potent to be had.'

Aunt Ebba settles back on the pillows as if this has been her argument from the very beginning.

Gisa is clutching the swan brooch so hard that her fingers hurt. She drops it into her lap and rubs her palm. The outline of the swan is indented in angry red lines in her flesh. He has already branded her with the mark of a sin she has not yet committed. And it feels like a seal upon her soul.

Chapter 9

There once were twins who had great powers. When one twin turned his right side to a locked door, it would immediately fly open, but when the other twin turned his left side to an open door, it would at once slam shut and lock.

Trust me, if you've been born the bastard son of a whoring English nun, and you've spent all your life being kicked around like a stray dog until you finally end up as a slave to a wizened old crow, you will discover that your first taste of power is as intoxicating as the finest wine on the king's table.

I had sniffed that wine before when I had written notes on behalf of ladies wanting to arrange secret trysts with their lovers, or begging letters for men desperate to settle gambling debts. But those brief tastes of power were nothing, mere wisps of a lingering perfume that merely hints at the pleasures that might be had. Those who dictated the secret letters to me were prepared to pay a few paltry coins for my silence, but no more, for even if the truth came out, what harm would it really do? But now that I finally held the weighty secret of a man of Philippe's stature in my inky fingers, I felt utter exhilaration. It gives you confidence, does power, confidence to take whatever you want from the world.

For a start, I no longer paid any heed to old Gaspard.

I'd said nothing about my discovery, but knowing that I had a deadly weapon in my hand meant I had nothing to fear from him. He could hardly have me dismissed, not with what I knew. In the past, I'd always sneaked out when I could, or idled whenever his back was turned, but I'd always been obliged to make a pretence of obeying his querulous commands. Now I had no intention of being used as his slave for one hour longer. You should have seen the look on the ancient one's face when I refused to fetch our supper.

'Not tonight,' I said, pert as a tavern wench. 'I'm going to eat in the Great Hall, but if I see a maid, I'll try to remember to ask her to bring you something. Can't promise when that might be, though.'

His jaw fell so slack you'd have thought a butterfly had roared at him. I was halfway out of the door before he had recovered enough to hurl his stick after me and yell at me to return, but the stick clattered harmlessly against the closing door and I found myself whistling as I bounded down the stairs. I couldn't afford to push Gaspard too far, not yet anyway, for I wasn't about to reveal to him what I'd learned. That news was for only one pair of ears.

But I soon discovered that it is easier for a mouse to bell a cat than for a lowly apprentice like me to meet in private with a nobleman such as Philippe. Indeed, one of the scullions from the kitchens or a stable boy would have had more chance of speaking to him. In the past, whenever I'd been summoned with Gaspard to the *salle basse*, the lower hall, in which Philippe received the peasants, so that we could record the judgements he made in their affairs, or even to the hall above, the *salle haute*, to record the contracts he had made with other nobles, we might as well have been at the town fair. There were always crowds of men, women and servants milling about, not to mention their dogs and hawks, snarling and shrieking.

Since his rise at Court, Philippe was far too busy to stroll alone in the gardens. Even when he was walking between the main house and his private chambers in the tower, he was always surrounded by petitioners trying to beg favours, or arse-lickers, like Charles, pretending to marvel at his every word, as if he shat gold coins and pissed rubies. Try as I might, I couldn't catch Philippe alone.

I even contemplated sending him a letter begging for a private audience. I'd written and read enough letters in my time to know how to flatter, but he received a hundred such requests a week from men he considered far more important that his librarian's whipping boy, so it might be weeks or months before he summoned me, if he bothered at all. More likely, he'd simply ask Gaspard what I wanted, and he would doubtless tell him I was a fool and to ignore me. I might have been hanging around for months. But ironically it was the lickspittle, Charles, who gave me my chance in the end.

Charles was a distant cousin of Philippe's, the poor relation. He was his father's third son, so he was never destined to inherit much from his own family, unless his brothers had the decency to die before their father. But Charles had a modest allowance and enough noble blood running through his veins to ensure that, if he'd entered the Church or had managed to display even a little prowess in the jousting tournaments, he'd have risen swiftly enough. If I'd had half of his advantages, I'd have been a bishop or knight by his age and amassed a small fortune in spoils from either blessing people, slaughtering them or both.

But Charles was as lazy as a cuckoo and was far more

interested in marrying wealth and position than trying his hand at building it for himself. All the women in the château seemed to find him attractive and charming, with his immaculately curled hair, cow's eyelashes and elegant flattery, especially Amée, who allowed him to fawn over her and actually seemed to like it. Why do women fall for such oily arse-wipes? I'd never be seduced by a pretty face if the woman behind it was as blatantly vacuous as that slug-brain.

As I said, Charles had never bothered to apply himself to anything, and when Philippe foolishly entrusted him with inspecting some properties he owned, he hadn't even known which records he would need to take with him to check that all the goods and livestock were accounted for, the boundaries and buildings in good order. With a languid wave of his paw, Charles instructed old Gaspard to have me bring him whatever he might need. The ancient one, anxious as ever to please, had me running around like a ferret in a rabbit warren, pulling out ledgers and boxes, until there was such a great heap of them that not even a warhorse could have carried them. He meticulously sorted them until he had a leather bag full of what he considered the most important, changing his mind several times before sending me, staggering under the weight of it, to deliver it to Charles. It was then that I saw my chance.

I, being only an ignorant apprentice, somehow *misunderstood* the instructions and took the records directly to Philippe, on the pretext that I'd thought he'd want to go through them with Charles before he set out. To my relief and delight, I found him standing alone in his chamber, pouring over a long parchment scroll stretched out on a table. I managed casually to let slip that Charles hadn't known which books he wanted and I'd been obliged to spend hours selecting them for him. I hoped my diligence would impress Philippe, while, of course, reminding him that Charles was a half-witted goose to whom no father should entrust a stray kitten, never mind his only daughter. But I was not congratulating myself for long.

Philippe barely glanced at me and, with a flick of his finger, indicated that I could set the bag down near the door. He said he intended to send for Charles later that evening to give him his final instructions; Charles could take the records with him then and study them overnight.

I derived considerable satisfaction from the thought of Charles having to lug that heavy bag all the way over to the Great Hall and spend the night wading through the mountain of dusty records. Not that he would, of course. He'd call for a servant to carry the bag and not give the ledgers a second glance. But I'd learned long ago that life was much more bearable if you indulged in the odd fantasy or two about the way things *should* be. But I had more pressing matters on my mind.

Philippe dismissed me with a curt gesture and bent once more over the scroll on which were inscribed the details of roads and rivers. He was so accustomed to servants doing exactly what he asked that he had turned away without waiting to see if I had retreated. Like a conjuror, he imagined that, at a simple sweep of his hand, I would simply vanish. And his authority was such that I found myself obediently walking to the door, even as I was telling myself not to be such a fool. Here was my one chance to speak to him alone. I might never get another.

I turned with my hand on the latch. Though I had been rehearsing this for days in my head, now that I was face to face with the man, I couldn't think how to begin. My mouth felt as if it was full of sand and my legs were trembling.

'My lord, I have to speak with you on . . . on another matter.'

I saw a slight frown of irritation crease his brow, but still he didn't bother to look round, his finger tracing down the length of the scroll. 'What is it?' he grunted. 'Out with it.'

'Some days ago you asked my master Gaspard to search . . . for a certain document.'

'So,' he said curtly, 'who do you imagine I would ask to look for documents – my cook?'

I came close to losing my nerve, but I forced myself to continue.

'I believe . . .' I swallowed hard, then said firmly, 'I *know* the document he brought you was a forgery. In the book . . . the book of records from St Luke's Church. That last account was not written by Father Vitalis.'

Philippe's back snapped upright. The scroll he'd been examining sprang back into a roll, jumped from the table and fell to the floor. He took a pace towards me, his expression so furious that I found myself pressing down on the latch ready to take flight.

'Shut the door,' he said, in a dangerously quiet tone. 'Come closer.'

I shuffled a couple of paces towards him. Living with Gaspard had taught me exactly how long a man's reach is, but Philippe was a younger and much fitter man.

'A book of church records.'

I nodded briefly, trying to force myself to stand still.

'And what makes you imagine that I would be interested in anything written in the church records?'

His gaze was fixed so intently on me that, though I had

been determined to look him in the eye as his equal, I found myself having to stare down at the corner of the table in order to be able to stammer out a word.

'The – the last entry, my lord, an entry concerning your great-grandfather's marriage to Countess Hélène and the birth of their son . . . that's what you wanted Gaspard to find.'

At the edge of my vision, I saw Philippe's feet stir and was unable to stop myself taking a step back, but he made no move towards me.

'I had not realised Gaspard had confided in you,' he said quietly.

I could hardly tell him I'd listened at the door, but if I said that Gaspard had told me all, the old crow would surely deny it. So I remained dumb. But, unwittingly, there in that chamber, I learned my first lesson about how to discover what you need to know. If you stay silent, neither confirming nor denying, men will eventually begin to talk.

Philippe sank down in the chair beside the fire. 'Then you know already that my enemies were circulating rumours that my grandfather's birth was not legitimate, which might have caused me some difficulties.'

Difficulties! Total ruin, more like. I'd be the first to admit I was as innocent as a newly hatched chick back then, but even I knew that the moment a man's entitlement to lands and hereditary rank is questioned you can't take a pace without treading on a hundred relatives, all clamouring to prove they have the greater legitimate claim.

'But now I have proof that my grandfather was the legit-imate son of Estienne, Le Comte de Lingones,' Philippe continued softly. 'The king is satisfied that all is in order, so that is the end of the matter.'

'The proof was the story in the book from St Luke's Church?' I asked, though I already knew the answer.

'Which Gaspard discovered in the attic,' Philippe said carefully, arching his eyebrows, as if daring me to contradict him.

'Which Gaspard *wrote* himself,' I countered.

'That's nonsense, boy!' Philippe was again on his feet. 'Any man can see at a glance it was written many decades ago. The book is old, the ink faded. Whatever madness has possessed you to think otherwise?'

'I saw Gaspard writing in that book, yet there are no new entries in it. The ink was made to look old. He didn't use iron-gall ink, he wrote with the older form of ink they used a century ago. I found the recipe, which he also must have read for it was among the books I fetched for him from the attic.'

As proof I recited the recipe from memory: '*Grind the seeds of goat-leaf and after let them boil in wine together with a rusted iron nail. This makes a green ink. But if thou wouldst make a black ink, add drops of vitriol till it turn black and also the sap of the hawthorn, so that will stay wherever thy pen does place it.*

'The base of that ink is green,' I said, in case Philippe hadn't got the point. 'So when it's old, the green tinge begins to show through the black again. Gaspard sent me to the still room for goat-leaf seeds for a purge, or so he said, but I know he used them for ink. By adding too few drops of vitriol, a little of the green hue would remain visible, so it would look as if black ink had faded with age. I can prove it to you. I can make that ink again and match it to the page.'

You have to admire men like Philippe: they have been

72

well schooled in the art of not betraying their emotions. Vital, I imagine, if you spend your life among the schemers at Court. But, even so, I thought I saw his face blanch a little, though it might just have been the flickering of the firelight.

'Gaspard is a loyal servant,' he murmured.

I had no idea if Philippe himself knew what Gaspard had done or if he, too, had been tricked by the old man. He wasn't stupid. He must have suspected something, but he'd been so desperate for proof that he'd probably grasped at any rope flung out to him that would pull him from the mire.

His tone when he spoke aloud again was chilling enough to freeze the flames in a blacksmith's furnace. 'But you, my young apprentice, are evidently neither loyal to your master nor to me. You say you saw your master writing. Naturally, he writes. That is his job. You say it was in a certain book. I have only your word for that and one book looks much like another from a distance. You say he sent you to fetch some seeds for a purge. Who gave you the seeds? Will this person corroborate what you have said? . . . No, I thought not. You can hardly imagine that King Louis would listen to the half-witted ravings of a disaffected servant and *English* boy to boot. And that is what they are, nothing more than the delusions of a mooncalf. The king has already accepted the evidence as true and he does not like to be made to look a fool.'

My face grew hot. The discussion was not proceeding as I had rehearsed in my head. But I wasn't going to slink away defeated, not yet.

'Surely then the king will like it even less if he's made a fool of by one of his trusted nobles,' I said quickly. 'What if your enemies who were spreading those rumours find out about the forgery and tell His Majesty? They'd be only too willing to believe my story and . . . and they'd pay well for such information,' I finished in a rush.

Philippe's mouth slowly widened into a humourless smile.

'Ah, now we cut to the heart of the beast. Gaspard, no doubt, told you that I generously rewarded his diligence in finding the record. And you thought, But I, too, spent many hours searching long and hard like my master. Indeed, perhaps it was you who discovered the book on those dusty shelves and, not unnaturally, you are thinking, But where is the justice in this? I also should have been rewarded for my pains, even though I am a mere apprentice.'

I gave a half-nod, uncertain whether he was mocking me or actually thought I had a point.

He paused, regarding me for a long time. A heavy silence descended on the chamber, broken only by the cracking of the logs on the fire and the moaning of the wind through the shutters. I could hear my own heart pounding in my chest. Was he going to pay me, have me thrown out or worse? It suddenly occurred to me that he could easily have me flogged bloody. The sweat was trickling down my forehead, but I daren't wipe it away for fear of drawing attention to it. I knew I shouldn't let him see I was afraid, but it was all I could do to stop myself blurting out that I'd made a terrible mistake and throwing myself on my knees, begging him to forgive me. I was on the verge of doing just that when he spoke again.

'You are an intelligent lad, quick-witted, observant. And it takes boldness to tackle the wolf in his own den. A young man with your gifts could rise rapidly if his talents were fully appreciated. I warrant you won't remain an apprentice for much longer. But I think you want to stride further than old Gaspard's feet will lead you. You want to be more than a mere scribe in my household, or you wouldn't have risked all by raising this matter.'

A surge of relief rushed through me. He understood!

'I could be of great service to you, Monsieur le Comte, if I had the chance.'

'I don't doubt that. But wits and ambition alone are not enough. If you seek advancement you must learn that those who can help you rise require two other qualities from the men they champion – discretion and loyalty.'

'You'll find no one more discreet or loyal than I am, Monsieur le Comte. I told no one, not a single person, what I knew. Not even Gaspard knows I've discovered his secret and I swear on the Holy Virgin no one will ever learn of it, if . . .'

He raised his eyebrows. '*If*. . . Yes, indeed, that tiny word on which have balanced the fates of whole kingdoms and the lives of thousands.'

His grey eyes bored into my own. 'Very well, then. We shall forget this foolish attempt at blackmail for we both know this nonsensical talk of a forgery was just a youthful and misguided attempt to bring yourself to my attention.'

He twisted the heavy gold ring on his finger, so that the blood-red garnet rippled in the firelight. 'I believe that if any man is to earn another's loyalty and trust, he must first demonstrate his own loyalty and trust in that person. So we shall offer trust to one another, you and I. I will entrust you with an errand that requires great discretion and secrecy. If you succeed, you will have earned my confidence and gratitude, and I am always generous in showing my gratitude, as you will have observed from the purse I gave Gaspard.

75

Perform this task well and I promise you that you will never again have to return to that tower to waste your life burrowing among dusty books.'

'Anything, I will do anything,' I blurted out. 'What is it that I'm to do? Only tell me and it will be done instantly . . . I mean perfectly. I won't fail you, I swear.'

And in that moment I meant it. I was not going to be flogged. Instead I was actually going to be promoted. I felt almost giddy at the thought, imagining myself day and night at Philippe's side, sitting at high table next to Amée in my new clothes – he'd obviously have to present me with new clothes: my limp rags weren't fit even for the servants' table.

He laughed. 'Patience. I will send for you again in a day or so and explain exactly what is required of you. In the meantime, tell Gaspard to wait upon me here. But, first, to seal our bargain, drink with me.'

He lifted a flagon of wine from the table, poured the wine into one of his own pewter goblets and held it out to me. 'Let us drink to your destiny. I predict it will be inter-esting, far more so than you could ever have dreamed.'

76

Chapter 10

He should be discreet and silent, revealing to no one
the truth of his works.

'Boys, this is Regulus, your new companion. You are to look
after him.'

Six pairs of young eyes gaze solemnly at the white-robed
figure and back again to the small child, who shrinks beside
him.

'But be warned. If I hear any idle gossip, or even a whisper,
that you have spoken of things about which you have been
told to keep silent, I will punish not just the offender, but
each and every one of you most severely. For he who listens
to idle chatter is as guilty as the one who utters it.'

The White Canon allows the full force of his glare to fall
on each of the faces in turn, noting those who quickly stare
down at the rushes on the floor or dart an anxious glance
at a companion. The boys believe he can see into their heads,
which indeed he can, for though they would never believe
it, he was once a child himself and he knows well what
strange and foul creatures wallow in the filthy middens of
a boy's mind.

Regulus clutches the wooden bowl, leather beaker and
bone spoon he has been given. He's been told that if he
loses them he will go hungry and thirsty, for he will have
nothing to put his meat and drink in. He wonders if he

must carry them all day and what will happen if his arms grow tired, which they already are, because he is gripping them so tightly. The canon pushes him forward.

'Felix, make room for Regulus at the table. I leave him in your care. See you instruct him well, for if he transgresses, it will be your back that will smart for it.'

A thin, gangly boy of about eleven years with lank brown hair and bulging eyes shuffles his buttocks along the bench, leaving a gap between himself and the next boy. Felix beckons Regulus to the space with a jerk of his head. The little boy tries in vain to scramble over the bench and sit at the table, but though the bench is low, he is still gripping the bowl, beaker and spoon, which he is afraid to set down. The other boys giggle. Felix impatiently stands, grasps him under the armpits, swings him over the bench and plonks him down on it, as if he was an infant.

'Put your bowl down,' Felix instructs.

But Regulus hesitates. He's hungry and he's afraid to let go in case they refuse to feed him. He glances along the length of the table. Each boy's bowl and beaker sit in front of him on the table. Still he worries. Suppose they snatch his.

'Everyone is waiting, Regulus,' the man with the frosted chin says. 'Set your bowl and beaker on the table, like the others.'

He obeys, glancing up first at the man, then at Felix, for reassurance that he has done it correctly, but neither gives him any encouragement.

At a sign from the white-robed figure they all stand. Regulus is hauled to his feet by Felix. The boys bow their heads and press their hands together in front of them.

'*Oculi omnium in te sperant, Domine . . .*'

78

Frosty-chin leads and the boys join in, though some are merely gabbling sounds that no Latin scholar would recognise. They take their places once more, save two of the boys who fetch a pipkin of herb pottage. The bowls are passed up and Regulus watches anxiously as his is whisked away to be passed along the row.

'It's mine!' He makes a grab for it, but Felix promptly cuffs him, pressing his finger to his lips and sternly shaking his head. Regulus anxiously marks the progress of his bowl, watching as a slice of old bread is dropped into the bottom and a dollop of the thick green porridge plopped on top. At last it is returned to him, with a slice of new bread. The boy takes a bite of the bread. He has never tasted anything quite like it. This is cheat bread, not by any means the finest bread that is made but when in your short life you have eaten nothing but ravel, full of bran and husks mixed with rye and beans, you may think yourself in Heaven when you first taste bread made from wheaten flour.

As the boys eat, a nervous-looking child stands at the low lectern in the corner, reading aloud. He rubs the metal amulet hung about his neck as if this will ward off disaster or the wrath of Frosty-chin, maybe both. Several times, the boy's stomach rumbles loudly as he smells the food he is not yet permitted to eat. Whenever he stumbles over a word, he glances anxiously at the white-robed man, afraid that if his tongue trips again he will get no pottage.

Regulus does not notice the hesitations. He is not listening to the words. He is too intent on spooning the cabbage and pease pottage into his mouth as fast as he can. He has to be prevented by Felix from devouring the stale bread lining the bottom of his bowl, which to Regulus's dismay is snatched from him and collected in a great basket. Felix whispers

79

that it will be given to the hungry who come begging at the alms-gate, but the boy is still hungry himself. He wonders where this gate is and if he can go there to get his bread back.

A bell tolls. Once more the boys scramble to their feet and stumble through the words led by the canon.

'*Benedictus sit Deus in donis Suis . . .*'

Frosty-chin surveys the room. 'You are free to indulge in such pastimes as you wish for an hour before Nones but, remember, no noisy games. Some of the brethren sleep at this hour and if any are woken by your balls or chatter, you will all be made to labour for them during this hour every day for a week.'

He sweeps from the room, closing the massive door behind him. The boys hesitate, then, as one, advance on Regulus, forming a circle around him.

'Where are you from?'

'When did you arrive?'

'Your parents dead?'

The questions fly at him and he can't answer them. No one has ever asked him where he comes *from* for he's always been there. There never was a past place, just a *here* and *now* and *is*.

'*Regulus.*' Felix pronounces it carefully, as if he was chewing a flavoursome morsel of meat. 'Who gave you that name? Your father?'

That is the only thing the boy does know. He knows it is not his name.

'Wilky . . . my name is Wilky.'

Felix's bulging green eyes blink slowly. 'Father John, was he the one who named you Regulus?' Then, seeing the blank expression on the child's face, he adds, 'You know, the man who brought you here . . . Him who was sitting just there.' He points to the chair at the end of the long table, which the white-robed figure has just vacated.

Regulus tries to think. Was it Frosty-chin who gave him this name? The night's events are as jumbled and hazy in his head as a half-remembered dream.

Finally he nods. 'And the man who cooks things in glass pots. He called me that too.'

'Regulus,' Felix repeats softly. He circles the child, frowning.

'What's it mean, Felix?' one of the boys asks, sensing this name is a weapon to be used.

'Don't you ever listen to your lessons, Peter?' Felix says. 'Last week, remember. Regulus – ruler, king.'

The boys see the joke at once and grins spread across their faces. 'Him, a king? That little maggot? What's he meant to be king of, then?'

'King of the beggars.'

'King of the codwits.'

'King of the turds.'

This game looks set to last a long time. The boys won't easily tire of coming up with new titles.

Only one of the small gang is not joining in and that is Felix. He knows only too well that if Father John chooses you and Father John names you, there is a good reason. Father John does not make jokes, far from it. He is always serious, deadly serious, and if the boy has already been to the dungeons, he must be special. And that is an honour no boy wants, not in this place. He's heard Father John speak the name *Regulus* before. They have been waiting for this boy for a long time.

'That's enough,' Felix says suddenly. 'Leave him be. You'll

get no chance to play any games if you don't go now. Hour'll soon be up.'

The boys stare at him, puzzled. Felix has never been known to stop teasing before. He's usually the chief tormenter, but they've no time to ponder the matter. Their one free hour in the day is far too precious to be wasted in here. They race each other to the door.

Felix stares down at the little boy, who gazes up at him from liquid blue eyes. Felix shudders. He would not want to be named Regulus for all the food on the abbot's table. Even at eleven years old he is already wise enough to know there are some titles in life you pray to every saint in Heaven you will never be granted.

Chapter 11

Devours his tail till naught remains.
This dragon, whom they Ouroboros call.

The summons came at dawn three days after I had confronted Philippe. I was beginning to think he had forgotten about me or had never had any intention of entrusting me with a task and had merely made promises to keep me quiet.

When old Gaspard returned from speaking with Philippe that night, he'd shuffled to his desk and ignored me as if I was one of the pigeons that flapped about the turret. I was used to the ancient one not speaking for hours at a time when he was absorbed in his work or his reading, but he always had something to say when he first returned to the tower, generally some complaint about me not working, but that night he didn't even look at me. I knew Philippe must have told him all I'd said and he was angry, hurt even.

Well, it was his own fault. If he'd offered to share the purse with me or told me what he was doing, I wouldn't have gone near Philippe, but if the old crow was determined to be so secretive and refuse to confide in me, his faithful apprentice, he could hardly blame me for reasoning it out for myself.

But I wouldn't have to put up with Gaspard's sulks or complaints or his vicious stick any more. Philippe had finally sent for me and I would never have to go back up that turret again. Gaspard could die up there, for all I cared, and probably would. In a few years someone would say, *I wonder what happened to old Gaspard?* And they'd find him, sitting mummified at his desk, the quill still in his hand, the ink turned to dust and the mice nesting in his beard.

'Adieu,' I said jauntily, as I turned at the door.

The ancient one lifted his head. He seemed to be struggling to speak, but nothing came out except a single word – *Vincent* – and, to my astonishment, I saw that tears were running down his papery old cheeks. Anyone might think the old crow was going to miss me. Well, I certainly wasn't going to miss him. I bounded down those stairs with all the joy of a colt let out to pasture on the first day of spring.

'I have a package I want you to deliver to a man by the name Albertus. A gift for the good service he has done me.' Philippe indicated a leather pouch lying on the table between us. 'His house is a mile or two beyond Ricey-Bas. The road through the valley will take you straight there. He's a man who prefers his own company. You will know his house by the ouroboros inscribed upon the wall. It resembles a winged serpent devouring its own tail. You will tell no one where you are going and you will give this package only into the hands of Albertus himself. Do not entrust it even to one of his servants. Then hasten back here.'

'Am I to take a horse from the stables?' I asked hopefully.

The town had to be at least ten miles away, maybe more, and on the few occasions I'd been there to buy new parchments and other supplies for Gaspard, I'd travelled with other servants in the back of a wagon. I didn't fancy walking that distance and back.

'Can you ride a horse?' Philippe asked.

84

He knew I couldn't. What chance did an apprentice librarian ever have to learn to ride?

'Can't be that hard,' I mumbled.

Philippe's face wore an indulgent smile, like the one men adopt when dealing with a small child who thinks he has said something clever but has merely shown his naïvety. 'When you return, I will see to it that you are taught the skills of horsemanship. In the meantime, Vincent, I have no wish to see you break your neck or, more importantly, damage the package. Besides, you are less likely to draw attention to yourself on foot. No one will suspect you of carrying anything of value, whereas mounted on one of the fine beasts I keep in my stables you would instantly be marked out as wealthy. But don't look so dismayed. I wouldn't expect you to walk there and back in a day. Take this.' He handed me a soft leather purse, which I could feel contained a few small coins. 'That should be more than sufficient to buy a comfortable night's lodging in the town before your return.'

Although I was still a little irked by having to walk, I could see the sense in what he said. To be honest, part of me was relieved he didn't want me to ride – the horses Philippe kept in his stable were huge, powerful brutes that even his knights found hard to control. But he could have sent a servant to drive me in a cart, at least as far as the town. Set against that, though, was the prospect of a night spent away from the château. All those inns and taverns, cockpits and girls! Actually, the more I thought about it, the more I realised Philippe was doing me the most enormous favour by making me walk. Otherwise I'd have missed what promised to be the wildest night of my life. After spending every night for the past seven years with Gaspard, even a sedate game of Nine Men's Morris with an elderly nun would have seemed thoroughly debauched, and I intended to do a great deal more with my freedom than play board games.

I heard the iron ring in the door turn and glanced round to see Amée entering, a small sack swinging from her hand of the kind that a farmer might sling over his shoulder when setting off for a day's haymaking. My heart began to pound at the sight of her. She always looked adorable, but today, in a sky-blue kirtle, her flaxen hair draped with a fine white veil, she was as beautiful and pure as the Virgin Mary at the Annunciation.

She crossed to her father and, stretching up on tiptoe, planted a sweet kiss on his cheek. I wondered how it would feel to have that soft mouth pressed against mine. I might never kiss her, but if I impressed her father, I would surely see her every day . . . and who knew?

Amée turned, with a dazzling smile. 'My father tells me you have a long walk today. I didn't want you to be hungry, Vincent, so I packed some food for your journey.' She held out the sack. 'I hope you will enjoy it. I chose everything myself.'

I didn't know what was in the bag and I didn't care. If she'd filled it with mouldy bread, I'd have thought it the finest food I'd ever tasted because she had picked it up with her own hands and put it in the bag for *me*. I could hardly have been more ecstatic if she had popped the food into my mouth with her own dear little fingers. Amée cared about me being hungry! She had risen at dawn to pack food for me . . . herself . . . with her own hands! I thought my heart was going to float out of my mouth. She had spoken my name. She had *remembered* my name! I was so stunned that it was several moments before I could stop gazing at her long enough to bow and thank her.

She nodded and, with another dimpled smile, slipped away through the door. I couldn't stop smiling. I bet she'd never got up at dawn to pack food for Charles.

Philippe coughed pointedly and I flushed as I realised I'd been standing there like the village idiot, grinning at a closed door. I straightened my face and scooped up the leather bag that I was to deliver, fumbling with the long strings with which I intended to tie it around my waist, concealing it beneath my cloak.

'Don't you want to know what you are carrying?' Philippe asked.

'I wouldn't dream of prying, my lord,' I said respectfully.

Philippe laughed. 'Yes, you would. Curiosity will get the better of you before you've gone a mile down the road. So, you'd better satisfy yourself now. It's safer that you do it here than examine it on the open road where others might see you. You have my permission to open it.'

Since he was ordering me to look, I could hardly refuse, so I loosened the drawstring and pulled out a small wooden box. It was a plain-looking object, not gilded or jewelled, not even painted, and decorated only by a carving of an ouroboros on the lid, the same sign that he had told me I would find on the wall of Albertus's house. I opened the lid and tipped out an object wrapped in a piece of soft white woollen cloth. Unrolling it, I found myself holding a heavy silver flask in the form of a bird's head with a thick curved beak and eyes inlaid with beads of polished black onyx. Every feather on the bird's head was so delicately engraved that each barbule could be distinguished, their lines no thicker than a human hair.

'The raven's head,' Philippe said, gazing at it with an expression of near rapture. 'Exquisite, is it not? A fitting gift for my friend, I think.'

I wondered what service Albertus had performed for Philippe to warrant such a present, for I could tell, just from the weight, that the silver alone was worth a fortune, even without the fine workmanship of the piece.

Philippe took it from my hand and with his fingertip caressed the smooth polished silver of the beak. 'You see what faith I am placing in you, Vincent. There aren't many men to whom I would entrust such a costly and rare object. Do not betray that trust.' His voice was suddenly as cold and sharp as a sword thrust. 'I do not forgive betrayal.'

Chapter 12

The spirit which is extracted from metals is the urine of children and of the sages, for it is the seed and primal matter of metals. Without this seed there is no consummation in our art.

The chapel is in darkness, save the candle flames trembling on the altar. The great pillars supporting the arches stretch up like petrified tree trunks, the tops vanishing into the shadows above. The breath of the little huddle of boys escapes as white mist from their mouths, as if their spirits are leaving their bodies. Somewhere, overhead, a great bell tolls.

Regulus is shivering in spite of the warm cloak they have given him. He pulls it up over his mouth and nose, trying to breathe through the wool, for the air is as cold and damp as if he was leaning over a deep well. Mighel, the boy with the amulet, is coughing and wheezing. He scratches frantically at the raw red patches on his arms. Father John frowns at him. He desists until he thinks Father John isn't looking, then surreptitiously rubs his arm against the wall, like a pig with an itch.

There is a sound at the great door behind them. Some of the boys crane their necks, but Father John clicks his fingers and they spin their heads back to face the altar as he motions to them to kneel on the hard stone flags.

The great door opens, but though Regulus turns, he can

see no one, for a broad panel of wood at the end of the aisle shields the doorway, and it is as well it does for the candles on the altar gutter wildly as if the flames are trying to tear themselves loose and fly up into the air.

Ten white-robed men emerge from behind the panel and process up the centre of the church two by two, their hoods pulled low over their faces. They are singing a psalm in Latin, though to Regulus, who has seldom been inside a church, it means less than the twittering of birds. He is unnerved by these faceless men. He had not realised there were so many men like Father John in this place. They have multiplied like maggots on a dead rabbit.

But by the time the incomprehensible service finally crawls to the end, Regulus has had to be shaken awake twice by Felix. The child is so sleepy, he can barely put one foot in front of the other. Felix propels him back to the chamber in which they ate, and pulls a straw pallet from the stack for him. He lays it neatly beside the row of others and tosses a blanket from the pile on top.

'I'm only doing this once, mind,' Felix warns. 'Tomorrow you fetch your own bed, else you'll sleep on the hard stones.'

Regulus isn't listening. He is desperate to lie down. Felix drags him over to the corner. 'That's the pot you piss in. That's the one you shit in. Don't forget. We'll all get punished if you get it wrong.'

Even half asleep, Regulus knows he has heard this warning before and panic wells in him again. What will the punishment be if he makes a mistake? Is it as bad a crime as poaching deer? He once saw a boy sewn into the hide of the deer he'd killed and sent running through the forest to be hunted down by the pack of hounds. He can still remember the baying of the excited dogs and the screams of the boy as their snapping jaws brought him crashing to the ground. Regulus shudders.

Father John glides silently in, and when all the boys are lying on their pallets, he blows out the candle. They hear the door close behind him. Regulus, exhausted, falls asleep as quickly as a new-born puppy, but not so the other children. They lie tense, waiting.

The bell tolls, echoing through the silent passages, like a stone dropped down a great well shaft. Huddled beneath the thin blankets, the boys silently count – *eight, nine, ten.* Still they lie awake. It is not safe to sleep yet.

As the air trembles with the last chime, the door swings open. Half roused by the bell, the sudden gust of chill air on his cheek makes Regulus open his eyes. A monstrous white bird hovers in the doorway. The boy tries to scream, but no sound escapes him. He pulls the blanket over his head, holding his breath, but the dust and fear make him choke and he stifles a cough. Has it heard him? Is it the lantern-man come to carry him off?

He hears a faint scraping, like a bird's claws, across the stone flags. The scaly feet are pattering nearer and nearer. He can hear them. Almost rigid with terror he presses himself down into the straw of his pallet, but that makes the straw rustle. There is a tiny shriek, like the cry of a mouse when the silent owl pounces, but Regulus is not the boy who cries out.

He pulls the blanket down just enough to peep out with one eye. A figure is bending over one boy's pallet, holding a guttering candle over the bed. Regulus sees it is not a bird at all, but a man dressed in white robes, his hood drawn low over his face. He drags the boy up from his pallet by his arm, and silently waits while the boy wrestles his shirt over his pale, skinny chest and gropes his feet into sandals, which he fumbles to fasten.

The robed man grows impatient. He seizes the boy by the shoulder, and propels him towards the door before his shoe is secure. The boy walks with a lopsided shuffle trying to keep a grip on his sandal, but on the steps leading up to the door, he loses it and it bounces back down, as if trying to flee back to the safety of the pallet. The boy turns, trying to retrieve it, but the robed man pushes him towards the door. As he lifts the candle to illuminate the iron ring, the light catches the boy's face. His cheeks are wet with tears, his face contorted, but he makes no sound as he is led out into the bitter night. The great door closes behind him.

Regulus dreams he is pissing into a giant pot, but it's running out through a hole and he can't stop it. Felix is shouting at him, *Fill it up! Fill it up!* But it's all running out. Beneath the blanket, something hot trickles down the sleeping boy's leg. The little king has wet his bed.

Chapter 13

Saturn is the planet of death: look, this one has brought
the black mantle of the raven's head.

There were two tracks that wound through the river valley
to Ricey-Bas. The broader one was favoured by soldiers on
the march and by men driving carts or women herding
squawking geese or plodding cows. This track followed every
twist and turn of the River Laigne, skirting fields of grain
and vineyards, and marked by numerous wayside chapels
where men might light a candle to their favourite saint to
pray for a safe journey and a good day's trading in the
market.

The higher track, on the opposite side of the river, was
much straighter, though steep, rough and narrow. It was fit
only for single riders and foot travellers. I agonised over
which would be the better route. If I took the broader track
there was a chance I could beg a lift on a cart, which was
certainly tempting. But the ground was sodden after the
rain and there was a risk of carts and wagons getting stuck
in water-filled ruts, with any passing man being pressed into
pushing it out. I'd no wish to spend my day with my shoulder
to a cartwheel, being splattered with mud and dung for my
pains.

I made for the river and parted with one of the precious
coins Philippe had given me to pay the ferryman to row

me across. At the start of the forest path, where the track parted company from the river, there was a small shrine to the patron saint of travellers, St Julian the Hospitaller, who had accidentally slain his own mother and father and spent his life running a pilgrim's inn as penance. But I passed without stopping. I didn't intend to waste a single coin or prayer on the fellow. I was only going out for a day's stroll after all, and when you have a man as powerful as Philippe as your patron and protector, you're hardly in need of the favours of a dead innkeeper, who was so witless he mistook his own parents for his wife and her lover.

The autumn leaves on the trees had turned every hue between buttercup yellow and ruby red, and as the wind rattled the branches, they spiralled up the hillside. Winter was not far off, but at least this year I'd be sleeping in the great hall before the huge fire, not in that draughty turret with the wind shrieking through the shutters and Gaspard's dry old bones lying between me and the miserly heat from the brazier.

The wooden box bounced against my thigh as I walked. If the surly ferryman had known what I had hidden under my cloak, he would have been far more polite to me, instead of treating me like a beggar. New clothes: that would be the first thing I'd demand from Philippe – and I'd hold him to those riding lessons too. I had a vision of myself leading the hunt for the stag, riding out ahead of the field and dazzling Amée with my horsemanship as I leaped boldly over fallen trees and ditches that her other suitors feared even to attempt. I patted the bag of food she'd prepared for me. She was the most wonderful girl.

Spurred on by my daydreams, I strode out confidently along that forest track. Running up and down all those steps in the tower had made me as fit as a hound of the chase, or so I thought, but I soon discovered it wasn't the best training for paths like these and I kept stumbling over tree roots concealed beneath the rain-sodden leaves or slipping on loose stones that had fallen down from higher up the slope.

In the first couple of miles, a few people passed me, making their way down towards the river crossing – two old women carrying live ducks in panniers, a crook-backed pedlar and a couple of children with bundles of kindling on their heads. They all grunted a greeting of sorts, but the wind was too sharp and the daylight too short to waste time in gossip. For the last hour or so the track had been deserted, so I was all the more startled when a voice rang out above me.

'Polecat, Polecat! . . . I's been a-waiting for you.'

I heard something slithering and crashing down the bank above me. I gave a shriek and almost slipped off the path. It was as if part of the forest had reared up from the leaf mould and formed itself into the crude shape of a man. It hurtled towards me and I retreated almost as fast. It came to a halt a few feet from me, its head tilted to one side, staring curiously at me.

'I's waited, Polecat. I's waited just like you said. Didn't tell no one.'

It was only then that I saw this was no forest sprite, but a man of flesh and blood, whose grimy skin was tanned to beechnut brown. He wasn't exactly dressed: his naked body was hung with rags of coarse brown sacking, woven through with leaves and twigs. His wild, matted hair bushed out from beneath the tattered remains of a cloth hood, decorated with bracken, feathers, withered flowers and what might have been an old bird's nest.

'You find the gold, did you, Polecat, did you?'

'I'm not Polecat,' I said hastily. 'I'm afraid you've mistaken me.'

The tree-man peered at me uncertainly through his shaggy locks. 'Polecat?'

'No, not Polecat, Vincent. My name is Vincent.'

'You seen him? You seen my Polecat? When's Polecat coming back?'

I had no idea who this friend or relative was, but I knew it would be futile to explain that. I wondered how long the poor old bastard had been waiting for this man – years probably, by the look of it. I thought it safest to humour the wretched creature. 'Polecat told me to tell you he's coming soon, very soon.'

I turned away, striding on up the narrow track on the steep hillside, and for a few yards the man kept pace with me, lolloping sideways through the leaf mould, as sure-footed as a mountain goat on the steep, slippery bank.

'Polecat's a-coming,' he sang over and over, like an excited child. Then, dropping his voice to a harsh whisper, he confided, 'When he brings the gold, I's going to buy a new hat . . . Sssh, sssh, don't tell them about the gold. Mustn't tell.'

'I won't,' I said, trying to quicken my pace to get away from him.

'You'll fetch the gold for me, Polecat?' His tone was suddenly anxious.

'I'm just going to fetch it now,' I told him. 'You wait here. Don't move. I'll be back.'

That seemed to pacify him, for he stopped following me, and when I cautiously squinted behind me, he'd vanished, as if he'd sunk back into the leaf mould from which he was formed.

96

After that, I saw no one. The trees grew closer together in that stretch of forest. The branches intertwined so that, even though the leaves were falling, it was like walking deeper and deeper into a cavern. Several times, I thought I heard someone walking behind me, feet shuffling through dried leaves, twigs snapping. Was that madman stalking me? But when I whirled round, the path was empty.

A worse thought struck me. Maybe a wild boar was preparing to charge or a wolf was stalking me. I suppressed the urge to run, knowing that if a predator was following that would only encourage it to give chase. But I'd come too far to turn back and take the other road. There was nothing for it but to press on and eventually, when no madman leaped out at me and no ravening beast sank its teeth into me, I was able to convince myself that the rustling was only squirrels and the footsteps just nuts falling in the wind.

My stomach growled and I pulled the sack of food from my shoulder. I was gratified to find that, in addition to fresh wheaten bread, the adorable Amée had furnished me with cheese, onions, apples, a roasted pig's trotter and two meat pastries. My only disappointment was that the leather bottle, which I had hoped would contain some more of Philippe's good red wine, had been filled with the white wine they issued to the servants, sour and as weak as nuns' piss. But perhaps that was to the good. A rich wine would only have made me drowsy.

The sun had swung well past midday, but I'd dared not stop to eat. I'd no means of telling how much further off the town lay and I certainly didn't want to find myself still in the forest when twilight crept in. So I ate as I walked, hoping that the smell of food wouldn't attract any animals.

Best to eat the pig's trotter first: then I could fling the bones behind me. If a lynx or wolf was following, that at least would distract them.

After the trotter, I devoured one of the pastries which was every bit as succulent as it looked, and after a good swig of wine to wash it down, I strode out again, blessing the sweet name of Amée. When I returned I would have the perfect excuse to seek her out and speak with her – just to thank her for the food, of course.

I tried to quicken my pace, but I was not accustomed to walking for miles, and I began to feel as if I was wearing lead boots. My legs would scarcely hold me up. A wave of cold sweat broke over me. I thought I was going to vomit. The path lurched under my feet, as if it had been transformed into a twisting serpent. I staggered, trying to keep my balance, but even the trees seemed to be tipping, as if they were slowly falling to the ground. I rubbed my eyes, trying to clear them. Everything was blurred, as if my head was under water.

I never saw the rope lying across the path ahead, only glimpsed the movement as it sprang taut at shin height, but by that time it was too late. I was already tumbling over it, sprawling face down on the path. A man sprang out of the trees, his staff raised above my head. But I had lived with Gaspard long enough to sense a blow when it was coming. I rolled out from under it and grabbed his ankle, jerking it upwards and sending him crashing to the ground.

I glimpsed his face screwed up in pain as he tried to right himself. But I barely had time to scramble out of his way when two more men were upon me, kicking and battering me with their staves. I covered my head with my arms, rolling myself into a ball, yelping in pain as the blows landed on my back and sides. I screamed out, pleading for them to stop, begging them to take anything I had, but spare my life.

I heard someone yell, 'Your knife, man, use your knife and finish the little turd.'

In desperation, I struggled to my knees and tried to crawl away, but another blow across my back knocked me flat again.

There was a roar somewhere above me. 'I's kill you! I's kill you if you hurt him!'

An arrow whooshed over my head. It must have struck one of my assailants, for he gave a sharp cry and the stave dropped from his hand. A second arrow followed and a third in quick succession, but both missed their mark. The men held their ground. Then I heard something lumbering down the hillside through the dried leaves, roaring like a wounded bull. With yelps of fear the men stumbled over me and ran. I was dimly aware of the distant sound of men tearing headlong through the trees, before pain and dizziness engulfed me and all the world grew dark.

I came to in a fit of coughing and tried to open my eyes. My eyelids rasped as if they were being dragged over sand. I could see nothing, except a flickering red glow. Two agonising sensations hit me in the same instant – the side of my face was burning and there was a searing pain in my ribs, as if they'd been pounded with a blacksmith's hammer. For one terrible moment I thought I'd died and was being tortured in Hell, but as I tried to pull my head away from the heat, I felt the cold, damp earth beneath me. I wasn't in Hell, then. I gritted my teeth against the pain of moving and shifted my weight, trying to make sense of where I found myself.

I was lying with my head dangerously close to a fire trench and my outstretched feet pressed against a large rock. By the glow of the smouldering wood, I could see I was in some kind of shallow pit excavated between two large boulders, with the rock that lay at my feet forming the back wall. The top was covered with a dome of densely woven branches. The fire pit guarded the narrow entrance to this hut, if such a basic shelter could even own a name, and was presumably intended to keep out any wild beasts that might be tempted in for food or shelter. I coughed again, clutching at my ribs, as the wind gusted the smoke back inside the hut.

Outside, the forest lay in darkness, but there was no way to tell the hour of the night. Just how long had I been unconscious? With my ribs screaming in protest, I tried to ease myself into a sitting position, and only then did I see that what I'd taken to be a heap of leaves was in fact a body, lying motionless beside me. It was the tree-man, the one who'd mistaken me for his friend.

It was as if time was turning backwards and fragments of broken images were rearranging themselves in my mind, like pieces of a shattered pot coming back together.

I'd been beaten, that much I remembered almost immediately, and it must have been the tree-man who had frightened off my assailants. But who had attacked me? Robbers! There was no shortage of those ready to prey on lonely travellers. Philippe had said I'd be safer on foot, so as not to draw attention to what I was carrying . . . As the thought struck me, I fumbled for the leather bag I'd hung around my waist and felt, to my utter relief, the hard outline of the wooden box inside. The small purse of coins hanging on the opposite side of my belt was still there as well. Neither the robbers nor my rescuer had discovered either one.

But my relief turned swiftly to puzzlement. The first thing footpads do is knock their victim off his feet, then, as he lies stunned, rapidly feel all over his body, cutting away any purses or ingots and running off before he has a chance to cry out. It was said that some thieves could do it so swiftly they were gone before he'd even landed on the ground. Why waste time beating your victim and risk being disturbed?

Stray words bobbed about in my head. One had shouted something – *Finish the little turd!* They'd intended to kill me! They were actually going to murder me. So it wasn't a robbery at all. But why? What was I to them?

I rubbed my forehead, trying to think. I saw the features of a disembodied face as if it was drifting towards me through the woodsmoke. It was the face of the man who'd led the attack. The features had been distorted with pain and rage as I'd sent him crashing to the ground, but now that the fog was clearing from my brain, I recognised him only too clearly. It was that bastard Charles, Philippe's arse-licker.

He must have got wind of the mission Philippe had entrusted to me and followed me, determined that I'd fail and be disgraced in Philippe's eyes. Charles certainly wouldn't want me to supplant him as Philippe's trusted man and he wouldn't think twice about stabbing his own best friend, let alone some lowly apprentice, not when the prize was Amée and all the fortune that went with her. Just wait until I told Philippe about this! He'd have the little weasel thrown out of the château in the clothes he stood up in, or even without them. I grinned to myself at the image. It had almost been worth taking a beating just to see that louse banished.

The smoke from the fire sent me into another coughing fit and I clutched my ribs against the searing pain. I tried not to groan aloud, though nothing seemed to disturb my snoring companion. I lay still, considering what to do. Should I return to Philippe immediately and warn him about Charles or deliver the raven's head first, as he'd told me to do? The question was, would Charles and his cronies be waiting for me further along the track, determined to finish what they'd started? I would be if I were them, especially since Charles was bound to think I'd recognised him. He'd apparently been so sure of killing me in the first attack that he hadn't even bothered to disguise himself.

Maybe the answer was to double back in the dark as far as the river, then cross over and take the lower path to the town from there. Always assuming I could find my way back, since I had no idea where the tree-man had brought me.

I wondered whether to ask him to guide me, but it was probably best to try to slip out without waking him. For I'd noticed that, in addition to his bow and arrows, a wicked-looking axe lay beside his right hand, where he could snatch it up at the first whisper of danger. If he was still suffering from the delusion that I was Polecat, he might not be keen to let me go, and if I told him I wasn't, he could turn nasty. Who knew if he'd even remember rescuing me? Suddenly roused from sleep, he'd probably think I was a stranger come to attack him.

A log in the fire pit collapsed, shooting red sparks into the darkness, and filling the sunken bothy with more smoke. But the tree-man didn't stir. It was a wonder to me he hadn't set himself ablaze long before now. He really was a sound sleeper. Still, doubtless you learned to be, living out there, with the creaking of the trees and the shrieks of unseen beasts as your only lullaby.

I'd lived rough for most of my early childhood, but always

in the town, sheltering in doorways or church porches or beneath a cart in the corner of some workman's yard. Towns never slumber. There are always footsteps and dogs barking, babies yelling from a nearby house, women shrieking or drunks roaring. I knew what town noises signified. But in the forest a rustle might be nothing more sinister than the wind stirring leaves, or it could be the last sound you heard before a boar ripped your belly open. I shivered. I had no desire to leave the comfort of the fire and venture out into that darkness, but my best chance of evading Charles was to move before dawn.

I attempted to roll over and ease myself onto all fours. It wasn't easy in the cramped space. It was all I could do to stop myself screaming at the pain in my ribs and back, and I couldn't prevent the odd gasp and squeak escaping. But as I struggled forward, my foot slipped under me, hitting the tree-man's leg. I froze, gasping for breath, but even the hard knock didn't wake him. If it hadn't been for his snoring, I would have thought him dead. Maybe he was dead drunk. I glanced down and saw that my sack of food lay across his legs. The leather bottle was on his chest and the crust of what looked like the remaining meat pie. He'd doubtless swigged the rest of the wine but, even so, the nuns' piss in that bottle wouldn't have been strong enough to send a baby to sleep.

At that moment the final fragment of memory slid into place. Just before the ambush I'd suddenly felt so drowsy . . . couldn't see properly. I was dizzy, staggering as if I was drunk . . . but I wasn't drunk! I'd been drugged, just as this man was now. Drugged by the food or drink Amée had given me.

But she couldn't have known, not my beautiful, innocent

103

Amée. Someone else must have put— Who was I trying to fool? She'd made a point of telling me she had packed the food sack herself, carefully selected the contents. Only she could have drugged it. Charles must have persuaded her to do it. He'd probably told her it was a joke and convinced her it would merely make me sleep so that he could steal the raven's head and deliver it himself to gain Philippe's favour and make me look a fool. I flushed with humiliation at the thought of the two of them laughing together at the stupid apprentice.

But Amée couldn't have known what Charles was planning. She wouldn't have smiled at me so gently and handed me that bag, knowing all the time she was sending me to my death. No girl could be that cold-hearted or cruel. And she wouldn't have been deceiving only me, but her father, too. Unless . . .

Each new revelation was like a punch to my throbbing head, but the last was the hardest blow of all. Suppose Amée had *not* deceived her father. What if she had done exactly what he'd instructed her to do? How else could she or Charles have learned that he was sending me on an errand unless he'd told them? The cold truth drenched me and left me shivering. Charles and Amée had acted on Philippe's orders. He had deliberately sent me on an errand from which I was never intended to return alive!

Chapter 14

Three species will suffice thee for the whole magistery:
the white smoke, the green lion, the stinking water.

Gisa stands in the Great Hall exactly where the manservant left her. She has not moved. She is afraid to, as if her slightest movement will be detected. She gazes around, trying to fix the details in her mind, as though her future might hang by a single hair of memory.

A small cage swings from an iron chain. A linnet sits huddled on its floor, its feathers fluffed out, its eyes closed. It looks so miserable that, for a wild moment, Gisa considers opening the door and setting it free. But how would it escape from the hall? Where would it go? They are both trapped.

In the centre of the floor, a fire crackles in the hearth, which is encircled by yellow and brown tiles and a ring of blackened stone. The blue smoke spirals lazily upwards to wander among the high beams and eventually trickles out of the small vent in the roof above. At one end of the hall a table and three carved chairs stand upon a dais. At the other end a long table and benches mark where lesser guests and servants dine. The long table is bare, save a bowl of apples spotted with black scab and soft brown patches, where the flesh is beginning to rot. Gisa wonders fleetingly why the servants have not removed them: surely a man as wealthy as Sylvain would not need to eat spoiled fruit.

But it is the walls that chiefly hold Gisa's attention or, rather, what is on them. For the lime-washed walls above the dark green wainscoting are painted with the signs of the zodiac – the scorpion with its stinging tail, the lion with dagger fangs, the bull with fire and smoke pouring from its nostrils. Behind the dais, the wall is painted with the flaming ball of the sun, borne aloft on the back of a golden eagle, while at the opposite end of the hall the silver moon is carried in a cradle of ribbons trailing from the beaks of two swans.

Gisa's hand strays to her shoulder, where the swan brooch holds her cloak in place. Her aunt Ebba had summoned her to her bedside and pinned it on, pinching her cheeks hard to bring some colour to their pallor. 'If an apothecary's family look sick, people will start to question his remedies,' she said, blithely oblivious to her own bedridden state. 'Now, remember, give the packages only into his hands, smile, curtsy and keep your eyes modestly lowered. Don't meet his gaze like a brazen tavern slut.'

Gisa still holds the basket her uncle had placed in her hands. It is heavy. The sulphur and quicksilver were sent ahead with the boy, leaving her to bring only the dragon's blood, but even so there are several pounds of it. She is afraid to set it down, knowing how valuable it is. Her uncle has told her she must wait until Sylvain has checked and weighed each piece, as he himself has already done.

A door set into the wooden wainscoting behind the dais opens silently. The smoke in the fire billows out in an arch, like a swan's neck, before straightening again. Gisa had not noticed a door for the wall appeared solid. That unnerves her even more. She feels that doors might appear anywhere without warning. Slowly he emerges from the wood panelling, his arms unfolding, like the wings of a black insect, as he extends them towards her.

'At last! I expected you days ago. You have it?'

'My uncle took great pains to obtain it.' She is always quick to defend him. 'You asked for the best, sir. The purest.'

He nods and steps down from the dais. She takes a step back, but for once his gaze is fastened not on her but on her basket. His long fingers pluck it from her and put it on the table. Then he lifts out each of the packages wrapped in sheepskins to protect the precious contents. He unrolls one, then peels back the inner parchment wrapper to reveal the dark-red shards. A fine film of crimson powder covers the pieces, where the fragments have rubbed together. Sylvain lifts one and blows on it gently, ensuring the precious dust falls back into the parchment. It is far too costly for the wind to play with. He holds the piece up in the light of one of the candles. It glows deep red, translucent, like an emperor's ruby. Gisa, as if she is drawn on a string, takes a step forward. She's seen dragon's blood before, but only as cakes of pressed powder, which were dull reddish-brown. She didn't know it could be as beautiful as this.

'*Edah amsellah,*' the man whispers. 'The tears of the dragon.' He examines each package carefully. 'Your uncle has bought well. These are of the finest quality.' He takes a small pair of scales and tiny weights from a pouch hanging at his waist and, holding the scales between thumb and forefinger, weighs each piece as if it were a nugget of gold. He methodically records the weight on a wax tablet, careful even to collect the powder and weigh that too. For a long time he works in silence. Then, without taking his gaze from his work, he says, 'Do you know where dragon's blood comes from?'

Gisa says nothing. Her uncle says it is the dried blood

of a slain dragon, which is why it is so hard to come by, and looking at these drops of glassy red, she believes him. But she fears her answer will sound foolish.

Sylvain's gaze flicks briefly towards her. 'There is an island of dragons far away in a distant sea, an island they call Dioscorida. But other monsters also inhabit this island. Elephants, which are giant beasts, taller than a house, with a long arm growing from their snout, tusks that curve up like boars' fangs, but much longer, and ears that are so large their young may shelter beneath them, like tents. The dragons and elephants are both such mighty beasts that they continually fight each other for possession of the island. The dragons are more agile and they can fly. They bite the elephants and suck out their blood in a single swallow. But the elephants are so heavy that when they fall dead they crush the dragons beneath them so the blood of the dragon mingles with the blood of the elephant. And as it dies, the dragon weeps tears of blood, these tears.' He lightly touches one of the dark-red jewels.

Then, dipping his finger into the crimson powder at the bottom of the parchment, he draws a wide circle in the centre of the long table. Without warning he bends and scoops Gisa up in his arms. She tries to push against him, but his grip is too tight and he is too strong. If this were a village lad, she would kick and scratch, but she is too afraid of offending him to offer any but token resistance. He lifts her onto the table.

'Step into the middle of the circle,' he instructs her. 'Tread carefully. Do not disturb the ring of dragon's blood.'

She is too afraid to move. She doesn't understand what this means, what he means to do. Circles can enchant the body and mind. Circles can call up evil spirits and demons. If you stumble inside a faerie ring in the woods, you will be snatched away, taken to another realm from which you can never return.

As if he can read her thoughts, he says soothingly, 'Dragon's blood is one of the most powerful protectors against the deep darkness and all the foul demons that are born from it. You will come to no harm, I promise.'

Still she hesitates.

'Do as I ask, Gisa,' he says softly. 'You do not wish to displease me. Your uncle has yet to be paid in full and this purchase will have cost him dear.'

He takes her hand to balance her and reluctantly she steps over the line of crimson powder. His skin is as cold as dead men's fingers. She braces herself against the dread of what she might see, where she might find herself. Her body is rigid. Her breathing stops.

But nothing happens. There is no blinding flash of fire or flood of blackness, no demonic scream or owl's screech. She is still in the hall. The fire still crackles. The candles still burn. He lets go of her hand and turns away from her, walking over to the hearth in the centre of the floor. He stands with his back to her and stretches his hands out flat over the blaze.

'Now, Gisa, close your eyes tightly, and turn slowly on the spot until I tell you to stop. As soon as you stop, point up towards the walls, but do not open your eyes. Keep them closed tight.'

She revolves, careful to turn towards the right, *deiseil*, as the sun moves across the sky. To circle the other way, to circle *widdershins*, against the sun, would bring down a dark curse. But she is still afraid of what this turning may do, what she may turn into.

He has let her revolve three times and still he says nothing.

Four, five, six, or is it seven, eight? She no longer knows. She is dizzy, disoriented, fears she will plunge off the table. But somehow she finds she cannot stop, not till he commands her.

'Stop and point.'

She stops, staggering slightly, trying to keep her balance. She lifts her arm.

'Yes,' he whispers. 'Yes! I knew it was so. I knew you were the one.'

She can hear the rapture in his voice. He is pleased, thrilled even.

Unbidden, she opens her eyes and stares to where her finger is pointing. Her hand is reaching out to one of the zodiac signs upon the wall – Leo, the golden lion. Its jaws are stretched wide as if it means to devour the other signs. Its teeth are as sharp as scimitars and its tongue as red as the tears of the dragon.

'The fifth rotation. Her lion, the *vas Hermetis* into which I must descend.'

He is speaking as if the room was empty and she had vanished. But she has not vanished. She stands awkwardly in the circle on the table, feeling sick and giddy. It has been nothing more than a harmless game, a game that children play. Except . . . except that when he lifts her from the table and sets her feet upon the floor, he suddenly grasps her shoulders, staring intently into her eyes.

'You must keep yourself pure, Gisa, for this sacred work. If you so much as look at a man or boy, if you let them touch you or kiss you, I will know. I will be able to see it in your face.'

Sylvain caresses the white enamel swan at her throat. 'You will sing only one song in your life, Gisa, and that will be when I demand it.'

Chapter 15

For deadly I can be and poisonous.

I was jolted from sleep by the sound of an ox-cart rattling over the stones and women screeching their gossip to each other as they walked beside it, in voices loud enough to be heard right across town. Instantly, I felt again each and every blow those bastards had rained down on me. The bruises had stiffened overnight and had not been eased by my long walk through the forest or sleeping on the cold, hard ground. Gritting my teeth against the pain, I forced myself to crawl out of the bushes where I'd taken shelter and peered about me.

The sun had long risen, and the smoke from the hearth fires and furnaces in the town hung in a heavy grey cloud above it. The wind had died down but, if anything, this day seemed set to be colder than the last. My throat was as dry as one of Gaspard's old ledgers and my belly rumbled, reminding me that I'd eaten nothing since that meat pastry the day before, and since the pie or the wine had been drugged, it was little wonder I was so thirsty.

Rage and indignation boiled in me again. Had Gaspard known what Philippe was planning? Had they been sitting cosily by the fire dreaming up ways to murder me? So that was why the old crow hadn't been able to look me in the eye when he'd returned from Philippe's solar that evening,

111

and after all I'd done for him over the years. I'd cared for that shrivelled wart better than any son and done most of his work, too. Well, they'd pay for it now. I was determined to see both of them begging on the streets before I was through.

After I'd slipped, or rather limped, away from the tree-man's shelter in the dark, I'd had time to think. I'd decided against returning to the river crossing. I knew if Charles proffered even the smallest coin to that sly ferryman he'd readily tell them I'd crossed back. It was probably him who'd told them which track I'd taken in the first place.

But I couldn't follow the forest path either for I was pretty certain Charles would be waiting for me somewhere ahead. So, I struck out through the trees, creeping over the brow of the hill, relying on the darkness to cover me. Mercifully the wind was roaring through the forest. Between the creaking branches and the rattling of the dried leaves, it sounded as if a herd of deer was thundering by, so I trusted it would mask any noise I made as I hobbled up the slope.

I don't know how long I walked. Pain and exhaustion numbed my senses, until I was blindly pushing through saplings and crawling up steep ridges, then stumbling and sliding down the other side. I was so dazed, I found myself staring dumbly at the flickering spots of yellow and red ahead of me, until I realised they were the burning torches of the distant town. I'd made it! And for now I was still alive. Unable to take another step, I'd crawled into the nearest clump of bushes and instantly fallen asleep.

Now, as I watched people passing along the track below me, I decided the best course was to join a group making their way into Ricey-Bas. If Charles was planning another ambush, even he wouldn't dare to attack me in front of witnesses. Once there I would make my way to the town's *burgeis* and tell them the whole story – how Philippe and Gaspard had conspired in forgery to deceive the king and, when they learned I was on my way to the town to denounce them, how they'd tried to have me killed. I would make no mention of my attempt to extract money from Philippe. That would only confuse matters and men in authority are happier if you keep things simple for them.

I had a glorious vision of the king's men-at-arms thundering into the château to arrest them and of the king's gratitude to me for my bravery in unmasking the rogues. A position at Court would surely be the least I could expect. My only twinge of anxiety concerned Amée. I'd no wish to see her suffer, even after what she'd done. I'd convinced myself her father had forced her to drug the food and she'd had no idea he was arranging to have me killed. She couldn't have smiled at me like that if she'd known – no girl could. So I would protect her. In fact I'd ask the king for her hand as my reward. And while she might, I supposed, initially blame me for her father's disgrace, when the king reminded her of how charitable my gesture was, how magnanimous my forgiveness, she would fall on her knees in gratitude that I was rescuing her from a life of degradation or seclusion in a nunnery, for it was certain no other man would take the daughter of an executed felon as his wife.

You probably think me as naïve and foolish as a newly hatched chick who wanders up to a fox and says, 'Mama?' And, indeed, I was back then. But look at it this way: though the seventeen years of my life hadn't been strewn with four-leafed clovers, I had managed to avoid most of the disasters that might have befallen a boy of my cursed nativity. And in the last few hours I'd even managed to evade Philippe's nasty little plot and the three assassins he'd sent to murder me. So, I think I could be forgiven for believing that Fortune was not averse to sprinkling a little of her luck on me, which, though I say it myself, I richly deserved. Fortune favours those who help themselves.

Besides, I'd lived for the past seven years among books and stories. They'd been my playmates, teachers, parents and priests. In books it's always the lowly woodcutter's son who dispatches the dragon and marries the princess; orphans outwit powerful wizards, and shepherd boys, armed only with sling-shots, kill giants who have slaughtered whole armies of warriors. Somewhere in a book I'd yet to read there had to be a tale of an apprentice librarian who defeats a wicked count and wins the hand of his beautiful daughter.

But, of course, the books do not record everything. Their writers carefully omit the stories about the dozens of hopeful woodcutters' sons who were burned to a crisp by the dragon's breath, or the shepherd boys whose heads were crushed like grapes or the apprentice librarians who . . . Well, let's not get ahead of ourselves. No, that morning, in spite of my throbbing bruises I was foolishly and stubbornly certain that I could take on, and triumph over, Philippe and all his minions.

I inched my way down the hillside towards the track, taking care to keep to the shelter of bushes and shadows. It isn't easy moving stealthily when you can hardly bear to move at all and have to stifle yelps of pain. But eventually I was within a few paces of the track and, so far, luck was with me: Charles and his hounds had not found me and they were, so I hoped, still lying in wait far back along the path.

The track here was broad and far better used than the higher stretches: besides the town, it led to several outlying farms and hamlets. It was evidently market day for a steady procession of people was ambling along the road. Some carried live chickens that swung, heads down, from cords over their shoulders, while others hefted panniers of fruit on their backs or balanced faggots of kindling on their heads. Ox-wagons and donkey-carts rumbled past, bearing barrels, planks, bales of fodder or a few late vegetables to sell in the town. The women, for it was mostly they who passed along the road, were chattering to each other, and wouldn't have noticed if the king and all his court had been standing among the trees.

I'd no wish to alarm anyone by lurching out at them from behind the bushes so I waited until an ox-cart, led by a woman and a young lad, had passed and the track behind was empty. Then, as quietly as I could, I crept out and began walking a few yards behind the cart, not so close as to make them think I was trying to rob them, but close enough that if I was attacked I could cry out.

A small child sitting in the back of the cart saw me limping along behind them. She smiled shyly and waved. I waved back. She must have said something to the woman leading the beasts, for she turned her head, regarding me curiously, then stopped the wagon. She walked a few paces back towards me as I approached. Her eyes narrowed in the glare of the bright autumn sunshine. 'What happened to you, lad? You look like you've been wrestling a herd of bears.'

I saw no reason not to tell her the truth, at least part of it. 'I was ambushed yesterday on the forest track. Three of them. I only got away because they were disturbed.'

She tutted angrily. 'Robbers are getting bolder by the day and the nobles who are supposed to protect us only shift their arses to do anything if it's one of them that gets attacked.

115

Quick enough to take our taxes, they are, but don't give a cat's turd for us the rest of the year. You want to report it to the Watch, soon as you get to the town – get a posse out to hunt them down . . . Meantime, you'd best ride in the wagon. Otherwise, by the look of you, the vultures and ravens will be pecking at your liver before the day is out.'

She helped me into the back of the ox-wagon and settled me down in what little space there was between baskets of round cheeses, eggs and nuts, flagons wrapped in hay, two young billy goats and the runny-nosed child. My stomach growled at the smell of the cheese and it took every mote of control I had not to break a piece off, but if I did, I'd probably be thrown straight back onto the road again.

Jolting along in the back of the wagon as it rattled over the stones was, if anything, more painful than walking, but since I scarcely had the energy for the latter, I accepted the punishment gratefully. At least lying down I didn't have to keep looking over my shoulder to see if Charles was about to leap out at me. He'd hardly attack me in front of witnesses. At least, I hoped he wouldn't.

We trundled unchallenged through the gates in the thick walls. The guards evidently recognised the woman and, at any rate, were far more interested in interrogating the pedlars in case any might be spies of the English king or could be conned into paying bribes to be allowed to pass with their packs intact.

I parted company with the woman and her children as soon as we reached the marketplace. She barely acknowledged my thanks for she was already hard at work shouting her wares, between yelling at the boy to mind his sister and tether the bleating goats to the wagon wheels, where passing customers could admire them.

The heavenly aroma of roasted meat, new bread, fresh-baked pastries and sweetened tarts drifted past my nose and set my mouth watering. Everywhere I looked men, women and children seemed determined to torture me by wafting delicious food within inches of my face. There were girls balancing trays of roasted sheep's feet, spicy blood sausages and boiled tongue on their heads, women selling eggs pickled in brine, men slicing thick wedges from great hams and children sucking dragées of hardened spiced honey. My stomach wasn't just grumbling, it was roaring.

I had intended to seek out one of the town's *burgeis* without delay and demand that he send word of the treachery at once to the king. Food, I told myself, could wait. Besides, there was a good chance that as I was bringing news of such importance I would be invited to dine as an honoured guest, especially if the *burgeis*'s wife took pity on me, as the woman with the wagon had done. I imagined a pretty young serving maid tenderly bathing me and the *burgeis*'s wife anointing my bruises with some sweet unguent before tucking me up in a soft bed and feeding me with 'whatever the poor boy fancies after his terrible ordeal'. But my stomach would not be satisfied by promises. It demanded food now, at once, immediately! And that was my undoing.

I limped up to one of the women selling roasted pigeon squabs wrapped in smoked bacon, which were just begging to be popped into my mouth. I dragged myself towards her, hoping that if I looked pitiful enough, she'd be generous. But she barely gave me a glance until I handed over a coin from the small supply Philippe had given me. She was about to tuck it away in the purse that dangled at her waist, but hesitated, glancing down at it again. She brought it close to her eye to examine it. Then she stared up at me. She turned to a woman standing behind her selling knives and prodded her in the back. She handed the coin to her with a jerk of her head in my direction.

The knife-seller also seemed to take an uncommon interest in the small silver coin. She gave me a long, hard look then lifted her head and started yelling.

'Here! That's him! That's the thief what stole the silver bird. See, here's the proof!'

She held up the coin between thumb and forefinger, although it was so small that I doubt anyone could have made out what it was. Heads turned and I glimpsed a few people beginning to move towards me.

For a moment I was too stunned by the accusation to do anything other than gape, but when I saw the expressions of hostility and greed on their faces I knew that any attempt at explanation would be useless. I felt a hand clutching my sleeve and, without even looking to see who had seized me, I grabbed the wrist and jerked the man forward so that he pitched head first into the roasted-pigeon seller. Then I ran.

'After him! There's a bounty on his head,' someone yelled.

I'd thought I was too stiff and battered to do anything more than creep along like some old dotard, but fear can make the body do what the will alone never could. I dodged around stalls, stacks of pots and animal pens. Fortunately the marketplace was crowded and those charging after me were as much hampered by the throng of people as I was. Most of the older men quickly dropped back and returned to their stalls, afraid to leave them unattended. But some youths, spurred on by the promise of a reward for my capture, were not so easily discouraged. Several times they almost caught up with me, but fortunately their way was frequently blocked by a stout goodwife dithering in their path or a man with a great pannier on his back, giving me just enough time to wriggle past and away.

The pain, which had been numbed by that first rush of fear, now flooded back and I knew my legs were about to give way. I ducked and crawled beneath a cart that stood behind a cloth-covered booth. I wriggled as far as I could into the shadow and lay flat, my limbs trembling with exhaustion, listening to the shouts of my pursuers as they searched for me.

I had badly underestimated Philippe. Even as I cursed him to the hottest fire of Hell, I had to admit that he was a genius. He'd planned for every contingency. Obviously not trusting that idiot Charles to make a good job of killing me, he'd made quite sure that if I did elude my assassins and reach the town, I'd be arrested as a thief. It simply hadn't occurred to me to examine the coins he'd given me. Why would it? But they must have been marked. Every man and woman in the marketplace had plainly been warned to look out for them.

And when I was arrested for theft, who would I be tried by? My master, Philippe, of course, because I was a servant at the château and he was the king's bailli. A smoked eel had more chance of swimming away than I did of not being convicted. I'd hang, there was no doubt about it. And, knowing Philippe, he'd probably have me flogged to the bone first.

I groaned. If I hadn't been aching already, I'd have kicked my own backside black and blue for ever opening my mouth. Why hadn't I just kept quiet about that wretched book? I was the most frog-witted, dung-brained idiot ever to draw breath. I certainly couldn't report the forgery to the *burgeis* now, even supposing I could get as far as the town hall. I couldn't hide under the cart for much longer either. The owner might return and drive off at any moment. By now someone would have alerted the Watch that I was in the town and they'd have started a thorough search.

I crawled forward and tried to wriggle out of my hiding place, only to see the face of a curious little girl staring upside down at me.

'What you doing?' she demanded.

I put my finger to my lips and flapped at her to go away, but instead she crawled under the cart with me, plainly settling in for a companionable chat. That was all I needed. Sooner or later her mother would miss her, call for her, and the child would lead them straight to me.

'What you doing?' she repeated.

'I'm playing hide and seek,' I whispered.

The child beamed. 'Can I play?'

'Of course, but we have to hide in different places, don't we? And if people start calling your name, you mustn't answer. You have to keep hiding and pretend you can't hear them.'

She nodded eagerly.

'Why don't you hide here, while I find another place? Do you know another good place to hide?'

The child sucked a grubby finger thoughtfully. She flopped onto her stomach and pointed between the wheels to a small yard squeezed between two houses.

'I hide in there when Mam's angry, under the stairs.'

Though I desperately wanted to run, I knew that would only draw attention to me, so I willed myself to stand up and saunter casually across. With every painful step I took I expected to hear a cry, but I reached the yard without anyone stopping me and slipped through the open gate.

Fortunately, the yard and the house appeared empty. Nothing stirred, save the family's washing, which flapped lethargically in the breeze.

From the stacks of casks and barrels in various states of completion, the yard belonged to a cooper and I saw at once what the child had meant. An open rickety staircase led up the outside of the workshop to the sleeping quarters above. The cooper had stacked his timber at the foot of the stairs and, in the space beneath the steps, you could crouch out of sight behind the pile of wood, though you'd be visible to anyone using the staircase. It was hardly much of a hiding place for a man, though it would indeed seem secure to a small child.

I was just deciding whether or not to try to creep away when I heard the Watchman blowing his horn for attention on the other side of the market and the hubbub of the marketplace quietened, though only slightly. Some announcement was being made, though most of the traders did not interrupt their business to listen. Any news would drift their way soon enough, if it was worth hearing. But I had a pretty good idea what that announcement might have been.

I snatched a woman's gown from a tree in the yard where it was drying and, for good measure, a length of linen cloth flapping beside it. Retreating behind the stairs, I began stripping off my clothes. I removed the bag containing the raven's head. For a moment, I was on the verge of hurling the cursed thing as far as I could throw it. But what good would that do? Whether I was taken with or without it, I'd still be branded a thief.

Very well: if they were going to hang that name around my neck, I'd live up to it. I'd take the raven's head, and Philippe would have only himself to blame. If they were

121

going to force me to make my own way in the world, I'd need all the valuables I could lay my hands on. Besides, I reckoned I'd earned it, all those years scribbling away as Gaspard's slave, keeping their secrets and covering their lies. And what recompense had I ever had for all my labours? Clothes so threadbare that even a beggar would scorn to wear them and food the pigs would have curled their lips at.

I fastened the leather straps of the bag around my waist and pulled the stolen kirtle over the top. You could have fitted me and a fat twin together into it but that was all to the good: it would conceal both the wooden box and my masculine shape. I wound the cloth around my head, and as I did so my arm brushed the stubble on my chin. Some might have called it little more than arse-fluff, especially since, like my hair, it was blond. But it would be enough to give me away, so I wound the tail of the cloth round my face, pulling it up over my chin, like a gentlewoman's wimple. Finally I tied my own clothes round my waist under the gown, which I hoped would conceal the hardness of the box if anyone brushed against me. So clad, I stumbled from my hiding place and edged out into the marketplace again.

Across the far side of the square, a group of men were fanning out and starting to search every wagon and booth, sweeping under carts with pikes and staves. With my head down, I sidled along the length of the square, keeping close to the buildings, and turned into the first street I came to.

It is an amazement to me that women can walk in skirts, never mind work in them. I couldn't seem to take two paces without the cloth wrapping itself around my legs. I was beginning to realise that they take tiny steps because a longer stride would have them sprawled face down on the cobbles in no time. I couldn't keep this up for long. As soon as I was clear of the town, I'd change back into my own clothes or it would take me all day to walk a mile.

As I minced round the corner, I saw ahead of me one of the town gates. For a moment I was elated. Freedom lay just yards away. But almost at once despair crashed in again for I saw that the carts, horses and men on foot were not passing through but slowing to a halt in front of the gates, forming an ever-lengthening line. The guard were searching everyone leaving the town and inspecting all the carts and wagons in which a fugitive might be concealed, even kneeling down to peer beneath them, in case anyone was hanging underneath. I'd little doubt they were doing the same at all the other gates. There was no way out except through those guards. I was trapped.

Chapter 16

He should reside in an isolated house in an isolated position.

'We've come to see our lad,' Hudde says.

He shuffles awkwardly in front of the huge wooden gate, trying to peer in through the iron grid at the man standing behind it. He hastily removes his hood as if he is in church or in the presence of his master, then just as quickly replaces it, in case he should seem too servile. His wife, Meggy, is watching him from across the other side of the track and she's told him to stand his ground.

'The brothers see no one at this hour,' the gatekeeper mutters. 'You got a message for one of them? Been a death in the family, has there?'

He, too, cranes his neck, trying to look over Hudde's shoulder to see who else might be with him. Caution and curiosity are both the vices and the virtues of a gatekeeper.

Uncertain how to reply, Hudde turns away to seek an answer from Meggy. She's balancing a small child astride her hip, while a little girl clings to her skirts. Her other three children are engaged in a noisy and boisterous game of tag, charging up and down the track. Meggy is too far away to hear the gatekeeper's words, but she sees the uncertainty on her husband's face and gestures at him to insist on seeing the boy.

'Well?' the gatekeeper demands. 'Do you want me to deliver a message or not? I've got better things to do than stand here talking to you all day.' If challenged, he would be hard put to name anything else he actually has to do, but he can tell Hudde is not the man to challenge him.

Hudde jerks his head in the direction of his wife. 'We buried our youngest a week or so back. She's grieving for him something terrible. Now she's taken it into her head there's summat amiss with our Wilky. Has these nightmares that he's in danger and is crying for her. I tried to tell her no bairn could be in a safer place. But she won't rest till she's seen for herself he's thriving. It's only the grief as has her fretting, but you know what women are when they get a notion into their heads.'

The gatekeeper does not know. Though he's only a lay brother, he's been an abbey servant for years, but even before he entered the cloisters, he'd never felt the slightest desire to have any dealings with those screeching creatures they call *women*. But he is beginning to grasp something of what this ignorant lump of a woodsman is trying to tell him.

'A boy – you mean a child, not one of the brothers?'

Hudde nods eagerly. 'That's it. Wilky, he's our boy. Came here a few months back.'

'No boy here of that name.'

Hudde's brow wrinkles. ''Bout this high,' he says, holding his hand flat as if he was touching the boy's head. Then he realises the gatekeeper can't see his hand. 'Just five summers, he is. His hair's the colour of . . .' he hesitates. He's not often called upon to describe such things. '. . . a ladybird, that's what it always put me in mind of. Course, without the spots.'

He laughs nervously for the gatekeeper is staring at him as if he is making no more sense than a chattering squirrel.

125

The lay brother wouldn't know a ladybird from a dragonfly and cares even less.

Hudde turns around and beckons to one of his sons. 'Jankin, come here, lad!'

The boy breaks off his game and comes running up. 'Our Wilky's almost the twin of his brother here, except Wilky's shorter and his hair's a mite redder.' He fondles the boy's rusty curls.

Before the gatekeeper can reply, a hand appears on his shoulder and pulls him aside.

'What is amiss here?' the white-robed figure demands.

They both stand away from the gate, deep in a whispered conversation. Hudde feels his spirits rise a little. He was beginning to fear the gatekeeper was half-witted, but here is the man who took his son from the cottage. He'll soon have things sorted.

Father John's face appears in the grille. 'Your son is well, Master Hudde, and making good progress with his lessons. If he was dead, you would have been informed at once. But I'll tell the boy you were asking after him.'

He raises his hand to close the shutter over the grille, but Hudde grasps the bars in both hands. 'We just want to see the lad, only for a moment or two. It's my Meggy . . . she's that upset about losing the babe. It would comfort her so to see Wilky.'

'I'm afraid that will not be possible,' Father John says. 'Many in the town have the bloody flux. We are permitting the boys to see no one from outside these walls for fear of the contagion. I'm sure you would wish us to keep your son safe and ensure that he's not exposed to any danger.'

'But Meggy and me aren't sick, nor the bairns. Look at them.'

As if to prove their father's words, the three children raced past the gate in pursuit of each other, yelping like a pack of overexcited hounds.

'But you told the gatekeeper that one of your children died only a week ago. We cannot be sure you do not carry the contagion. We will pray for the soul of the dead infant, but now you must return home. You may come again at Easter. He will be permitted to see you then. And I advise you not to enter the town or talk to any of the townspeople for fear you endanger your other children.'

The shutter is slammed so decisively that Hudde knows no amount of ringing the bell or begging for admittance will cause it to be opened again. He remembers the stories his grandmother used to tell, of children who were lured away by the faerie folk and led through a door in the hillside to a land beyond, but when their parents hurried after them to bring them back they found the door vanished and they were left pounding on solid rock.

Hudde paces slowly back towards his wife. The anguish on her face cuts him like a knife slash. She has cried enough these past days and he knows he has failed her. He tries to sound cheerful, to explain that the holy brothers are keeping Wilky safe. If a fever takes hold in such closed places it runs through them like a fire in a forest.

'But why couldn't they bring him to the grille in the gate? I wouldn't have touched him,' she sobs. 'I only wanted to look at him.'

Her husband doesn't know what to say to comfort her. 'Suppose women aren't allowed to look in,' he says, ''case the monks see them.'

It's all he can think of to console her, but they both know it's a lie. Monks see women all the time in the towns and villages. And many do far more than look.

Hudde plucks his little daughter from his wife's skirts and swings her up onto his shoulders. They trudge back along the muddy road. The children creep up behind one another and tickle each other's necks with dried reeds or shove each other into puddles. But for once neither Meggy nor Hudde has the heart to scold them and in the end, disconcerted, the children, too, fall silent.

They see a woman they recognise walking towards them, leading a milch cow by a rope halter, with a pail and stool slung either side of its back. She and Meggy have known each other since they were giggling girls for she lives in the very centre of the town where Meggy grew up. Fearfully, Meggy calls the children to her, forcing them to walk at the very edge of the track on the opposite side to the woman, as if she is a leper.

The woman is taken aback as she sees fear on the face of her friend. Alarmed herself now, she glances behind her, assuming danger must be following, but the track is empty, innocent of harm. She begins to tug the cow across the road, intending to offer the little ones some milk, warm and foaming, straight from the cow's udders, for they look tired and hungry, but stops, bewildered, when Hudde hastily steps in front of his family, holding out a hand, warning her to step no closer.

'Whatever's amiss?' she calls, really frightened now.

'I hear tell there's bloody flux in the town. We've been warned to stay away. Don't want the little 'uns getting sick. We buried our youngest just a week back. Meggy can't bear more grief.'

The woman's face crumples in sympathy. 'I'm right sorry to hear that, Meggy, God rest his little soul.' She crosses herself and hastily spits three times on the back of her fingers to ward off any curse that might pass from Meggy's family to hers.

'But what's this about the flux? Whoever was it told you such a thing? Why, thanks be to the Blessed Virgin, there's been no sickness in the town since the summer fever last year. You've no need to fret for your cletch, Meggy. I swear on my life, there's no flux in these parts.'

Chapter 17

*If an emerald is set before a toad's eye either the stone,
if of weak virtue, will be broken by the toad's gaze, else
the toad will burst if the stone is possessed of natural
vigour.*

'Stand aside, woman.' A guard pushed past me so violently
that I staggered into the wall. For a moment I could do
nothing but crouch there, gasping and hugging my sore
ribs.

'Mind who you're shoving, you clumsy great ox,' a woman
yelled at the man who'd knocked into me.

But he didn't bother even to turn as he elbowed his way
through the crowd at the gate who were waiting to be
searched before they'd be allowed to squeeze out of the town.

Two arms encircled me, helping me to stand. 'The guard
think they can do what they like. Don't care who they
trample underfoot.'

I was sprayed with spittle as my rescuer spoke, for her
mouth was crammed full of teeth that jutted out at odd
angles, like a rockfall, between her lips.

She stared at the bit of my face she could see beneath
the cloth wrapped around my head. 'By the looks of it that
guard wasn't the first to knock you about. Husband, was
it?'

I nodded, not daring to speak for I wasn't sure I could

manage a high enough voice. I'd never had reason to practise for a moment like this.

The woman shook her head grimly. 'And with his babe in your belly too,' she said, staring at the bulge beneath my skirts.

By good fortune, the bundle of clothes I'd tied about my waist had been pushed to the front as I'd fallen. I should have thought of doing that myself, for the guards would never search a pregnant woman, would they?

My rescuer looked at me sharply. ''Tis your husband's, I suppose.'

I nodded again, gazing down and sighing in what I hoped was a heartbroken and affecting manner.

The woman nodded towards the gate. 'You don't want to be queuing there in your condition. The Watch'll keep people hanging around for hours. Makes it look as if they're doing a thorough job of searching for the thief, which they're not. You come along with me, my little duckling. I know a quieter way out of the town and one your husband'll never find, that's for certain.'

Having no safe way to protest without giving myself away, I had no choice but to allow her to link her arm through mine and lead me through a maze of twisting alleys and stinking hovels till we reached a line of houses crowded hard against the town wall on the far side.

The street was so narrow that not even a sliver of autumn sunshine could squeeze between the dark houses. Pigs, chickens and skeletal dogs rooted through the offal and scraps that had been tossed out into the mud, squawking, snapping and snarling whenever they came too close to each other. A group of women with grizzling infants dandling on their hips or clinging to their patched skirts broke off their gossip to stare in silence at me as my companion hurried me along the street. With a wary glance up and down the road, the woman stopped at one of the buildings and, opening the door, pushed me inside.

I found myself in the long narrow ale-room of a tavern, crammed with half a dozen tables and benches. It was empty at this hour of the day, save for a couple of young women who were sprawled over one of the tables, engrossed in rolling knuckle-bones on which they had evidently placed a wager. Both were pretty, in a grimy sort of way. The taller of the two had sandy hair and a mass of freckles over her wide cheeks. The other was darker and plumper, her dumpling breasts pushed so high over the top of her gown that it was a wonder they hadn't escaped altogether.

They straightened as we entered. One of the girls snatched up the two small coins that lay on the table and scooped the bones into a small sacking bag, ignoring the furious glances of her friend.

'Aline! Barbot! I hope you've got the chickens plucked and stewing,' my companion snapped.

'Course we have, *Tantine*,' the dark-haired girl said, with an impudent grin.

'Then fetch a bowl of chicken and some bread. This poor creature's in need of a bite.'

The girl looked me up and down curiously. Then, with a grin spreading across her face, she ambled towards the door at the back of the room, her hips swaying.

I was so famished I'd have thrown myself into the arms of the hangman himself if he'd held out a piece of bread. I could think about nothing except food and when the girl returned with a steaming bowl of chicken stew, I almost snatched it from her hands and tipped it down my throat.

It was far too heavily salted and the chicken was stringy. A boiled shirt would have had more flavour. But when you are hungry enough the meanest dish tastes like a king's banquet.

'Eating for two, that's what it is,' my rescuer said.

'Two? I reckon she must have a dozen of them in there.'

I glanced up to see all three of them watching me with amusement and realised that I'd been shovelling the food down like a ploughboy. I tried to use my spoon more daintily.

As a woman I was sure I was expected to refuse another bowl, but even for the sake of maintaining my disguise, I couldn't bring myself to say no to a second or a third, but at last even I was satisfied.

'I reckon you'll want to sleep that off now,' *Tantine* said. 'We've a loft-room, all nice and quiet it is. Barbot'll show you.'

The dark-haired girl hitched up the front of her gown. 'Stairs at back.'

I was about to protest when I remembered my voice. Any attempt at a falsetto was doomed before I opened my mouth. Even experienced actors never made the women's roles sound anything other than comic and I'd had no time even to try it out. So I settled on a hoarse whisper, hoping they'd put it down to shyness or my delicate condition.

'You said you'd show me a way out of the town. I must be on the road before dark. How do I get out?'

Barbot pointed to the window at the back of the room. I peered through. Behind, a courtyard enclosed a chicken coop and pigsty, which were pressed up against a couple of small huts that I took to be a brew house and kitchen. These in turn were leaning against the massive town wall, which ran along the back of the yard. There was no gate. A squirrel or polecat might have bounded up those great stones with ease, but even with a grappling iron I couldn't have scaled them, which is hardly surprising since the whole point of a town wall is to stop people getting in or out.

'I can't climb that, not in my condition,' I whispered, patting my bulge for good measure.

Barbot giggled. 'You go under, not over, stupid.'

'Hold your tongue!' *Tantine* rapped, and spittle sprayed out in a great shower from her crooked teeth. Her niece's grin was instantly replaced by alarm. Those teeth could evidently bite, and bite hard. But when she spoke to me again it was with a soothing tone.

'Why don't you rest for an hour or so, my little duckling? You're as weak as whey and you'll be needing all your strength when you're out on the road. I'll fetch you myself soon as it's safe and show you the way out. And don't you worry, your husband will never think to look for you here.'

I was desperate to get out of the town, but I could see that no amount of argument would persuade her to act sooner. Instead, I allowed Barbot to lead me out into the courtyard and up an outside staircase behind the inn to a dusty chamber tucked under the thatched roof. It was impossible to stand upright except along the centre. A couple of stained and stinking pallets lay side by side and a few small chests and boxes were stacked in the corner. I guessed it was where the girls entertained their customers for, though no one had ever offered me such entertainment, I knew that inns sold more than wine and pottage.

I was about to press Barbot further about the route out of the town, when I heard footsteps outside on the wooden stairs and Aline pushed open the door with her hip.

'*Tantine* sent this in case you're thirsty.' She set a flagon and beaker down on one of the boxes.

I'm certain I wasn't meant to catch the look that passed between the two girls, but something in Aline's expression set my heart pounding with dread. As her aunt had done, she urged me to sleep, assuring me that I'd be roused as soon as it was time to leave. She poured a beaker of blood-red wine and thrust it into my hand. 'Drink this. It'll put hairs on your chest.'

Barbot gave a nervous laugh, but Aline grabbed her hand and dragged her from the room. My face grew hot. Did they know? I heard them fumbling at the door, before they clattered down the wooden stairs. I tried the door. It opened a crack, but no more. They'd tied it shut. Was that to keep me in or inquisitive neighbours out?

I sniffed at the wine. It was strong and spicy. I'd been desperately thirsty before I'd even reached the inn and the salty stew had made it worse. It was an old trick to encourage customers to buy more wine, but this wine smelt and looked much better than any I'd expect to be served in a place like this. It seemed as good as the wine Philippe had poured for me from his own flagon that day I'd confronted him in his chamber. I'd be surprised if any of the customers who frequented this midden of an inn could afford to pay for anything of quality. But that only made me more suspicious. I'd been drugged once and wasn't going to fall for that one again. Had the tavern-keeper guessed who I was and was even now on her way to the Watch so that she could claim the reward for my capture?

But with the beaker in my hand, my thirst became torture. I knew that, sooner or later, I wouldn't be able to stop myself taking a gulp. Even if I only rinsed my mouth with it, who knew what poison those witches had put in it or how quickly it would take effect? The only safe thing to do would be to get rid of the wine before I gave in to temptation. I daren't throw it on the floor in case it dripped through the boards and betrayed me, so opening the nearest chest I tipped the contents of both flagon and beaker onto the ragged blanket inside.

I had to get out – out of the inn and out of the town – but I knew every gate was being watched. There was only one small window in the chamber, little wider than the slits in the turret that, just a day ago, had been my home. I squinted through the gap. The three women were standing in the courtyard, deep in conversation. Several times I saw them glance up at the door. It was clear I was the subject of their earnest discussion. As I watched, *Tantine* handed something to Aline. Both moved too swiftly for me to see the object clearly, but I was certain I glimpsed the flash of a long blade.

I quickly drew back from the window. They had no intention of handing me over to the Watch. The silver bird's head must be worth far more than any reward offered for my capture. And, dead or alive, I was worth the same bounty. They could claim the raven's head was not in my possession when they found me, steal the bird and claim the reward as well. Cold sweat trickled down my back. Those witches were going to murder me as I slept.

Chapter 18

*Thy body I will bury that it may putrefy and grow and
bear innumerable fruit.*

Shrieking and whooping, the boys dodge between the bare
fruit bushes and run towards the great wooden cross that
stands in the centre of the vegetable garden. They are brandishing the stoutest sticks they could steal from the abbey's
wood pile. Today they do not resemble Father John's obedient
little scholars, for they have tied cones of straw to their
heads and their faces are blackened with soot. Cloaks of
straw hang ragged and moulting from their shoulders.

The boys are oblivious to the biting cold, though their
breath puffs out in white clouds, as if they are rampaging
dragons. Every blade of grass and slender twig is gilded with
frost. The winter sun, pale as the moon in the blue sky,
glints on each tiny crystal of ice covering the flagstones and
walls. The whole garden dazzles so brightly, the boys have
to squint to see, but they know exactly where they are going.

On any other day, they would never dare to leap or shout,
but today, on the feast of St Stephen, even Father John is
prepared to indulge them. But as they near the tall wooden
cross, they motion each other to silence. They rise on tiptoe
and creep towards it with exaggerated strides, suppressing
giggles, which explode once more into raucous laughter as
little Mighel slips and crashes down onto the icy flagstones.

The hard bang to his knee brings tears to his eyes, but he tries to grin as if he doesn't care and, scrambling to his feet, he clutches the tiny amulet of St Michael he wears about his neck, holding it tightly to make the pain go away. As the throbbing subsides, he limps after the other boys.

They are already clustered about the foot of the cross, which is mounted on a heap of large stones, and it is on these stones that they focus their attention.

'Is it still there?' Peter whispers.

'How can I see with your pudding head in the way?' Felix grumbles, pushing him aside. He kneels down, oblivious to the melting frost soaking his knees. 'Straw's still there,' he announces.

And it is. Straw has been wedged into every small gap between the stones. Felix did it himself last night, when it was dark, with Father John's grudging permission. He glances up. 'Everyone ready?'

The boys nod eagerly, crowding closer to the stones and raising their sticks high in the air. Felix pulls out one of the plugs of straw. The boys hold their breath, waiting, their gaze fastened on the tiny dark hole. Nothing happens. Felix pulls out another plug. Then, after a pause, he removes yet another twist of straw. Finally there is a flutter and something small and brown emerges at their feet.

The tiny wren finds itself surrounded by a dense forest of legs. It tries to fly upwards, but the sticks beat down. Most miss the bird, a few almost hit Felix as he scrambles out of the way, but before long, as is inevitable, one of the flailing sticks catches the little creature, breaking its wing. The next blow leaves it lifeless on the sparkling, frosted ground.

Boys all over the land are hunting the wren today, for

there is not one who does not know how the blessed St Stephen, on his way to be stoned to death, managed to escape his captors, and how the heathen wren betrayed him by waking his guard with its shrill cry. Stephen is in Paradise now, but all the same, the wren must be punished for all eternity as a warning to the heretics and pagans who would dare to murder Christ's holy saints.

The other boys are cheering and punching the air to celebrate their triumphant victory, but Regulus alone is not grinning. He stares miserably down at the tiny bundle of feathers. Once, he trailed after his elder brothers as they roamed through the forest, like real huntsmen, following a wren, before hunger and cold drove them home. The little bird hopped and flew low in front of them, always just out of reach, leading them deeper and deeper among the trees. They never caught it. Regulus wonders if his brothers are out there, somewhere beyond the high wall, hunting today. If he called out, would they hear him? Would they come?

This is not much of a hunt at all. The boys know where the wren takes shelter and they made sure that it couldn't fly away with the dawn, for unlike the village boys, they can't follow it as it hops over a wall or flies up into the trees. This is the best they can do.

'Bring the bier,' Felix orders.

Regulus, in deference to his name, has been accorded the honour of carrying the bier. It is a wheel the boys have fashioned out of plaits of straw, festooned with strips of rag, for there are no ribbons to be found in the abbey with which to decorate it. The wheel is impaled on the tip of a long willow pole. Regulus, with Peter's help, lowers the end of the unwieldy pole to the ground.

Felix reverently scoops the tiny creature up in both hands,

though he could easily have held it in one. He ties it to the edge of the straw wheel, with a strip of rag bound about one tiny leg so that it dangles upside down, its wings outstretched as if it tries to fly even in death. The other leg, broken, hangs limp against its feathers. The needle-sharp beak is open. The eyes gaze sightlessly into the dazzling sun.

On Felix's orders, Regulus walks carefully up the path, holding the slender pole as high as he can. The boys follow in solemn procession. The wren is so light that Regulus keeps fearing it has dropped off and the other boys fall over him as he stops to squint up. Felix tells him to walk straight, else they'll batter his head with their sticks.

In the abbey there are no neighbours to beg treats from. The White Canons will not give them nuts or coins. Beggars and widows will come to the abbey today, but they will crowd about the alms-window, demanding their own treats, as is their due on the feast of St Stephen. But the boys are not permitted to go near that gate. Instead Felix guides his little band to the kitchens and hammers on the door. The boys begin to sing, their voices ragged, their teeth chattering.

> *The wren, the wren, King of the Birds,*
> *On St Stephen's Day was caught in the furze.*
> *Though he is little, his honour is great,*
> *Come out, come out and give us a treat.*

The door opens and one of the lay brothers waddles out. He is clad only in a sleeveless tunic and short breeches, for the kitchen is always steaming hot. He shivers in the sudden chill. He thrusts out a wooden platter on which are a few pieces of *payn ragoun* – pine nuts, mixed with ginger and breadcrumbs, covered with boiled honey. It is a rare treat

140

indeed. The boys tug the hard sticky morsels from the platter and cram them into their mouths, each trying to grab the largest piece before his fellows.

Regulus, forced to hold the tall willow pole with both hands to balance it, watches in dismay as the pieces vanish before him, like snowflakes in a fire. He is on the verge of flinging aside the pole and grabbing a piece, but the lay brother, eager to be back in his warm kitchen, pulls the last piece from the trencher and rams it halfway into Regulus's mouth, then firmly shuts the door. The sweetmeat is too big to chew and Regulus is afraid to bite down in case the end falls to the ground and is trampled. He tries to suck the sticky mass and breathe at the same time, which is not easy, so that by the time Felix and the boys have led him back to the vegetable patch, he is scarlet in the face and almost suffocating.

They bury the little wren in the bare earth close to the irrigation stream, which flows in under the high wall. Felix plays priest, solemnly reciting what bits of the Latin burial service he can remember. He tears up a tuft of grass and dips it in the icy stream, flinging sparkling jewels of water on the tiny grave, as if it is holy water from a branch of hyssop.

Regulus, relieved of his burden, chews his honeyed pine nuts slowly, trying to make the heavenly sweetness last for ever. Their mouths and fingers sticky, the boys cast off their straw hats and cloaks and race away to play. There are no lessons today, and they mean to make the most of every hour of freedom outside, until their toes are numb and fingers so stiff and swollen they ache with cold.

At night, as he shivers beneath the blanket trying to get warm, Regulus thinks about his namesake lying out there in the frozen earth like his brothers. Maybe the bird is not dead after all, but merely trapped, as it was inside the stones beneath the cross. The wren lives down in dark holes. Perhaps now they have put it back in a hole it will wake up.

The boys enjoy only one glorious day of liberty, before they are again imprisoned by their studies. The long hours spent in the gloomy dorter poring over copy tablets seem to shuffle by twice as slowly as they ever did before. But finally they are released for their hour of play. Regulus hurries back to the vegetable garden. It is deserted for there is no work to be done at this season.

He crouches down and scrapes away with his fingers at the frozen earth. He must free the little bird. He must get the heavy soil off its soft feathers. But he cannot find it. He digs deeper with a twig. But the wood keeps snapping. He finds a stone and hacks the ground with it. Nothing! He digs in another place, another, until there are tiny grave-pits all over the bare earth, but the wren is not there.

A rapid chittering makes him glance up. A tiny brown bird darts across the bare earth into the shelter of a black-currant bush. Regulus's heart thuds in his chest. The wren has woken up. It has crept out of the ground while they slept and it's free. In relief and excitement, Regulus scrambles up, eager to fetch the others to come and look. But he stops himself. What if they kill the bird all over again? He sees the sticks thumping down, hears the boys roar and shriek as the tiny creature falls. He will not tell them that it lives, that it escaped them. That will be his treasured secret.

He covers the little pits, pushing the earth back with numb fingers, so that they cannot see the bird has escaped.

He hugs the secret to himself as he walks back to where the boys are chasing the ball. He is relieved, elated.

The earth makes creatures well again. When you are sick you are put to bed, and when you are *very* sick, you are put into the earth to make you well. That's why his brothers were put into the earth. And soon they will climb out again, just like the wren. He has seen pictures on the church wall of men and women clambering out of their graves, because the earth has made them better.

He starts to run joyfully towards the ball. Then something catches his eye. He stops, staring at what lies entangled in the gnarled roots of a tree. He edges across and peers down, gazing at a bedraggled heap of brown feathers. The tiny broken body has no head, only a gory stump of a neck, but tied about one tiny fragile leg is a narrow scrap of rag.

Chapter 19

To a black raven am I akin
Such be the wages of all sin
In deepest dust I lie alone

The hardest thing in the world to do is simply to wait. I knew that *Tantine* and her little vixens might return to cut my throat just as soon as they thought the drugged wine had rendered me senseless, or that the watchmen might, even now, be on their way to seize me if I had mistaken the purpose of that knife, but either way, I dared not make a move in daylight.

I'd already decided there was only one way out of that loft-room and indeed out of the town, but I would have to wait until the cover of darkness to try it and in the meantime I had to stay alert for the slightest creak that might mean someone was mounting the stairs.

Even an hour spent in a woman's gown convinced me that if I was to move with any speed it wasn't going to be in skirts. But I didn't want to risk changing back into my own clothes, for by now the whole countryside probably had a description of them. I rummaged in the second chest and found an assortment of less than savoury garments, but I forced myself to pull on a short tunic and breeches that stank of onion, which, trust me, was the least offensive odour of the many fragrances on offer. I bundled up the woman's gown I'd stolen together with my own clothes and another spare tunic from the chest. I was learning that being able to change my appearance could prove useful.

I set to work with my knife, trying to hack a hole in the underside of the thatch. I selected a point in the far corner, where the roof was low and where I hoped it wouldn't immediately be seen by anyone looking up from the court-yard below. Thatch looks flimsy, but, believe me, it's not. It had been packed down tight and the straw was scythe-sharp. In no time I was sweating like a spit-boy and my fingertips were raw and bleeding.

By the time I had finished it was growing dark and the tavern was filling with drinkers. Shouts of laughter and raucous voices rose up from beneath me. I knew I couldn't leave it much longer. I was convinced by now that *Tantine* and her imps had not sent for the Watch for they would have been here long ago, which could mean only that they intended to slaughter me, take the silver flask and claim the reward for my body. Philippe would certainly not trouble to enquire closely into the manner of my death.

A gale of chatter wafted out as the back door of the tavern opened below me. My stomach contracted. Was this it? Were they coming? I tiptoed to the slit window and peered out, listening hard for any creaking on the stairs. Aline was crossing the courtyard, dangling two wine flagons in her hands. She vanished inside the far hut, and a few minutes later she emerged with the weight of the full flagons balanced on each hip. So that was where it was stored.

All the time I'd been stabbing away at the thatch, I'd been puzzling over that wine. It was far too good for a place like this. I doubted they'd had a customer in a dozen years who could pay what it was really worth. Neither did I imagine for one moment that *Tantine* could afford to buy the wine at its true value from the merchants who supplied it, not even for the purpose of drugging fools like me. It had to have been stolen, which meant they weren't bringing it in through the town gates.

As soon as the door to the tavern below me closed, I crossed to the hole and, using the knife hilt to break the last crust of the thatch, pushed my bundle out ahead of me and wriggled out behind it, trying not to yelp at the pain in my ribs as I dragged myself over the edge of the hole. I lay flat on the sloping roof, reaching down through the hole to cling to the beam below and praying the section of thatch on which I was pressing my full weight wouldn't simply slide off onto the ground.

I shivered in the cold breeze. The night was cloudy and dark. Here and there, trickles of oily yellow light spilled from beneath ill-fitting shutters and the open doorways of the buildings that crowded either side of the tavern. The cries of bawling babies and yelling mothers intermingled with the shouts of men and barking dogs. I glanced up at the town wall, just in time to see a guard shuffling along it. I buried my face in the mouldy straw until he'd passed by.

It was too far to drop to the ground and, desperate though I was, I couldn't steel myself to face a heavy fall on top of my bruises. My only hope was to try to lower myself onto the rickety staircase. I slung my bundle over my shoulder and inched forward. But as soon as I pulled myself up into a crawling position I found I had nothing to cling to but handfuls of thatch. Solid it might have seemed from underneath but, on top, the straws pulled out as easily as hair from a mangy dog. As I slid inexorably downwards I finally understood why people say you should never grasp at straws.

146

I managed to twist myself sideways and landed with a crash on the top of the wooden stairs. The pain as I hit my already bruised side sent white lights bursting in front of my eyes, but it would have been very much worse had the bundle of clothes not softened my fall.

I curled into a ball, lying as still as I could, sure that the sound would bring people running, but the door below me remained shut. Evidently the noise of the revellers in the tavern and the banging and shouting from the houses round about had masked it. I'd decided that my best chance of crossing the courtyard unobserved would be immediately after the girls had fetched fresh supplies of wine. Then they would be occupied inside the tavern at least long enough to empty their flagons. So I waited.

I lay in the darkness at the top of the steps until I was so cold and numb I wasn't sure I could walk even if I wanted to. Finally, just when I was convinced they were never coming out, the door opened and yellow light rolled across the stones of the courtyard. I heard footsteps tripping across the yard, and a muffled curse as the girl slipped on some piece of filth. I rolled up as tightly as I could and pulled the bundle over my head, praying that if she glanced up as she walked back to the door she would see nothing that looked human in the darkness. Presently, I heard her returning across the yard. Her footsteps suddenly stopped and I braced myself for her shriek to warn that I was escaping.

But instead a man's voice called out below me, 'Barbot, where are you, my lovely? I'm dying for a kiss.'

'Best send for the priest then, 'cause I'll not be saving you.'

Her footsteps started again, and the light was sucked back in as the door closed behind her.

147

This was it. I had no idea how long it would be before she or Aline re-emerged, but I could delay no longer. As quietly as I could I clambered down the stairs and hastened across the yard to the hut I'd seen the girls enter. The door was unlocked and I slipped inside. A single horned lantern hung from the centre of the room to provide enough light for them to refill the flagons. A keg rested on its side, raised on a rough wooden cradle. Three more kegs stood against one wall. A broken bench, coils of rope, fowling nets, brooms, hammers and other assorted tools lay in jumbled heaps against the other walls.

I went immediately to the far wall of the hut that I knew lay hard against the town wall. I pressed and tapped the length of it, but there was no sign of a door or an opening. I was almost sick with dismay, for I'd been so sure that that was the way they were bringing in the stolen wine. I was suddenly aware of the sound of my own footsteps and glanced down. In a miserable little hut like this, I'd have expected the floor to be nothing more than beaten earth. But it wasn't. It was flagged. *Under the wall*, Barbot had said, not *over* it and not *through* it.

I dropped to my knees, running my hands over the cold stones trying to find a ring or some means of lifting a trap door. But I could feel nothing. A wooden mallet lay on top of one of the barrels, which was probably used to broach the sealed casks. I began to tap my way across the floor, until I heard it, the hollow echo beneath one of the flags. I ran my fingers around the edge, trying to find a finger-hold.

I was so engrossed that the footsteps outside had almost reached the hut before my mind registered the sound. With only a whisker of time to spare, I flattened myself behind the door as Barbot wandered in. She set her flagons on the floor and, pulling the wooden bung from the barrel, let the wine stream into one. She was so close that, even behind the door, I could smell the cooking fat on her hair and the rosemary she'd sewn into her gown to make some lover return to her.

But, to my horror, the door she'd thrown open began to swing closed under its own weight. As soon as she turned to leave she would see me standing there. I was still holding the wooden mallet. I raised it. I swear, I meant only to protect myself, threaten her into silence if I had to, but she must have sensed the movement behind her. Still crouching on the floor, she half turned her head. The mallet smashed into her temple even as she was opening her mouth to scream. Her eyes opened wide in shock. She crumpled onto the floor and lay still, the blood-red wine trickling over her neck.

I kicked the door closed and stepped over the prone body, not daring to look at her to see if she was alive or dead. I was trembling with the fear and horror of what I'd done. I began to gag and had to force myself not to vomit. I knew it would be only minutes before she was missed and someone, probably that drunken oaf who'd called for her earlier, would come looking.

Frantically, I searched though the jumble of nets and tools until I found myself grasping an iron mattock on a long wooden handle. I shoved the sharp end of the iron under one side of the hollow flagstone to prise it upwards. It was heavy, but I was able to lift it high enough to grasp the edge and pull it, grating, across the floor. Underneath, just as I'd hoped, was a dark hole. Cold, damp air rolled up as if from a well. I snatched the lantern from its hook and dangled it down inside. But I could see little except puddles of water glistening on the earth floor below me. I had no idea if this was simply a cellar or was indeed a way out.

Still gripping the lantern, I flung the mattock back onto the pile of nets and tools and eased myself over the edge of the hole, wincing as the sharp edge grated over my rib-cage.

'Barbot! Where are you, girl? There's customers want serving. If you've fallen asleep in there again, I swear I'll swing for you this time, God's blood, I will.'

I heard footsteps coming towards the hut. I dared not hesitate. I dropped into the mud. Then reaching up, I dragged the flagstone back over the hole. It fell into place just as the door of the hut was flung open.

Chapter 20

Wherever there have been crudities and excrements they have been purged and destroyed by being suffused with its water and the body has been led back to clarity and perfection.

The great bell tolls – one, twice . . . The dozing boys stir fitfully. Some jerk awake and lie in the icy darkness counting silently – *three, four . . . knock at the door.* But there will be no knock, no warning, if he comes.

Little Peter curls himself into a ball and prays. Prays – as do they all – that if the door opens tonight and Father John comes padding softly along the row of boys, the canon will not stop at the foot of his pallet. Peter silently begs for it not to be his shoulder that Father John shakes, not be him who is led out through that door. *Not tonight, please. Take Felix, or Regulus or Mighel. Take anyone else, but not me!* But what chance do a boy's stammered prayers stand against the army of Latin invocations from the white-robed priests? The Blessed Virgin will never hear his feeble plea above such a mighty surge.

Sometimes down in that shadowy dungeon, which is nearer Hell than Heaven, they make Peter drink bitter liquids till his guts burn as if he's swallowed hot iron. If he gags, they clamp his mouth shut, tip his head back, so he is forced to swallow again what has risen up in his throat. Other times the liquid is sickly sweet. He does not mind that so much,

151

except that afterwards his legs give way beneath him. He crumples to the floor and lies helplessly on the cold flags, staring upwards at the stone arches that twist like serpents, while the floor below him melts into a lake teeming with monstrous crabs that tear his skin with their pincers. He cannot fight them off. He screams, but there is no sound.

He never remembers being returned to his bed, and in the morning when he drags himself from his pallet, head pounding, legs as heavy as tree trunks, he wonders if he's dreamed it, until he sees the other boys' wary glances in his direction. Then he knows he was the one who was taken.

Peter shivers. He is cold beneath the thin blanket, but he no longer even admits that to himself. Last week he wished he could be warm and Father John knew what he'd wished for. He always knows what each boy is thinking, and he punishes each sinful thought.

That night there'd been no goblet in Father Arthmael's hands. Father Madron stripped Peter of his shirt, and Father John pushed him naked into a wooden box, so small he could only fit if he sat with knees drawn up and head bent. The box grew warm, then hot. White steam gushed up through the holes beneath him until he was struggling to breathe, trying to claw his way out, sobbing in panic, tears and sweat running together down his cheeks. Then came the moment of utter relief when the door swung open and they dragged him out, slippery as an eel, into the cool air.

Holding him in a great basin, they scraped the sweat from his naked body with sharp slivers of black stone, which left shallow, stinging cuts across his back and thighs. His legs were scarlet from the watery blood running down them. He thought they would skin him, like he'd seen a flesher skin a goat.

'Every drop,' Father Arthmael urged. 'Collect every drop

of bloody sweat. It is a precious fluid, the dew of a child that purifies the soul, and I must begin the distillation at once, while it still contains the spirit.'

That night Peter remembered being returned to the dorter – the icy air on his wet hair as he was pulled through the courtyard, the smart of the coarse blanket on his newly washed cuts, the sobs he tried to stifle in the straw of his pallet. Father John had paused and turned back. Peter cringed, but the priest crouched and gently stroked the boy's damp hair.

'Hush now, sleep. It is over.' He bent closer and whispered, 'You must understand, Peter, Father Arthmael does not do such things from cruelty. He seeks the greatest secret a man can possess. He has studied and conducted his experiments for many years, testing each substance carefully, harvesting the living essences from the young, which are the seed and primal matter of the universe. And now he believes he is close, so close, to achieving what he seeks. Nothing good can be gained without sacrifice, Peter. Remember the suffering of Christ and all the saints. They submitted joyously to pain and you must follow their example. Dry your tears and give thanks to the Blessed Virgin that you have been chosen to play a part in this great work. And remember, Peter, you must say nothing about what happens in the laboratorium, not even to your fellows. I shall know if you do and I *will punish*.'

Peter shivers as the bell tolls again. Then he feels it. The blast of cold air as the door at the top of the dorter steps swings silently open. He shuts his eyes. If he cannot see Father John, then Father John cannot see him. The soft pad of sandals advances down the row of pallets towards him, measured, slow steps.

Not me! Not me! Take someone else tonight, please . . . please!

The footsteps pause. Peter's eyes are screwed so tight they hurt. He waits. He grasps the blanket tightly over his chest as if it is a shield. He can hear the rasp of Father John's breath in the darkness, smell the incense on his robe. The little boy waits for the hard fingers to clamp like a claw upon his arm.

Then he hears a gasp that is not his own, the rustle of the straw pallet next to him as another boy is pulled from his bed. But Peter dare not open his eyes. He hears two pairs of sandals on the stairs, feels the breeze from the door as it opens and closes. Only then does he release his breath and a surge of relief washes over him, like a warm bath.

Little Mighel knows better than to resist. He stumbles over the uneven flagstones, Father John gripping his shoulder, pushing him forward into the impenetrable darkness. But even though he knows full well where they are going, still he jerks back when they reach the heavy wooden door hiding the stairs that spiral down and down into the great red maw of that chamber. The child is seized with panic. He tries in vain to wrench himself from the hand that grasps him. He cannot help it, even though he knows there is no escape, knows that it will only lead to punishment and pain. Father John bends his head close to Mighel's ear.

'Come along, boy, you know there is nothing to fear. Father Arthmael is an abbot, the servant of God. It is your duty to obey him as you do me, for we know what is best for you. You have been here before, Mighel, and you know that the sooner you do as you are asked, the sooner you can sleep.'

Mighel has been here before and he does now what he did then. He pretends he is not here. They are not here.

He reaches for the amulet of St Michael and the dragon hanging round his neck, the one his father gave him long, long ago, before he went to sea. His father told him it would always keep him safe. Nothing could hurt him as long as he held on to St Michael. His father promised, and his father never lied.

Mighel clutches the amulet in his fist so fiercely it hurts. St Michael will make the staircase and the dungeon vanish. He will slay Father John, Father Arthmael and all the canons with his spear and when Mighel opens his eyes he will be back in his own bed again, safe.

Father John turns the iron ring. The door swings open. The staircase has not vanished.

Chapter 21

The wind carried it in its womb, its nurse is the earth.

I swung the lantern around and discovered I was in a low, wide tunnel, which branched off in three directions. The sides and roof were sweating beads of water, which dripped down into the slimy puddles on the floor. Wooden props had been wedged in at intervals to hold the roof up, but small mounds of stones and soil marked where there had been falls. I'd spent half my life up in a turret looking down on the earth, and now, in that tunnel, I felt like a skylark trapped in a rabbit warren. In spite of the chill, damp air, I was already gasping for breath and sweating in panic at the thought of the weight of rocks pressing down on me. It was all I could do to stop myself bursting back up through the trapdoor again.

Above me, I heard *Tantine* give a little scream. 'Barbot! Barbot, you silly girl, what have you done now?'

She roared for someone – anyone – to come and help. There was a pause. Then it sounded as if a herd of cattle was stampeding above me. Clods fell from the roof, covering me with a shower of dirt. I had to move and quickly, too. If Barbot was still alive and started to talk or they began searching for her attacker, *Tantine* was bound to think of the tunnel.

But which way should I go? Moving around beneath that

156

trapdoor had completely disoriented me and I no longer knew which way I was facing. Where was the town wall? Panic seized me: what if I took the wrong passage and got trapped?

I found myself gripping the wooden box that swung at my side. And as if I could feel the raven's beak pointing the way, my thoughts cleared. The footsteps of the men summoned from the tavern were approaching from my right. I shuffled round so that the sounds of running feet were behind me. That meant I had my back to the courtyard, so if one of these tunnels did lead out under the town wall, it would most likely be the one in front of me.

Ducking as low as I could, I stumbled forward round the curve of the tunnel, praying that it would not get any narrower. I kept having to remind myself that if they could roll kegs of wine up this tunnel the walls would have to remain at least wide enough for that. But I did not like the way the floor was gradually sloping down. The last thing I wanted was to go deeper.

Was I under the wall yet? I must be. But that was far from comforting. All the height and weight of the towering stone wall were pressing down on this small tunnel, which, at that moment, seemed as fragile as a sparrow's egg. I had to get out of there. I edged forward, but the gap had vanished and the feeble yellow light of the lantern struck only a wall of earth. There was nothing but a blank wall in front of me! This was a dead end. I was trapped and I found myself paralysed with fear. My legs would not go forward or back. Then I heard the grating echo of a stone being dragged across the flags. They'd opened the trapdoor. They were checking the tunnel.

I slipped and slithered in the slimy mud as I edged towards

the wall ahead of me, hoping desperately to find a hollow in which to conceal myself. I heard the soft pad of feet, the splash of a puddle. Someone was creeping along the passage behind me. I suddenly realised the glow from my lantern was shining back up the tunnel, leading them straight towards me. With trembling fingers, I lifted one of the horn panels and snuffed out the candle. The tunnel was instantly plunged into darkness. I stood rigid, holding my breath, but the footsteps kept coming and I could just make out something red flickering along the wall. Whoever was approaching was carrying a burning torch.

Sick with fear, I turned away from the light and, sliding my right hand along the rough surface of the side of the passage, stumbled forward. I held out the other hand in front of me expecting any moment to collide with the end of the tunnel, but instead I felt the side wall against which I was pressing bend sharply right into a second branch of the tunnel, whose entrance must have been concealed in the shadows as I'd approached.

A rush of cold air and the sound of running water burst in my ears. I glimpsed flashes of white and black shapes. I could make no sense of it, until it dawned on me that I was staring out through the branches of a wind-whipped bush into the moonlit river beyond.

There was a yell and curse behind me. I guessed whoever was following me had just tripped over the lantern I'd abandoned. I darted forward, searching for somewhere to hide. It was too dark to see exactly where I'd emerged. I stepped forward expecting to feel solid ground, but the bank fell away sharply beneath me. My shoes were caked in the wet, slimy mud from the tunnel and could get no purchase on the grass. I seized a low branch to steady myself, but it broke off in my hand. One foot slid out from under me. I crashed to the ground and slipped straight down the muddy bank. Before I could grab at anything to stop myself, I plunged into the river. The icy water closed over my head. The shock drove the remaining breath from my body and, choking and gasping, I was swept away.

Chapter 22

*His father took him to his heart and swallowed him
out of joy and that with his own mouth.*

Regulus is dreaming, dreaming of a little boy he once knew
called Wilky. Wilky is running for his life through the forest,
trying to reach the safety of his little cottage before the
lantern-man catches up with him. He can hear the lantern-
man coming closer, the crackle of the twigs beneath his feet,
his rasping breath. He daren't turn and look at him, but he
knows he is there.

The boy can see his brothers and sisters playing outside,
see his mother sitting in the doorway, plucking pigeons. He
tries to scream for them to save him. But no sound comes
from his mouth. He waves frantically, but his family ignore
him. His legs won't move. They're stuck fast in the earth.
His bare feet are burrowing down into the ground, his toes
are growing long and thin, wriggling out like white roots.
And he can hear the clanking of the chains. The lantern-
man is almost upon him!

Somewhere, far above him, the abbey bell is tolling.
Regulus jerks awake, drenched in sweat, trembling. All
around him, the shock-headed boys are trying to rouse themselves from their beds, feeling for their cold leather sandals
with sleep-warmed toes, their eyes still closed. Not one wants
to rise, but they fear the punishment that will fall upon

them all if they are not dressed and ready to be marched to the chapel for Prime when Father John appears.

'Where's Mig?' little Peter whispers.

He kneels by the straw-filled pallet next to his own, tugs back the blanket in case Mighel might somehow be concealed beneath it, though not even the shadow of his friend could be hiding beneath that thin crumpled cover.

Felix takes charge. 'Anyone seen Mighel? Has he gone out already?'

He enunciates the name firmly, though still in a whisper. Father John does not approve of the shortening of any saint's name that has been bestowed on a boy. It is disrespectful to the saint, whom they should bless each time they have cause to use his name.

One of the boys runs to the door and tries it, but it is still locked from the outside, as it always is at night, for boys, as Father John well knows, will get up to all kinds of mischief or worse if allowed to roam the abbey unsupervised.

Peter still kneels disconsolately beside the empty bed. 'He hasn't come back,' he says, staring miserably at the hollow in the pallet that still bears the outline of the boy, curled up like a woodlouse. 'Father John chose him last night, I heard him, but he didn't bring him back.'

The boys freeze. Tiny threads of fear snake from one to another.

'Did anyone see Mighel come back?' Felix demands.

They shake their heads. They heard the door open. They heard Father John's heavy breathing as he padded on almost silent feet across the room. They heard the rustling as he shook someone, the slap-slap of the chosen boy's sandals crossing to the door. But they had their eyes shut tight, pretending to be asleep. They fell asleep for real only when the selection had been made, only when the door had closed and they were still lying in their beds. They were safe then, at least for that night.

But Peter knows where Father John stopped. He hangs his head, awash with misery. It is his fault Mighel is gone. He'd made it happen. He'd wished that Father John would choose Mighel instead of him. Father John knew what he'd wished for, he always knew.

Felix sees the anxious faces of the younger boys and knows they are waiting for him to tell them what to do, what to think. 'Get dressed quickly, all of you, before Father John arrives, and no one say a word about Mighel . . . I'll try . . .' he adds uncertainly.

They dress in silence, rolling away their blankets, stacking their own pallets in a neat pile in the far corner, as they have been taught. Mighel's pallet alone remains on the floor. They stare at it, unwilling to touch it, in case it might be cursed, in case they, too, vanish. Felix no more wants to move it than the younger boys, but he knows as the leader he cannot show fear. Besides, he will get the worst of it if Father John discovers the room unprepared. He takes a deep breath and heaves the pallet on top of the others. Now it is as if Mighel was never here, never one of them. Even the hollow where he lay has been shaken away, his shape erased. He is expunged.

The door opens and Father John stands at the top of the small flight of stairs. His white robes billow in the cold draught that enters with him. With the pale dawn light behind him, he is faceless, as if a hooded robe has reared up in the doorway without anyone inside.

The boys line up hastily as he closes the door and glides down the centre of the room, jerking up chins to see if faces have been washed, grabbing wrists and checking for dirty fingernails. All the time, his grey eyes dart back and forth, his gaze quartering the room, hunting for anything that might be out of place.

As Father John passes each boy and moves on down the line, Felix sees that boy's eyes swivel towards him, waiting. A row of anxious faces stare at him, willing him to ask what they are all desperate to know. He is afraid. Loose tongues are punished, he knows that only too well. But is it forbidden to ask a question? He is the leader. The boys look up to him. Their respect is all he possesses. His mouth has gone as dry as a cinder.

'Please, Father John. Mighel is missing . . . absent. Is he . . .' Felix tries to think of a reason to offer Father John that will cause no offence. 'Is Mighel sick, Father? Should we pray for him?'

Father John pauses in his slow perambulation and turns towards him. Felix is greatly relieved to see there is no anger in his face.

'You should pray for every boy and man in this abbey, Felix, sick or not. Pray for their souls day and night.' A smile twitches at the corner of his mouth. 'But since you are concerned about the welfare of your fellow pupil, which is to be commended, I can set your fears at rest. God be praised, Mighel enjoys good health. But his parents came for him. They wished for him to return home and help in the family business. We are sorry to lose him but, naturally, if the parents ask for their son, we must let him go.'

Felix sees relief spreading across the faces of Peter and the younger boys. More than relief, a brilliant flash of hope that one day soon their families will come for them. They are grinning, almost bubbling over with delight, after their fear. If Mighel can go home to his family, then it could happen to any of them.

Little Regulus is hugging himself as if he already feels his mother's arms clasping him to her. His parents promised they would come to visit him. They have not come yet. But now that Mighel's family have taken him home, his own parents will come soon, he knows it. Maybe they will even come today.

Only Felix does not smile. He feels a cold, painful lump in his gullet. For he alone remembers that Mighel is an orphan, with neither kith nor kin to care for him. His father's ship was lost at sea, his mother dead of a fever. Felix is certain that wherever Mighel is now, he is not safe in his mother's arms – at least, not in this world, he isn't.

Chapter 23

I am light and I am dark; I am born of earth and of heaven; I am known and I do not exist.

If you can imagine squelching through a forest in the middle of the night, sopping wet and chilled to the marrow, teeth chattering and ribs screaming in pain, you'd think that you'd be feeling utterly wretched. At the very least, you'd think you were having a bad day. But when the alternative is certain death, even these dire miseries seem little more than trifling inconveniences compared to the exhilaration of finding yourself alive and free. And I found myself in just that crazed, euphoric state, to the point that, had I not been so weak, I might have started leaping about like a lunatic and baying at the moon. Not even the rain dampened my spirits, for when a man has been half drowned in a river, how much wetter can he get?

I stumbled on for as long as I could, putting as much distance as I was able between myself and the town. Only relief and elation drove me on, for my body could barely keep itself upright, but eventually not even the fear of pursuit could force it to take another step. I collapsed into the nearest hollow, made a feeble attempt to cover myself with dried leaves and shivered into an exhausted sleep.

I woke in damp clothes to an even colder dawn. Then, and only then, the reality of my situation dropped on me, like a great boulder. I couldn't return to the only home I'd ever known. I was a wolf's head, a fugitive, an outlaw. If any man, rich or poor, beggar or priest, discovered who I was and hacked me to pieces on the spot, the law would reward him for doing it. If I was captured alive and taken for trial, I would certainly be executed, if not for the theft then for the murder of the girl, if she was dead. I felt a pang of guilt about that, but reminded myself that Barbot would willingly have helped her aunt to cut my throat if I'd given her the chance.

I had no friends or kin, no work or shelter, and all I possessed were a few paltry coins. Not that the size of my emaciated purse mattered, for even had it been stuffed full, I couldn't risk spending a single denier. It was plain from the reaction of the roasted-pigeon seller that the coins Philippe had given me were marked and I'd no doubt word would spread quickly to all the neighbouring towns and villages. Even if a lonely cottager innocently accepted one in payment for food or lodging, it would be like leaving a trail of blood across the countryside for Philippe's hounds to follow.

It wasn't quite true that all I possessed were the marked coins. I still had the silver raven nestling against my thigh in its little box, and some might have considered that made me a wealthy man indeed. But, like the coins, it might as well have been a box of cow shit for all the use it was to me. I certainly couldn't sell it anywhere in those parts.

I drew the box from the leather pouch. I hadn't looked at it since the morning Philippe had made me unwrap it in front of him. That had been only two days ago, but it seemed like two years, for so much had happened in those few hours. Everyone I had trusted had deceived me, and I

166

wondered if the silver flask, too, had been a trick. Perhaps it was only made of base metal, or maybe Philippe, by some sleight of hand, had substituted a stone for the flask before returning it to me.

But in the cold, grey haze of the breaking dawn, the head was more wondrous even than I remembered. The light, flickering through the branches of the swaying trees, glinted from the silver feathers so that they looked as if they were being ruffled in the breeze. I turned the flask upside down so that the raven's head was upright. The polished black-onyx eyes had a gleam in them that almost made me believe they were staring back at me. I ran my finger down the long, sharp curve of the beak.

The harsh cry of a bird shattered my contemplation. It came again, the rapid *pruk-pruk-pruk* of a raven, so close to me that for a moment I thought it had come from the silver bird in my hand. The alarm call sounded again, and I glanced up to see a black raven sitting in the branches of the tree above me, its gaze fixed on the forest slope below.

Then came the creaking of leather and the jangle of harness. Three or four men-at-arms on horseback were winding their way through the trees below. I recognised Philippe's livery at once. Two men on foot ran in front of the riders, each holding a pair of hounds on long leashes that were quartering back and forth, sniffing the ground.

My heart galloping like a charging warhorse, I shoved the raven's head back into its box and slipped it into my leather pouch. Rocking myself forward into a crouching position, I watched the progress of the riders, unable to decide whether to make a run for it or to try to hide. Either way the limiers would surely pick up my scent and drag their handlers straight towards me. I had climbed up to this vantage-point in the dark and I couldn't remember which route I'd taken up the hillside, but I was sure any moment the limiers straining on their leashes would find it and follow.

The flapping of wings above my head made me glance up. The raven launched itself off the branch, flying straight down towards the first of the riders. Startled by the raucous cry and closeness of the large bird, the horse shied and reared. The bird circled the beast, repeatedly clawing at its head as if it meant to scratch out its eyes. The rider fought to drive it off with one arm and regain control of his mount with the other, but it was no use. The terrified horse plunged down the side of the hill and thundered away through the trees towards the river, the rider clinging to its mane.

The other horses, seeing their companion galloping away, bolted after it. The limiers, convinced that the hunt was in full spate, began barking and straining so fiercely on the leashes that one broke free and rushed after the horses. The handlers slithered and tumbled down the slope, trying desperately to regain control of their dogs. Whether they did manage to retrieve them I never knew – I certainly wasn't going to hang around to find out. I fled.

From that moment on, I was certain of only one thing. If I had any hope of living long enough to reach my eighteenth birthday, I would have to leave France: with Philippe's fortunes rising steadily at the king's court, his reach would shortly extend to every corner of the kingdom. And as his wealth and power grew, so would my threat to him, for as long as my head remained on my shoulders.

Chapter 24

*Both the vessel and the receiver must be chosen carefully
according to the nature of the thing to be distilled.*

Gisa sits at the bench in the apothecary's shop. The shutters that form the counter have been fastened for the night,
blocking off the sight of the street outside, but not its
sounds. Two pairs of feet clack over the cobbles; the rattle
of the wooden pattens tied over the thin-soled shoes echoes
from the buildings. Their owners chatter as they pass.
Fallen words, cast adrift from their sentences, drift through
the cracks in the door, but Gisa ignores them. She is
straining to hear what is being said above her head in the
solar.

The *unguentum basilicon*, which she has been sent to
prepare, lies in the clay bowl, only half mixed. It must be
stirred twelve times to the right, and twelve to the left, after
each drop of myrrh is added. She knows this without ever
having to be reminded, but tonight she keeps losing count.
All her thoughts are fettered to the room above.

The voices above are too muffled to pick out anything
but her own name. First comes her uncle's soft, measured
tones, then her aunt's strident ones, but she cannot hear
Lord Sylvain's voice, though she knows he is up there. A
chair creaks on the boards above and footsteps cross the
floor, but not to the stairs. Her uncle must be fetching more

wine. He bought it especially for his visitor. Uncle Thomas prefers ale.

In church Gisa always prays for the souls of her dead parents. As instructed by the parish priest, she prays for her aunt and uncle too, even though they are not dead, though she guiltily reflects that her prayers might be more sincere if Aunt Ebba had departed this life. At each confession, she is reminded to beg the Holy Virgin to help her live in obedience, duty and virtue, as befits a grateful orphan. But the words Gisa is murmuring now are not any her priest would approve of. She is praying fervently to St Ursula and to every other virgin saint she can name that Sylvain is not asking Uncle Thomas for her hand in marriage. And that if he is, Uncle Thomas will refuse, though she knows this last plea would require a miracle far beyond the talents even of the Virgin Mary: Aunt Ebba wants this match, and when she is determined to have something, the entire army of the heavenly host could not turn her aside.

Aunt Ebba has changed her mind entirely about Gisa leaving her. A few days ago she was adamant she would waste away and die if her niece was not there to care for her. Now she has decided she could easily obtain another willing orphan from the nuns, a child who would gratefully perform all of Gisa's duties and more. Not that she will need the orphan's services for long – if her niece marries a baron, Aunt Ebba fancies she will be invited to dine daily at the manor and will soon reside there permanently. She is Gisa's mother in all but name, and in her frail state of health cannot be expected to languish uncared for in a damp, poky room while her niece plays the lady in splendour.

Gisa's heart is pounding again as the door opens above her. She hears two pairs of footsteps descending the stairs.

She rushes out into the courtyard before they reach the shop, shrinking into the darkest corner. She doesn't want to hear the news. If they don't utter the words, it cannot happen. But words, once spoken, seal a man or maid for life or death. Crouching outside in the darkness, she hears the door to the shop open and close, then the sound of the brace being slid into place.

But she knows that, sooner or later, her future has to be faced. She edges back into the shop. Her uncle is standing by the door, his head resting wearily against the wall. From upstairs, Aunt Ebba calls shrilly for some hot metheglin to soothe her soured stomach after the wine. She does not sound happy. Uncle Thomas lifts his head and grimaces.

'You'd best fetch her some. Your aunt has suffered something of a disappointment.'

A bubble of joy and relief rises in Gisa's chest. She cannot suppress a smile. 'You mean I am not to go to the manor?'

Uncle Thomas rakes his beard. 'Not as the baron's wife. I am sorry if you were hoping . . .' He hesitates. 'But he did come to ask for you. It seems he needs someone to assist him with some work in his laboratorium. He believes that the skills you have acquired working in this shop are precisely what he requires. He has offered a handsome payment for your services . . . perhaps too generous for what he *says* he wants from you.'

'Uncle, please don't send me!' The panic, which had ebbed away, now surges back, greater than before. 'Tell him I cannot be spared. You can find him an apprentice, a journeyman with far more skill than me. You must know a dozen—'

Her uncle holds up a hand to silence her. 'I suggested as much to him myself. But he is adamant. I'm sorry, child. I cannot afford to refuse. It is not simply a question of the money he is offering, but what he would do if I cross him. He could ruin me in a week, not merely by withdrawing his own custom, that would be loss enough, but he could stop anyone in these parts coming to me with just a word. Besides . . . your aunt demands that we accept.' He shrugs helplessly, begging for her sympathy. 'What can I do?'

Gisa crumples onto the stool, not even registering her aunt's increasingly shrill demands for her immediate attention. Unbidden, her hands reach for the half-finished pot of *unguentum basilicon* and she stirs it mechanically, as if she is twining the cord that will become her own noose.

Her uncle lays a hand upon her shoulder. 'He wanted you to live at the manor, Gisa, but I told him I would not agree to that. I have insisted that you return here each night, so you will sleep safely under my roof. He was not pleased . . . but I insisted.'

Uncle Thomas repeats the phrase as if he is begging to be forgiven for doing her a grave wrong, the nature of which neither of them as yet understands. Gisa knows he wants her to thank him, to tell him that she is happy to go and all is well. But she can't. She won't. She cannot forgive him and he will never forgive himself.

Chapter 25

Under the Astrological House of Pisces, the Fish.
Port of Hondsdamme

This dragon seize and slay with skilful art within the sea,
And wield with speed thy knife.

'And what use would I have for a sprat like you on board a ship? Climb a rigging, can you? Tie a rope? Man an oar? You'd be clinging to the sides and squealing, "Mama!" before we were clear of the harbour.'

The ship's master squinted down at me as if he was blinded by bright sunlight, even though the space under the ship's castle was as gloomy as a church crypt. The constant dazzle of sea and sun gives sailors permanently screwed-up eyes and it certainly didn't make any of them look friendlier, particularly the ship's master. Not only was he built like a blacksmith, the features of his face looked as if they'd been hammered out on an anvil. His nose was bent sideways and his leathery skin pitted with such deep dents above the grizzled beard that shrimps and small fish could easily have taken shelter in them. I could tell at once he was a man who wasted no energy in smiling and that was just as well, for any attempt would have sent small children shrieking to hide behind their mothers' skirts.

He cracked the knuckles of his great hairy fists, which would probably have taken my head clean off my shoulders if he'd landed a blow, but I'd met dozens of men like him as I had crept my way closer and closer to the coast, and I wouldn't be thwarted by this bull.

'I can assure you I have no intention of swarming up any rigging,' I said. 'I am on official business.'

With a flourish I pulled a parchment out of my shirt and offered it to him. Having watched him supervising the loading of cargoes yesterday, I was certain he couldn't read. I saw him glance about for the clerk, but I'd taken care to wait until I'd seen him heading towards one of the warehouses with the quartermaster before I'd sauntered up the gangplank.

'I am to be granted passage by order of King Louis. See there.' I tapped at an impressive flourish on the scroll.

I glanced around pointedly, as if fearing we would be overheard, and drew closer to him, though I wished I hadn't for he stank of rancid pork. 'I am to deliver a package to one of the English barons loyal to our king's cause. It must pass unseen. That's why His Majesty wants it carried by someone who will not be suspected of being a king's messenger.'

The ship's master raised a cynical eyebrow, looking at my ragged clothes. 'No one's going to suspect you, that's for certain. Take me for a fool, do you? As if the king would send a mudlark on his errands!'

'And would I be in possession of such a document if I wasn't on his business? You recognise the king's seal, don't you?'

I dangled the heavy red wax seal in front of his bloodshot eyes. It was a good piece of work, though I say it myself. I'd abstracted the parchment from one of those scribes who hire themselves on street corners to write charms or letters for those who cannot do it for themselves. The wax was from a stolen candle that some pious pilgrim had left at a wayside shrine, which I'd melted and coloured with berry juice. I'd seen enough letters sent from the king to Philippe bearing the royal seal to be able to whittle a passable copy, which I had impressed into the wax. It wouldn't have fooled anyone who'd seen the real thing, but I wagered the ship's master had not, though he plainly recognised the coat of arms.

He peered closely at the wax seal, then back at me. I could see he was beginning to waver. But he needed something more to convince him. Dare I? What if news of the stolen silver flask had spread this far and all the ships' masters had been instructed to keep a look out for the thief and murderer? The box hanging at my belt stirred, as if something was moving inside it, something that was urging me to trust my instincts and show him. I drew the man deeper under the castle deck.

'You must swear that you will reveal to no one what I am about to show you. The king would have both our tongues torn out for this.'

Curiosity burned in his eyes and he nodded.

'This is what I am to deliver to the English baron. It's a sign from the king, a coded message.'

I pulled the box from its leather bag and opened it, peeling back the woollen wrapping just long enough to let him glimpse the silver raven's head. That must surely convince him I was no mudlark, if I had something so fine and valuable in my possession. I had hoped he'd be impressed, but he seemed almost bewitched by it, gazing at it with something approaching awe. I tucked it safely away again.

175

He sucked in his breath. 'King Louis sends the sign of death to England?'

'The raven warns of war between the false king and the true one. King Louis sends word to those loyal to him to make ready for battle. The raven is the sign that they must gather all the information they can about which of the English nobles will support him and where King Henry plans to muster his defences.' I winked at him. 'A cunning symbol, don't you think? The old gods used to send the ravens out across the world as their spies to bring them all the news.'

'Then the king makes ready to take the throne of England again?' the ship's master asked eagerly. 'I said all along what King Louis should do is land north of London and march south. And if an army set sail from Scotland and joined forces with him, the nobles in the north would march with them and they could take London by the heels before the boy-king could cast aside his hobbyhorse. Our Louis has the stronger claim by far and what right-thinking man would want a snivelling boy on the throne when they could have a seasoned warrior, especially when that boy has the devil's blood running in his veins?'

I shook my head wonderingly, as if I was astounded by his cleverness. 'That is exactly His Majesty's plan. You think as a warrior does. The king will like that. And, of course, to carry out that plan the king will need ships and men to captain them, men who have shown their loyalty to him and share his reasoning. Men who know where an army might safely land in England along the northern coast,' I said, hoping I was not laying it on so thickly that he'd grow suspicious again.

He tapped his grimy nails against his teeth for several

moments. Then, with a final glance at the seal, he nodded. 'I suppose it would do no harm to let you aboard . . . But I can't treat you any different from the other passengers, no better rations or sleeping quarters, case they start complaining and the captain asks questions.'

'I wouldn't want you to,' I said hastily. 'It's vital I should not draw attention to myself. I'll tell everyone I'm on a pilgrimage.'

I'd watched a friar bargain for passage for a party of pilgrims earlier in the day and, by the sound of it, he was making a handsome profit – he told his pilgrims that the ship's master was charging considerably more than in fact he was for the voyage and plainly he would keep the difference.

The master gestured to where the other passengers were already claiming their little portion of the deck on which to sleep and I hurried to do the same, before the most sheltered spots were taken. I settled myself where I could keep a close watch on the ship's master. I was confident he had believed my story, but if he started to have doubts or someone alerted him that a wanted man might be trying to gain passage, I had to be ready to flee. There were a few occasions when I tensed and my heart pounded as I spotted him deep in conversation with men on the quayside, though they never glanced in my direction.

But it was only when the mooring ropes were untied and a wide stretch of water opened between ship and shore that I could finally relax. I had done it! I had escaped Philippe. He would never be able to reach me in England, unless, of course, King Louis really did take it into his head to make another bid for the English throne. But by then I would have vanished into the heart of the country and have made my fortune. And there is no better disguise for a poor man than wealth.

Almost as soon as we were clear of the harbour, the rain began to fall, a light misty rain but, driven by the wind, it soon had all the passengers soaked and scrambling to find a place beneath the aft-castle. The sailors had stretched a canvas from the wooden platform at the stern as far as the mast, but this was more to protect the cargo than the passengers.

The last time I had been on a ship crossing from England to France I had been a boy, and either I had forgotten just how violently a ship could lurch and roll or, being a child, had been indifferent to it. I remembered slipping under the blankets of the soldiers as they lay wrapped on deck and burrowing into their broad backs for warmth. They had not kicked me out, using me as a puppy to heat their own bodies. But this time, returning to my homeland, there was no one to share a blanket with. I shivered. This was only the first night. How was I to endure a week of it, or longer if we were becalmed? But, judging by the wind howling like a demon in Hell through the rigging above, there wasn't much chance of that. It was far more likely we'd be dashed to pieces on some cliff.

'The raven flew off the ark, Lugh,' I muttered. 'And he didn't bother to return, so you'd better grow some wings and save yourself.'

I'd found myself talking to the silver raven these past few weeks, like some men talk to their dogs. Halfway to madness, I know, but when you're alone and on the run, you need someone to grumble to, someone to ask, 'Shall we take this track or that one?' Otherwise, you fear you'll forget how to speak and be found wandering about, wild-haired and naked, as crazy as the tree-man.

There were days when I was so lonely I thought I'd died in those woods, but didn't know it. You hear of spirits who haunt the forests trying to find their way home, believing they're still among the living. I'd even seen them some nights, drifting pale as moths among the dark trees. But they don't speak. So as long as I kept talking, I knew I must be alive.

Lugh, as I'd named him, after the ancient god, was an attentive listener. He'd peer at me from out of those glistening black eyes and I could almost swear he was about to answer. He was better than any priest when it came to confession and I'd had much to confess during those long weeks on the run. Theft, of course, I was certainly guilty of that – clothes left to dry on bushes, food and blankets from unattended cottages, and then, as I travelled further away from Philippe's château, there were the pies and roasted sheep's feet I stole from crowded market stalls, and the trinkets I scooped up and slipped beneath my cloak. The latter I sold for a few coins in the next village or exchanged for a beaker of wine and, when the snows and frosts started to bite hard, to pay for a night in a flea-ridden tavern in the poorest quarter of a town.

There were other sins too – a girl on a farmstead. She caught me stealing and threatened to tell her father if I didn't come to the barn with her. She had the face of a cow with large brown eyes and a wet tongue that seemed too big for her drooling mouth. I'd always imagined my first time would be with a noble woman, with Amée to be exact. I had spent many hours up in old Gaspard's tower, imagining every moment of our coupling from me carrying her to a bed covered with snowy white linen to the soft, slow caresses that would coax us, inch by inch, up to the heights of ecstasy.

179

But this slut dragged me down in the piss-soaked straw and was pulling up her skirts before I could stop her. I certainly wasn't her first, that I can assure you, and I staggered away feeling as if I'd been slobbered over by a large smelly dog. During those long nights in the turret, I'd often feared I would die a virgin. After that encounter I was sorry I hadn't.

But as I hastened away from that stinking barn, I came to the third and what would prove to be the most fateful decision I would take since the night of the ambush. Up to then I'd survived by stealing bread from old women who were probably hungrier than I was, being chased by slavering farm dogs and dragged into barns by amorous she-trolls. And every time I stole, I risked being caught and mutilated for that crime at the very least, even before they discovered I was also a man with a price on his head. All that effort and danger and for what – a piece of rancid ham or a stinking tunic that was only fit for an arse-wipe? I wasn't suited to the life of petty crime. And it was Lugh who reminded me where my true talents lay.

My change of fortune came a few nights later. I'd hidden in the darkest corner of a wayside inn and was trying to make a small jug of sour wine last for as many hours as I could, just so that I could stay out of the rain. A man was sitting at one of the tables nearby, making idle patterns with his spoon in some rabbit stew, which he'd barely touched, while all the while my mouth was watering at the sight of it.

Finally, he pushed it away and I swallowed my pride to ask if I could finish it. He shrugged, which I took as yes, and I gobbled it down as rapidly as I could, before the gimlet-eyed innkeeper's wife noticed. I was wiping up the last juices from the wooden bowl with my finger when the man gave a great sigh. I looked up to see him gazing despondently into mid-air, like a frog who had discovered his favourite pond had dried up.

'Something troubling you?' I asked.

I felt obliged to enquire since he'd given me his stew, but I wasn't much interested in the answer. If this man had money enough to waste on food he wasn't going to eat, whatever trouble was vexing him couldn't be half as bad as what I was enduring.

'A woman,' he said morosely.

'You love her, but she doesn't love you – is that it?'

I'd read about such cases, youths so love-sick they couldn't eat or pretended they couldn't, refusing their food with great sighs and groans, in the hope that the object of their infatuation would take notice and have pity on them. But this man looked a trifle old to be afflicted with love-sickness, for he was grey and running to middle-age fat.

He shuddered. 'Love her! I'd rather bed a sow.'

Having recently had my own encounter with the she-troll, I knew just how he felt.

'Then what is the problem?' I enquired cheerfully.

'I'm betrothed to her. She's a widow and I borrowed a good deal of money from her husband before he died to repair my mill. It's been handed down from father to son for generations, has that mill, and needed a new waterwheel and beam, as well as new grind stones. But the widow's set her heart on marriage and she's as good as said she'll demand the return of all the money within the month unless I wed her. I'd pay her the money today if I had it, but it'll take me at least three years to scrape it together, for the harvests have been so poor these past years. If she insists on her

181

money, I'll be forced to give her the mill itself in payment and make myself a beggar, so I've no choice but to wed her.'

He raised his face to me with an expression of such hopelessness in his eyes, it was like staring into the face of a man on the gallows as they put the noose about his neck.

'I was married once, years ago,' he continued. 'Wife ran off with my brother on our wedding night. I've not looked at another woman since, more trouble than they're worth. I'm content with the quiet of my own hearth and the company of my cats. But once this widow gets her talons in me, I'll not have a moment's peace again. She'll nag me from morn to night. She's already started, and we're not even wed yet. She's insisting I must get rid of my poor cats, for when she moves in with me, she is bringing her pack of vicious lapdogs. Between them yapping and her yammering, I'll not be able to hear myself think. I'll end up drowning myself in my own mill pool.'

'What you need,' I told him, 'is a tale to convince her you'd be the wrong man to marry, but also to make her pity you.'

'And where am I to find such a story?' he asked bitterly.

'I might be able to help you there,' I said.

I thought hard for a few moments. Then, pouring myself a beaker of his wine from his flagon, which was much better than my own, I began: 'I reckon your story should go something like this . . .

'Many generations ago in this valley the grain grew in abundance. But the women had to grind it by hand and it took most of the day just to produce enough flour for the next day's bread. They had no time to tend vegetables or livestock or even to mind their children. So your ancestor resolved to build a water mill next to the river, so that the women could bring their wheat to be ground into the finest flour.'

The miller nodded morosely. 'That's how it came about, so I was told.' He frowned. 'But what's the use of telling me what I already know? That'll not rid me of the widow.'

'Patience and I'll tell you something you *don't* know . . . Your ancestor and his sons laboured long and hard to build the mill and at last one evening it was completed and the miller eagerly anticipated the coming of dawn when he would begin milling his first sack of grain. But that night they heard a terrible roar and shrieking, and a huge wave swept down the river, smashing the mill wheel to pieces. They were baffled for there'd been no storm or rain in the night. But so great was the need for a mill in the valley, there was nothing for it but to patiently rebuild the wheel. But the very night it was finished, the water in the river began to race so violently that the wheel spun itself into kindling.

'Refusing to be defeated, the miller and his sons rebuilt the wheel for a third time, and on the night it was completed the miller decided to sleep on the riverbank and watch over his wheel to see what transpired. The night was warm and tranquil. The moon shone brightly and the stars glittered in the indigo sky, and he almost drifted into sleep. Then, at the midnight hour, the water began to foam and churn. The miller hastily backed away from the bank, fearing there was a great beast in the river.

'But, to his surprise, he saw a woman, with skin as white and shimmering as a pearl, rising out of the water. She was naked and her long hair floated out about her. She was the most beautiful woman the miller had ever seen . . . until she opened her mouth and began to scream in rage. The sound was so shrill it brought tears of pain to his eyes, and when he glimpsed the three rows of dagger-sharp teeth, he fell to his knees, shaking with fear.

'"You miserable tadpole, is it you who have trespassed upon my river?" the naiad screeched at him.

'The miller was so afraid he could hardly speak. But, trembling, he told her that he had built the mill to help the villagers and without it they would surely starve.

'The naiad hauled herself out onto the bank and the miller was even more terrified to discover that below her waist her body was covered with thick green scales, and instead of legs she had the writhing tail of a great serpent. She slithered across the ground towards him. The miller scrambled to his feet and tried to run, but her scaly tail lashed out like a whip, wrapping itself around his knees, bringing him crashing to the ground. The miller dug his fingers into the grass, but the creature was so strong that she dragged him towards her with the coils of her tail.

'The miller shut his eyes, certain that he had lived his last day on earth. The naiad wrapped her cold, wet arms about him and he was sure she meant to devour him, but instead she caressed and fondled him. The miller was powerless to resist her advances for her great thick tail was coiled tightly round his body, binding him fast.

'Finally, when she'd had her lustful way with him, the naiad said, "I will make a bargain with you. I will not destroy your mill, if you pay me rent for my river. Every year on this night you shall tether a fat cow on this spot. And when you die, your sons and grandsons must do the same and I shall keep your mill safe. But if you or your descendants ever neglect to bring me my tribute I shall take their first-born son to be my husband."

'When the miller had sworn a solemn oath that he would

do as she asked, the naiad kissed him on the lips, a kiss so icy and terrible that he felt as if all the breath had been sucked from his lungs. Laughing, she uncoiled her tail and slithered back into the water.

'The following year the miller did exactly as he was bade and tethered a plump cow on the riverbank. In the morning he found the rope cut as if it had been bitten through and the ground churned up by the cow's thrashing hoofs. But all that remained of the poor animal were the blood-stained tail and horns. The miller and his sons were so chilled by the sight that they resolved never to forget the tribute. Nor did they, and the mill wheel kept turning.'

I paused and my unwitting host shifted his buttocks on the wooden bench. He frowned, puzzled.

'It's a good tale to wile away a winter's evening,' he said, 'but how will it help me get out of this marriage to the old widow?'

'I'm coming to that,' I said, 'but my throat's dried up with all this talking.'

My companion took the hint and waved his empty flagon at the tavern-girl, who carried it off to refill it. When she returned, and after I'd taken a long swig of wine, I resumed my story.

'Every year since that night down through the generations, the tribute was paid as the naiad demanded, until your father's time. He didn't believe in naiads, but he continued to leave a cow by the river, afraid to stop in case it brought ill fortune. But times were growing hard, and one particular year, when you were just an infant, a plague of insects swarmed through the valley, eating every green stalk down to the bare earth. Men and beasts alike went hungry. Your father could not afford to waste a good cow that year, so

185

he picked out the skinniest, most sickly beast and began to lead it to the river. As chance would have it, a neighbour with whom he'd quarrelled passed him on the road and jeered at him.

'"There's not enough meat on that scrawny beast to keep me fat this winter."

'He went off chuckling to himself. And your father began to wonder – was it his neighbours who'd been taking the cow each year and laughing at him behind his back? Determined not to be taken for a fool any longer, he turned and led the cow home.

'Though he was sure it was his neighbours who were making off with the cows, still your father lay awake all night worrying just in case the legend might be true. But come dawn, the mill was still standing and the river was as calm as a nun at prayer. Your father rubbed his hands in satisfaction. He had been right all along. The legend was no more than a silly tale to frighten children and he'd waste not a single cow more on it.

'All was well for several years. You grew up and when your father died you became the miller. You fell in love with a pretty maid and were overjoyed when she consented to become your wife. She was a beautiful bride and you couldn't wait for the wedding feast to end and the wedding night to begin. But no sooner were the two of you alone in your cottage than you heard a great roaring as if a huge wave was rolling down the river. You ran out into the darkness to check the mill wheel, but it was undamaged and the river was no higher than before. It must have been rocks falling up in the hills that you'd heard. But you wasted little time pondering about that, for it was your wedding night and your adorable bride was waiting. You hurried back to the cottage.

186

'Your bride had extinguished the candle, but by the dim glow of the damped-down fire you could just make out the outline of her head on the pillow and her arms stretched out to receive her new husband. You ran to the bed and jumped in, but the arms that embraced you were wet and cold, her leg rubbing against your bare thigh felt as if it was covered with thick slimy scales, and when she pressed her icy lips upon yours it was as if she was sucking the breath from your body.

'Alarmed, you sprang from the bed and in your haste you trod on something warm and sticky lying on the floor. With trembling fingers you lit a candle and saw that what you had stepped on was a blood-soaked hand, bitten off at the wrist. To your horror, you saw a ring on that dead hand, the very one that, only that afternoon, you had slipped onto your wife's finger. The hand was all that remained of your beautiful bride. Aghast, you stared at the bed and saw a naked woman resting against the pillows, with skin as translucent and gleaming as a river-pearl, while beneath the blankets something slithered and coiled. The woman held out her arms to you.

'"Come to your new bride, my husband. I've been waiting for you."

'As her lips parted in speech, you saw the three rows of dagger-sharp teeth and they were crimson with fresh blood.

'You fled to the door, but you couldn't move as fast as that serpent's tail. It lashed across the room, twisted you in its coils and dragged you back into her cold wet bed.

'And ever since then, each year on the anniversary of your wedding night, the naiad slithers from her icy river, creeps into your cottage and into your bed. Neither bolt nor bar can keep her out for she is far stronger than any of them and you are forced again and again to spend the long dark night in her dreadful embrace.'

187

My companion was now green in the face and staring at me in horror, as if he thought the creature might actually be waiting for him in his bed when he got home that night.

I patted his arm bracingly. 'There, you see? Now, all you have to do is tell the old widow that if you were to marry her, the same dreadful fate would befall her as your first wife and you love her far too much ever to allow that. Furthermore, the naiad has told you that if you should try to leave your cottage, and escape her, she will cause such a terrible wave to surge down the river that it will not only sweep away your mill but flood the whole valley, destroying everything in its path. So you're forced to carry on living in the cottage alone and suffer this yearly torment to save the village. You'll need to groan and look distraught. Sob, too, if you can, and I guarantee the old widow will feel so sorry for you she'll cancel the debt on the spot and never mention marriage again.'

He gazed at me for a moment, visibly shaken, dropped a few coins on the table to pay for his meal, and tottered from the tavern. I scooped up the coins before the tavern-girl could lay her hands on them, then bought myself another flagon of wine and a bed for the night in their barn.

But I had learned three things from that encounter. First, negotiate a good price before you tell them the tale or they just toss you a coin as if you were a storyteller at a fair. Second, don't tell a story that gives your customers night-mares. And third, Philippe, Le Comte de Lingones, was not the only man in the world badly in need of a good tale to rid himself of a pressing problem. The world abounded in such men and it seemed to me that a sharp-witted lad might make a passable living by giving them exactly what they needed, even if they didn't yet know it.

I knew these men wouldn't all fall into my lap as easily

as the miller had done. Like Philippe, most men hide their shameful secrets. The trick was to discover what a man, or woman, come to that, was afraid of losing most in this world and what they needed to conceal. I had to ferret out their dirty little secrets as I had done with Philippe, then, like an angel stretching down from Heaven, drag them up out of the flames of Hell. It had all gone wrong with Philippe, but that was because I'd come to him as a lowly servant, a gullible boy. I would not make that mistake again. A man of substance is not to be so lightly dismissed and that is what I would become, just as soon as I reached England and sold the silver raven.

The rain was lashing down harder than ever and even though we were still hugging the French coast the ship was bucking and tossing, like a maddened bull. Most of the passengers were regretting ever having eaten supper. It was going to be a miserable voyage, but I comforted myself with the thought that luck was still on my side. I had eluded Philippe and escaped the gallows. I'd talked my way into being given free passage on the ship and as soon as I sold the raven I would have more money in my purse than even I had dreamed of. As I told you, Fortune favours those who help themselves. I was the proof of that.

I swallowed hard, trying to fight down the first wave of nausea that rose in my gullet as the ship bucked ever more wildly, but as I pulled the blanket over my head, I thought I heard the rapid *pruk-pruk-pruk* alarm of a raven calling above the creaking sails and crashing waves. But whoever heard of a raven flying over the sea? I reached for the wooden box and held it tight against my chest. I could have sworn it was trembling, almost as if the box was an egg and the creature inside it was beginning to hatch.

189

Chapter 26

A chicken egg decays and from it is born a live chicken, thus the living animal comes forth from the decay of the whole.

Regulus darts along in the shadow of the wall, the wet blanket in his arms. He means to wash the tell-tale patch in the stream that runs through the small vegetable garden, before Felix or Father John discovers it.

The last time he had wet the bed he had tried to hide the blanket in the middle of the others, but that had led only to more trouble, more humiliation, greater punishment – sitting, hungry, in the corner of the dorter, watching the others eat, the piss-soaked blanket on his head, before finally being sent to wash not only his blanket but all the others he had contaminated. He had been permitted nothing to eat or drink for the rest of the day.

'Wetting the bed is not just filthy and disgusting, but a wicked waste of urine,' Father John had thundered. 'Even animals do not soil their own nests. You are lazy, boy, too idle to get out of a warm bed and use the pot.'

I'm not lazy, Regulus had wanted to tell him. It happens in his dreams, his nightmares. He cannot help himself. By the time he wakes it is too late. But he had said nothing: no words would burst through a throat closed tight with tears.

The boy stops suddenly, as he sees two of the white-robed canons standing yards from him in the early-morning light. He quickly crouches down. They are talking with their backs to him. They haven't seen him, but they are standing between him and the little stream.

Keeping low he edges back along the wall, desperately searching for some other route. He sees the door in the wall, stretches up to turn the iron ring-handle with one hand. It moves a little, but not much. He drops the wet blanket on the ground and uses both hands to turn the stiff ring. It isn't locked. Cautiously he pushes the door open, just a crack, and squints through the gap.

He is still not certain which places are forbidden and which are not, but he has another reason to be wary. He remembers the first night he came being taken through a door, a door that led down into a chamber deep below the earth where flasks bubbled and a magpie flew at him. At least he thinks he remembers that, but he has had such strange, wild dreams, he can no longer be sure if it happened in his sleep or his waking. He dreams he is pissing and wakes to find that he has. Are dreams real, then? But, real or nightmare, he is afraid of what lies behind these identical doors now, afraid that the next one he opens will lead back to that place, to that cell in which they shut him up all alone.

But through the narrow gap he glimpses not a dark chamber, but grass and branches and wrinkled trunks. The place beyond the door is full of trees. His face breaks into a grin and he has to stop himself shrieking in delight. He has found the way out, the way back to the forest. Dragging the blanket behind him, he slips through the door as swiftly as a mouse darts into its hole and pulls it shut behind him.

But as soon as he is on the other side of the door, his smile vanishes. In that fleeting moment between him peering through the crack and stepping through the door, it seems to him that great high walls have sprung up all around the small patch of trees. And the trees are barely trees at all, not the great towering oaks and swaying elms of the forest, but stunted, gnarled and bent as old men, like the apple tree near their cottage at home.

The heavy cloud of disappointment that has enveloped him lifts briefly. He is a good climber. He can climb any tree in the forest – at least, he can in his head. He could easily climb up any of these twisted trunks and scramble over the wall. But even as he stares around, searching for a likely tree, he can see the branches are too low, too far away from the walls. He knows, without trying, he'd never be able to reach.

There is a pool, though. The water in the stream that feeds it runs in under a low gap at the bottom of the wall. A frog could come and go as it pleased, but not a boy, not even one as small as Regulus.

He wanders to the pool and dips the damp patch of his blanket in the cold water. If it doesn't smell of piss, maybe no one will notice. It is only as he tries to wring the water out that he glimpses someone moving at the far end of the orchard. Not a white-robed man, but a boy, a boy he knows. Felix is searching for something on the ground, walking back and forth across the grass, like a hound quartering in search of a slain bird. Regulus tries to bundle up the blanket and conceal it behind his back, but it is too big and heavy and just as he tries to edge back towards the door, Felix raises his head.

For a moment neither of them moves. Then the blanket

slips from Regulus's hands and tumbles onto the grass. He is still trying to gather it again when he feels Felix tugging on the other side of it. Regulus cowers, afraid that Felix will start yelling, will call Father John – everyone – to come and look at the evidence of his sin.

But Felix does not call out. Instead he takes the blanket from the boy and he wrings the wet patch out. His long fingers are far more adept at the task than Regulus's. In silence they watch the grey drops splash onto the grass. They sparkle in the sun, before they are pulled down into the earth.

'Shouldn't be in here,' Felix says.

Regulus guesses that means him.

'Bury them here under the grass . . . the White Canons,' Felix says, but as Regulus continues to stare blankly at him, he adds helpfully, 'When they die . . . When Father John dies, he'll be buried here too, all the brothers will. It's what makes the trees give lots of fruit, see. Roots burrow into their corpses, suck up all the juices.' He jerks his head towards the trees. 'You'll see come autumn. Trees'll be thick with apples, pears, too. We help to pick them. There's loads. Best you ever tasted.'

He chuckles. 'My father used to say corpses are food for worms, but he was wrong. The White Canons are food for us. Next time Father John punishes you, tell yourself, *One day I'll be eating you. Everyone'll think I'm just biting into a nice juicy apple, but really it'll be your bones I'll be crunching.* That's what I think when he locks me up. Then I don't mind what he does to me.' Felix grins and lifts his chin defiantly, as if trying to convince himself he really doesn't care.

The idea of eating Father John doesn't make Regulus laugh. In fact, the very thought of eating an apple now

193

makes him feel sick. He stares at the ground, picturing all those men lying beneath the grass. He wonders if he walked over someone's body as he crossed the grass. He's suddenly afraid to take another step in case a dead hand thrusts itself up through the earth and grabs his leg, angry at being trodden on.

He shudders. 'Is that what you were looking for, a dead body?'

Felix looks surprised. 'How did you know?'

'Saw you searching the grass over there.' The boy points to the far side of the orchard.

Felix grunts. 'Thought maybe there'd be a fresh grave. Guessed this is where they'd bury Mighel, if he was dead.'

'He's not dead. His mam came for him and took him home,' Regulus reminds him, convinced Felix must have forgotten. 'Father John said.'

'But they didn't 'cause Mighel doesn't have any parents. Father got killed by pirates and his mam's dead too. That's why the priest in the village brought him here, he told me so, 'cause there was no one else to look out for him. And you heard old Crabby – he said Mighel wasn't sick, so he's not been taken to the infirmary.'

Regulus giggles. He's never heard Felix call Father John anything but his name. He sobers quickly, seeing the grim look on the older boy's face.

'Maybe he's in the room on the stairs that lead down into the ground,' Regulus says. 'That's where I slept the first night, leastways . . . There is a room, isn't there? A real room?'

He gnaws his lip, realising that Mighel has been gone for days. Has he been locked in that terrible dark place all this time?

194

Felix shakes his head. 'Room's real, all right, but Peter got taken down to the cellars again three nights ago and he reckons the door of that room was open when he passed, 'cause I asked him, and he swears it was empty. And Mighel wasn't in the cellars either. I reckon he's been taken.'

The little boy looks up at Felix, his blue eyes full of anxiety. 'Did the owl take Mighel? My brothers died in the night. The owl ate their souls. The charcoal-burner's wife told Mam she heard it cry in the night. Can the owl get into our room?'

'Wasn't the owl took him,' Felix says savagely. 'It was the wizard. They gave him to the wizard. Sometimes he comes to the cellars. I've seen him when old Crabby drags me down there in the night. He's a friend of Father Arthmael – heard them talking about the time when they were students together in France, years ago, but' – Felix wrinkles his nose – 'I don't reckon they like each other much. I've seen 'em look like they'd kill each other, if they had half a chance.'

'Why does the wizard come to see Father Arthmael if he hates him?'

Felix shrugs. 'Father Arthmael gives him things . . . flasks and boxes.'

'Why, if he doesn't like him?'

'Wizard brings him scraps of parchment . . . for the boxes, like they're swapping eggs for butter in the market. Says he's copied them from pages in some book. I reckon Father Arthmael must really want them 'cause when he gets one he shoves it inside his robe, like it was a gold coin and he's afraid someone'll steal it.' Felix shakes his head irritably. 'Anyhow, what does it matter why he comes? He has the evil eye, I know it. He could do worse things to you than Father Arthmael ever could, just by looking at you.'

Felix reaches down and grips the front of Regulus's shirt, almost lifting him off his feet. 'If old Crabby comes for you in the night and there's another man waiting, a man dressed all in black, you scream and yell your head off. Wake the whole abbey if you have to. Run and hide if you can. They'll punish you, but it's better than being taken by him. He'll turn you into a bird and keep you locked in a tiny cage to sing all day. That's what he's done to Mighel. Wizard's turned hundreds of people into birds – that's what the gatekeeper said. I heard him. Cages of birds all over his house, that's what he reckons.'

Regulus remembers the magpie that flew at him in the chamber. Was that really a boy?

Felix, still gripping his shirt, gives him a little shake. 'But you mustn't tell anyone what I told you, none of the other boys and especially not Father John. If you do I'll . . . I'll cut your throat when you're asleep and I'll tell Father John you wet the bed again too. Swear?'

Regulus nods as vigorously as he can with Felix half choking him. 'Swear . . . I swear, Felix, by . . .' He tries to think of the most binding oath he's ever heard. 'By the Holy Virgin . . . by all the virgins ever.'

He isn't sure what a virgin is, but he knows there are a great many of them, for one of the boys read a story from the lives of the saints while they were eating supper, a story about St Ursula who took eleven thousand virgins on a ship and sailed away. Regulus doesn't know how many eleven thousand is either, but he's pretty sure it's more than all the trees in the forest, maybe more than all the trees in the world.

Felix seems satisfied and releases him.

'You won't tell, will you, about the bed?' Regulus asks

anxiously. This threat is far more menacing than merely having his throat cut.

Felix nods. He holds out his little finger and the boy wraps his own round it.

'Brothers,' Felix says. 'I'll keep your secrets and you keep mine.'

Regulus smiles. For the first time since he came here he feels safe, even after what Felix has told him about the wizard. Felix is going to be his big brother from now on. He will protect him because they share a secret, and Regulus would sooner die than betray Felix.

Chapter 27

Under the Astrological House of Aries, the Ram. Norfolk, England

If it be cast onto Earth, it will separate the element of Earth from that of Fire, the subtle from the gross.

We anchored in the port of Lynn Episcopi, Bishop's Lynn, on the late-evening tide, but no one was allowed to disembark until the following morning. We were obliged to wait until the bishop's official had been rowed out to inspect every keg of wine and plank of timber we were carrying. It was his job to collect the tolls and taxes to be paid, and you could tell at once he was a man who enjoyed his work. If he spotted even the smallest splinter that wasn't actually part of the ship, he'd find some reason to tax it. He even inspected the passengers' bundles in case he could unearth anything to tax there. Fortunately for me, he didn't actually search our bodies, so Lugh was safe, nested in his little wooden box beneath my cloak.

As we'd tossed and rolled our way up the east coast I'd become more despondent by the hour. When I'd last lived in England as a boy, it had been in Winchester in the south, which in my memory was bathed in eternal summer, a town surrounded by sweet water-meadows where cattle grazed and corn ripened in the sun. But this coast, when I could glimpse it at all between the swirling clouds of dank mist, appeared to consist of nothing but bleak marshes and low, scrubby hills, inhabited only by flocks of half-wild sheep. From the stench of the smoke wafting across from the hundreds of little huts that lined the seashore, the entire population appeared to survive only on rotten fish cooked over fires of dung and seaweed.

The sight of the port of Lynn did nothing to lift my spirits. It seemed that the denizens of Hell itself had risen from the nether regions to lay siege to the town. Great waste heaps of sand and silt encircled the city and the air was choked with steam rising from huge copper pots and the smoke of dozens of roaring fires, whose flames bathed all in a devilish red glow. Half-naked men and boys loomed in and out of the mist, like the spirits of the damned, straining to push sledges and handcarts through the sand or staggering under the weight of sacks hefted on their backs.

'What are they doing?' I asked a man leaning on the gunwale beside me.

'Salt,' he said tersely. 'That's what my master's sent me to trade for. This ship will be crammed to the masts with it going back. They make brine from the sand and boil it off in those vats. Filthy work, but it's made this town's fortune. Ships and salt – 'tis all you need to make a wealthy man, though only for them as owns them, of course, not for those poor bastards carrying the loads.'

'God has ordained each of us our place in this world,' a voice said behind us. 'To question that is blasphemy.'

I turned to see the friar. The long fringe around his tonsure was blowing straight up from his head in the wind, which made him look like a startled goat. He gave me an oily smile. 'Have you decided to join our pilgrimage to the shrine of the Blessed Virgin at Walsingham, Master Laurent?'

I almost looked behind me to see who he was talking to, until I remembered it was me. Naturally I'd changed my name. I was hardly fool enough to use the name I was known by in Philippe's household, but it was taking me a while to get used to answering to it.

'After we have enjoyed all the delights that Walsingham has to offer,' the friar continued, 'I shall be guiding my little band of pilgrims to Bromholm Priory where they may touch a fragment of the true cross. It has worked many miracles – lepers cleansed, the sight of the blind restored and even the dead raised to life.'

'I hope my father doesn't get to hear about that,' my companion said, with a grin. 'Cost me a fortune to bury him first time around, and knowing that old tight-purse, if he rises from his grave he'll be wanting his pigs back 'n' all, including the ones we've eaten.'

'The relic also drives out demons from the possessed,' the friar added, glaring pointedly at each of us in turn, as if he thought we might both be in need of a good exorcism.

I must confess I was sorely tempted to go to the shrine, though not because I was seized with a sudden attack of piety. Shrines attracted sinners with guilt on their consciences. They might confess all to God, who would absolve them of anything from gluttony to mass murder for a price, but man is far less forgiving of the weaknesses of his fellows and those sinners would still need tales to cover those dark secrets.

'Is Walsingham close by?' I asked.

The friar plucked at his lower lip. 'Less than thirty miles away. There's a stable in the town where we can hire good horses. So, even riding at a pace that will suit the women,

200

we should be comfortably installed in the pilgrims' lodgings by nightfall tomorrow, provided, of course, we are permitted to leave this ship within the hour.'

That thought seemed to remind him he was in a hurry and, without another word, he sped off in pursuit of the ship's master, demanding to know when we would be allowed ashore.

The man at the gunwale snorted. 'So they're not planning to crawl to Walsingham on their knees, then. Doesn't believe in suffering on his pilgrimage, does he?' He gave me an amused glance. 'Are you really planning to go with them? I'd not have marked you as a relic-kisser.'

'Thought it might be a good place to earn a few coins,' I told him, though it was a few well-stuffed purses I was really after. I'd had my fill of struggling to earn mere pennies.

But first I'd need to sell the raven's head if I was to hire a good horse and buy some decent clothes. I'd need to arrive in Walsingham looking like a wealthy man. That way I'd be admitted to the better lodgings where the rich pilgrims stayed. The poor didn't have much to lose in this life, so they wouldn't pay for tales to cover their guilt, but the wealthy had both salt and ships or, in this case, secrets and money.

But the salt-buyer shook his head. 'You go near a shrine and the only money you'll be seeing is what's going out of your purse 'cause there'll be none going in. Those monks are there to fleece the pilgrims, not give them coins. They won't even allow the mongers to sell the crowds food or ale while they're waiting in line unless the sellers pay the monks half their profits for the privilege. That friar's as bad. I've met his type before. Those pilgrims'll be lucky if he hasn't filched the breeches off their backsides before they get there.

He'll charge them each an ungodly sum to guide them there and that'll only be the start of it. I'll wager he's in the pay of that stables too. They bribe him to bring the pilgrims to them, so they can charge twice what it's worth to hire one of their broken-winded nags. And whatever he promises, they won't reach Walsingham by tomorrow night. That'll mean another night on the road and another handful of coins for the friar from the innkeeper who puts them up.'

A shout from the ship's master made us both turn round. The last of the bishop's men was lumbering down the creaking gangplank to the quayside and we were finally free to disembark. My companion heaved his belongings onto his back and clapped a heavy hand on my shoulder. 'If you need good honest work, take my advice, stay here in Lynn. There's a tavern in the town close by the river they call Purfleet. Woman who runs it goes by the name of Ibby. Tell her Martin, steward of Foxby, sent you. She can usually find work for a willing lad.'

I thanked him politely, but refrained from telling him I had no intention of working for my supper – at least, not by washing pots or turning a spit in some poxy inn. I had my heart set on much bigger prizes than that.

I took my time exploring the town. The harbour was crammed with ships bringing in wine from Germany and France, figs, oil and leather from Spain, dried fish and live hunting falcons from Norway, spices and dyes from the Far East, and countless bales of sable, beaver and Arctic squirrel pelts from the great fur market of Novgorod, all to be loaded onto carts or river boats and dispatched to every corner of England. Seamen and merchants thronged the streets, laughing and quarrelling in a dozen different languages.

Buildings seemed to spring up even as I passed them. Makeshift hovels were being torn down to be replaced with great warehouses, and fishermen's huts chopped to firewood to make room for the houses of wealthy merchants and sea captains.

Several times I was elbowed into the open sewers by merchants and their clerks, who strode down the middle of the street, ostentatiously showing off the sumptuous fur linings of their woollen cloaks by artfully folding back the edges. Great jewelled clasps flashed on their tabards, and their sword hilts were more elaborately gilded than a saint's reliquary, though the men who wore them were so portly I doubted they'd be able to pull the swords from their sheaths without slicing open their own bellies.

After I had been rudely shoved aside for the third time, it occurred to me that the reason I was being treated like a beggar was that, after weeks on the run and days being drenched and wind-tossed at sea, I probably looked filthier than a dog-shit collector and doubtless smelt as bad. I knew I couldn't attempt to sell the raven's head if I appeared to be a man who couldn't even pay for his next meal. They'd immediately suspect that the silver bird had been stolen and I could hardly prove it hadn't.

So, there was nothing for it but to spend the very last of the coins I had carefully amassed on some new clothes. The best I could afford was a moss-green tunic with a reddish-brown tabard to wear over it. They were both much plainer than I'd hoped for, but at least they fitted me well and were not stained or torn. I'd no money left to buy new hose, but I hoped the tunic would cover most of the holes.

The salt spray had made my hair so sticky and matted, I couldn't pull my stolen comb through it. It felt like a thorn bush growing out of my head. Much to the amusement of some small boys, I stripped almost naked in a quiet back alley and steeled myself to tip buckets of icy water from a well in the street over my head, in an effort to rinse the salt from my hair and skin. My teeth were chattering violently by the time I'd finished, but there was one good thing to be said for that vicious wind: it dried hair quickly.

Dressed and groomed as neatly as I could manage, I set about finding a likely-looking shop in which to sell the silver flask. I needed someone who had the money and good taste to pay for the bird, but was not so respectable that they would enquire too closely into its origins.

I found one such shop near the church of St James. A curious hairy creature with an imp-like face and almost human hands and feet squatted in a tiny cage that hung outside it. When anyone approached it shrieked and gibbered, rattling the cage and grimacing, stretching out its paws through the bars as if trying to drag the customer in. It certainly drew attention to the shop. I glanced in through the dark doorway. A man sat at a bench, repairing a large silver buckle. The shelves that lined the shop were crammed with all manner of objects, from copper platters to pewter goblets, silver bowls to candle spikes in the form of manikins or animals.

I swaggered inside, trying to exude an air of confidence. He glanced up as I greeted him. I swept my hand in a grand gesture around the shelves. 'You are a skilled craftsman, Master. You fashioned all these?'

He grunted, unimpressed. 'Some. Others I buy from the ships.' He nodded towards a pair of copper bowls decorated with delicate silver trees and exotic birds with sweeping tails. 'From India those are, finest we've ever had. Just the thing if you're looking for a gift to impress.'

204

He laid the buckle aside. 'Getting married, are you? Wedding gift for your lovely bride, is it? She'll give you the wedding night of your dreams, if you buy this for her. Fair melt into your arms, she will.' He pulled down a round silver mirror.

I stared into its highly polished surface. It had been quite some time since I'd seen my own reflection, and for a moment I fancied I was looking at a painting of a stranger. My skin had always been as pale as a grass blade trapped beneath a stone, from having been kept in the turret through the summer, but was now tanned, and my wispy beard was golden against my brown face.

The silversmith turned it over so that I could admire the back, which was engraved with what seemed to be a small cottage, a woman's head hovering above it.

'The Holy Shrine of the house of the Virgin Mary at Walsingham, that is.' He leaned towards me, as if he was about to impart some great secret. 'I tell you, they don't sell anything half as fine as this in Walsingham itself and what they do sell will cost you three times as much for half the quality.'

'You're a man of exquisite taste,' I said. 'And you know good craftsmanship when you see it. I'd be most interested to hear your professional opinion of this.'

His face settled into a resentful scowl as soon as he realised I was selling not buying and, replacing the mirror, he returned to his seat behind the bench. He bent his head to his work, plainly indicating I should leave and stop wasting his time. But I refused to be discouraged. Glancing round to ensure the shop was empty, I turned my back to the door and pulled out the box. I carefully unwrapped the raven's head and placed it on the bench directly in front of him, where he was forced to look at it.

'Interesting piece,' he said, with a casual indifference, but I could tell from the gleam in his eyes and the way his fingers darted towards it that he thought it far more than that.

He lifted it and examined it carefully, running his finger over the smooth polished beak. 'Selling it, are you?'

I shrugged. 'I might be persuaded to part with it, for a good price, though it has been in my family many years.'

'I'd have a hard job selling it on. Ravens are unlucky. There's not many would want this in their house.'

But the expression on his face was one of almost pure lust. I could see how much he coveted it and knew he was just trying to find an excuse to offer me far less than the bird was worth.

'But the *head* of a raven protects a house and a kingdom,' I said. 'It is said that the great King Arthur didn't die but became a raven so that he could watch over his people, and that King Brân could turn himself into a raven to spy on his enemies. When he died they buried his head on Tower Hill in London, facing France, to keep this sweet isle safe from invasion.'

'Didn't work, though, did it?' the silversmith said sourly. 'Louis the Lion took England just the same.'

'Only part of it, and he was driven out from all in the end.' The mention of King Louis brought my erstwhile master painfully to mind. 'Besides,' I added quickly, 'everyone knows a raven on the roof brings prosperity to the house.'

The silversmith gave an appraising glance at my plain clothes. 'If it's that lucky, I'm surprised you want to sell it.'

'I'm embarking on a long voyage,' I said airily. 'My uncle is a wealthy woad merchant in Picardy. His business has grown so much that he wants me to join him and help him expand still further. But, alas, silver and seawater don't mix. I'd hate such a lovely object to be damaged or even stolen in my travels. So, reluctantly, I must part with it.'

The silversmith nodded. I couldn't tell if he believed the tale or not, but I guessed he was prepared to accept any story, just as long as it was vaguely plausible. He doubtless found it helped business not to enquire too closely into the origins of some of the things he was offered for sale.

We began to haggle, like marketplace crones, him starting, as I knew he would, at a ridiculously low price and me at an outrageously high one. As we bargained he continued to examine the head, holding it close to a candle the better to admire the fine engraving. I could see how much he desired it. We had almost met at a price on which we could shake hands when he froze, then thrust the silver head back at me.

He turned away, flapping his hands as if he was trying to shoo away a wasp. 'I can't help you. I can't buy it.'

Thinking this was just a tactic to bring the price down again, I tried to press him, holding out the head so that the beak turned to gold in the light of the flame. But I could tell something had changed. He was shrinking away from it, holding up his hand to shield himself from it, as if warding off the evil eye.

'The signs,' he muttered.

'What signs?'

'Haven't you seen them? There . . . hidden in the feathers. Look at them closely with the candle behind them. Turn it at an angle. See? Can you see them now? The swan, the scorpion, the sun, the moon, the tomb itself. They're all there. It's the marriage of death!'

I peered at the raven's head, trying to make sense of what

he was saying. And then I suddenly saw them too. In daylight, the head appeared to be covered with nothing more than the intricately engraved feathers, but in this interplay of flame and shadow, some of the lines stood out in relief and I saw now that tiny symbols were hidden there – a flame, a lion, a boy.

I glanced up at him. He had taken several paces back from the bench, as if I was holding a live viper. 'I don't understand,' I said. 'What do they mean?'

The silversmith shook his head. 'Go! Go! Get it out of my shop,' he begged. There was no mistaking the fear in his voice. This was no bargaining tactic.

Bewildered, I began to rewrap the head in the white woollen cloth. But then, as I was folding the last piece in place, the raven's eye winked at me. I know you'll say it was just a trick of the light, nothing more than shadow cast by the guttering candle flame, but I swear to you, on my own miserable life, I saw that eyelid move.

My hands were trembling so hard, I could scarcely get the head back into the box. I hurried from the shop. As I passed the gibbering imp in the cage, I heard the silversmith's voice cry out behind me, 'Get rid of it, boy. Hurl it into the sea. It will be your death if you don't.'

Chapter 28

*Take his brain, grind it up with very strong vinegar or
with a boy's urine, until it turns black.*

The manservant looms over Gisa as she proffers her name.
He does not hide his contempt. He is a giant of a man,
thighs thick as her body and neck corded like that of an
ox. Coarse black bristles poke out from his eyebrows, chin,
nose and ears, as if he is a hollow skin that's been overstuffed
with horsehair.

'You are Master . . .?' she asks, trying to placate him with
the courtesy of a title.

His sneer deepens. He is not appeased.

'Odo. Plain Odo. The *master* is waiting for you up in his
laboratorium.'

He leads her through the walled courtyard and the Great
Hall, with its painted walls, to a door at the back of the
hall disguised as part of the wooden panelling. She emerges
into the manor grounds, which appear to be entirely enclosed
by a high wall. In most manorial grounds the eye would be
drawn to the herb garden or the orchard, but here both
herbs and trees alike cower beneath a grim, square tower,
which stands alone in the centre of the grounds, its black
shadow stretching out, like an accusing finger, to touch the
walls of the manor house.

The tower has a flat roof and on top Gisa can just make

out a metal cage, like the gibbets in which they hang the corpses of executed prisoners, though this one seems to be full of wood. She decides it must be a beacon of sorts, to be lit as a warning of invasion, like the one on the bell tower of the parish church. Will the French invade again? Aunt Ebba is certain they will and certain she will be ravished if they do.

Odo grunts, jerking his head towards the heavy oak door in the base of the tower. 'I've unlocked it. He doesn't like to be kept waiting.'

'Aren't you going to tell him I'm here?' Gisa asks.

The manservant's hairy nostrils flare. 'Announce you? As if you were a noblewoman?' His tone makes clear which of them he believes is the superior. 'I never go up there, not when he's working. If he needs something heavy removed or brought in he gives instructions . . . *clear* instructions. There are rules. Those who don't learn them fast are not here long.'

Odo turns back into the Great Hall, then seems to remember something else she must be told. 'When the master's dismissed you for the day, you'll leave through there.' He points across the garden to a narrow door set into the wall of the manor grounds. 'I have the key.' He says this as if he wishes her to understand that he controls every gate and door. He, and he alone, has the power to release her from this prison.

He retreats inside and the door to the Great Hall slams shut, but Gisa does not move. She has no desire to enter that tower, but as she glances up at the high windows, she thinks she sees movement. Perhaps Sylvain is standing up there looking down at her, watching, waiting.

Her legs have turned into twin pillars of salt. She has to

drag them across the grass. As she reaches the entrance she hesitates. In spite of what Odo has instructed, she feels compelled to knock, but there is no response. Can Lord Sylvain even hear the beating of her small fist all the way up there? She twists the iron ring and pushes. The door to the tower is as stout as that of a great castle's and she has to lean her full weight on it to open it. She edges inside, expecting . . . She has no idea what to expect. All the same, she fears whatever might be in there.

But she finds herself standing in nothing more alarming than a bare, dusty room, containing only a neat stack of logs, some sealed barrels and sacks of what smells like horse dung. A straight wooden staircase runs up one wall, leading to the open trapdoor in the wooden floor above.

Gisa calls out, but there is no reply. There is no rail or rope to hold, so pressing her hand against the wall to balance herself, she inches up the staircase and emerges through the trapdoor into a second chamber. Shelves run around this room, crammed with many small flasks and jars, and beneath are stacks of chests and boxes. Every jar and box is labelled, not just with words but also symbols in the form of circles, lines and crosses, with the signs of the sun or moon and the different houses of the zodiac.

Though Gisa does not understand the significance of the lines and circles, she knows the signs of the zodiac well, for every plant and mineral her uncle uses in his shop must be collected in accordance with astrological rules. Every illness is governed by a planet and therefore its cure is to be found in a herb ruled by the same planet or by the opposite one. These heavenly bodies govern the health and fortunes of the meanest beggars and greatest nations alike. They cannot be ignored, so Uncle Thomas says.

Gisa longs to examine the contents of the jars, but she hears footsteps crossing the wooden boards above her and, though she is trying to put off the moment for as long as possible, she dare not tarry. She must face Lord Sylvain sooner or later. In this chamber, too, a wooden staircase runs up the side of the wall and, with a lump in the centre of her chest, as if she has swallowed a great stone, she begins to climb.

As her head rises through the hole in the floor, the first thing that strikes her is the heat in contrast to the chill of the chambers beneath. It is emanating from a glowing charcoal fire burning in a round copper bowl balanced on three legs, the feet of which are fashioned into giant eagle claws.

A huge glass flask, like a bird's head with a long glass beak, is suspended over the fire. The inside is clouded with dense red steam; it condenses at the top of the flask and trickles down through the beak-like projection into a series of tubes and vessels ranged in a cascade down a set of wooden steps to the floor. Gisa is so fascinated by this waterfall of glass and hissing steam that she has almost forgotten her new master, until he speaks.

'You must come earlier in future. There is much to be done, much for you to learn. Time is the most costly ingredient of all. It must not be wasted.'

Sylvain is standing in front of one of the small slit windows. He seems more like the shadow of a person than flesh and blood, for the light behind him throws his face into darkness, save his eyes. They glitter, an iridescent green, like the flies that swarm over corpses in summer. He is clad in a plain black robe. The hem trails on the dusty boards and the folds are caught about his waist by a broad black leather belt, whose silver clasp is formed from two interlocking snakes. In his pale, bony hands, he is twisting a length of white cord.

Gisa staggers back, almost falling through the trapdoor, terrified that he means to throttle her. Sylvain lunges at her and grabs her, jerking her towards him as she is about to collide with some glass flasks on the floor behind her.

'You must take care as you move about. If a flask breaks it will mean the ruin of months of work. And tie your hair back with this.' He hands her the cord. 'Otherwise the flames may catch it.' He reaches out and strokes back a strand of long ebony hair. 'We don't want you to set yourself on fire . . . not yet, anyway.' He smiles as if he means this as a joke, but his tone makes it sound more like a prophecy.

She catches again the faint smell of urine that always clings to him, but cannot tell if it emanates from his clothes or the flasks, maybe both. He watches her as she fumbles to pull back her hair with the cord, her fingers made clumsy by his unblinking gaze. When he is satisfied, he steps back a little and regards her, pressing his fingertips together as if she is a painting or a piece of sculpture and he the artist creating her.

'First I must impress upon you that you are never to speak of what you do here, or what you see. My work must be carried out in secret, for there are many in this world who would seek to take what I have learned. Kings have held men captive for years to gain such knowledge. Popes have sold their souls for it and countless lesser men have killed and been killed in pursuit of it. But the royal art must not be perverted by greed. Unlike Father Arthmael, I seek only life itself, but he seeks a power greater even than the grasp of kings or popes. He will not succeed!'

Sylvain is not looking at her now. He is declaiming to an invisible army, swearing an oath before a holy shrine she cannot see. 'Some of what you see, my child, may make you afraid, revolted even, but you must remember that all life is born of corruption. The reborn can rise only from death and decay. Resurrection springs only from the tomb. Just as the fly is generated from the mud, the eel from the slime of the fishes and the tree from a seed buried in the dirt, so it is from filth that we shall draw forth the greatest treasure of them all. Do you understand?'

Gisa nods, as she knows she is expected to do, but she does *not* understand.

'The day will come soon when you will beg your uncle to let you remain by my side night and day, for you will desire nothing more than to become part of this great work.'

She tries to suppress a shudder, fights to keep her face impassive. She will never, *never* beg to be with him, not even for a single hour, let alone a whole night. But her years of massaging soothing unguents into the intimate caverns and hairy crevasses of her aunt have taught her how to keep her revulsion concealed.

'But today we will begin the work where all must start, with the *prima materia*, the spring of putrefaction. And to do that we must prepare the white water and the red. In the chamber below you will find the seeds of moon poppy and moonwort with bunches of dried lunarie. Can you recognise these plants?'

'Of course.'

He nods approvingly then turns to the table and selects a large glass flask. 'You will place the seeds in this flask and carry it up to the roof.'

With a single finger, he gestures towards a ladder that is

propped against the wall. Above it is another trapdoor, like those through which she has already ascended except this one is closed.

'The poppy and moonwort seeds you must spread at the bottom of the flask,' he continues. 'The stems of dried lunarie you will stand upright in it and arrange them such that any dew that falls from the moon tonight will run down the white discs of the lunarie and fall upon the seeds beneath. See that they are well protected from the wind. Alas, it is not a task I can perform, for it must be a maid who collects the dew . . . a *virgin* maid.'

His gaze fastens on hers, as if he has the power to see deep inside her soul, and though she has not the slightest reason for guilt, she suddenly feels as if that soul is dirty, contaminated. But as soon as he dismisses her, she is awash with relief, grateful for any task that will take her away from him. He stands too close, always too close.

She descends to the chamber below, cradling the wide glass flask. She works her way methodically around the shelves, ignoring the minerals, the scrapings of grave mould, the dried insects, powdered shrews and desiccated organs of frogs and foxes, mice and moles. All of these she knows from the apothecary's shop – indeed, her uncle has supplied most of them. She recognises her own writing on many of the labels, though not the strange symbols that have been added. One wall of the chamber is dedicated to plants, and here she finds what Sylvain has asked for, seeds of moon poppy and moonwort and the dried stems of lunarie, with their silver-white, parchment-like discs.

Now she must climb back up the ladder to the roof, but it will mean passing through his chamber again. It will mean squeezing past him. She tries to delay the moment. She

215

makes another circuit of the chamber, peering into jars, opening boxes, pretending she is still searching, should he glance down through the open trapdoor. She tries to memorise the location and contents of each of the containers in case she should be required to fetch something else. She rehearses what each thing is used to cure as she used to do in the apothecary shop, when she was trying to learn. She finds the kind of comfort in the repetition that a nun might find in reciting a familiar prayer.

Ashes of a young kite's head – that prevents gout. Does her new master suffer from such an affliction? She hasn't seen him limping. *Dried viper to counteract the snake's venomous bite.* She reads the labels she wrote in the apothecary's shop and each is like the strands of a rope, holding her fast to the safety of the shore – *turpentine, myrrh, gum-elemi, quicksilver, alum, sulphur, brimstone.*

A wooden box catches her attention. This one has no label. It did not come from her uncle's shop, of that she is sure. The tops and sides are carved with a repeating pattern of the hooked sun-cross. It is too ornate to be used in a store room. Surely it should be on display in the house. She raises the lid. It does not occur to her not to do so.

She sees a mass of bones and the shining white dome of a skull. That it is a human skull momentarily startles her, but it does not frighten her. On the shelves of her uncle's shop a jar contains the powdered skull of a suicide, a well-known cure for the falling sickness. And in another of Uncle Thomas's small caskets are fragments of the skull of a hanged man, with a piece of the rope used to dispatch the poor wretch. These ease the agonies of those afflicted with blinding headaches. Apothecaries regularly purchase the heads of felons from the executioners, while the less scrupulous obtain their

216

supply much more cheaply from the enterprising youths who steal them from the maggoty corpses in the gibbet cages. Legal or otherwise, there is always a lively trade in cadavers.

But Gisa can see at once that this is not the skull of a hanged man or, she devoutly hopes, of someone who committed self-murder, for it is far too small. The owner of this little skull never lived long enough to become a man. These are the bones and skull of a young child. And the bones are fresh. They have not been dug up from some ancient grave. She has seen enough human and animal remains in her uncle's shop to be sure of that.

How did these bones come to be in the tower? Children die of many things – fevers, starvation, accidents. Death is an all-too-common visitor to many households. But why was an innocent child not given a Christian burial or, if the poor mite was unbaptised, at least laid to rest somewhere close to a church where the shadow of the Holy Cross might fall on it? Apothecaries do not trade in the bones of children.

Above her, she hears the heavy tread of her new master, pacing up and down before the flames in his copper pot. She knows he is waiting impatiently for her. She shivers: the tower room, which was cold before, now feels as if it has been encased in ice.

Chapter 29

A dragon springs therefrom when exposed in horses'
excrement for twenty days.

A bald man with a face like a sow's arse thrust his leg out between the benches in the ale-room, barring my way and nearly tripping me.

'Here, muttonhead! I'll have some of that sweet rabbit, and Hugh here, he wants eels. Bring strong ale now and plenty of it. Think you can manage to remember that, codwit? And hurry up before my belly jumps out of my throat and goes hunting for its own meats.'

Hugh winked at him. 'Maybe we should put a tar barrel up his arse and set fire to it. That'd make him dance more lively.'

All the men at the table roared with laughter. I forced my lips into a rictus grin, as if I shared the joke, and headed for the back door of the tavern that led out to the kitchens.

Another hairy-fisted man grabbed my thigh as I passed his bench. 'Here, where's my rabbit? I asked for it an hour since.'

He'd asked for it barely a *pater noster* ago, and if he kept grabbing my leg like that he'd be wearing the rabbit stew in his crotch, which might at least dampen his ardour even if it didn't cool it. One of the serving girls gave me a sympathetic glance as I wrested my leg away. They had it worse. They were fighting off hands all night.

218

Mistress Ibby squeezed around the table with two brimming flagons in each hand. It was little wonder she'd muscles like a blacksmith. 'Did your old master not teach you how to carry more than one dish at a time?' she snapped. 'You'd best take over in the kitchen and send the girl in here.'

If she thought my skills were any more suited to basting and stirring, she was going to be sadly disappointed, but I couldn't afford to tell her that. I'd given her the impression that I'd worked in the Fiery Angel. Apparently it was one of the busiest pilgrim inns on the road to Becket's shrine at Canterbury. I'd learned the name of the inn from the friar on the ship – he'd boasted to his little flock of having stayed there. There wasn't a shrine in England the man hadn't visited, or so he said. I'd told Mistress Ibby it was the most commodious and best-appointed place in those parts, where all the wealthy pilgrims stayed, which was what the friar had said. I didn't suppose for one moment it was true, but Canterbury was so far from Lynn I gambled she wouldn't know that.

Working as a scullion in a piss-poor quayside tavern had most definitely not been my idea. I had intended to sell the raven's head immediately, dress myself as a gentleman and make for Walsingham or some other place where I could make my fortune inventing stories for those who'd reason to fear their sins might soon catch up with them. That had been my plan, but I was now beginning to believe that the raven had hatched another, one that was very different from my own.

After the encounter with the silversmith, though somewhat shaken, I'd continued to try to find a buyer for the bird's head. I'd tried shopkeepers, both English and foreign merchants, and even some of the wealthier pilgrims. All

219

admired the craftsmanship. Each was fascinated by the object. Most appeared to covet it. Then, as I was on the very brink of parting them from their money, they would recoil and thrust the head back at me, as if I had dropped a scorpion into their hands.

No one else noticed the tiny symbols the silversmith had seen, though I saw them more distinctly with each passing day. But some swore the bird's eyes blinked at them, others that they heard a raven cry out, or felt a throbbing as if some invisible heart was sending blood coursing round the disembodied head. Some men said the metal became burning hot in their hands, others deathly cold. A few could not explain their fear, saying only that they could tell it was unnatural, cursed, an object of death. Foolish as it sounds, I was beginning to believe the raven did not want to be sold.

I made one last attempt to offer it to a captain aboard his ship, persuading him that it would be the ideal object to trade for a good sum in a foreign market or else take home as a gift for his wife. He, too, seemed interested and we had just got around to naming a price, when a sudden and violent gust of wind came out of nowhere. It tore through the ship's bare rigging, rocking the hull, so the great ship juddered and convulsed at its moorings as if it was about to break its back. None of the other ships in the harbour was touched by the gust.

Even beneath his deep tan, I could see the blood drain from the captain's face. He flew into a rage, accusing me of cursing the ship by bringing a raven aboard. He said every seaman knows that a raven flying too close to the seashore is an evil omen, for its croaking cries up a storm. On reflection, I was lucky that when he threw me bodily off the ship it was onto the quayside, not straight into the sea.

After that, I dared not risk trying to sell the raven's head again in Lynn: I was afraid word might spread about the strange object, and the last thing I wanted was tales of it being carried by some ship's crew back to France and to Philippe.

In the meantime, I had taken the salt-merchant's advice and sought lodgings at the inn at Purfleet run by Mistress Ibby, telling her I had a little business to conduct in Lynn and would settle with her as soon as it was concluded. I fully intended to do as much, once I'd sold Lugh. But when I discovered no one in those parts would buy the wretched bird, I knew I had no hope of paying what I owed for my bed and board – I'd not a coin left to my name. There was nothing for it, but to try to creep out of the inn at first light, before anyone was stirring, and make for the next town before they'd realised I'd gone.

But, for a woman, Mistress Ibby showed remarkably little faith in her fellow man: no sooner had I tiptoed down the stairs than I ran slap into the twin mounds of her gargantuan breasts, which alone would have been enough to kill a man, without any need for the knobbly cudgel she was bouncing against her palm.

'Off for a stroll before breakfast, Master Laurent? Dawn's not broke yet. Even the gulls are still abed.'

'Couldn't sleep, Mistress Ibby, and I wanted to make an early start. Always up with the lark, that's me.'

'Mostly I find men don't sleep when they've summat on their minds. Perhaps there's summat troubling you, Master Laurent, like the money you owe me for bed and board, not to mention the wine you've been supping like a lord. I dare say you've been worrying about how you're going to pay me. You *were* intending to pay me, weren't you, Master

221

Laurent, not sneak out of here like a common thief? 'Cause if that thought ever crossed my mind, I'd have to call the bishop's constable and have you charged. Owns everything in these parts, does the Bishop of Norwich, including this inn, and he doesn't take kindly to being cheated. Not what you'd call a forgiving man, the bishop.'

She held out a meaty hand for the money. Her palm was so calloused and thickened with scars, she looked as if she could easily grip a red-hot iron without flinching. A useful skill were she ever to find herself tried by ordeal for murder, and I could well believe she had been – several times.

Not wishing to be dragged off to languish in some dank dungeon, I could see no alternative but to tell her my story and throw myself on her mercy.

'Mistress Ibby, I confess I cannot pay you, though I swear on the Holy Virgin that I had every intention of doing so. The truth is I've been crushed by ill fortune. I was to have met my father here. He sent me word he was arriving by a ship and I was to see him safely ashore and accompany him to the shrine at Walsingham, for he's blind and near-crippled and cannot travel alone. He wanted to make the pilgrimage for his soul's sake. He knows his end is near. But the ship has not put into port. I don't know if it's lost, or merely delayed. I couldn't sleep for worrying about my poor, help-less father. I was just on my way to the quayside again to ask if anyone had seen his ship or had word of it.'

Any woman with so much as a mote of compassion in her would have taken pity on a desperate lad, particularly one who might be about to discover he was an orphan, but Mistress Ibby merely stood there, arms akimbo, eyes steel-hard and lips pursed as tight as those of an abbess who'd caught one of her nuns in bed with a monk.

For several moments she stared at me, before the corners of her mouth began to twitch as if she was trying to suppress a laugh. 'I'll give you credit for the tale, lad. Most can come up with nowt better than – *I was robbed*. Even known some to give themselves a black eye just to make it look convincing. But I'll say to you what I say to all of them. If you don't want me to call the constable, you've got two choices. You give me what valuables you've got, and if they'll cover what you owe, I'll say no more about it, or if you've nothing worth the selling, you'll have to work off what you owe.'

I hesitated. The only thing of value I had was the raven's head, but that was worth far more than I owed. If I surrendered it, I'd be left with nothing. I still entertained hopes that I could sell it if I travelled inland. Those living along the coast were bound to be infected with the fears and superstitions of the seamen who, as everyone knows, are a strange and contrary breed. They refuse even to utter the word *pig* in case it brings them misfortune, and though all normal men carry a hare's foot to protect them from colic and ague of the bones, the sailor thinks his ship is doomed if anyone should bring a hare's foot aboard.

I shrugged helplessly. 'I regret I've nothing valuable to offer as surety. If I had I would willingly give three times what I owe. But as soon as my father arrives, he'll pay you handsomely when I tell him you've entertained me as if I was your own kin.'

'That so, is it?' she said, in a tone that suggested she thought it more likely the King of England would take her as his wife. 'I'll tell you what, while we wait for this poor, blind father of yours to crawl here, why don't I find you some work to do, just to pass the time, like?'

She looked me up and down as if weighing up what tasks

I might be suited to. There was some talk of midden heaps that needed clearing, which might have led me to mention my work at the Fiery Angel in Canterbury. Chatting to convivial customers in a warm ale-room sounded infinitely preferable to digging out some stinking dung heap in the cold and rain. How hard could it be to serve a few mugs of ale? Flatter the men, flirt with the women, and they'd be bound to stand me a drink or toss me some coins. But I'd have no chance of earning any extra money if I was shovelling shit and stinking like a beggar's backside.

And so it was that I found myself working for Mistress Ibby, mostly in the kitchen, scrubbing a mountain of pots or acting as scullion for the girl who did the cooking. After a few days up to the armpits in grease, my eyes stinging from the fumes of burning fat, my chest and arms blistered to the bone from cranking the spit over a roaring fire, I wished I'd chosen the peace and cool of the midden heap.

But Ibby was not ungenerous to her servants: the pallet on which I slept was much warmer and more comfortable than my old one in Gaspard's turret and at least there was always plenty to eat, for she let us eat our fill of whatever was left after the paying customers had departed. After the weeks I'd spent hiding in rain-soaked forests and ruined barns, I'd learned to appreciate the comforts of a full belly and a warm fire to curl up beside, as the sea wind rattled the shutters.

Gradually, I even worked my way back into the ale-room as I learned to carry several flagons at once, like the girls, and to ladle pottage onto the customers' trencher-bread without landing hot dollops in their laps.

It is easy to find yourself becoming woven into a repeating pattern of days, so that you scarcely notice you have become entangled in a net. You mean to move on, but it is always the next day, then the next. And I don't know how long I might have remained working in that inn had it not been for a chance remark I overheard one night as I was serving customers in the woodsmoke fug of its ale-room.

At first I was so preoccupied with remembering what I was to fetch from the kitchen that it wasn't until I was walking towards the courtyard door that my mind registered what my ears had heard or, at least, the import of it. The three men at the table had drained the best part of two flagons of cider, and their voices were growing louder, as was their recklessness. The wretch they were pillorying was none other than Lynn's bailiff, a man by the name of Robert de Drayton, and what they were saying about him was not merely enough to have him dismissed from his post but to put him on the gallows, if the crime could be proved. As I stood in the sharp wind of the darkened courtyard, the realisation drenched me like a pail of iced water – never mind those sinners at Walsingham, right here in Lynn was a man in dire need of a story and he'd have the money to pay handsomely for it, too.

That night, after the maids and Mistress Ibby had gone to their beds, I stretched my pallet out before the banked-down fire of the ale-room and, carefully unwrapping Lugh from his wool-lined nest, I recounted all I'd learned about the bailiff. 'So all I need now, Lugh, is a story – a story for which Robert de Drayton will pay the earth to silence those braying tongues.'

And I swear I saw a glint of malicious pleasure in the old raven's eye.

Chapter 30

*There are four degrees of fire: the first slow and mild as
of flesh or embryo; the second moderate and temperate,
as of the sun in June; the third, great and strong, as of
a calcining fire; the fourth, burning and vehement as
of fusion.*

The white-robed man sidles into the chamber and, bending
his head, mutters something in Father John's ear. Regulus
recognises the intruder as Father Madron, who came to the
cottage with Father John to fetch him here. He looks scarcely
older than Felix, all bone, with sharp cheekbones and knobbly
wrists. All the boys are darting curious glances at the pair
as they whisper together, trying to hear without raising their
heads from their wax-coated writing tablets. Father Madron
steps back a pace and waits, sliding his reddened hands into
his white sleeves.

Father John coughs and lifts his head, peering down the
row of boys. 'Felix, Peter and . . .' Father John pauses, his
gaze stalking round the table. All the boys are intently
studying their tablets, or their fingers, trying not to draw
themselves to Father John's attention, all except Regulus. At
the mention of Felix's name, Regulus's head jerks up and
he glances anxiously at the older boy's face. Felix has become
his soothsayer.

When his mother wanted the future told or an omen

interpreted she would visit the old charcoal-burner in the forest. He was too old and eaten up with ague to build the charcoal hearths himself any more, but he would watch the earth-covered mounds and tell his sons where to pour a pail of water on the hearth for fear of it opening up, and when to break the crust. They had been making charcoal themselves since they were knee-high, so they hardly needed their father to remind them, but he did anyway.

But none of his sons could read the future in the cooking fire, like the old man. Ask him a question and, depending on what you wanted to know, he'd throw a feather or a nut, a blackbird's egg or a forked twig into the embers and watch how it burned. Did it smoulder or pop? Did it shrivel or flare or twist? It was all written in the flames, he'd say. As the sailors used the stars to find their way across the raging oceans, so he used fire to guide him through the dark world. Regulus loved to watch the old man muttering away, pointing to a shape in the flames. The boy could never see anything at first, save red embers, grey ash and charred black wood, but the old man would trace a shape in the air with his twisted hands.

'There, boy, see it? A fish leaping – that there's a good sign. Goats and pigs'll all drop a good litter this year and chickens'll lay plenty of eggs. Reckon your mam might drop another bairn 'n' all.'

Once he'd outlined the shape in the air, Regulus could see it, too, as clearly as if a real fish was swimming through a red sea, a fish with a black head and a fiery eye.

Now, instead of reading fires, Regulus reads Felix's face. If Felix looks unconcerned the boy's breathing eases, but if the skin is puckered between Felix's sandy brows Regulus's heart starts to race. He studies him now, but Felix looks

227

more sullen than fearful. Regulus is relieved. He doesn't want anything bad to happen to Felix. As long as Felix is here, he is safe.

'And Regulus,' Father John says.

The boy starts violently. He's been so concerned that Felix has been chosen, he never thought his own name might be called.

'You are excused lessons this morning. Father Madron has need of you. Off you go.' Father John flicks his hand in an impatient gesture. Felix scrambles to his feet and the other two boys follow. They trail after Father Madron out into the grey morning. The canon shivers in spite of his thick robes.

'A spiteful breeze this morning, boys,' he says. 'But we'll soon be out of it.'

If anything, the outside feels warmer to the boys than their dorter, for they are rarely permitted a fire, but none-theless they quicken their pace to keep up with Father Madron, who is plainly anxious to be back inside.

Regulus keeps glancing at Felix's face, but there is no old man's hand hovering above it to make the reading clear. They stop in front of a low oak door, which looks like all the others in the abbey until Father Madron opens it and Regulus sees the stone staircase winding down. Then he knows. Then he remembers. Panic-stricken, he edges close to Felix. The older boy briefly squeezes his shoulder.

'It's daytime and there's three of us,' he whispers. 'It's only at night, alone, you have to worry.'

Regulus feels a little better, but not much. He presses his hand to the wall as they descend in single file behind Father Madron. They pass the door to the room where he slept, or tried to sleep, that first night and then they are in the vaulted chamber. *Day* and *night* have no meaning down here. Only the flickering torches and fragile candle flames hold back the tide of darkness. But this time no braziers burn and the thick black liquid in the bottom of the glass flasks is still and cold.

The magpie squats at the top of the shelves. It gives a swift *chacker-chacker* and turns its back on them, annoyed at being disturbed. Regulus wonders if it has ever flown free in the forest, if it has ever seen the sun.

Father Madron clears his throat and his prominent Adam's apple bobs up and down, making him look like a snake that has swallowed a mouse. He points at Felix. 'You're a good strong lad. The dung in all these containers needs taking upstairs and tipping on the midden heap. It's old and the heat's gone from it. We'll need fresh. And then the water needs emptying from that vat.' He indicates a huge wooden vessel, like a giant barrel, resting on six small stone pillars. The open top is high above Regulus's head and he cannot see inside. 'There's a wooden bung underneath it. Pull it out and the water will drain away down that gully beneath,' Father Madron continues. 'Then collect fresh water and wash the vat out thoroughly. Don't spill any on the floor. If any of the fathers should slip . . .'

Father Madron leaves the threat of what will befall Felix unspoken and it is the worse for that.

'Why can't the lay brothers do it?' Felix grumbles. 'They're the ones who are supposed to carry water and shit.'

Regulus is startled. He's never heard Felix or any of the boys challenge Father John. They wouldn't dare. Father Madron takes a pace forward, his face flushed. Regulus is afraid he is going to hit Felix.

'The lay brothers are not permitted down here,' he says,

then adds, with an attempt at authority, 'Besides, I dare say Father John selected you because he believes you might benefit from a lesson in humility and I see he was correct.'

It is Felix who flushes this time. He opens his mouth, but the mention of Father John seems to remind him that it is not wise to risk further defiance. Sullenly he heaves up one of the containers of dung, deliberately brushing it against the back of Father Madron's white robe, leaving a thick brown stripe. The young canon appears not to notice. Peter and Regulus catch each other's eye, a fit of giggles bubbling up in both of them.

Father Madron regards them suspiciously, but seems to conclude their laughter is caused by Felix being reprimanded. 'There's no cause for you two to smirk. You boys will not find your task any less instructive. Father John selected you both because you are the smallest. You two will clean the well of the furnace at the top and also underneath, where the fire usually burns. A vessel cracked in the well above and the contents ran through the holes into the fire chamber beneath. You'll have to crawl through the stoking hole and scrape the inside clean so that the fire will burn clear. It's been extinguished for many hours and the furnace is cold now. But you'd best strip off your clothes. They'll get filthy and, besides, they might catch on something and trap you. Peter, you're a little bigger. You'd better take the top. Regulus can crawl into the hole.'

Regulus stares at the tunnel that leads into the bottom of the furnace. He is not even sure it is wide enough to wriggle through. How big will it be inside? What if he gets stuck and can't get out? He is close to tears.

'You heard what I said,' Father Madron snaps. 'Take off your clothes or you'll be in there all day.'

Regulus fumbles hopelessly with the knot that fastens the top of his tunic. Fear makes him clumsy. After watching him for a few moments, Father Madron slaps his hands away and begins to undress the boy himself. Regulus does not resist. He has been here long enough to know that it is useless.

Peter is already wriggling out of the last of his clothes. He does not want Father Madron to change his mind and send him through the hole.

'Regulus, you'd better wait until Peter has finished, else the soot he dislodges will fall through the holes and choke you. You can fetch a besom and be ready to sweep up any dirt that falls out of the fire hole.'

Peter grimaces as Father Madron inserts his cold hands under his naked armpits and thighs and swings him up in his arms, depositing him in the well of the furnace. The young canon hands the boy a scraper and a brush. Peter, crouching awkwardly in the narrow space, sets to work. Powdery soot and burned fragments begin to tumble down the holes in the base and trickle out of the stoking tunnel beneath.

Clumsily, Regulus sweeps it into a pile, but the dust refuses to lie still, swirling up again each time he moves. His legs and hands are black with it.

Father Madron has moved to the other side of the pillar, where he is replacing bottles and boxes on the shelves, but each time Regulus looks up he sees the man's head turned in their direction. He is watching them intently. Regulus thinks it is to ensure they are working hard. He will tell Father John if they are not. The boy tries to make the cloud of soot behave, but it will not lie still.

'Wet it,' Felix hisses.

Regulus flushes. He can't piss on it. Not here, while Father Madron watches. But Felix dips his hand in the pail of water he carries and sprinkles it on the soot. It forms little clumps that cling together long enough for Regulus to collect them. He is grateful.

Soon, much too soon, Peter sings out that he has finished. Father Madron peers over the edge of the furnace to inspect his work, pointing out odd places he has missed, but finally he sets a stool beside the furnace and tells the boy he can climb out. He does not seem so eager to lift Peter out now that he resembles an imp from Hell, rather than a cherub.

Regulus laughs, for Peter's eyes in his blackened face look startlingly white. He does not look like Peter at all but an actor in the Christmas mummers' play. Peter grins back, but Regulus's smile freezes as Father Madron takes the scraper and brush from Peter's hand and gives them to him. He gestures to the narrow opening at the bottom of the furnace.

'In you go, boy.'

Regulus edges towards the furnace. Father Madron pushes him down until he is crouching on the floor.

'Lie down and wriggle in,' Father Madron urges. 'It's not dark in there. There's plenty of light from the holes.'

Regulus peers at the tunnel. It looks dark. 'What if I get stuck?'

'Peter will hold your ankles and pull you back out when you ask him to,' Father Madron says. 'The sooner you get started the sooner you'll be out,'

Regulus feels something pressing on his backside, pushing him in. He thinks at first it might be the sole of Father Madron's shoe, but then he feels fingers moving against his goose-pimpled skin and knows it is a cold hand pressing against him. He wonders if Father Madron has a birch, like

Father John. He can almost hear the whistle of it above his naked rump. He crawls rapidly inside.

The tunnel is not long, two or three foot maybe. A faint light filters down into the fire chamber ahead of him. Regulus wriggles in a little further, though not too far in case Peter cannot touch his feet. He starts to cough. The stone is not hot, but it is still warm to the touch and that is enough to remind Regulus of where he is. Suppose someone lights a fire while he is in here? The scar round his finger suddenly burns, like it did that night he fell into the hearth. The flames of the torches on the walls are dancing over the holes above his head. He can't breathe. He's growing hotter. The flames are licking down the holes now. Sweat greases his naked body. He will be roasted alive. He starts to scream.

Something seizes his ankles, but in his panicked state that only makes him more frightened. He thinks they are trying to push him further inside, shut him in. He is kicking, thrashing, sobbing. He feels himself being hauled painfully backwards over the rough stone, until at last he is lying on the floor beneath the great vaulted ceiling, coughing and choking. The tears mingle with the sweat on his face, the warm blood from his scraped and stinging elbows and knees trickles over the soot-blackened skin.

Felix and Peter stare down at him, their faces wrinkled in concern. Felix swiftly presses his dung-grimed hand over Regulus's mouth.

'Stop bawling,' he orders. 'Madron'll hear you. He's just stepped out, but he's bound to be back soon. Here, give me the scraper.' He prises it from Regulus's hand. The boy stares in surprise for he didn't even realise he was still gripping it.

'If I scrape off what I can reach from outside that will do. Madron can't get his head in there, never mind his fat hairy arse, so if the bit just inside the tunnel looks clean, they'll think the rest's been done. Peter, go and keep cave by the door – listen out for him coming back. And, Regulus, you wipe that snot off your face, so he doesn't see anything's amiss.'

Both boys obey instantly and Felix works hard, so that when Peter comes scampering back to warn of approaching footsteps, a sizeable pile of ash, soot and fragments of some hard black substance lie outside the stoking hole. Just in time, Felix pushes the brush into Regulus's hand and clambers up onto a stool to heave a bucket of clean water into the vat. As he predicted, Father Madron kneels down to peer into the entrance of the stoking tunnel, but the pile of debris appears to convince him that the job has been completed.

Once the boys have swept up, Father Madron releases them, sending them to the lavatorium to wash away the soot – 'Thoroughly, mind. Ears too.'

He hands Felix three worn linen towels and a clay pot of soft soap, which stinks of rancid fat. Peter and Regulus are instructed to walk naked while Felix carries their clothes so that they do not soil them. Not that his clothes look much cleaner than their skin.

The wind is even sharper now. A fine misty rain is falling and both the little boys shiver, but Regulus doesn't care. He feels almost elated at having escaped the chamber. Although he was terrified in the furnace, the vaulted room itself has lost some of its nightmare horrors. Without the glowing fires and the boiling, bubbling vessels, without Father John and Father Arthmael with the burning eyes, the cellar now seems little more than a big store room. Even the magpie stayed on its shelf, emitting only the occasional *chacker* of irritation. Regulus begins to wonder if the room was ever quite as frightening as he remembers, or if it has somehow got mixed up with a bad dream.

The boys' teeth chatter uncontrollably as they rub the soft soap over themselves and splash icy water on their goose-pimpled skin. They quickly rub themselves dry, leaving more grime on the towels than in the tub of black scummy water, and try to pull clothes over damp skin.

'Do we *have* to go back yet?' Peter asks, plainly thinking that staying outside, even in this freezing rain, is preferable to returning to one of Father John's Latin lessons.

Felix screws up his eyes as if he's considering the matter, then gestures towards a dark corner where the branches of a tree will shield them should anyone happen to glance out of the upper windows. They scuttle across, and hunker down, wrapping their arms about their legs for warmth.

'You know that big vat I had to empty and clean,' Felix says. 'Well, it wasn't just water in there. It stank of shit and I reckon someone had been sick in it too.'

Regulus wrinkles his nose, but he's come across far worse things left to fester in tubs. He is a son of a forester, after all.

'That's why I didn't see it at first,' Felix continues, 'with the water being all cloudy, and I reckon they didn't either. I only saw it 'cause it got caught on a jag round the edge of the drain hole. Saw the glint of it after the water was gone.'

He pauses dramatically, waiting for the question from his audience and they do not disappoint him. They know what storytellers expect of their listeners.

'What was there, Felix?'

'Did you find something?'

Felix lifts his foot and fumbles around inside his shoe. He is holding something in his clenched fist. Slowly, like a magician at a fair, he uncurls his fingers. Lying on his palm is a small amulet, hanging from a broken leather strap. He turns it over and the heads of the two little boys bump together as they lean in to peer at it.

'Emblem of St Michael, that is,' Felix says triumphantly. 'See, there's the dragon under his feet and the hand of God stopping him killing the monster.'

Peter thrusts his knuckles into his mouth. Felix is watching him closely. 'You've seen it before, haven't you?'

Peter nods solemnly, without taking his fist from his mouth.

'I'm right, aren't I?' Felix says. 'It's Mighel's, isn't it? He told me his father gave it him before he went off to sea. Right proud of it, he was. Said his father promised him it would keep him safe.'

Regulus jerks away as if he has been stung. The little tin emblem hasn't kept Mighel from harm, like his father had promised, because he's been taken by the wizard who turns boys into birds, else he's dead. But he's not safe. His father lied. All fathers lie. They say they are going to come to see you, but they don't. It's all a trick to make you behave, but even when you try to be good, they never, ever come. Anger boils up in Regulus and he almost blurts out his indignation, but he stops himself in time. Peter doesn't know about Mighel, and Regulus can tell from his face he hasn't guessed.

'What's St Michael doing in the vat?' Peter asks. 'Why didn't Mig take it home with him?'

Felix glances sharply at Regulus. Regulus nods and lowers his eyes. Their secret pact holds.

'I expect his mother hugged him when she came to get

236

him,' Felix says to Peter. 'Probably hugged him so tight, the strap broke and it fell into the water. That's what mothers do, don't they, hug you till you can't breathe?'

There is a look of aching hunger on the older boy's face as if he is thinking of something sweet he knows he will not taste again.

''Sides,' he adds, with forced cheerfulness, 'he doesn't need old St Michael and his sword to protect him now 'cause he's safe at home, isn't he? His mother'll look after him now.'

Chapter 31

For the womb of that woman is full of poison. So let there be dug a grave for the dragon and let the woman be buried therein with him.

'What is it you want, disturbing me at this hour,' Robert de Drayton demanded, 'and in my own home too? You told my servant you'd important information for me. Come on then, cough it up. But I warn you, if this is some frivolous request for me to settle a dispute in your favour, you'll find your back smarting at the whipping post for wasting the time of the bishop's *prepositus*.'

I suppose Drayton imagined using the Latin title of *prepositus* instead of plain *bailiff* would make him sound more important, especially if he thought he was addressing an unlettered pot-boy. I was sorely tempted to answer him in a stream of fluent Latin, which, thanks to old Gaspard's tutelage, I could easily have done. But I'd learned long ago in Philippe's employ that it doesn't sweeten the temper of these little puff-toads if they think you know more than them.

He was only lording it over me because he'd recognised me from the tavern. But even if he hadn't known where I worked, a blind man in fog could have told him, for the clothes I'd selected so carefully when I'd first tried to sell the raven's head were now stained with spilled food, pitted with holes from burning sparks and reeked of hot fat and sour ale. But if this evening's work went well I would soon be dressed as a man of substance.

To flatter him, I bobbed my head as respectfully as any lowly servant. 'I thought you'd want to know at once, Master Robert, that there are some disturbing rumours circulating in the taverns about you. Not that I eavesdrop, of course, but when men are merry and the tavern's crowded, voices become raised, and you can't help but hear things.'

'Rumours? What rumours?' the bailiff blustered. But it was plain from the flushing of his face and the alarm in his eyes that he had a pretty good idea of what was being whispered, and not just whispered – shouted.

'Of course, I don't believe a word of it myself,' I assured him. 'And neither, I'm sure, does the bishop for he'd have never appointed a man to such high office in Lynn if there was even a hint of something untoward in his past.'

Drayton's neck was now as red as a cock's wattle. 'I've done nothing, nothing to give my lord the bishop any cause to doubt my honourable stewardship of his town.'

'The rumours are no more than a wicked slander,' I told him soothingly. 'What they're saying is ridiculous.' I laughed. 'You'll never believe this, but they are actually claiming that three years ago you murdered a girl in Wiggenhall. I ask you, how do these outrageous tales ever get started?'

'That is a foul lie!' The bailiff leaped from his chair and paced around his chamber in great agitation. His fists were clenched, but that didn't disguise their trembling. 'If they had a single grain of evidence why didn't they arrest me three years ago?'

I shrugged. 'From what I heard, the girl's body has only just been found. Apparently her brother was away at sea when she disappeared. The neighbours thought she'd simply moved away. It was common knowledge she was walking out with a man and several neighbours saw her go off with him the day she disappeared. Later the man returned alone with a cart and loaded her few possessions into it. He told one of the neighbours that they were going to be wed in his own town. The villagers had no reason to doubt him, at least until her brother came home. He was adamant his sister would have left word for him about where she was living, and when he searched the cottage he discovered neck-laces and other precious things her mother had left to her, still concealed in the hiding place they used. He was certain she would never have left them behind if she had gone to be wed.'

Drayton snorted. 'Hardly proof that the girl was dead. I dare say she hid the jewels to prevent them becoming her husband's property on their marriage. Knew her brother would find them and intended him to look after them for her. Plenty of women try to keep a little money or some trinkets concealed from their husbands, so as to have some means to support themselves if he turns out be a drunkard or abandons them.'

'That must be how it was, Master Robert,' I said. 'Pity the brother didn't think of that, but apparently he wouldn't let it rest. Said he kept waking in the middle of the night to find the ghost of his sister standing at the foot of his bed, water streaming from her. He was sure she'd been murdered and her spirit was trying to show him where the corpse was so that it could be given a Christian burial. He did what most men do when they want to find the drowned. He hollowed out a loaf of bread, filled it with quicksilver and floated it on the river. It led him straight to the spot where her corpse lay. It had been dismembered, put in a basket, weighted down with stones and dropped to the riverbed. Course, by the time they'd fished her out, the flesh had gone, but he knew her by her bones for she'd an extra finger on her right hand, as her mother had before her.'

Beads of sweat were standing out on the bailiff's forehead, and he kept plucking at the skin on his throat as if it was closing up. 'What's this got to do with me? I know nothing of any girl.'

'When her brother came to the Moot House to report the murder, he saw you there and recognised you as the man who was courting his sister. That's what they're saying in the tavern, that it was you who murdered the girl, Master Robert. I was sure you'd want to know straight away,' I added, giving him my most innocent look. 'I knew you wouldn't want to let such rumours go unchallenged. They could be most damaging to a man in your position.'

'It's bilge-water!' Drayton said furiously. 'I've passed through Wiggenhall, like hundreds of other men, but I've not paid court to any women there, much less murdered one.'

'After three years it is all too easy for a man to mistake why he recognises a face,' I said soothingly. 'You probably look familiar to the brother if he's seen you pass through the village on some occasion. A man may think he's met a woman in a tavern, while the truth is she looks familiar because he's seen her at the fair. But the trouble is, if the idea is put to him that they met in a tavern, that is what he will swear to and therein lies the danger for you. If the rumour reaches the bishop he'll summon the girl's neighbours to testify. And since they have already heard the brother's tale, they may easily make the same mistake about believing they saw you with the girl.'

The bailiff seemed to deflate like a pricked bladder and crumpled down into a chair, his head buried in his hands. Even his skin sagged. I could feel the waves of misery and despair emanating from him. I let him stew for a few minutes, to allow the full horror of his situation to sink in, knowing he'd be all the more grateful when I dangled the key in front of him that would help him escape from his hell.

'So what have you come for?' he muttered. 'You want money, I suppose, a bribe to keep silent and not to report this to the bishop.' He laughed bitterly. 'You've not got the brains of a cockle if that's why you're here. You said yourself, rumours are spreading all over town. If the bishop hasn't already heard, he surely will before the week is out.'

'Which is why you need to have a story prepared that will save you from the gallows,' I said quietly.

'A story that proves I didn't kill the girl?' he asked bitterly. 'After three years, how can any man be certain where he was on a particular day? I doubt even the neighbours will be able to agree what day she went missing.'

'So that's why you don't deny you killed her. You admit it with tears and sobs, if you can manage it.'

His head jerked up and he glowered furiously at me. 'That's your answer, is it – confess to murder? Why don't you just fetch me the noose now and save the town the cost of a hangman's purse?'

'You admit to killing her,' I said, 'but you make them bless you for it.'

'What?' he demanded. 'What on earth are you drivelling about? Explain yourself.'

But I'd learned from my mistake with the miller – demand the money first, a good deal of it, and only then part with the story.

We engaged in a lively bout of haggling, as you can imagine, but he was desperate, and when a man has seen the cold shadow of the gallows dangling over him, he'd sell his own wife in the marketplace to save himself. Only when I had his money safely tucked into my purse did I begin.

'You frequently have cause to travel between Lynn and Downham as part of your duties and, as you passed through Wiggenhall on one of those journeys, your horse stumbled outside the door of one of the cottages and you were thrown heavily to the ground. A girl came running out and helped you inside to recover.

'She had a strange beauty about her.' I waved my hand vaguely at Robert. 'You'll have to describe her, but make sure you mention an unusual quality in her eyes – wild, unblinking, couldn't tear your gaze from them, that kind of thing. And teeth, emphasise the sharp white teeth . . . She did have teeth, I trust?'

He nodded glumly. I could see that so far I had not helped to reassure him. In fact he appeared on the verge of asking for his money back. I hastened on with the tale.

'She was all gentleness, caring for you with such tenderness you might have been her husband instead of a stranger, plying you with mead and meat, so that before long you began to doze off by the hearth. When you woke it was dark. The girl was standing in the open doorway in the light of the new moon, clad only in a thin shift, her feet bare on the cold earth floor. Her hair hung around her in a silver mane and the light from the fire caught her eyes, which glowed bright green. You thought her the most beautiful woman you had ever seen, but for reasons you couldn't understand you were deathly afraid of that beauty.

'When daylight came, some of the enchantment of the

night had faded. In the sunlight, she was a comely enough woman, but her charms were no greater than those of a dozen young girls of your acquaintance. Nevertheless, you were grateful to her for all her kindness, though you had no reason to call on her again.

'Yet somehow over the next few weeks you found yourself returning several times to that cottage, inventing excuses to ride through Wiggenhall, even though it took you miles out of your way. And every time, the same thing happened – however hard you tried to keep awake you'd fall asleep in the heat of that soporific fire, waking to find hours had passed and the girl standing barefoot in the doorway, staring out at the moonlight.

'But one night, when once more you had fallen asleep by her hearth, the resin in a burning log exploded from the wood with a loud bang. The sound woke you. As you turned in your chair, you saw that you were alone and the door to the cottage was flung wide open. You heard a shrieking and howling outside as if a dozen wild beasts were bounding through the forest in pursuit of their prey. Fearing for the safety of the girl, you dashed out of the cottage towards the marshes.

'The moon was three-quarters full and shadows of birch trees writhed in the silver pool of its light. All around you the deep bog sucked and gurgled. The shrieking and howling grew louder, but you were so terrified for the girl you pushed aside your own fear and plunged onwards. You burst out from the trees and almost fell into the waters of a black lake.

'In its centre was a small island on which grew an alder tree. Ferrets and foxes, cats and wolves, all the size of men, were bounding and leaping about the tree. There were other strange creatures besides – a goose-footed man whose beard

244

writhed as if each hair was a long white worm, a youth with the antlers of a stag and the tail of goat, a woman with a scorpion's tail, and a naked girl, whose head was that of a gaping toad.

'But even above the howls of bestial delight, you heard other cries – screams of pure terror. For hanging from the alder tree by their limbs were two monks. Their robes had been ripped from them and the foul creatures prancing below them were tearing mouthfuls of flesh from their living bodies and rasping their bleeding skin with long tongues. The monks were shrieking for mercy, but the only mercy that would be shown them was death, which would not be swift in coming.

'You fled back through the marsh pools to the safety of the cottage. Trembling, you huddled beside the fire until exhaustion drove you into sleep. In the morning you told the girl all that you'd seen and she soothed you with kisses.

'"Such a terrible nightmare," she murmured.

'And in the bright morning light it did seem that it must have been nothing more than a dream. Nevertheless, you were left with such a chill of death in your bones that you resolved never to venture to that village again.

'But the moment you were away from Wiggenhall, the desire to return grew ever stronger, and as the days passed you could think of nothing else save the girl. Finally, you could stay away no longer, so you went once more to her cottage. But that night, as soon as the girl fell asleep, you drew a circle, sun-wise, with your knife-point in the ash in the hearth, quartering it with a cross. Then you took some of the ash and repeated the sign on the stone of the threshold so that neither witch nor demons could enter through the door.

'You fell into a deep sleep, but you were awoken by a great shrieking and howling. Grasping your knife, you rose and edged closer to the open door and, to your horror, the foul demons you'd seen a few nights before were circling the cottage in the moonlight, cackling and baying. They called to you in mocking voices, trying to reach in through the door to drag you out, but as their arms stretched over the sign on the threshold, they howled in pain as if they'd been burned.

'You staggered back from the door. But the girl wrapped her warm arms about you. Her hot breath caressed your cheek. "Come, we shall show you such wild pleasures as you have only dreamed of. You ache to possess me. Come into the moonlight and I shall give myself to you. I am hungry for you. Ravenous!"

'At that moment the earthy scent of her body was so intoxicating, the desire burning in your loins so fierce, that you allowed yourself to be led towards the door. A howl of delight rose from all the foul creatures capering outside. Gently, gently, she drew you on towards their tongues, their talons, their teeth.

'But as she stepped into the doorway a shaft of moonlight struck her and at once a great pelt of spotted tawny fur burst from her milky skin to cover her back. Her heels grew long, her feet turned into great cat paws and the embers of the firelight caught the green animal glow of her eyes. Her face and arms, which were still covered by the shadow of the cottage, were human, but wherever the moonlight touched her, she was lynx.

'With a shriek, you dragged yourself from her grip and pulled out your knife. She lunged forward to seize you again. You called upon St Hubert, patron saint of hunters, and

246

plunged the knife into her throat. She fell forward into the cottage, and as the shadows covered her, the fur vanished and the most beautiful girl in the world lay bleeding at your feet. She lifted her arms to embrace you, then fell back dead.

'Outside the cottage, there was a shriek as if a thousand seabirds were circling. Then the earth began to bubble and the foul creatures sank into it, as if they were being sucked down into a mire. You smelt a stench of sulphur and glimpsed the hellish glow of the flames far below leaping up to swallow them. Then the ground became solid once more and all was silent and still.

'You knew you couldn't bury the body – if any unsuspecting person walked over the ground where she lay, they, too, would become a were-lynx. There was only one way to prevent her spirit rising and wreaking terror on the helpless villagers of Wiggenhall and that was to dismember the corpse and imprison it beneath running water, for evil spirits cannot escape moving water. But it had to be done before the sun rose, else the evil spirit would leave her and enter another.

'Dawn was not far off so, though you were deathly afraid, you cut up the body, placed it in a basket and dragged it to the river. You arrived just as the thin grey line marked where the sun would rise. Frantically you searched for rocks to weigh it down, knowing that if a single ray of sun touched the sky before she was beneath the water, her spirit would enter you and you would become the beast she had been.

'With your last remaining strength you pushed the basket far out into the river. The water gurgled in and, as the first shaft of sunlight crept over the horizon, the basket vanished beneath the water.'

Robert de Drayton was grinning, like the demon cat herself, by the time I'd finished my tale, and he was still smiling as he dismissed me. But my smile was bigger than his, for my leather purse now felt satisfyingly weighty and in the morning I would be once more on the road, ready to seek out any who needed my unique services, provided, of course, they had the money to pay for them.

Chapter 32

*A king stands with naked sword while his soldiers slay
the falling children and take from them their blood.*

As soon as little Peter descends the last stone step into the
flickering red glow of the dungeon he senses that something
is different. Whenever he has been led down here before,
Father Arthmael has been occupied, swirling some dark liquid
in a flask or peering at a scroll by the light of a candle. He
seldom troubles to glance up as the boy descends, as if
Father John is delivering nothing more than a sack of dried
bones or a vial of quicksilver.

But tonight Father Arthmael is deep in conversation with
another man, one whom Peter has not seen before. This
man is not a White Canon. It is as if he is the shadow of
a White Canon or the hole where one should be, for he is
dressed in a long black robe, embroidered with a silver band
that undulates about his throat. Both men turn and stare
as Father John pushes Peter towards them.

The man in black steps forward, his head tilted. 'Hardly
a babe,' he says. 'The book specifies a male-child of two.'

'King Herod's slaying of the infants in Bethlehem,' Father
John murmurs.

The pupils of Father Arthmael's eyes contract as he flicks
his gaze towards Father John. 'St Matthew did indeed study
the royal art, of that we can be sure. There are many great

mysteries hidden in his gospel, but you are no master of them, Father John. God in His mercy and wisdom has granted you other talents.'

Father John respectfully inclines his head towards his superior, but his fingers dig suddenly and painfully into the boy's arm, making him squeal. Peter knows his teacher is angry, though he senses for once that he is not the cause.

A chill smile flickers across the face of the man in the black robes. 'Father John may not have had the good fortune to study under the Great Master in France, as we did, but in his ignorance he has nevertheless stumbled upon a truth. I would have thought that you of all men, Arthmael, would have paid heed to the instructions of your holy gospel. After all, it is God you claim to serve in this work, unlike us honest sinners who do not need to conceal our ambitions behind clouds of incense.'

Peter holds his breath. The words make no sense to him, but the insolence in the man's tone is unmistakable. In spite of his fear, the boy is almost gleeful. He stares up at Father Arthmael, expecting bolts of fire to dart from his eyes and reduce the black-robed man to ashes. But Father Arthmael does not even raise his voice.

'Either you failed to learn what the Great Master taught or God has deliberately blinded you, knowing to what evil you intend to put this sacred art. Like Father John, you see the word but not what it hides. You think the object is of more substance than its shadow; the line is more significant than the space it encloses. The number two does not refer to the age of the child, it is the symbol of opposites. Sulphur and quicksilver are antagonistic, but they may finally be resolved and united in the one that is both male and female. The Great Master's book and the gospel both speak alike

250

of sun and moon, king and queen, who will together bathe in the blood of the children and rise as one in rebirth.'

The black-robed man laughs. The sound surprises Peter for Father Arthmael is not smiling. The man fingers the silver snake that coils around the high neckline of his robe. 'Strange, is it not, that of all four of the Great Master's chosen disciples the Master should leave his book to me? Not to mighty Count Philippe, or loyal Albertus, or you, holy Arthmael, but to me, the one whom you say does not know how to interpret its words. Was our Great Master mistaken? Did your omniscient God blind him, so that he placed the greatest secret of mankind in the hands of a fool? Which do you doubt, Arthmael – the wisdom of the Great Master or the wisdom of God?'

'He intended it to be shared by all four of us,' Father Arthmael snaps, his voice rising for the first time. High on its ledge, the magpie stirs and gives a cackle of alarm. 'He intended that his four disciples should continue to study the book together and learn from each other. But you took it and smuggled it to England.'

'If I hadn't brought it to safety, Count Philippe would have stolen it from all of us. As we both know, he has an unfortunate habit of taking whatever he covets. Do you think Philippe would have shared the words of the book with you, as I have done?'

'Page by grudging page.' Father Arthmael glares at him. 'And only when you need to obtain the precious substances from the boys placed in my care. You haggle over the sacred knowledge like some tanner's wife in the marketplace, bargaining for a piece of offal.'

Father John coughs pointedly. 'The boy . . .'

Both men look vaguely startled as if they have forgotten

Peter is there. For a moment, the boy hopes, prays even, that he will be returned to his bed.

'Well?' Father Arthmael demands. 'Do we use this boy or not?'

The man in black hesitates, then gives a curt nod. 'Proceed. Time will prove which of us is correct.'

Father Arthmael nods. 'Remove your clothes quickly, boy. It must be completed before the abbey bell rings for Lauds at daybreak.'

It is Father John who finally pulls the shirt over Peter's head, as he cowers and pleads. Father Arthmael has turned his back and is preparing something on a table at the far end of the chamber, half hidden from view by one of the pillars. The man in the black robe is holding out a scrap of meat towards the magpie high on the ledge. The bird watches him curiously, head tilted, but does not fly down.

His hand gripping the boy's arm, Father John leads him towards a large copper laver with a short metal tube running from it, which is in turn connected to an empty glass flask. Peter remembers the suffocating steam box, remembers the basin in which they scraped the sweat from his skin with sharp stones. He won't go back inside that box. He won't!

Wresting himself from Father John's grasp he dodges round him and races towards the spiral steps, but the man in the black robe grabs his hair and holds him fast till Father John can seize his arm again. Peter wriggles and shrieks, bites and punches. The magpie flies madly round the vaulted ceiling, uttering wild cackling cries of alarm. Peter fights valiantly with all his strength, but he is no match for two grown men. They lift him by his wrists and ankles, still thrashing, and dump him in the copper laver.

Father Arthmael paces slowly towards him. Glinting in

his hand is a thin sharp blade embedded in a bone-white handle. They are going to skin him. This time, they really will. Peter screams, arching backwards away from the blade, but the grip on his arms only tightens.

'Stand still!' Father John hisses. 'Otherwise you'll hurt yourself. Do as you are told and soon you will sleep again.'

Father Arthmael runs his cold fingers down the back of the boy's soft thigh. Peter shudders and whimpers in fear. The fingers pause. Peter squeals at a sudden sharp jag into his bare flesh. The pain is gone in an instant, but he feels something hot running down the back of his knee, hears it splash into the copper bowl. He stares down at the trickle of scarlet that is meandering across his toes. But before he can fully grasp what the red liquid is, he feels a little stab in his calf, minutes later, another in his arm.

The light in the chamber is growing very bright, as if someone has lit a hundred candles. The little boy is vaguely aware of the blade jabbing into his flesh again, but it no longer feels like pain. He no longer tries to resist. His head flops, too heavy to hold up. His legs buckle. He is a tiny fragment of bread floating in a warm bowl of soup. The room suddenly becomes dark. The voices of the three men are muffled, as if his head is buried deep beneath a thick blanket. He is back in his bed. He is falling asleep. He drops into nothing.

They dump the limp body on the floor of the dungeon, slippery and scarlet as a babe torn from the womb. Father Arthmael and Father John kneel either side of it. Making the sign of the cross over the little boy, they recite the prayers for the dead hastily, but reverently, careful to omit not a single word, so that his spirit cannot rise and condemn them for their neglect.

Heaving himself painfully to his feet, Father Arthmael drains the last drop of blood from the copper laver into the clear glass vessel. The man in the black robes holds it up to the candlelight, tilting the glowing ruby liquid carefully, as a wine-merchant might inspect the first drawing from a newly broached keg. Father Arthmael takes the flask from him and just as carefully divides the contents between two smaller flasks, holding them up side by side, to ensure the measures are equal. They are stoppered and laid in separate baskets, each lined with straw. The man in black picks up one and walks towards the stairs. Father Arthmael follows.

Father John hesitates, looking down at the crumpled little body on the cold flags. 'What is to be done with the remains?'

Father Arthmael turns his head slightly. 'Father Madron will come later to clean the laboratorium. He has his instructions. Come, Father John. Lauds is nearly upon us and it would not set a good example if we were to be late for the Divine Offices.'

Chapter 33

Under the Astrological House of Taurus, the Bull.
River Yare, Norfolk

The decomposition of a basilisk generates scorpions. In the dead body of a calf are generated bees, wasps in the carcass of an ass, beetles in the flesh of a horse, and locusts in that of a mule.

As it transpired it was not hard to find men and women in dire need of a story to save their skins. I travelled east, searching out inns and taverns, town stews and the pilgrims' halls in monasteries, and in every place I sat quietly and listened. I soon discovered that monks and lay brothers gossip worse than any fishmonger's daughter. They've nothing else to occupy their minds or their tongues, save their prayers, and since they never vary, the monks can recite them as piously as old St Hubert himself, while letting their thoughts amuse themselves with any salacious tattle that blows through their draughty cloisters.

Lugh and I learned of wealthy knights in whose fathers' veins ran not one drop of noble blood, of women miraculously pregnant when their husbands were away at the wars, of abbesses caught with lovers, of thieves and fraudsters who had cheated their poor brothers out of their inheritances and their sweet sisters out of their dowries. Any titbit I purloined I squirrelled away. Then I made a few discreet enquiries. Was the person wealthy? What did they stand to lose? I carefully calculated how desperately they needed a way to silence the gossips or defend themselves against their accusers. Then I'd invent a story. It wasn't easy. I had to work for my money. There were days when I squeezed my brain until my thoughts ran dry, but could think of no tale, however fanciful, that would exonerate the guilty. Then I'd lie down to sleep with Lugh close by, and in my dreams I'd hear the harsh croak of the raven and the tale would begin to form itself as I slept.

I'd see the characters wandering towards me as if the raven had thrown a rope of silk about them and was drawing them closer. I'd watch them cavort like jesters for their lord, while his bright black eyes looked on, compelling, commanding them to reveal their tale. And when I woke, the story lay nestled in my head, like an egg waiting to be broken open, its gold spilled out.

I became more daring. Why wait for gossip? Why put myself to the trouble of spending hours and hours hanging around on the off-chance I might hear something? If I could invent the stories, Lugh whispered in my ear, I could invent the rumours too. It was easy to discover the men of wealth and influence in any town – they're not exactly known for their reticence: they proclaim it, shout it, flaunt it from the gilded carvings on their houses to the cordovan leather on the fine steeds they ride.

A croak from Lugh, a wink of his black-onyx eye, and we had identified our next little milch cow. Then all it took was a word in a tavern here, a whisper in the market there, and before you knew it, an ugly rumour had taken hold and grown great wings all of its own. I sent my whispers out as tiny nestlings and they came flapping back to me as strapping eagles. How these birds of mischief do grow!

It matters not a jot if the scandal be true or false, for the commonality are only too willing to believe the great and good are all villains and rogues. They positively drool when the mighty start to teeter off their thrones, and are only too eager to give the added push that will send them tumbling into the dung heap. Hint that a man has stolen a girl's virtue, and the townsfolk will suddenly recall a dozen other virgins he cruelly wronged. Whisper that a woman's grandmother stole a pewter plate, and a whole chest of silver will be reckoned to have gone missing.

Having started the rumour, all I had to do was wait just long enough for my quarry to grow desperate, then stroll in with a tale to restore their good name and, with it, their appetite and their sleep. If they wanted the tale discovered in some ancient chest, I could easily oblige, just as old Gaspard had done. My tales glittered with immortal beings, demons and merfolk, noble knights and holy men, daring rescues and deeds of courage that any family would be proud to name as their own, and for which they would be glad to pay. After all, if you are going to invent a past, why not make it a thrilling and glorious one? Who wants to boast of a dull old hearth-hugger for an ancestor?

Things were going well, better than well, and I saw no reason why they should not continue that way, until the day I arrived at the river. I'd been planning to make my way south to try my luck in some of the wealthier towns. Men can easily hide their vices in the bigger cities, but it's in the market towns where gossips' tongues wag the fastest, and rich merchants fear most to lose their reputations.

But no sooner had I resolved to head south than ill-luck seemed to beset me. Within moments of turning onto the road, I trod on a nail that pierced the soft leather of my shoe and was driven deep into my foot. I managed to pull it out, but my foot was throbbing like the devil and my shoe was slippery with blood. A carter, who passed me on the road and saw me limping, took pity on me and allowed me to scramble up beside him. I think he was glad of conversation to break the monotony of the journey.

He was jovial enough at first, but as the miles crept by, he seemed to grow uneasy. I caught him giving me sideways glances as if he thought he might unwittingly have given a ride to a revenant or a demon in disguise. I knew the cause only too well. It was Lugh! He was stirring in his wooden nest beneath my cloak, snapping his beak rapidly and giving deep creaking calls, which sounded as if the wood was cracking beneath us. Several times the driver pulled the horse to a standstill and leaped off in alarm to examine the wheels and shafts, clearly fearing the worst. I shook the box and tried to muffle the sounds beneath several folds of my cloak but it was to no avail. Lugh would not be silenced.

Then that wretched bird gave the raven's *pruk-pruk-pruk* of alarm, so raucously and so close to the carter that he almost fell off his seat. Almost at once the raven's head was answered by a flock of six curlews flying over us, each calling shrilly in turn. At that, the carter jerked his horse to a halt. The sudden and violent tug on the reins made the poor beast rear in the shafts and come close to overturning the cart. The driver turned, his face blanched beneath his tan. 'Off! Get off!' he shouted, prodding me with the stout handle of his whip. 'Bad luck, that's what you are.'

'What have I done?' I asked, bewildered.

He gestured wildly at the empty grey sky. 'Called up the Six Whistlers, that's what. Searching for the seventh, they are, and I reckon you're it. It was you they was answering. I heard 'em clear as well water. Death you are, death and disaster.'

He gave me another violent shove that sent me tumbling off the cart and I landed on my backside in the dirt. He threw my small sack at my head, then brought the whip down on the horse's back and drove off as if the hounds of Hell were baying behind him. I only just managed to roll over in time to escape being crushed by the cartwheel.

'This is all your fault, Lugh!' I said, as I dragged myself to my feet and tried to brush the mud off my clothes. 'What did you have to start screeching for? You've just lost us our ride!'

But Lugh neither stirred nor croaked. He lay so still anyone would have thought he was only a lump of silver.

The place where I'd been so ungraciously dumped by the carter was a desolate spot. We'd been so busy chattering that I hadn't fully taken in my surroundings, but now I saw that I was on a raised track that ran close to the banks of a broad river. In every direction there was nothing but sucking marsh-land and black, reed-fringed pools. In the far distance, perched on tiny islands, were clusters of mud-coloured hovels, distinguishable from the marsh that surrounded them only by the thin plumes of mauve smoke that rose above them. We'd seen a few of the inhabitants earlier, paddling around the twisting waterways in flimsy coracles, fowling or catching eels. Their skin and clothes were the same hue of brown as the oozing mud that had spawned them. They'd stared sullenly at the cart as we'd passed them. I was sure that if I'd made any sudden movement they would have plopped into the water like voles and vanished. I couldn't see much chance of them offering me a bed for the night or a bite to eat, but I didn't relish the prospect of spending the night on the lonely marsh track.

There was nothing for it but to start walking in the direction I'd been travelling with the cart and hope that I'd stumble across some wayside inn or remote abbey where I could seek shelter for the night. But my injured foot was throbbing painfully and, after hobbling along for a mile or two, like some old crone, I feared I'd be spending the night on the marshes after all. I'd not seen even a single cottage along the track, except those far out on the marsh islands, and the sun was already sinking low in the sky.

So, you can imagine my relief when I spotted a man punting across the river towards me, heading for a rough wooden jetty. I hurried down the bank as fast as my foot would allow and limped over the boggy ground to the river's edge. But all my enquiries about inns and abbeys were met with a silent shake of the head.

'Marsh it is all the way along the Yare. Marsh till you reach Norwich that way or the isle of Yarmouth t'other. Take you days to reach either one on foot, and by the look of it, that foot of yours might not make it at all. Closest town's on t'other side of the river. Langley, they call it. I reckon you'd be best making for there.'

'But there must be places for travellers to stay along the track,' I protested.

'Maybe, maybe not. Never set foot on track, me. River takes me anywhere I want to go. What'd be the sense in walking, when she'll carry you?' He pushed his fingers under his hood and scratched his head. 'Course, I could take you across to t'other side, if you've the money to pay. Three pennies it'll cost you.'

I'd hesitated. I'd been wary of ferrymen ever since that little rat had told Charles and his henchmen which road I'd taken. Threepence to cross the river was sheer extortion and, for all I knew, there was an abbey just round the next bend in the track with a warm pilgrim hall and an infirmarer who would treat my foot.

'You want to cross or not?' the boatman demanded. 'Make up your mind 'cause owl-light's not far off and I'll not work the river then, too dangerous. All manner of outlaws hiding out in these parts, and if they don't cut your throat, it's liable to be ripped out by the great black shuck.'

I knew he was only trying to scare me, but even without devil-dogs and cut-throats, the marsh was no place to go blundering around at night. 'You can take me across,' I reluctantly agreed. 'But the crossing is only a few strokes. It's not worth more than a penny. I could swim it.'

He snorted. 'I'll not stop you. The bailiff pays me fourpence for every drowned body I fish out of the water.'

We finally settled on twopence, though I knew I was being robbed.

He steadied me as I climbed into the rocking punt. We were halfway across the river when a curlew rose up from the reeds and flew low over our heads, shrieking like a soul in Hell. The seventh Whistler had cried out and the wooden box hanging at my belt suddenly burned as cold as ice.

Chapter 34

Making her fair as Luna, she coils anon towards the
splendour of the sun.

Gisa climbs up the wooden steps, keeping close to the wall
and treading as softly as she can in the hope that the stairs
will not betray her with a creak. If Sylvain is lost in his
books or sublimations and she can reach the store room
without him hearing her, she can work for an hour or two
before he descends or calls her up to his laboratorium. Even
when he is absent her body is always tense, her ears straining
for the sound of his tread.

At night her body aches as if she has been harvesting
all day in the fields. The work she does for Sylvain is not
hard. It should not make her muscles sore, but whenever
she is in the tower her body is always rigid, like some
child's poppet carved from wood. Only when she is alone
in her bed, when Aunt Ebba's querulous demands have
finally given way to her snores, does it feel as if a great
stone has been lifted from her ribs and for a few hours
she can breathe freely again. But dawn comes too quickly.
The hours of the night melt as swiftly as snowflakes on
her cheek.

Gisa's heart jolts as she emerges through the trapdoor.
This morning Sylvain is not safely occupied among his
steaming flasks but is standing in the store room, *her* room,

his hooked finger tracing along the line of labels on one of the shelves.

A great book lies open on the table. She has seen him studying it many times. The words twist and wind between symbols on the page, sometimes circling the tiny images like chains, as if they've been put there to prevent the strange beasts crawling out of the book and creeping away.

Some of these images she understands – drawings that describe the arrangements of flasks and distillation tubes or astrological diagrams showing which signs belong to water, or fire, which signs oppose each other and what they govern. But there are other pictures she does not understand – rows of spherical flasks, which Sylvain calls the philosopher's eggs, each containing a serpent, lion, salamander, pelican or the disembodied head of a bird, the beasts rising and falling amid tears of liquid or floating flames.

Sylvain continues to search among the boxes. 'Grey wolf, I need grey wolf.'

Gisa is puzzled. He is searching the shelves on which the minerals are stored, but surely he must know that all the animal substances, including the wolf's hair, testicles, tongues, hearts and suchlike are stored on the opposite wall, for he arranged them thus. She gestures vaguely towards them, hesitating for fear she is seeming to correct him.

'The parts of the wolf . . . are over here, my lord.'

He turns to stare at her, frowning, and for a moment she fears she has angered him.

'Ah, no, little swan. It is antimony I seek.' He taps the great book. 'The noble art is written in code to deceive those who think themselves wise. The arrogant believe they can read it, just as they think they can read the mind of their God. They cannot.' A spasm of savage anger contorts

263

his face but only for a moment. He traces his finger over the spider crawl of letters. '"The sun must be devoured by the green dragon,"' he reads. He glances up, smiling. 'You understand that?'

She shakes her head, knowing he does not intend that she should.

'The sun, *sol*, represents gold and you know there is little that can consume gold, save *aqua regia*, the king's water.'

'*Aqua regia* is red, sometimes yellow, but never green,' she blurts out.

If she had uttered those words at home Aunt Ebba would have flown into a rage. Women should not know about such things, far less question them. But Sylvain looks far from angry. He is staring at her, his mouth slightly open and a distant, almost lustful expression in his eyes, which she cannot interpret.

'*She* said that too,' he murmurs to himself. 'Those were almost her exact words.'

He paces across the chamber towards Gisa. She is staring at the floor, willing him not to come closer, but he does. He slides his fingers beneath her chin and raises her head. She tries to pull away, terrified that he means to kiss her, but instead he examines her face as intently as he searched the shelves, as if he expects to find the antimony there.

'You share her thoughts, but what else, Gisa? Do you have her desires too? Her treachery?'

His tone has grown hard again. His cold fingers tighten around her jaw, almost lifting her off her feet. His hand presses against her throat. She gasps for breath.

His hand drops and he walks back to the book. 'You are quite correct. *Aqua regia* is red, as I shall show you, but when I do, you will observe that it turns green as it devours

264

the gold. That is what the scholar meant by the green dragon.'

Gisa, anxious to drive him back up to his own domain, hurries to the shelves, lifts off a box and hands it to him. 'Antimony . . . grey wolf,' she says, opening it to reveal the silvery-grey lump. 'Shall I grind some for you?'

He nods. Then, seeing her gaze straying again to the strange drawing in the book, he closes it carefully and cradles it in his arms. 'This book intrigues you, I think?'

'My uncle does not possess a copy.'

Sylvain's lips twitch into a thin smile. 'No other copy exists.' He holds it out. 'Feel the binding.'

Suddenly conscious that her hands have grown sweaty, she rubs them against her gown before touching the leather cover lightly with one finger. The cover is adorned with a golden sun haloed by great flames and the hide stretched over the wooden covers beneath is softer and smoother than any calf or pig skins that bind her uncle's books. But, then, not one of them is as valuable as this book.

'Soft, is it not?' Sylvain says. 'As well it might be, for it's bound in the flayed skin of the man who wrote it.'

He laughs, as she snatches her hand away. 'There is no higher soul than that of man and it is from man that the stone of eternal life must be drawn. Therefore the book that contains the knowledge of that stone must be wrapped in human flesh. No matter how sick a man might be, no matter what his deformities, his healing lies within these pages.'

Gisa's head jerks up. 'This book tells you how to heal any condition? Even something physicians cannot cure? You are sure?'

Sylvain laughs again, for the expression on her face is one of undisguised hunger. 'Though a man be already crossing from this life to the next, though he lies buried in his grave, what is written here will restore him to such perfect life and health as even the angels have never known.'

Gisa hurries along the path in the cold shadow of the wall of the manor grounds. She cannot escape the feeling that the stones will suddenly open like the panels in the Great Hall and she will be dragged back inside. It is only when the wall ends that she slows her pace. For a mile or so, she can breathe easily. There are no walls here. Only stunted birch scrub and willows flank the track and beyond them the red-gold glints of light from the setting sun as it catches the breeze-riffled water of the marsh pools.

But all too soon another wall looms up beside the track, separated from it by a water-filled ditch – the great, grim walls of Langley Abbey. Their shadow, too, stretches cold and dark across the track, oozing out towards the distant town, where the smoke from the hearth fires rises into the chill evening air.

Gisa hesitates. She has no wish to linger here, but no desire to return to her uncle's house either. Aunt Ebba will be waiting on her throne of pillows, querulous, impatient, demanding to know every detail of the furnishings of the manor house with which she intends to regale the endless stream of goodwives who are ravenous for the smallest scrap of gossip. She will not believe Gisa if she tells her she does not enter the house.

'Help me! Lady . . . help!'

The cry is so tremulous, so faint, that Gisa thinks she has mistaken the words for the call of some marsh bird. But it comes again. She spins round. She can see no one, but she's certain it is a child's voice. Is it coming from behind the abbey wall?

'Who's there? Come out where I can see you.'

She has heard tales of drowned souls or malicious spirits who call from the marsh pools to lure the living to their deaths. She does not quite believe them, but now, in this half-light . . .

'Stuck . . . I'm stuck.'

The cry is coming from somewhere low down. Gisa walks along the lip of the water-filled ditch peering into the thick green water. She sees something and scurries towards a dark shape a few yards ahead, until it resolves itself into a rotting tree-trunk.

A tiny movement catches her eye. It is probably just a scrap of cloth fluttering in the breeze, yet she moves closer. The fingers of a child's hand are poking out through a drainage hole between two massive stones in the base of the abbey wall. Gisa kneels on the edge of the ditch, leaning over as far as she dares.

'What are you doing down there?'

'Hid under the big vat . . . heard someone coming so I crawled down the hole where the water goes . . . into the tunnel . . . but there are lots of tunnels, full of mud and water . . . It was dark, so dark . . . saw light . . . but hole's too small . . . can't get out.'

The child's teeth are chattering violently. Gisa can see little of the boy's muddy face, but what she can see is smeared with streaks of blood, as is his hand. He is hurt, though she can't tell how badly.

'Can you find your way back to the hole you climbed into?'

'It's dark . . . don't want to go back into the dark and—'

'I'll get help.' Gisa begins to struggle to her feet. 'I'll fetch the White Canons. They must know other entrances to the drainage tunnels beneath their abbey. They'll soon have you out.'

'No, no!' the boy sobs. 'They'll kill me. Don't tell. Please don't tell.'

She does not believe anyone would kill the child, but there is no mistaking the abject terror in his voice. Something terrible must have happened to drive a little boy to hide himself down there, something that the child is far more afraid of than the dark.

'Hush now. I won't tell anyone, I promise. But we'll have to think of some other way of getting you out. Stay by the hole. I'll fetch you some food and . . .'

And what? What else can she bring to help him? The boy needs warmth. His wounds will need tending, too, else cold and wet will kill him in hours. She must fetch an iron crow as well, or something she can use to prise out one of the stones. There is no such tool in her uncle's shop, but she's seen one in the blacksmith's forge. If she could take it while he is at supper . . .

'I'll be back as soon as I can,' she promises. 'Do you have a name, so I can call to you when I come?'

She can barely make out the whispered sob of his reply. 'P-Peter.'

Chapter 35

He should avoid having anything to do with princes
and nobles.

I limped into the market square, trying to walk on the heel of my left leg. The ball of my foot, where the nail had gone in, was hot and painful. The whole foot was beginning to swell alarmingly. I needed a good physician to draw the poison from it. A night spent sleeping in a leaking goat byre, which was the most luxurious shelter I could find, had left me cold, aching and in a foul humour.

But my mood was slightly lifted by seeing that I had arrived in Langley on market day. Now, I do enjoy a lively market, not that I'd gone to many when I was walled up in old Gaspard's turret, but as a child in Winchester I'd loved watching the jugglers and dancing bears, dark-skinned merchants in their colourful robes and pink-cheeked fisher-girls prising open their oysters to tempt goodwives with the plump, glistening flesh. Every way you turned you'd catch a whiff of something different – exotic spices and roasting pork, perfumed Castile soap and fresh peaches. But the market at Langley held no such excitement.

It reeked of necessity not pleasure, of cabbage not cinnamon. In one corner, faded women were selling off whatever they could spare from their tofts, a couple of thread-bare chickens, a few onions or some dried peas scooped up in wooden bowls and trickled into a sack held by some gimlet-eyed hag, who would shriek as though she was being ravished if she thought her measure short by so much as one withered pea. Butchers proffered hunks of meat so dry I'd have sworn they'd been trying to sell the same piece for a month.

The salmon and cod fish smelt none too fresh either and even the carp gasping in their barrels of green water looked ready to hurl themselves on the ground to end their misery. There were a few beasts on sale, mostly unwanted billy kids or cows and goats that had ceased giving milk, but there was scarcely enough meat on their sharp bones to feed the most ascetic of hermits.

The most animated section of the market was occupied by the craftsmen and those who had sailed their tiny craft downriver to Langley from the neighbouring villages. They shouted their wares, proclaiming the cheapness of their threads and needles, axe heads and knives, pots and pails, oxen yokes and leather belts. All sturdy and serviceable, but fashioned without any attempt to decorate them, and I could see why: the few goodwives and men who rooted about the stalls were as dully clad and unadorned as the pails and beakers they were haggling for. There were only two qualities the Langley folk considered – would it stand up to hard wear and was it cheap? They'd no money to waste on anything as frivolous as beauty.

The wooden box rocked beneath my cloak. Lugh was growing restless.

'You're right,' I murmured. 'There doesn't look to be a man in these parts with spirit enough to get a nun with child, or a wife with the energy to care about it if he did. As soon as I find someone to tend my foot, I'm off to find a town with more life about it, for where there's life there's scandal.'

What I should have done, of course, was to heed the warning of the Seven Whistlers and hobble out of Langley just as fast as my one and a half feet could carry me, but if the beetle could see the boot about to descend on it, it wouldn't hang around waiting to get crushed. So, fool that I was, I limped up to a goodwife who was dragging a small tow-haired child by one hand and a skeletal cow by the other and enquired politely if there was a competent physician in the town.

She studied me for an age, her eyes narrowed, as if she was weighing up the merits of the numerous physicians Langley had to offer. The child and cow tugged her fretfully in different directions, but she ignored them. 'You don't want to waste time on physicians. They only send you to fetch physic from the apothecary. May as well go to him straight off. That way you'll not be charged twice.' She jerked her chin towards the street that ran off the square. 'Try the apothecary up yonder street. He's a good 'un. Saint, if you ask me. What he has to put up with from his wife would drive most men to murder. Most husbands would have sent her packing long since and got themselves a new woman, one as could cook and clean, instead of lying about expecting to be waited on.'

Now that the woman had started, she was like a broached keg. The gossip flowed out of her and I began to fear I'd never get away.

'Course, he used to have his niece to help him. Quiet little thing she was, plain as pease pottage.'

I thought this a trifle unkind, given that the straggle-haired gossip had a face that resembled a badly carved gargoyle. 'My thanks,' I said, turning away to face the street she'd shown me.

But she was far from done talking. She'd sold me her knowledge, and she was determined I should pay the price by listening. She stepped in front of me so that I was hemmed in by woman, cow and child.

'I was telling you about the girl. Queer affair, if you ask me.'

I hadn't, but she ignored that minor point. She leaned closer. Her breath smelt of onion and, for some inexplicable reason, wet dog.

'This niece of his is working up at the manor. But the old baron's only ever had manservants in the manor for as long as anyone can recall. A woman's not stepped over the threshold since his wife ran off and left him. Not that any women from these parts would venture near him. Cruel as the east wind, so they say. But now, after years of keeping away from townsfolk, the old baron's sent for the apothecary's niece to work for him, if you ever heard of such a thing. And what does he want with her? That's what I'd like to know. Whatever it is, it can't be decent, for the girl has told her aunt Ebba nothing about what she gets up to in the manor, save he asks her to grind and mix things.

'"What things?" Ebba asks the girl.

'"Herbs," the girl says.

'"Is he setting up his own apothecary shop now?" she asks the girl.

'But the girl tells her aunt she doesn't know.' The woman snorts in disbelief. 'How can she not know what's she's mixing? And if there's mixing to be done, why can't one of his manservants do it? Course, I reckon Ebba encouraged the girl to make sheep's eyes at him in the hopes he'd wed her. Ebba's always been one to hanker after roast swan when anyone else would be grateful for a bite of boiled chicken. But it stands to reason, a man as wealthy as the baron wouldn't wed a girl like that, especially when her father . . . Well, you know what they say about her father.'

I didn't, but at that moment I was far more interested in the wealthy baron than some penniless girl's father. In fact, I was so interested that the throbbing in my foot had almost vanished. Curiosity is better than any apothecary's draught for relieving pain.

'You said this man's wife ran off? Who with?'

The woman gave me an impatient glare, as if I'd entirely missed the point of what she was telling me.

'Osle doesn't like folks enquiring into his business and he's not a man you'd want to go annoying.'

'Osle – is that the baron's name?'

She glanced around furtively, lowering her voice to a whisper. 'Sylvain's his name, but there're some names as are best forgotten.' She tugged at the child's hand. 'Come along now, don't dawdle, there's a heap of things want doing at home.' She jerked the cow and child forward, as if they'd been delaying her. 'You want to plough a wide furrow round Osle, you do. Wide as you'd plough round the devil himself.'

But I had no intention of ploughing any furrow, unless it was straight to this baron's door.

I found the apothecary's shop by following my nose. The pungent scent of dried herbs and tallow trickled out through the shutter, which had been lowered into the street to form the counter. A tired-looking, grey-haired man was leaning over it, handing a jar to an old woman, who was cupping her ear the better to hear his instructions. He repeated them several times, but finally she abandoned the attempt to understand. She heaved her drooping dugs round in the direction of the marketplace and the rest of her body waddled after them.

The apothecary gazed after her, sorrowfully shaking his head. 'She hasn't understood a word of what I told her to do with the unguent. And she refuses to bring her daughter with her to help her. You'll see, she'll be back next week complaining it's done her no good.'

He seemed suddenly to realise he was addressing himself to a stranger and peered at me anxiously, as if I might take his comments amiss. I explained about the injury to my foot. He regarded me warily, as if trying to decide whether this might be some trick, but when I started to take off my shoe in the street, he finally nodded. 'You'd better come inside and let me look.'

There seemed to be a great many bolts to be drawn before the door was opened, then fastened again as soon as I'd limped through. The shop was small, and so dark I could barely make out the shapes of the jars and bottles on the highest shelves and was forced to duck beneath bundles of herbs and twigs swinging from the beams. An ancient yellow thigh bone of some animal lay on the table, beside a bowl of dried mice, another of desiccated worms and some shrivelled black things that looked as if they might be the dried hearts or livers of hares or cats.

The apothecary led the way to the rear of the shop, where a rough-hewn bench had been placed before a tiny window that overlooked the yard at the back.

'Please sit and remove the shoe.'

I plucked at the laces around my ankle till they were loose enough to slide the shoe off. Once free of the constraints, the throbbing intensified and my foot felt as if it was swelling so fast, I wondered if I'd get the shoe back on.

I hauled my leg up on the bench so that the apothecary could examine it.

He flexed my toes and prodded the wound in the ball of my foot, ignoring my gasps of pain and keeping a firm grip on my ankle as my foot jerked at each touch.

'I should send you to the physician. Master Alfred objects to me treating his patients.' He shrugged. 'I cannot blame him. I'm depriving him of a living, but even a king would blanch at the fees he charges – and as for his treatments! Sometimes I think he is still living in the days of the Saxons, like his namesake.'

'I'm not Master Alfred's patient,' I said. 'I arrived in Langley today and I'll not be staying long. I swear he'll never know you treated me.'

The apothecary smiled wearily. 'All the same, we'd best close the shop. You never know who might peer in.'

He bustled outside into the street, lifting the counter up so that it fitted over the open window as a shutter, then returned and refastened the door. Lighting a candle at the fire burning in the hearth, he collected a wicked-looking iron implement shaped like a small spear, with a long glass tube that opened out at one end into a small glass sphere.

'Perhaps I should see the physician after all,' I said hastily. 'I wouldn't want to get you into trouble.' I tried to thrust my swollen foot back into my shoe.

He pressed me firmly back onto the bench. 'Have faith, young man.'

Faith had never been a particular virtue of mine: I preferred always to trust what I could see, and seeing the apothecary advance towards my exceedingly tender foot with that sharp little spear was not helping to turn me into a believer.

'I will make the tiniest of incisions so quickly you will feel nothing but relief. Then I will draw a little of the poisoned blood.'

He straddled the end of the bench, clamping my foot between his knees. He was right. The sharp prick as the blade pierced the swollen flesh was almost at once followed by an immediate easing as the warm, sticky fluid oozed out.

He held a snip of cloth to the candle flame till it caught fire, dropped it inside the glass sphere and quickly pressed the end of the long glass neck over the incision. The mouth of the glass tightened hard against my skin and I felt a strong, sucking sensation. He'd neglected to warn me that that part would hurt. I yelped as he slid a finger against the edge of the glass and levered it off. It came away from my skin with a pop, and as he held the glass up in the light of the candle, I saw the sphere now contained watery blood and yellow pus.

'Does your foot feel easier now?' he asked.

To my surprise, I found it did, though it was still tender.

'I'll dress it with an ointment that will draw out any remaining foulness. You must apply it morning and night for three days. After that you should return here, so that I may look at it again. It would be foolish to walk any distance on that wound. It will only inflame it the more. Stay in Langley till it is healed.'

'Are there any passable inns in the town?' I asked him.

He shrugged. 'I have no use for them myself. Better ask in the market.'

He smeared a thick layer of some dark green ointment on my foot. It smelt of fat and bitter herbs, but didn't smart. In fact, it was soothing.

276

'I was thinking of visiting a certain baron who I'm told lives in these parts,' I said casually. 'A friend asked me to call and enquire how he does. He goes by the name of Sylvain. Does he live far from here?'

The apothecary's hand paused in mid-air and a great gob of the sticky ointment plopped onto the bench. 'You know Lord Sylvain?'

'I know of him only through a friend and it's been many years since they met. Is he in good health?'

The apothecary rose abruptly and went to a shelf, pulling down a box containing strips of linen. 'I do not discuss the health of my customers.'

'I wouldn't dream of asking you to break any confidences. I only meant that my friend hopes he is well. I trust he prospers? I believe my friend said he was newly wed,' I added, in the hope that he would be drawn into correcting me.

The apothecary did not meet my eye, seemingly absorbed in the all-engrossing task of bandaging my foot. 'Is that why you came to my shop, to learn of Lord Sylvain?'

'Hardly – you've seen my foot. It was relief from the pain that I wanted.'

His fingers worked deftly, but his lips remained firmly pressed together.

I glanced along the shelves, noticing the array of poisons sufficient to lay waste an entire army. At the very least this apothecary was usurping the physician's role behind his back, which Master Alfred would not take kindly to if he discovered it. I briefly contemplated reminding the apothecary of that and maybe hinting about the poisons too, but I thought better of it. I couldn't afford to upset him. I needed his services to heal my foot far more than I needed his money.

If the wound turned foul, Sylvain would be the least of my concerns. Besides, I could probably learn all I needed from the well-oiled tongues in the local inn: judging by that woman in the marketplace the whole town was gossiping about the baron.

I treated the apothecary to one of my most carefree smiles and prattled on about the wars in France, the rowdy behaviour of the foreign pilgrims, the late spring and anything else I could think of that would make it appear my enquiries about Sylvain were nothing more than inconsequential chatter to pass the time.

All the while, however, my mind was working feverishly. A missing wife, a wealthy man who shut himself away with only men for company and who was now brewing up Heaven knew what with the help of a young girl. If there wasn't a scandal here already, one was crying out to be invented and a great big juicy one at that. The question was, how best to get close to this Sylvain long enough to convince him he badly needed my help?

He was plainly not a man to frequent the inns or stew-houses. And I guessed from what little the woman had said that a stranger, even one bearing a message, was unlikely to be admitted to his house, never mind be granted a private audience. But perhaps the message might be carried another way. Yes, the more I thought about it, the more I was convinced I'd been shown exactly how to get inside the baron's deep and well-lined purse.

Chapter 36

He who wants to enter the divine realm, must first enter his mother's body and die therein.

Lord Sylvain is watching her again. She can feel it. When Gisa can hear neither his feet shuffling on the boards above her nor the clink of the glass vessels, she is afraid. In the silence, in the stillness, she knows he watches.

He has arranged two silver mirrors at angles in her store room beneath his chamber and hung a great silver ball in his own chamber above the trapdoor. He says they are to reflect the light, to help her work. But whenever she is in his chamber, she stares into the silver ball and knows that it captures the reflections of the mirrors in her room below, imprisons them, so that he can watch her chamber as if it is land floating in air. He can see the bench where she grinds the herbs and the stairs she climbs. These objects are distorted. Things she knows to be small appear monstrous. Straight lines are bent into graceful curves. She knows she, too, must be grotesquely twisted inside that silver ball. But why does he watch? Is he afraid she will steal from him?

Her face flushes hot with guilt, for she has stolen and she means to do so again as soon as she can, a little fragment of dragon's blood, some myrrh, galbanum and opanax to make the *unguentum apostolorum*, which she has been reading about in his books. She needs it for the trapped boy.

Gisa has found a plank to bridge the ditch and reach the hole where the boy lies beneath the wall. She conceals the plank among the trees. It must not be seen. For the past three nights, as soon as she can slip away from Aunt Ebba, she has brought stolen food and small ale to the boy, blankets thin enough to feed through the hole and a shirt of her uncle's, to cover his naked body. She took the iron crow from the blacksmith while his back was turned, and worked until her hands were blistered, but not one of the great stones would move or even splinter. But she will free him.

He lies on a narrow ledge inside the tunnel, just inches above the oozing mud and water. The labyrinth of channels is the bowel of the abbey, carrying away the filth draining from its latrines, wash houses and middens. But Gisa has seen the dried refuse and green slime covering the ledge on which the boy lies. If it rains hard or the river bursts its banks, the tunnels will fill to the top. And there will be no way out for Peter. Every day she glances anxiously at the sky.

But the boy may not survive long enough to drown. He is weak and growing weaker from loss of blood and the cold. Raised red lumps, and scarlet Y-shaped marks cover what she can see of his face and arms where the midges and leeches have fed on him, and the mice that scuttle along the ledges have nibbled his hair. Yet, tormented though he is by the creatures that infest the tunnels, he is far more terrified that the White Canons will find him again. Every day he begs her to tell no one he is here.

Jumbled fragments of nightmares tumble from his mouth as he gobbles the stolen food – *blood and magpies, furnaces that burn and floors that turn to water*. Yet, if she asks him to tell her more, so that she can try to make sense of it, he presses his hand to his mouth.

'Mustn't talk. Mustn't tell . . . He'll know . . .'

And through the long days and longer nights, the child is alone in the tunnel, his mouth pressed desperately to the wind that blows across that pitiful square of light, while she lies awake in her narrow bed, tunnelling through the weight of her thoughts, searching for a way – any way – to release him.

The sun moves round the slits in the chamber of Sylvain's tower, piercing each in turn and sending a thin blade of gold to touch the wall opposite. When the sun shines through the fourth slit, the bell on the door at the bottom of the tower will clang. Gisa hastens down the wooden stairs where Odo has left their midday meal in a basket covered with fresh white linen. She carries it up to Lord Sylvain. He washes his hands in the laver with perfumed soap and gestures for her to do the same.

Then they eat – roasted plovers, snipe, egret and curlew, re-dressed in their coats of feathers as if they were about to take wing. Eggs boiled in herbs and spices until they are scarlet or green. Roast larks' tongues arranged around glistening beads of rosehip jelly, like the petals of strange flowers. Fruits preserved in honey, nuts dipped in spices. On fast days they eat scarlet lobsters, sea-swine and coffins of lampreys, washed down with purple wine.

Sylvain chooses what Gisa will eat, offering the morsels to her on the point of his knife, studying her face as she takes the first bite of a new dish, waiting until she has swallowed before he selects something for himself, as if he must be satisfied she has consumed it all . . . as if he knows she really wants to steal it for the boy.

Today there is a whole round cheese among the roasted

birds. Sylvain breaks it open. The stench chokes her for inside the cheese is rotten, almost liquid, and wriggling with tiny white worms.

'See, the maggots are generated by the corruption and decay of the cheese. This is their womb and it will be their tomb.'

He scoops a dollop of liquid cheese and wriggling worms up in his fingers and pops it into his mouth. A white worm escapes from between his lips and jumps to the floor. He digs his fingers into the maggoty cheese again, pushing the wriggling mass towards Gisa's mouth and laughs when she recoils. But, for once, he does not make her eat it.

'You know that all things are composed of four elements. Tell me their qualities,' he orders, his smile suddenly vanished.

'Fire is hot and dry. Air is hot and moist. Water cold and moist. Earth cold and dry.'

It is a question a mere child could answer, or at least a child who has grown up in an apothecary's shop, for every cure depends upon knowing which illness has arisen from heat and may be cured by herbs that are cold, which decoction has dry properties and which moist.

He nods. 'Then what is the ultimate desire of the human spirit?'

She falters. *Then* implies a connection and she can see none.

He is waiting. He plucks the flesh from a heron's breast and stabs it with his knife. It hangs there, impaled. She senses his impatience, fears his anger.

A phrase from her Psalter pops into her mouth. 'Body and soul together shall rise from death and be with God and have joy that lasts for ever.' Does he think her ignorant of the holy faith?

Sylvain frowns, and she knows she has not given him the answer he wants. 'The elements – think of the elements, Gisa, fire and air. What is the body but earth and water? Earth and water cannot rise. The body must be purified through fire and entwined with the spirit, which is air. Only then does it cease to be moist and formless and may rise up through each of the four elements. Purified, it may ascend through the seven planets, through the realm of the unborn souls, through the nine choirs of angels, through the pure spirits. It must rise beyond all the realms until the dry soul is reunited with the fire that is the Divine, which is far beyond this God, this creature with a human face that priests like Arthmael have fashioned. Do you understand? There is not one death, but four. There is not one resurrection, but four.'

She stares at the boards beneath her feet. She has never heard Father Roland talk of these four resurrections. Would he declare this heresy? Yet how can she refuse to listen? Lord Sylvain is her master.

Sylvain reaches out and takes her hand, which she has left carelessly within his reach.

'Soon you will see the first death, Gisa, you will watch it. You will feel the power of it and then you will understand.'

She pulls her hand away, afraid of the fire that burns too brightly in his eyes. Her father is dead. She does not want to see death.

Sylvain carries each dish in turn to one of the windows and begins to push the remains of the food out through the slit. Birds appear as if they have been waiting. Gulls and ravens, jays and jackdaws swoop down, hopping across the grass, snatching greedily at the flesh that once flew like them.

'Stop! It is a waste!' Gisa is angry. If the boy could only eat this meat Lord Sylvain is so wantonly throwing away, he might recover.

Sylvain jerks round, staring at her, as if a rabbit has snarled at him. 'Do you want to eat it?'

She shakes her head. She wants to explain about Peter. Beg him to help. He is powerful enough to keep the boy safe from the White Canons, but would he? She watches the last of the meat fall.

Shafts of sunlight creep, slug-slow, around the tower, slithering through each narrow window in turn. The last gap is always the longest of the day, when the sun seems to have fallen asleep in the sky, but at last it reaches the slit. She hears the distant ringing of the church bell for Vespers and, glancing out, sees the great bulk of Odo plodding across the grass towards the door in the wall to unlock it. She throws her cloak about her shoulders. But just as she is about to hurry down to him, she hears Sylvain's footsteps descending the staircase above her.

In silence he inspects the various herbs she has left to steep in spirits of wine, dipping glass rods into the flasks, smelling, tasting, drawing the rods slowly over his long pale tongue. She waits in a fever of impatience, glancing agitatedly at the sky. She must get back to her uncle's house to find food for the boy, but is afraid to depart until she is dismissed.

Finally he turns. 'It is well done,' he says. 'You are diligent and you learn quickly.'

He takes a pace towards her and draws his finger across the throat of the white swan brooch on her cloak. She blushes at his proximity, at his smell. The same long cold finger slides beneath her chin to raise her head, so that she is forced to meet the intense gaze of those poison-green eyes.

'I told you when you came here that nothing you do or see is to be discussed outside this tower, not with my servants, not with your aunt and uncle, no one.'

'But I haven't, I swear,' Gisa says, suddenly alarmed that he is accusing her.

'I do not need oaths to know that you have kept your silence. I can read it in your face. Besides, I would be told at once if you had broken your word. There are many outside who ascribe what they cannot comprehend to the devil's work and others who would seek to use what I do for their own ends. So, I remind you to keep silent. I would not wish to see you suffer as your father did.'

'My father?' Gisa is startled. 'My aunt and uncle have told me little of him, how he died. Can you tell me?'

His fingers stroke the soft skin of her cheek. 'If, my little swan, you do all I instruct you to do, you will not need to ask, nor will I need to tell you. You will know. Oh, yes,' he whispers, 'you will know it in your body and your soul.'

He releases her and she runs down the stairs so fast that she almost slips. Her skin crawls where his fingers touched her face.

She hurries down the track, away from the manor, trying to make sense of what he has said. But she cannot. Her father suffered, Sylvain said. Was he talking about her father's death or something that happened before he died? And how will she know what that was without being told?

'Your pardon, mistress, but you dropped this!'

A young man steps out from the shadow of the trees. He bows and hands her a ball of yellow cowslips.

She takes it before his words penetrate her thoughts. Then she realises what he said and thrusts it towards him. 'You're mistaken. I didn't drop this. I've no time to make cowslip balls.'

He shrugs and grins, but does not take back the ball. 'Pity – a beautiful maid like you should have nothing else to do except make cowslip balls to discover her future husband.'

The young man is mocking her. She knows she is not beautiful, not even pretty. Aunt Ebba has told her often enough, and all of Aunt Ebba's friends agree. Gisa walks away from him down the track, though she can't bring herself to drop the delicate blossoms.

She is approaching the hole beneath the abbey wall where Peter is hiding, but she deliberately looks the other way for, in spite of his limp, the young man is keeping pace with her and she dare not draw the stranger's attention to the boy's hiding place. She must hurry home and return with food for the child.

'. . . baron shouldn't make you work so hard,' the young man is saying. 'But, then, old Sylvain was always a hard master.'

Startled by his use of the name, Gisa's thoughts are jerked away from little Peter and she looks at the young man properly. He's tall and spindly, with hunched shoulders, like a sapling that's grown bent in a fierce wind. He certainly doesn't have the muscles of a farmer or a sailor, but he is no clerk either: the bleached gold of his beard and hair is startlingly bright against his tanned face. His deep blue eyes are rather too close together and his nose a little squat, but he has an easy smile, as if he is greeting an old friend. But he is not her friend. Gisa knows by sight every young man

286

who buys and sells in the marketplace, hefts the loads or tends the horses, and he is none of those.

'You work for Lord Sylvain?' she asks.

'No, sweet maid. But we have a mutual friend. In fact, I've been trying to call on your master. I have a message from a noble knight, which I am instructed to deliver only to Lord Sylvain's ears. But that manservant of his won't let me see him. You know him? Giant of a man, face as sour as a barrel of pickles. Looks as if he thought he was biting into a sausage and found himself chewing a turd instead.'

Gisa giggles. That's exactly how Odo looks.

'Not much liked, is he, that master of yours? Most people seem afraid of him. Still, I suppose you can't expect a man to be as merry as the Lord of Misrule when his wife has run off. But I dare say you've got to know him, seen a different side of him. I never believed those rumours about him. Someone actually told me he has a daughter he keeps locked up in his tower, only lets her out to walk at night.'

Gisa feels the young man's sharp glance, but doesn't turn her head. Only this afternoon, Lord Sylvain was telling her to say nothing of his business and now here is a stranger asking questions about him. Is this another of Sylvain's tests?

She turns down a snicket between the backyards of the houses, trying to shake off the young man. It is not possible for them to walk two abreast here, because of the deep open sewers that line the path, but still he limps after her.

With relief she reaches the gate to her uncle's yard and pulls it open just wide enough to edge through.

'Gisa!'

She turns, taken aback that he knows her name.

'Would you take pity on me and ask the baron to grant me an audience? My ship sails soon and I must be aboard.

I swore a solemn oath on the Holy Cross of Bromholm to deliver the message to Lord Sylvain and my soul will be cursed in this life and the next if I fail.'

'Why don't you write the message or ask a scribe to write it for you? Odo would give him that, I'm sure.'

He takes a step towards her, lowering his voice. 'This matter is so secret and delicate, I cannot entrust the words to a scribe. Your master would not want anyone else to know of it.' He leans towards her, and gently takes the hand that still grasps the ball of cowslips. 'Please,' he whispers. 'My name is Laurent. Ask him. Beg him. I shall wait outside the manor all day tomorrow, in the hope that you can persuade him. I know you can. You could persuade the sun to shine in the middle of a storm.' He gazes earnestly into her eyes. 'I will wait for you, Gisa. My very soul is in your hands.'

He smiles, and his smile makes her blush, though she doesn't know why it should. But she gives him no reply. She slips through the gate, closing it firmly behind her. As she crosses her uncle's courtyard, she pauses by the well to sprinkle drops of water on the cowslip ball to keep it fresh. She reminds herself that the flowers don't belong to her. She still believes he has given her the cowslip ball by mistake, but all the same it reminds her of his smile and she doesn't want either of them to fade.

Chapter 37

The third day again to life he shall uprise, and devour the birds and beasts of the wilderness, crows, popinjays, pyes, peacocks, and seagulls, the phoenix, the white eagle and the griffin of fearfulness.

Even through the box, I felt the raven's head tremble with excitement, its beak drumming on the wood, urging me to hurry. For the first time since I'd had the silver head in my possession, I sensed it was willing to let itself be sold. All I'd heard about Sylvain's love of birds convinced me he would be just the man to buy Lugh and would probably pay me far more than the head was worth, no questions asked. I was almost whooping with excitement: if I succeeded in selling him both the raven's head and a story, I'd come away with such a weighty purse, his story would be the last I'd ever need to tell.

I'd done well enough out of my stories, enough to buy a bed and a warm meal most days. But I'd had enough of eking out a living on the road. I wanted to be invited to the tables of the wealthy to dine and to have men bow to me as I passed them in the streets instead of looking through me as if I was a wraith. One really heavy purse was all I needed. Then I could buy myself a house, invest in a cargo or two and wait for money to come flowing to me, instead of having to scratch around for it. But there was little point in the raven's head leading me to a rich man's door where I might make my fortune, if I couldn't get inside. That was where a woman would be far more use than a bird.

I quickly realised the apothecary's niece would not be bribed into helping me by a promise of money, and she was not like the tavern wenches, who could be flattered into refilling my flagon behind the innkeeper's back. But young Gisa had one weakness. Her neighbours and customers agreed she was a tender-hearted creature who would not see anyone suffer. That was the snare I would use to catch her.

But, all the same, I knew it wouldn't be easy to coax her to do what I asked. I'd seen her hurry from Sylvain's gate, stopping only to draw breath when she thought she was safely out of sight of that tower. It was plain she was as afraid of Sylvain as the rest of the townsfolk. I'd have to work hard to persuade her to pluck up the courage to get me through those gates.

But if ever a man was in need of reinvention, Sylvain was, especially after my rumours began to trickle around the town. The people already thought him a strange, sinister figure, but by the time I had dropped a little hint here and prompted a vague recollection there, they were starting to believe he was the horned one himself, who could command the winged demons to snatch babies from their cradles or drop polluted blood into the wells to bring sickness and death to any who crossed him. I was so convincing, I even frightened myself and had nightmares in which Sylvain flew like an owl from the top of his own tower.

But each time I drew Lugh from the box, the raven's head whispered to me – *He's the man who will make your fortune* – and I believed it. For Sylvain was rich, there was no doubting that. It was said even his servants lived in luxury, eating the finest food, drinking French wines, their loyalty amply rewarded by the generous corrodies he'd bought for them at the local abbey, which, in old age, would keep them in the kind of comfort a bishop would envy. Clearly, here was a man who was prepared to pay for silence and pay most handsomely. I could not walk away from a chance like that.

The morning after my encounter with Gisa I prised myself off my pallet at the inn, at a ridiculously early hour. I didn't even stop to eat. Shivering and hungry, I made my way to the end of the snicket that ran behind the apothecary's shop and leaned against the wall, yawning. A watery light was seeping up over the thatched roofs and the morning star still hung in the sky. Grey smoke spiralled up through the roofs of the cottages as women stirred fires back to life. Men and boys stumbled along the track on their way to the fields, and a handful of travellers were setting off early for distant towns, but most did little but grunt in my direction. Several times the click-clack of wooden pattens roused me, but none of the footsteps was Gisa's. I was on the verge of turning away, fearing she had taken a different route, when I saw her coming towards me, a small sack dangling from her hand.

She was a slender little creature with hair as dark as Lugh's eye, at least what little I could see of it from the wispy tendrils around her temples. Though she was as yet unmarried, her hair was bound up under a cloth wound round her head as kitchen maids do to keep it from catching on the cooking fires. Her brows and long lashes were black against her white face, her lips full but almost bloodless, and there were dark circles beneath her large eyes. That gargoyle in the town had described her as plain, but she was far from that. She was like an outline of the painting of the Holy Virgin that an artist had sketched in black and white, but not yet filled in with colour.

Amée had been beautiful and she knew it. She knew how to glance up suddenly from beneath her lashes to drown men in the depths of her blue eyes, knew how to thrust her reddened lips into a pout so you ached to kiss them. This girl made no attempt to use any of her charms. It was as if she was determined not to be seen, much less admired.

Gisa gave a slight start of recognition as she caught sight of me, and tried to hide the sack she was carrying beneath her cloak. I fell into step beside her and she quickened her pace.

'Will he rail at you if you are late?'

'There's much to do,' she answered.

I could feel the raven's head stirring in the box, tapping with his beak on the wood with such force I was surprised Gisa didn't turn her head or ask what was making the noise. As we drew level with the abbey walls, she seemed to become even more agitated, and strode ahead as if desperate to lose me. But I would not be shaken off so easily.

'Will you see him today?' I said, hurrying to catch up.

'I see him every day.'

'Then will you take pity on me, sweet Gisa, and ask him to receive me? He will thank you for it, that I promise, when he knows the nature of my business.'

I felt a little twinge of guilt in telling her that. He wouldn't be grateful at all. What man is, if he thinks you are trying to squeeze money from him? But on the other hand I would probably be doing her a favour if he flew into a rage and dismissed her. Anyone could see she hated working for him. She'd be much happier back in her uncle's shop, gossiping

292

with the women and flirting with the boys, assuming she had the first idea how to flirt. I continued to try to persuade her as we trailed up the road beyond the abbey and the marshes, but she never once turned her head or answered.

'Ask him today, I beg you. There isn't much time before my boat sails and I couldn't bear the shame if I broke my sworn oath to my poor friend.'

We were approaching the wall that surrounded the manor grounds. She quickened her pace again, making for the little bridge over the ditch that led to a low door in the wall.

'I'll wait by the main gate all day,' I called after her. 'I'll maintain my vigil day and night if I have to, so that I may fulfil my vow to such a noble knight. I couldn't live, knowing I had betrayed his trust.'

I glanced up at the sky, hoping it might threaten rain. It would encourage her to take pity on me, if she thought I was standing outside like a hound, miserable, wet and shivering. But the dew on the grass was already sparkling in the first rays of sun and if anything it looked set to be the first warm day of spring.

She glanced back at me and pressed her finger to her lips, inclining her head towards the door. I guessed that someone was standing behind it and hastily drew back out of sight as it was opened from within. Gisa slipped through and I heard the key grind in the lock and the beam rammed home to brace it. Whatever Sylvain was doing behind those walls, he certainly had no wish to have anyone burst in on him.

I made my way round to the main gate. The two great iron-studded doors in the courtyard wall were firmly shut, but I had no intention of tolling the bell for admittance. That great brute of a manservant had already slammed the door in my face once. I was not going to give him the satisfaction a second time. On the other side of the track was a small grove of birch and willow. There I found a moss-covered stump, which, though rotten with fungus, was marginally drier than the boggy grass, so I settled myself down on it to wait.

I'd had the foresight to thrust some bread, slices of dried apple and the end of a ham shank into my scrip the night before, and it was as well I had, for my stomach was complaining loudly about its missed breakfast. The bread was so hard it could have taken a man's eye out if it had been fired from a sling. But after I'd gnawed what I could, I wiled away the time by chipping bits off to throw to the birds pecking at the leaf buds in the trees. They ignored the crumbs.

Hours shuffled past. Occasionally a boy came staggering along the track bent double beneath a load of fodder or a bundle of kindling. An ox-cart would rumble by, or an old woman totter past, clutching a chicken or an armful of herbs. They stared at me curiously and some laughed, gesturing towards the closed doors.

'Your backside'll have taken root and you'll be pushing leaves out of your ears afore you see that door open.'

I smiled politely and ignored them. Midday came and went. After my early start that morning, I found my eyelids drooping and my head nodding onto my chest. I had repeatedly to shake myself awake. Then it was mid-afternoon and the distant bells for the None prayers were ringing. I was beginning to realise I was going to have to work a lot harder on persuading Gisa to speak to her master. But how?

Giving a woman a bunch of ribbons or a cheap necklace might be enough for most, but I'd seen the enamel swan brooch Gisa wore on her cloak and knew that nothing I could afford in the marketplace would even come close to matching that. Besides, I was pretty sure even a gold necklace wouldn't work on her. Maybe if I asked her to come for a stroll along the river and spun her a story . . . My thoughts drifted into tales of wounded knights and holy quests, and I had almost drifted off to sleep again when something jerked me awake. It took me a few moments to realise it was the sound of the door opening.

The manservant lumbered out and peered up and down the track, like an ogre who's caught the scent of human blood. I leaped to my feet and hurried towards him. His thick black eyebrows formed one continual line above his nose, which gave him a perpetual scowl.

'You Laurent?'

'*Master* Laurent,' I corrected, in what I hoped was a tone of authority.

It produced only a sneer. 'The master wants to see you.'

I was sorely tempted to make some sarcastic comment about him having told me Sylvain would never have me admitted, but I've learned you should never annoy servants. They have all kinds of subtle and devious ways of getting back at you, not least poisoning their masters against you. So I contented myself by stalking past him, as if I was grossly insulted at being kept hanging about for so long.

He led me through the courtyard and into the Great Hall, which was empty of people, but not of noise. A dozen cages hung in the breeze from the open casements, each containing some exotically coloured bird that was doing its best to out-sing its neighbours. A few fluttered hopelessly against the bars, trying to fly up into the wide blue sky they could see but not reach.

But the birds seemed colourless compared to the splendour

of the hall. Here was a man who had wealth, but didn't flaunt it in vulgarity. The wall paintings of the astrological houses, exquisitely executed in vivid reds, greens and blues, glittered with subtle touches of gold leaf. The great shell-like lavers on their stands were sculpted of finest bronze, and the iron candle spikes on the walls were in the form of horned stags or twisted nests of scorpions.

At one end of the hall was a raised dais, while at the other, below the hearth, was a long table on which stood a huge enamel and gilt cup, covered with a lid and studded with semi-precious stones, which would have been the envy of many a cathedral. But it was not decorated with scenes from the life of Christ. Grotesques that were half man, half woman wandered over the surface. There was a man with the sun in the place of his head and a woman with the moon instead of a face. One panel showed a king being boiled alive in a cauldron, while in another, a king and queen lay side by side in a tomb. I could make little sense of it, unless it depicted the life of one of those strange saints like St Christopher, who was born with the head of a dog and devoured men before he was converted.

'You admire my chalice.'

I spun round. A man was standing on the dais behind me. He was dressed in a flowing black tabard, trimmed with fur and girdled at the waist. Beneath it his robe was white. Though he was in his own hall, his hands were encased in close-fitting gloves of black kid, decorated with strips of silver embroidery. His hair, if he had any, was concealed beneath a tight black coif fastened beneath his chin. He was a man whose age was impossible to guess.

I bowed. Without taking his gaze from me, he lowered himself stiffly into a chair placed ready in the centre of the dais. He was staring intently at my hair and then his gaze slid over the rest of my body, as if I was a horse he was appraising for bloodstock. For a moment there was an expression of greedy excitement in his eyes, like you see in the eyes of men when they are looking at a woman who arouses their lust. I felt my face growing hot. But it was gone in a flash and his face became expressionless again.

When he finally spoke, his voice was cold and hard. 'Gisa tells me that you approached her last night and again this morning seeking an audience with me, when you had already been refused admission by Odo. Did you think the girl would tell you something that Odo would not?'

'My lord, I wouldn't dream of asking any servant to betray the confidences of their masters. Indeed, what would be the point? If a servant was perfidious enough to do such a thing, whatever they said could hardly be relied upon. I trust the girl told you that I asked her nothing, save only that she might beg you to speak with me, since your manservant seemed disinclined to convey the message.'

He clasped his gloved fingers together and rested his chin upon them. 'But you have been asking others about me in the town and sharing your own more *colourful* thoughts about me with them.' His tone held no emotion, which made it only more chilling.

Who had told him? I couldn't imagine any of the townspeople dropping into the manor to exchange pleasantries and gossip. Was he simply guessing? I tried to remain as calm as he was and not be flustered into hasty denials. I decided to treat it as a statement rather than a question and say nothing.

The birds had fallen silent and I became aware of the loud buzzing of flies. The source was a solitary bowl on the long table that might once have contained fruit of some kind, now rotted to a heap of brown slime covered with white mildew. Odo's talents evidently didn't run to clearing tables. I was surprised Sylvain tolerated such laziness in his servants.

We both waited. After a long pause, the baron raised his eyebrows as if I had surprised him.

'Gisa said you'd sworn an oath to a knight to deliver a message. You doubtless thought she would find such a fable romantic. You underestimate her, Master Laurent. She is an intelligent girl, not a moonstruck milkmaid. She told me of your approaches because she knew I would wish to be informed about someone trying to gain access to this manor. And, I suspect, because she thought she might have been seen talking to you and was anxious to tell me before others did. My servants are chosen for their loyalty.

'But let us put an end to this game, before I find you standing in my bedchamber in the middle of the night. What is it you want from me? Money to invest in some great enterprise, a ship of exploration, perhaps? Are you offering me a miraculous elixir, which I can possess for a fortune? Or are you another adventurer who claims to know the whereabouts of my lost daughter? I warn you, Master Laurent, I have heard them all, which is why I have given instructions that no more men, like you, are to be admitted to waste my time.'

'And,' I said, 'that is precisely why the rumours about you multiply like mice in a tithe barn. They will devour all that you own if you cannot kill them. The townspeople say your daughter lies imprisoned in the tower while her suitors languish, chained up in your cellars, blinded and castrated. They speak of you conjuring demons and sending them out to wreak vengeance on any who cross you.'

Sylvain gave a snort of laughter. 'You think I don't know what is said? Mothers have always told their children stories of the black shuck and terrible tatterfoal that stalk the lanes after dark in order to frighten their offspring into returning home in good time for supper. For the same reason, if these wild tales frighten the townspeople into leaving me in peace, why should I care what is said of me?'

'Because if these rumours continue to grow, peace is the one thing you will not be able to buy. Already there is talk of men storming the manor to rescue those they believe imprisoned inside and to cast you down from the top of the tower, so that you can work no more magic.'

Sylvain's eyes flashed, but it was anger I saw in them, not fear. 'And why do you warn me of this? Have you come to offer your services as a guard?' He gestured contemptuously towards me. 'Unless you have hidden strength in those skinny arms, I doubt you could fire an arrow far enough to reach a practice butt, or even draw a sword from its scabbard, never mind wield it in my defence.'

'If you employed my services you would have no need of any guard to defend you,' I told him. 'I could put a stop to this before the men had even gathered. I could make them admire you, defend you even. I have done as much for many others. I can weave a tale that will explain all the mysteries men have conjured about you and this place. One that if spread around the town will make them leave you in peace for ever.'

'A child's tale! And for that you'd charge handsomely, I've no doubt.' He pushed back the chair and rose. 'I dare say you have been able to blackmail others, Master Laurent, discovered some crime, planted the seed of fear in them, then, like some saintly gardener, destroyed the deadly weed in one stroke so that they fall on their knees in gratitude. But you have overreached yourself this time. Go, frighten the puffed-up merchants or the clerics who are stealing taxes or fornicating with the bishop's bastard daughter. But if you attempt to threaten me again, you will be joining those fictitious suitors who lie – what was it you said? – blinded and castrated in my cellar, except in your case I'd be only too willing to prove the rumours true.'

He turned abruptly and strode towards the door. But I'd been expecting that. I knew it would take more than the threat of a rampaging mob from the town to unnerve a man like Sylvain. I waited until he had his hand on the iron ring.

'And if the rumours of magic should reach beyond the town, Lord Sylvain? If they should reach a bishop's ears or the king's court, they would certainly attract attention from the Church or the Crown who might consider them worth investigating. Young King Henry knows many in his kingdom still believe Louis of France to be the rightful King of England. Henry is certain that some are using sorcery to aid the French king's cause and turn the English against him. He looks for traitors everywhere among his nobles and seeks to curb the power of the barons, who so ruthlessly tried to tame his own father. He mistrusts them all. So if he were to learn that one of those barons, who owns lands so close to the ports that trade with France, was practising the dark arts, he might send men to discover if these rumours were true. I fear that what his spies would be told by the towns-people would only make King Henry believe his fears were fully justified.'

The iron ring of the door fell from Sylvain's gloved hand and dropped back into place, swaying as if an icy wind were blowing it. He turned back, his face pale with anger. The cold fury in his eyes almost sent me fleeing from the hall. I thought he was about to spring like a wild beast and tear my throat out with his teeth. I found myself stumbling backwards as he leaped from the dais. But I didn't move quickly enough. His gloved fist struck out, catching me on the side of the head, knocking me into the great oak table. The last thing I remembered was his glittering eyes staring down at me and the flash of a steel blade in his hand.

Chapter 38

The eagle flying through the air, the toad crawling on the ground, chained one to the other, are the magistery.

Lord Sylvain utters not one word when Gisa finally plucks up the courage to climb up to his workshop to tell him about Laurent. His expression betrays nothing of his thoughts. He works on as if she has not spoken and Gisa half wonders if she really has, or if she has only imagined what she would say.

Only hours later, in the afternoon, when the None bell chimes, does Sylvain leave the tower. He does not return. Gisa works on alone, until the distant bell for Vespers rings out across the water meadows and Odo unlocks the gate. Outside, Gisa peers up and down the track, but there is no sign of Laurent. Maybe he's given up, or perhaps Sylvain is even now speaking with him, but that surely can't be. Three hours have passed since Sylvain left the tower.

Gisa walks up the road towards the abbey, pausing frequently to look over her shoulder, hoping that Laurent is on the road behind her, hurrying to catch up. She finds herself wanting to walk with him again, which startles her. She realises, with a sudden flush of her cheeks, that she wants Laurent to like her. But the moment this thought solidifies in her mind, she tries to banish it, as if Sylvain will know.

She cannot shake off the feeling that Sylvain sees everything she does even when she is not with him, as if there are invisible mirrors and silver balls hovering over her wherever she goes. When she undresses in her uncle's house at night, it is as if her fingers are Sylvain's fingers touching her naked body, unthreading the laces on her kirtle, pulling her shift from her bare shoulders. Even under the blankets in the dark, she does not lie alone. He follows her into her dreams. She shudders.

As she draws level with the abbey walls, Gisa steps off the track, peering up and down the road to ensure she is alone. She drags the plank from its hiding place and slides it across the ditch to the hole at the bottom of the wall. This morning, while her uncle was distracted by a customer who hammered on the door before breakfast, Gisa stole bread, cheese and a mutton bone with a good deal of meat still clinging to it. It is a feast for one so small. She wanted to give it to little Peter this morning, but she'd had no chance, with Laurent following her. She pulls the small sack from beneath her cloak.

'Peter,' she whispers, kneeling down to peer through the gap in the stones.

She hears a whimper, but he does not answer. She can see his dim outline in the tunnel. He's lying on the ledge, facing away from her. He moans softly.

She pushes her fingers through the hole and can just touch the back of his neck. She thinks he must be cold after lying there all night, but his skin is hot. He is burning up.

'Peter! Peter!' she whispers more urgently, trying to prod him, but her fingertips barely reach him.

He stirs all the same and struggles to sit up. His eyes, when he stares up at her from the darkness of the tunnel, are unnaturally bright, feverish. A bloated leech hangs from his lower lip. It plops down into the foul green water below. A trickle of watery scarlet blood runs from the bite and meanders down the boy's neck, but he is too listless to notice.

Gisa pushes the food, piece by piece, through the hole. He tries to hold it, but his grip is too weak and the cheese drops into the foul water.

'Eat the bread, Peter, you must eat.'

He seems barely interested in the food, but grabs the neck of a leather bottle when she holds it to the hole, sucking on the small ale it contains with such a fierce, raging thirst, she fears he will choke. Her mind searches through the herbs and physic she knows that will ease a fever. Is it caused by his wounds or the foul vapours from the drain? He cannot survive down here for much longer. But she does not know whom she can trust. Laurent? Even if he would help, he could no more protect the boy from the White Canons than her uncle. The child belongs to the abbey. Only one man has the authority to stand up to them, and him she trusts least of all.

If she can make little Peter strong enough to move, he can search for another way out. She will bring him candles. They will use a thread, so that he can find his way back to the hole. But he is too weak even to struggle off the ledge.

Furious with herself at her own helplessness, she drags out a small wooden shovel she has hidden in the sack. Last night as she lay in bed, it came to her that she could dig down into the bank below the hole. The stones at the bottom might be smaller, looser. But even as she scrapes away the weeds and earth, she can see that the stones beneath are much bigger than those above ground. But still she hacks away in frustration, until the wood snaps.

Peter is still sucking at the leather bottle, whimpering in misery and frustration for it is empty. She drags it away from his mouth and he presses his face to the gap, begging for more, but she has none. The bread and mutton bone lie untouched on the ledge.

'Please eat,' she urges.

He bites off a tiny piece of bread, moving it round and round in his mouth, but his throat is too dry and sore to swallow it. 'Man in the black robes come back . . . Saw him in the dark . . . Don't tell him. Don't tell.' Peter starts to cry, but softly.

'The White Canons, they were searching for you?' Gisa asks. She glances hastily up at the high wall, afraid their voices might carry.

'Snake man,' he mumbles. 'Don't let him find me. Don't let him . . . He stings.'

Gisa gnaws her lip. The child's wits are wandering. The fever is taking hold. She will have to make up a draught and bring it back tonight. She cannot wait till morning. But what excuse can she make to Aunt Ebba?

A soft grey moth-light envelops the apothecary's courtyard. In the shop, the candles have been extinguished. Business is concluded for the day. She can hear her uncle's footsteps on the boards above and the querulous voice of Aunt Ebba, but she does not go up. She searches in the twilight of the shuttered chamber, trying to remember the order of the herbs on the shelves and praying her uncle has not moved them.

Evil faces leer down at her. Hairy creatures with many legs sway from the beams, and imps peep at her from the corners of the room. She knows the shelves hold nothing more sinister than jars and dried herbs, bones and boxes, and in daylight that is all she will see and wonder then how she saw them prance and grimace, but tonight they do.

She opens the small chest in which she keeps her few belongings. The cowslip ball is wilted, shrivelled. Why didn't she take some of the blossoms to dry and press while they were still fresh? It is too late to preserve them now. But why should she want to anyway? It was never her posy. A pool of misery wells up in her and she aches with a loneliness she has not felt so intensely since they dragged her father away.

Chapter 39

Take a white tree surrounded by dew, build around it
a round, dark house, put in it a man stricken in years,
a hundred years old, lock him in so that neither wind
nor dust shall penetrate, and when he eats of the fruit
he will become a youth again.

When I woke, I thought I'd been struck blind. I tried to lift my right hand to my eyes, but I found I couldn't raise my arm more than an inch or two, as if it was chained. My left hand seemed normal, though. I felt my eyes. Several layers of thick linen strips had been bound about my head, like a blindfold. God's blood, had he actually done it? Had that bastard really blinded me? I fumbled at the folds of the linen, trying to peel them back, but a strong hand gripped my arm, dragging it away from my face.

'Don't try to move. You're hurt. You must lie still.' It wasn't a voice I recognised.

'What happened? Where am I?'

I was struggling to piece together little fragments of images. Something black . . . black sleeve . . . the flash of a blade . . . a two-headed man. God's arse, was I in Hell?

I fought to sit up, but again the hand pushed me down. I heard the rustle of a straw mattress beneath me. But only as my body moved against a linen sheet did I realise I was naked. There was nothing unusual about being naked in bed, but when you are blindfolded and there is a strange man sitting next to you, you feel as vulnerable as a live chicken stretched out on a butcher's block. I clutched the sheet that covered me, clamping it firmly under my armpits.

I heard the creak of a chair as the man shifted his position. 'You're in the house of Lord Sylvain. You stumbled and fell. Your right arm is broken, but it has been bound in cloth and covered with a paste of grated comfrey root, egg white, flour and fat. It has set hard and will hold the broken bone in place, but you must try not to move it. If you accidentally strike it on something, the cast will shatter and the broken bone will move. That will be painful,' the man added unnecessarily.

I had no intention of waving my arm around, but I was rather more concerned about my eyes.

'Am I blind? Tell me!'

'Your head struck the edge of the table when you slipped. Blood has gathered in your eyes. They have been bathed in green coriander mixed with a woman's breast milk. But you must keep them closed and covered. If you look upon so much as a candle flame while they are so inflamed, it will indeed blind you permanently. And I am sure you do not wish for that. You must try to lie completely still and not sit up or make any sudden movements of the head until you are healed. A servant will come to attend to all your needs presently.'

'Aren't you a servant?' I asked.

He laughed as if I was an idiot. 'I'm a servant of God, but I am most assuredly not a servant of Sylvain.'

I was affronted. How was I supposed to tell? I couldn't see him. 'A monk, then? An infirmarer? Did you set my arm?'

'I do not set bones,' he said coldly. 'I am the *abbot* of Langley. We are an order of Premonstratensians. Some call us the White Canons. I had business to conduct with the baron and, learning of your accident, I thought I should visit you before I left and offer my prayers for your recovery. Sylvain tended your arm. He is a skilled bone-setter, which is fortunate for you. Those who fall into the hands of the unskilled have been known to lose limbs and, indeed, their lives when a bone has been badly set.'

I heard the wood of a chair groan and guessed that he was levering himself to his feet. He intoned a Latin blessing and reminded me again to lie perfectly still. His sandals padded softly across the boards. It was only as the latch on the door clicked shut behind him that I realised there were a hundred things I hadn't asked, like where exactly I was in the manor and was it night or day and just how long had I been there? I called out, but he didn't return and neither did the promised servant appear.

The abbot might be a servant of God, but either he had lied to me or the baron had lied to him about what had transpired in the hall. I hadn't stumbled, Sylvain had punched me, and if I hadn't blacked out, he would have knifed me too. Maybe he had! I was sure I'd struck the table with the side of my head, not across the front. God's arse, Sylvain had stabbed me in the eyes! Gingerly I touched them through the bandages. Both eyeballs seemed to be intact and they didn't hurt when I pressed them. Come to think of it, neither did my broken arm. Was I drugged?

Panic seized me, blind panic in every sense. Only the insane fear that if I pulled off the bandages my eyeballs would roll out onto the floor stopped me doing just that. Then I heard a familiar gurgling croak. Lugh! I reached down to where the leather scrip should be, but it was gone. Hardly surprising, since I'd been stripped of all my clothes.

But the gurgling croak sounded again, harsher this time. Lugh was still here somewhere close by my head. Where was he? Where was I, come to that?

Take deep breaths, calm yourself.

'It's all very well for you to prattle on about calm, Lugh. You can see where you are!'

Hardly. I am in a box, remember. Think! What did you hear?

'I'm thinking! Creaking floorboards, so we're probably not in a cellar. An upper room, a small chamber, because it didn't take the abbot many steps to reach the door. So I'm locked up in that tower of his. He's going to keep me locked up and starve me to death, like his daughter's suitors! He's already blinded me, like them.'

You invented that story yourself, remember? Shouldn't go believing your own tales. You also said he castrated them. Not done that yet, has he? But if I were you, I wouldn't mention chopping anyone's cods off again – it might give him ideas. But why would he bother to set your arm if he meant you to die? He'd just toss you down on the bare boards and leave you to your agonies.

'Maybe he is afraid I'll scream and be heard outside. Then the townsfolk really will storm the manor.'

He could have gagged you and tied . . .

The raven fell silent and, moments later, I heard the latch lift on the door and someone entered the chamber. He lumbered towards me. I found myself holding my left arm up to defend myself, though it would have been of little use. The fragrant smell of cooked meat and herbs drifted over my nose, closely followed by rancid fat and raw blood.

'Who is it? Who's there?' I called out in panic.

'Pipkin they call me, just old Pipkin. Course, it used to

310

be *young* Pipkin when they firstly called me that, on account of me being the smallest scullion in the kitchen and always needing to be stuffed with food. Now look at me, size of an ale barrel. Firkin, that's what they ought to call me, but Pipkin it is and always will be, I reckon, till they plant me in the ground.'

I heard the thump of wood close by my head as he set something down. The smell of meat and herbs was stronger now, but so was the stench of stale, raw blood.

'I've a drop of good beef broth here,' Pipkin said. 'Master says you're not to move. So you open your mouth and I'll spoon it into you, as if you was an old gammer.'

The smell had suddenly made me ravenously hungry. When had I last eaten?

'How long have I been here?'

'Don't rightly know. Master sent for me this morning. Told me you was here and what I was to cook you to help you mend. Don't ask questions of the master, we don't. He can't abide it. And good positions are hard to find at my age, so I does what I'm told and says nowt. Open your mouth.'

I did as I was told and allowed him to trickle the broth into my mouth. Although it was already barely warm, he blew wetly onto each spoonful in case it burned me. I couldn't even recall being fed as an infant. I think as soon as I was weaned I must have learned to grab whatever food was lying around else I would have starved. It was hard trying to swallow, lying flat with my head raised only an inch or two on the pillow, and Pipkin wasn't exactly fitted to be a nurse-maid, so between the two of us, half the broth ended up running down my neck and soaking into the pillow.

Pipkin grunted as he ineffectually dabbed at me with a

cloth that stank of raw onion. 'Tell you what, I'll fetch a bit of hollow horn with me next time. Then you can suck it down like a babe.' His fat, calloused fingers fumbled with my left hand and I jerked it away indignantly, wondering what on earth he was doing. 'Here, take this.' He was trying to force whatever it was into my hand again. 'It's a leg of chicken. I reckon you can gnaw on that without sitting up. Only don't tell the master. He said you was just to have broth, but what you've got down you wouldn't keep a fly fed.'

There was no more to be got out of Pipkin, for either he didn't know or wouldn't tell. I learned only that I was being housed in a small chamber that had once been a private chapel in the manor, which, he told me, with a long-suffering sigh, was a good way from the kitchens and up a steep flight of stairs too.

I gnawed gratefully on the chicken leg after he'd lumbered out of the room. The pillow was unpleasantly wet, and cold, fatty broth does nothing to enhance the smell of sodden feathers, but that was the least of my concerns. I had plainly been here one night, maybe more, for it had been late afternoon when I'd spoken to Sylvain. The question was, how long would I remain and what exactly was Sylvain going to do with me when I was well, assuming that I did recover? But I soon gave up trying to think about it. Although I had not long been awake I found a great drowsiness creeping over me, a numbness that seemed to spread up from my feet. Before I could even begin to fight it, I had sunk into sleep again.

This was to be the pattern over the next few days, or was it weeks? I had no idea. I would wake to find that my bed linen or bandages had been changed, but had no recollection of it, save for vague snatches of distant voices, which might have been dreams. From time to time Pipkin arrived to feed me more broth, which I was managing to swallow without too much mess now that we had mastered the art of using the hollowed horn. I'd ask him questions, but his answers were so vague and rambling I could make nothing of them. Even Lugh was silent. Had they stolen him?

It was only when Pipkin was feeding me that I was convinced I was awake at all. Most of the time I was floating in some dark warm lake, or running through trees with flocks of ravens screaming after me, or wandering lost through a town, opening door after door only to find half-naked women with men's heads growing from their bellies trying to pull me in.

Then one day, I don't know how long after, I woke and for the first time there was nothing pressing on my eyes. I blinked and realised I could see light. Cautiously I moved my head. It took a while for my eyes to focus, but when they did I could see I was in a tiny circular chamber. There were no windows, and the only furniture was the bed on which I lay, a chair and a small table. A candle burned on what must have once been a stone altar of the chapel and by its light I could dimly make out a sun, moon and stars decorating the domed ceiling. The rest of the chamber had been painted white, though clearly not for some time: there was a patch of black mould at the bottom of the wall.

After gingerly touching my eyeballs several times to ensure they were firmly fixed in their sockets, I sat up. I regretted it at once, for I felt as if I was back on board the ship in a violent storm. The floor and walls were lurching up and down so violently, I thought I would vomit.

As I eased myself down, I realised I was using my right

hand. The cast was gone. There was no pain. Lying on my back I lifted it up to examine it. For one terrible moment I thought someone had cut off my own arm and sewn on the arm of some old man or even a dragon. The skin was scaly, disgusting. I almost tried to fling it away from me, as if it was some dead thing, but the fingers were moving and it was suddenly terribly itchy.

'The skin is thin. I advise you not to scratch it.'

The voice, coming out of nowhere, startled me so much I almost tumbled from the bed.

The latch on the door lifted and Sylvain entered.

'I will give you a soothing oil to rub on the arm. In a few days the skin will recover.'

I shrank back, pulling the blankets over my naked chest. How had he known what I was doing? Could he see through walls? It occurred to me that Sylvain could have been in many times while I was sleeping. He probably had been, if he'd removed the bandages and cast.

He handed me a beaker. 'Sip this slowly. You're doubtless thirsty and you look a little dizzy. It's only to be expected, after you've been lying here for so long.'

'How long have I been here? I haven't been able to tell day from night with my eyes covered.'

'Nor could you anyway, in here. There are no windows and the walls are so thick you cannot hear the church bells. It was built so that the one who prayed here would not be aware of the passage of time or of the world outside. When we reach into the higher planes, we pass beyond time. Only the body is governed by time, but that, too, I will change.'

I could tell that I wasn't going to get a straight answer from him. But in any case how long I'd been in the chamber

314

hardly mattered. The only thing that concerned me now was how quickly I could get out of there.

'Are you going to let me . . . am I free to leave?'

Sylvain walked slowly to the chair, drew it a little way from the bed and sat down before he answered.

'Why should I wish to detain you? I didn't ask you to come here. You came to me, Master Laurent, with a proposition. You wanted to construct a story that would satisfy the town's curiosity about me. So, when you have recovered your strength, I suggest you begin. There is only one condition – that you reside in my house as my guest until your task is completed. You have a habit of talking in your sleep, Master Laurent, and I suspect you are over-fond of good wine. Oh, don't worry, you will have all that you could wish to drink and eat, but in this way, if you begin to babble indiscreetly, it will be of no consequence.'

A tangled woolly fleece seemed to have taken the place of my brains and I was having immense trouble grasping what he said. But as the words slowly sank in, I began to realise he was offering me a job. Not only that, but I was to be entertained as his guest until I'd finished.

A distant part of me was screaming, Leave! Get out of here while you still can. He half blinded you, broke your arm. What might he do next? The man is dangerous, ruthless. Everyone warned you of that.

But he healed you. Tended you in his own house. He could have dumped you out on the road, left you to die there, and no one would have been the wiser. They'd believe you'd been set upon by robbers. Think of the money you could earn from this story and the comfortable living you'll enjoy while you compose it. You could spin this out for weeks.

315

But I can't think of a single word.

You will. You always do. He does not expect you to start until you are stronger.

Lugh! That was Lugh talking. I glanced round the small chamber. Then a glint of light caught my attention. Sylvain was holding the raven's head in his hands. I could have sworn they had been empty when he had sat down. But my head was so dulled, I couldn't be sure of anything.

He held the silver head up to the candlelight. 'Exquisite! And the symbols so cunningly concealed. The raven that flies in the night. The bird that flies without wings. As soon as I saw it I knew you had been sent to me. You must forgive my suspicious nature, Master Laurent. I have been wronged by so many men that I find it hard to trust anyone and see only greed and malice in every heart. I was angry when you came to me, thinking you were nothing more than a common blackmailer. But now I sec you came only with a desire to help me and I swear that your true intentions will be most fittingly rewarded.'

He rose and, crossing to the altar, placed the raven's head upon it beside the flickering candle. The silver turned to gold in the yellow light and flashes of scarlet seemed to light up each of the symbols so they burned brightly in the shadows. Then they became nothing more than tiny reflections of the candle flame.

'You will work in this chamber. Tomorrow I will have my servants bring you clothes, ink and parchment – all you require. You must be sure to tell them of anything you desire to make your stay more comfortable. In the day we will work, but in the evening we shall talk, you and I.' And before I could utter a word, he swept from the room.

I tried to convince myself that I was delighted. I had got

316

exactly what I wanted. But I couldn't squash the little worm of disquiet that was wriggling deep inside me. How long had I been lying in that chamber? I reached up to touch my beard. Its length might give me some clue. Only then did it penetrate my fuddled mind that my beard was gone. I'd been freshly shaved and even my hair was shorter now than when I had arrived, I was sure of that. I was more than a little annoyed. I'd been fond of that beard.

My eyes were beginning to adjust properly to the light now. I gazed back up at the dome of the heavens painted on the ceiling above. It was only then that I noticed something else in the painted sky, directly above the bed. The sun, moon and stars were positioned in swirls around some object in the centre, like angels clustered round the throne of God. But this was no throne, nor was it God. It was a shining glass flask, shaped like a tear, with something black suspended at its heart. Clutching the edge of the bed for support, I shuffled to the altar to fetch the candle and examine it more closely. With a jolt that set my heart pounding, I saw that the black object inside the flask was the head of a raven. Its beak was opened wide as if it cried out a warning, and from its mouth a long forked scarlet tongue quivered in the flickering candle flame, like a viper poised to strike.

Chapter 40

Dissolve the king or the queen in the red blood of children, then the sun and moon will take their bath in it, for this well is inexhaustible.

Sylvain is standing in the open doorway of the tower, waiting, as Gisa walks towards him across the garden from the door in the wall. Her shoes crush bitter chamomile and her skirts brush against the low hedges of sweet lavender and rosemary that frame the medicinal herbs. She doesn't know why she should be so conscious of these fragrances today, when she has walked this route so many times, but something has changed. She shivers, glancing up, as the early-morning sun vanishes behind a cloud that resembles a great dragon. An omen, but is it good or bad? She doesn't know.

She senses Sylvain's excitement even before she draws close. There is tension in his frame. His fingers flex and clench, as if his hands might drop to the ground and scuttle off by themselves.

'The raven who flies without wings in the blackness of the night and in the brightness of the day. It has begun! Death and life, corruption and resurrection, you will witness them all.' His lips are drawn back from his teeth in an exultant grin, but there is a fevered determination in his eyes, as you see in the eyes of the naked beggars who slash themselves with sharpened flints and scream that the world is ending.

'First there is something you must see. Come. Come!'

He grips her upper arm and marches her towards the manor house, but not to the path that leads across the garden to the Great Hall. Instead they turn the opposite way to the narrow turret built on the corner of the house. He leads her through the door and up a long spiral of stone steps, until they emerge into a bare chamber.

The walls of this room are painted with a dark landscape. On one side is a depiction of a tower, like Sylvain's tower in the grounds, only much higher. A menacing storm-cloud hangs above it and a bolt of lightning strikes down at its roof. The sky in the painting is swarming with flying beasts – dragons, griffins and birds of every kind. There are eagles and hawks, screeching swans and crows with human faces, while peacocks trail their magnificent tails over the ground below.

Naked figures, male and female, as tall as the tower itself, wander through a landscape of rocks and mountains. Some are twined with serpents, others lead lions. Corpses clamber out of tombs. Babies, dangling from the fists of warriors, are being slashed with swords and great arches of blood from their wounds spurt into wells that overflow and run in streams across the earth.

Gisa spins round, unable to make sense of any of it. It must be a depiction of the Last Judgment, yet which are the righteous souls and which the sinners? Where is the throne of God and His angels? Here, Heaven and Hell have sprung up on earth and are at war.

But Sylvain ignores the paintings and eagerly beckons her over to the far wall, pointing to a squint hole. Putting his finger to his lips, he motions her to peer through. She is staring into a circular chamber. A man lies in a bed, his eyes closed, his hands limp. A linen sheet is drawn halfway up his bare chest, which rises and falls in deep sleep. Soft yellow candlelight glints on his golden hair. He looks familiar, but there is something odd about him too.

With a jolt she suddenly realises it is Laurent. But he is clean-shaven now. That is what looks so strange. The lower half of his face is paler than the tanned skin of his cheeks and forehead. She turns, her mouth open to speak, but Sylvain shakes his head warningly. She puts her eye to the hole again, unable to resist another glance. Laurent's lips are slightly parted and his eyelids flutter, as if his eyes beneath are looking at things she cannot see.

She'd thought him long gone. Has he been lying here all this past week? Each morning and evening she has walked below this blind room without even knowing it existed, much less that he was in it. It is as if she has looked into the solid rock of a mountain and seen a new world hidden inside it. But why is he sleeping at this hour? Is he ill?

Sylvain lets her watch for a few moments more, then pulls her away and leads her back down the stairs and out into the grounds. She can feel his gaze on her face. What is he trying to read there?

'Master Laurent is staying here. He is undertaking some work for me. You will enjoy his company, I think. But such pleasures cannot interrupt our work. Perhaps one evening you might wish to stay after we have finished to sup with Laurent . . .'

He says no more. Does not ask her for an answer or specify a day. The suggestion merely hangs in the air for her to pluck or not.

They reach the tower and she steps aside so that he might enter ahead of her, for he is her master.

He stands close to her, always too close. 'Today all I have striven for will be set in motion, like the first trickle of water that turns the mighty wheel of the mill and then the stones begin to grind. I must prepare myself, cleanse myself. You will help me.'

He closes the door of the tower, plunging them into deep shadow. She hears the key grate in the door. He is locking them in. Panic rises in her and she has to stop herself yelling at him to unfasten the door. What does he mean to do?

Brushing past her, he bends down and tugs at an iron ring recessed into the third step of the wooden stairs, a ring she has never noticed before in the gloom of the chamber. The three lower steps lift upwards, like a trapdoor, revealing a hole that glows red as if a great fire burns beneath their feet, but there is no heat. A wave of cold, damp air rolls up from the shaft beneath. Sylvain beckons to her and, as she inches closer, she sees a set of wooden steps descending into the maw below. For a terrible moment she fears he is going to shut her down there. She backs towards the door even though she knows it is locked and the key hangs about Sylvain's neck. But without even glancing at her, he edges down the staircase, calling her to follow, and she does. She dare not refuse.

The chamber beneath is round and small, the floor made of beaten earth, the walls rough stone. Four candles burn on spikes on the walls above her head, each flame shielded by a translucent blood-red stone, which she recognises as dragon's blood. The red light is so dim she cannot see the expression on Sylvain's face, only the glitter of his eyes.

In the centre of the chamber there is a long stone trough,

like a coffin, almost covered over with a slab of stone, which has been pulled away from one end. She can see the glint of water inside, or she *thinks* it is water. It is hard to tell in the ruby light.

Sylvain faces her across the trough. 'I must descend into the first death. I must be cleansed. It has taken weeks to prepare the *aqua vitae*, the water of life that springs from death, the water of the flood that drowned the boy. It has been distilled many times over, till there is nothing left of his body. Only the pure essence of his spirit remains. Now you must add the drops of the distillations you prepared from the moon plants you gathered the first day you came to me. The essence of the moon, gathered by a virgin, added to the death of innocence.'

She does not understand. Who has drowned? Where did the boy drown? Peter swims into her thoughts, but he is not drowned, though daily she fears it. Besides, Sylvain does not know about Peter. He speaks in riddles. These are just words, symbols like *grey wolf* and the *green dragon devouring the sun.*

He hands her the flask. 'Pour it all in.'

She hesitates. This is too simple. Surely he brought her down here to do more than this. As she tips the liquid into the stone trough, Sylvain unfastens the neck of his robe and pulls it over his head. She gives a little cry of alarm for he is naked beneath. Her hands shake as she empties the last drops. She can see almost nothing of his wrinkled body in the dim light, but still she looks away, ashamed, embarrassed, fearful that he will force her to undress too. And what then? What then will he do to her?

'When I am inside you must pull the lid into place so that it covers the stone coffin. Then you must wait with

322

me. Whatever you see or hear, you must not be alarmed. It is the cleansing and I must endure it. When the last candle has burned away and extinguishes itself, you will push back the lid and release me. But not before then, however much I might scream and beg you to let me out, for I must pass through the terror. But if you do not release me as soon as the last flame dies, I shall drown.'

He places his hands about her small neck, massaging her throat with his thumbs. She shudders at his touch and the closeness of his naked body, the stench of stale urine on his skin.

'See how much I trust you, little swan. I am putting my very life in your hands.'

She jerks away. 'What if I cannot move the lid? Odo is far stronger.'

'Only a woman, a *virgin*, may do this.'

She can feel his stare on her body, as if he is peeling away the layers, stripping off her clothes, her skin, and burrowing deep inside her to assure himself she is still a virgin.

She turns her face away as he grasps the edge of the trough. She hears the sharp intake of his breath as the icy water touches his skin. She hears the water slap against the stone as he eases himself down inside the coffin.

'The lid.'

She does not want to see his eyes staring up at her out of the blood-red water. She goes to the far end and pushes the lid forward. Although it is heavy, it slides easily, as if the surfaces have been greased. It fits perfectly, seals stone to stone.

The red light flickers in the chamber, making the stones of the wall undulate, as if they, too, are liquid. She longs to run up into the light and air, even though she knows she cannot escape the tower. But she cannot see how thick the candles are through the shards of dragon's blood to determine how long they might burn. Suppose they go out while she is upstairs? Suppose she cannot open the stone coffin again? Panic seizes her and she wants to drag the lid off at once, just to be sure that he is not already drowning. But the fear of his wrath stays her hand.

She can hear voices, faint murmurs, snatches of words, as if people are passing by outside the tower. She cannot understand what they are saying. The muttering grows louder, and she realises that what she can hear is not coming from above her but through the walls around her, as if a great crowd is crawling through the earth towards the cellar.

The muttering gives way to discordant shrieks and moans. Dull echoing thuds shake the walls, as if bones are being struck violently against the stones, as if the dead are trying to break through the walls. Terrified, Gisa races up the stairs, but before she can reach the top, the three steps above her fall back into place with a crash and the staircase is plunged into instant darkness. She pushes and pushes against the wood above, but it will not yield.

Behind her the din stops abruptly and in the same breath, the first candle is extinguished.

Using the wall to guide her, Gisa edges down the stairs, feeling for each one with her foot until she reaches the bottom steps, which are illuminated by the glow of the candles inside the chamber. Something is moving on the dark earth floor. It is liquid, thick, glowing in the red light. Water is seeping up through the floor, creeping up the walls. It will rise and rise until it fills the chamber. It will flood the stairs. She is trapped!

She turns to try again to open the trapdoor above her

and then, at the edge of her vision, she sees the liquid is forming itself into a ring about the chamber, a ring of quicksilver. It swells and a great silver head rises from it, with huge black eyes and a long viper's tongue that flickers in and out, tasting the air. The snake slithers towards the stone coffin, wrapping its coils around it, squeezing until the edges of the stones begin to splinter.

The second candle goes out, leaving a wisp of smoke. The snake vanishes.

The creaking of a rope makes her look up. A naked man is hanging from a noose above the stone coffin. He is struggling to free himself, gasping and wheezing, trying to force his fingers behind the rope biting into his neck, but he cannot loosen it. He spins round, thrashing on the rope, his eyes bulging, his face swollen purple and black in the red light. His features are so distorted she cannot recognise him, but yet she knows him. She searches desperately for some means of cutting him down. She scrambles on top of the stone coffin, trying to reach him, to lift his legs, support his body, but as her fingers almost touch him, he is jerked upwards out of her reach. She stares up into the dark dome. She cannot see what he is hanging from. It is as if she is staring down into the deepest well.

Then she hears a scuttling, the sound of a hundred sharp claws. The rope is alive with mice that swarm down it and over the choking man. He opens his mouth to scream but no sound comes out except a dreadful gurgling. He is thrashing, trying to fling the mice off, but they are eating him alive, stripping the flesh from his limbs and face. Gisa shrinks back in horror. There is nothing she can do to help him.

The third candle is snuffed out. The space above her is empty.

The chamber is almost in darkness. The single flame cannot push back the shadows as they flood towards it. Gisa bends to lower herself off the coffin and onto the ground. Then she freezes. Something is standing on the stairs, where the shadows are deepest. It moves, unfolds, rises up. Two bat-like wings open like a cloak, revealing a woman's body with great pendulous dugs and a swollen belly. Her long hair whips and writhes about her head as if she is being buffeted by a violent wind. The woman slowly lifts her head to gaze at Gisa. Her face is gaunt as a skull, and a black fire blazes in the sockets of her eyes. Her wings flex, their leathery skin rasping on the stones behind. She opens her mouth and shrieks in fury, the scream so high-pitched that Gisa thinks her ears bleed. The wings beat wildly as if the creature means to fly at the girl. Gisa throws herself from the stone coffin and crouches on the floor, cowering against the wall, her eyes clenched shut, her hands over her ears, as a whirlwind rages around her.

The chamber is plunged into perfect darkness. The air is still and silent.

Gisa remains on the floor, too afraid to move, too afraid that the woman might still be in the chamber somewhere, waiting like a bird of prey for the slightest sound, the tiniest movement and then it will pounce.

All the candles are extinguished. She must move. She must find her way to the stone coffin or Sylvain will drown. Maybe he is already dead. But she cannot leave him. She cannot get out of the tower without him. What if she cannot open the trapdoor? No one knows where she is. No one will hear her calling. No one came running when that woman screamed.

She listens for the rasp of those wings. She hears only

326

the beating of her own heart, the clawing of her own breath. She drops to her knees, one hand outstretched, feeling for the stone of the coffin. She crawls through darkness. She crawls for what seems like an eternity. And still she cannot touch it.

Chapter 41

It is the body which retains the soul and the soul can shew its power only when it is united to the body.

Finding my beard had been shaved off without so much as a by-your-leave annoyed me. I'd been proud of that beard. It had taken long enough to sprout and there were times, when I was growing up, that I feared it never would come in, despite the copious amounts of bears' grease I rubbed into my chin to encourage it. But I knew it was common for physicians to prescribe cutting off a patient's hair to conserve their strength or stop their brain becoming fevered. Perhaps it was the same with beards, and at least they hadn't shaved my head.

But they had shaved something else! Something I only discovered when I eased myself out of bed to use the piss-pot. I hadn't looked before. I'd had no reason to, so it wasn't until I put my hands to my cock to point it in the direction of the pot that I felt a very short prickle of stubble where for several years there had been a bush of coarse hair. I stared down, but there was no mistaking it: I had been shaved all around my cods. The thought of which of them might have done it made me blush hot and shudder at the same time. Sylvain, Odo and Pipkin. I didn't know whose hands I least wanted fumbling around that very delicate part of me with a sharp razor. Had Sylvain ordered it, not wanting to take the risk of me bringing lice or crabs into his bed? I must say I was more than a little affronted.

I searched the room for the clothes I'd been wearing when I arrived, but there was no sign of them. Perhaps they'd been taken to be washed and mended, which was at least a courtesy of sorts, though after all those weeks I'd been lying in bed surely they'd been laundered by now. Unless, of course, Sylvain had had them burned, thinking they were lousy too.

A long loose scarlet robe hung over the chair next to the bed, with linens and a pair of leather shoes. I could only assume they were intended for me to wear, and when I reluctantly dragged them on, I was forced to admit I'd never before worn woollen cloth that was so fine and soft. But I wasn't accustomed to a long robe – at least, not since I'd disguised myself as a woman in Ricey-Bas – and I was sure I was going to trip over.

I was barely dressed when I heard a fumbling at the door. I expected it to be Sylvain, but it was old Pipkin. I recognised his voice and the smell of the stale fat, blood and onion that wafted before him, like a page announcing his arrival even before he was fully in the room. I'd half a mind to ask him who'd shaved me so intimately, but I decided I really didn't want to know.

It was the first time I'd actually seen Pipkin, for he'd not come to the chamber since my eye bandages were removed. I discovered he was indeed as rotund as an ale-barrel, as he'd claimed, with at least three chins, though goodness knows how many more he might have secreted beneath the neck of that grimy tunic. What I hadn't pictured was that he was as bald as a hardboiled egg, or that his eyes wandered, quite of their own accord, in different directions, as if they'd quarrelled bitterly and were determined to have nothing more to do with each other.

'Good to see you on your feet,' he said cheerfully. 'At least I won't be having to cook up any more of those broths, or feed you like an old gammer.'

He set down half a loaf of bread, a jug of wine and a whole roasted pheasant. My head was clearer now. But how long had I been asleep this time?

'Is this dinner or supper, Pipkin?'

He shook his head, amazed at my stupidity. 'Noon bell's only just rung. Why would you be wanting your supper now?'

He gazed hungrily at the roasted pheasant, which glistened under the lard, honey and spices with which it had been lavishly basted. A little stream of saliva trickled from the corner of his mouth.

I pushed the platter towards him. 'I won't eat all of this.'

Actually, I was so hungry I could easily have devoured it all for I felt as if I'd had nothing solid in my belly for weeks, but I was willing to sacrifice a little meat in the hope of winkling some information from him.

He didn't wait to be asked twice but, drawing up the chair, lowered his great hams onto the groaning wood. He took out a sharp knife, sliced off a large chunk of pheasant, and began gnawing at it, like a bishop devouring the first meat after the Lenten fast.

I pulled off a leg and sank my teeth into it. It tasted even better than it smelt. 'I suppose the baron's ancestors built this place,' I said casually.

I knew it was no use asking direct questions about Sylvain, but I reckoned Pipkin might just give something away if I crept round the subject.

330

Pipkin waved a pheasant bone in the air while he swallowed the mouthful he was chewing. 'Not his family, it weren't. But the master's been here a good long time, over thirty years or more, I reckon. It was afore the abbey were built anyway. I reckon Father Arthmael only came here 'cause of the master . . . seems they knew each other years before.

'But the master was none too pleased to see his old friend here at first, that I can tell you. Tried every which way to get the building stopped, but the abbot was determined. Then, a few years after, something changed. I couldn't fathom it. The master started paying calls on Father Arthmael, spending half the night at that abbey, like they was blood brothers. But I dunno,' Pipkin wiped a rivulet of grease from his chin and frowned, 'those two always put me in mind of two beggars I saw once. One of 'em blind, the other'd no hands. Fought like two cats in a sack, each convinced the other was cheating him, but stuck together 'cause they couldn't do without each other.'

'I can't imagine Sylvain having much time for a saintly abbot,' I said. I was about to add it was as likely a friendship as Lucifer and the Archangel Michael sharing a jug of ale, but I stopped myself. I didn't want that remark getting back to my not-so-genial host.

Pipkin chuckled. 'I doubt you'll find many in these parts who'd call Father Arthmael *saint*. He's another who keeps his place locked up tighter than a castle under siege. The White Canons go out teaching and preaching, but no one ever goes in. They don't let pilgrims or travellers stay there. I heard one time . . .'

Pipkin paused and leaned forward as far as his great belly would allow. I thought at first he wanted to be sure we were not overheard, but it was to pour himself a good measure of wine.

'You were saying about the White Canons,' I prompted him, as he hacked yet more meat from the bird.

'Queer lot.' Pipkin shook his head dolefully. 'All these different orders squabble like cocks on a dung heap, thinking their way's right. I've known monks to draw swords on each other afore now, but generally if a friar or monk is passing through, no matter what his order, they'll always offer him a place in their guest hall and a bite to eat. Leastways, that what's my cousin says – he's a Benedictine. Keep a good table, they do, unlike some.

'But he told me two of his brothers were coming this way in the middle of winter. It came on to snow so hard that if there'd been a black dog standing not a hand's length from them they'd not have seen him. So, finding themselves close to Langley Abbey, they ride up and ask for shelter for the night. The gatekeeper tells them they've no room. I ask you, how can there be no room in a place that size?

'"We'll sleep in the stables with the horses then," the Benedictines say. "Any place to shelter out of the snow."

'Quick as a ferret down a rabbit warren, the gatekeeper comes back at him, "We've a fever among some of the brothers. The infirmarer says no one's to be admitted for fear of the contagion."

'Well, you'd have thought he'd have told them that straight off, if it were true, wouldn't you?' Pipkin said, pausing to take another bite. 'The Benedictines were too afeared of blundering into the marsh in the snow to try to make it to the town, so they ended up sleeping in some riverman's cottage. And they were none too happy about that, I can tell you, for their own pigs are given better fare than the riverman could offer them. They don't let a fellow monk in, yet my master's round there day and night. Makes no sense, does it?'

'You make no sense, you old fool.'

The hunk of pheasant in Pipkin's hand shot out of his greasy fingers with such force it hit the wall opposite. He lumbered to his feet, as Odo barged into the room, carrying a small sloped writing box under one arm and a narrow table to stand it on under the other. He set both down as Pipkin blundered towards the door.

'You know what the master says about gossiping,' Odo growled. 'If he heard you, he'd rip your tongue out and kick your fat arse out of the gate for good.'

'And what do you think he'd say if he knew about the whore you sneak in here when he goes off to the abbey?' Pipkin retorted.

'I've never brought a whore in here, you dung-brained scullion!' Odo's great hands clenched into fists and he took a menacing step towards Pipkin who, I discovered, could vacate a room with a surprising turn of speed for such a stout man. 'As if I'd keep company with a whore,' Odo muttered furiously. 'Anyway, he can talk. The goats get nervous whenever they see him, and I don't mean just when he's a knife in his hand.'

But from the guilty flush that had turned his face an unbecoming puce, it was evident that, whore or not, Odo was smuggling some female or other into the manor when his master's back was turned. I'd have to remember that. You never knew when these little secrets could be turned to good use.

Evidently still seething, he gestured towards the writing box. 'Master says all you need for your writing is in there.'

333

He strode from the room, still muttering away to himself furiously. Cooks as talented as Pipkin were hard to come by, so I only hoped that he'd found some place to conceal himself out of sight until Odo's temper had cooled.

I opened the writing box to find rolls of new parchment, bundles of uncut quills, a quill knife, pots of dried gall-inks and small dishes on which to mix them. Sylvain did indeed know exactly what was required. I doubted that my former master, Philippe, would have had the faintest idea what a scribe needed, even after all his years of dictating his letters to Gaspard, any more than he would have known what ingredients went into the dishes he demanded from his cook.

Still hungry, I picked over what little meat Pipkin had left on the bird and devoured the bread. Fortunately there was still a good measure of wine left, and I sipped it as I tried to think of a story. Sylvain was in the habit of going to the abbey. So . . . he might be a secret monk, a holy man . . . No, that wouldn't do. If what Pipkin had said was true, then the townsfolk were as suspicious of the White Canons at the abbey as they were of Sylvain.

It was no good. The air in the windowless chamber was stale and heavy with candle fumes. My eyes were already aching from peering through the dull light. The room smelt musty and little wonder: I could have sworn the small patch of black mould I'd noticed near the base of the wall when my bandages had been removed had more than doubled in size. Either I'd slept longer than I thought, or else my memory was still far from clear. I needed to see daylight, breathe some fresh air.

I tried the door, convinced it would be locked, but as I lifted the latch it swung open without so much as a squeak or groan, which somewhat unnerved me. The hinges had been well oiled and the wood too. No wonder Sylvain had been able to enter my chamber without waking me. But that little jolt was nothing to the one I received when I saw what lay on the other side of my chamber.

The room was bare, save for a painted landscape that ran right round the walls. Some of the figures were similar to those on the chalice I'd seen in the Great Hall, but as I wandered round I began to notice other creatures too, which were disquietingly familiar – a lion, a swan and a scorpion – the same symbols that were hidden in Lugh's feathers. The very ones that had made the silversmith thrust the raven's head back at me in such alarm. But I still couldn't understand why. Such images were common on shields and crests. Even in churches it was not unusual for the painter to work animals and objects into the biblical scenes that made some punning reference to their patron's ancestors or deeds.

Now, there was a thought. Maybe I could get an idea for a story about Sylvain from these walls. I wandered around them several times, but soon thought better of it. If any bishop or townsman saw these images of two-headed people and dismembered corpses, they'd more than likely drag Sylvain out and hang him on the spot.

I tried the door on the opposite side of the chamber and discovered that it, too, was unlocked. It opened onto a spiral staircase. Holding up the skirts of my robe, I descended gingerly, partly because I was still dizzy, but also because at any moment I expected to encounter Odo or Sylvain himself. But there was no sign of either. Perhaps Odo was too busy chasing Pipkin around the kitchen with a meat cleaver. I supposed there must be other servants – a place this size could hardly be maintained by two men – but as yet I'd neither seen nor heard any others.

I emerged through a low, narrow doorway into some well-kept gardens, with trees and a herb plot, neatly bordered with low hedges of lavender and rosemary. A dead rabbit lay on a stone a few yards away, maggots swarming over its gaping belly. A cat or fox must have dragged it there.

But I had taken no more than a step outside when the door to what I took to be the Great Hall opened. I drew back hastily. A man clad in a long white robe strode towards the tower that dominated the grounds. His head was down and he seemed deep in thought. I guessed this to be the infamous Father Arthmael. I hastily retreated behind the turret door, fearing that if Sylvain was looking out of his tower he would see right across the garden to where I stood. I wasn't sure if I was permitted to wander outside and I didn't want to give him any excuse for locking me in. I huddled just inside the door, leaving it open a crack so that I could watch the abbot enter the tower. With luck, Father Arthmael would keep Sylvain occupied, leaving me free to explore.

Father Arthmael turned the great iron ring in the tower door, but it didn't open. He tried again, this time setting his shoulder to it. He banged and called Sylvain's name. Then he bent down to examine a basket that lay on the threshold. Picking up the skirts of his robe, he ran back across the grass towards the house. This time I could hear him calling for Odo, who came charging out of the house, like a bull stung by a bee.

'The door is locked,' Father Arthmael shouted to him. 'And the basket of food has not been touched. Sylvain always comes down for it when the noon bell strikes and it is long past that. I fear there may have been an accident.'

They hastened back to the door.

Odo was fumbling with a bunch of keys that dangled on a great iron ring from his belt. As soon as the key had turned in the lock, Father Arthmael gestured to him to stand aside and rushed in. Odo hesitated, peering in through the open door and calling out several times, but not entering. It was quite some time before anyone emerged. Father Arthmael came out backside first, and bending low. It wasn't until he swung round that I saw he had his hands under Sylvain's armpits and was dragging him. Sylvain was naked except for a black robe that had been hastily tied around his hips. Blood-stained water dripped from his corpse-pale limbs.

Odo crouched down and, with Father Arthmael's help, managed to hoist Sylvain over his shoulder. The man's head and arms dangled limp as a dead rabbit. Odo set off towards the house, staggering slightly under the weight, with Father Arthmael scurrying behind.

I stood at the foot of the stairs, not knowing what to do. Should I follow them or scuttle back up to my chamber and pretend I'd never left it? I was on the point of doing just that when I heard a cry and saw Gisa running from the tower. She managed to get as far as the nearest apple tree, when her legs crumpled beneath her and she collapsed to the ground.

Chapter 42

Nigredo: the Black Death — All flesh that is derived from the earth must be decomposed and reduced again to the earth which it formerly was.

Gisa feels the hand touching her shoulder, then withdrawing just as suddenly, as if its owner doesn't know whether to lift her up or not.

'Did you faint?'

'No,' she snaps, indignant at the very idea.

She's seen her aunt swoon dramatically on numerous occasions and always swore she would never do something so silly. But she is more angry with herself than the questioner, because she knows she came close to it. She lifts her head and finds herself staring at the young man, who only that morning – was it only that morning? – she had seen lying on the bed in that hidden chamber. She can only stare at him. After such horror, her mind cannot seem to grasp what he is doing here.

She pushes herself up until she is sitting, her knees drawn up. She is dismayed to find that she is so shaky she cannot trust herself to stand.

Laurent crouches down, peering anxiously at her. 'Sylvain, is he dead? . . . Was there an accident?'

She rubs her eyes. The light is cruelly bright after the utter darkness. 'Accident? No, there was no accident. It . . .'

She cannot think of a word, a phrase, even a whole book, that would give a name to what she has just witnessed, that would begin to explain the terror of not being able to find the stone coffin, of not being able to open the lid, and when she did, hearing no sound, no splashing, no breathing. Having to grope in the darkness for the gap, plunge her hand into the icy water and feel for his cold face beneath. All that time not knowing if the creature from Hell was behind her, creeping towards her as she reached out to Sylvain.

Then the utter relief as the stairs lifted and the precious grey light washed in. One of the White Canons had come pounding down the staircase. He'd heaved the stone lid wider and dragged Sylvain out, his wet body flopping heavily onto the earth floor. The light filtering down the spiral staircase was not enough to see much, save that Sylvain's eyes were wide open as if he was staring at some great horror above. Gisa had glanced up, fearing the hanged man was still dangling above her.

The canon had curtly demanded she hand him Sylvain's robe, which he had tied hastily about the man's loins, but not before Gisa had glimpsed . . . It had been covered so fast she must surely have been mistaken . . . Even now, as she buries her face in her knees, she is fighting to make sense of what her eyes saw, or what she thinks they saw, in that dangerous and deceptive half-light, yet at the same time trying to banish the image from her head.

And the blood in the water . . . Was it Sylvain's? Somehow in her head it merges with the blood on the face of the little boy trapped beneath the stone wall. Is she remembering him? Maybe spending so long in the red light of those candles has confused her eyes into seeing a film of blood covering everything.

339

Laurent touches her again on the back of her bent neck and her head jerks up. He looks contrite at having startled her. Awkwardly he extends his hand and she allows him to pull her up. Then, though she is grateful for the touch of his warm hand enveloping hers, though she wants to cling to him and blurt out the whole nightmare, she immediately pulls her hand free. She stares at a small frog that sits camouflaged against the mottled grass, only the flick of a tongue betraying it as it catches a mayfly. It gulps, but the hair-thin legs of the fly still thrash between its lips.

The door opens and Odo comes striding across the garden. He looks anxious, then relieved to see them standing there. Holding one of the massive keys on his chain straight ahead of him, as if he was charging into battle with a pike, he hurries past them and, with evident relief, slams the door of the tower shut and locks it. He ambles back.

'Will he live?' Laurent asks.

Odo nods. 'Already sitting up. Father Arthmael's tending him.'

'Am I . . .' Gisa stammers. 'Did he say if I was to go?'

In her mind it is not a question, but a desperate prayer for release. She cannot return to the tower, not today, please not today.

Odo looks at her with the same expression of contempt at her stupidity he always wears, if ever he is forced to speak to her. 'Didn't you see me lock the tower? But I'll ask if he has any orders for you before you go. Wait here.'

They watch him saunter back towards the door to the hall. Gisa glances up at Laurent, then quickly looks away before he notices.

'You've been staying here—'

'What happened in there—'

They both speak at the same time, then, with embarrassed smiles, both gesture for the other to continue.

'I thought you only came to deliver a message and you had a ship waiting in port,' Gisa says.

Laurent looks bemused, then seems to remember. 'That's right, but I had an accident . . . in the Great Hall. Sylvain . . . I slipped, broke my arm and injured my eyes. Didn't Sylvain mention it? Been lying up there these many weeks while my arm mended.' He gestures vaguely in the direction of the windowless room. 'My ship will have long sailed by now, so Sylvain has asked me to stay on to help him with some documents.'

'Weeks?' It's Gisa who frowns now. 'I only spoke to you a few days ago, on the road outside the gate . . . when you asked me to persuade my master to see you.'

But after all that her eyes and ears have been tricked into seeing and hearing today, she cannot be certain of anything. She's heard stories of demons disguising themselves as young men to trick maidens into selling their souls to the devil. Is he the seventh magpie? No, he is all too human, a man who is mocking her, trying to make her look foolish. Yet when she glances up at him, it is not ridicule she sees in his face but confusion.

He stares down at his right arm, pressing it with his left hand, feeling the bones. 'It must be far longer than that. I admit I was sleeping much of the time, but my arm was set in a cast, couldn't move it. Broken bones don't knit in days, do they? Unless there's a miracle. I mean, the abbot said he'd pray for me, but I didn't actually believe . . . Are you quite sure it was only a few days ago? Easy to forget when you last saw someone.'

Someone, yes, Gisa thinks, a customer coming into the

shop, a beggar in the marketplace, but not you. Not you. I've looked for you every morning and evening since you vanished. But she doesn't say any of this. She casts around, trying to think.

'Look. You remember you gave me a ball of cowslips. See there, by the strawberries, the cowslips are still in bloom and the strawberries are only just beginning to flower. If weeks had passed the flowers on both would be over by now.'

'But I don't understand . . . how . . .'

She glances to where he is looking and sees the great hulk of Odo lumbering towards them.

'Odo, how long—' Laurent begins.

Suddenly she is afraid for him. This is a question that must not be asked.

'How long will it be before the master is fit to work again?' she interrupts quickly.

Odo does not appear to notice the startled look Laurent gives her.

'I'm his steward, not his physician. Master pleases himself when he works.' Odo stares morosely at Laurent. 'He says you're to return to your chamber – he's too tired to have you join him for supper tonight. He'll have meat sent up. As for you, girl, you're to come tomorrow same as usual. Father Arthmael has a task for you. The abbot'll be here to instruct you himself in the morning.'

Limp with relief, Gisa stumbles towards the gate in the wall. Only her trembling legs prevent her running to it and pounding on it to be let out. Even though they are in the garden, she feels that the walls are closing in. But as she turns, Odo shoots out a massive hand and grips her arm, his fingers and thumb completely encircling the slender limb. 'Master says I'm to give you this, a gift for your services today.' Odo's mouth curls in a sneer as if he is picturing exactly what kind of services a young girl might perform for an old man. 'Says I'm to tell you to take heed of its meaning, *girl.*'

Odo thrusts a small package at her, wrapped in a woollen cloth. It is heavy, too heavy to be another brooch. Gisa wants to throw it to the ground and run, but the manservant stands in front of her. Plainly, he has no intention of opening the gate to the world beyond until she has unwrapped it and he is satisfied she has understood. Reluctantly Gisa peels back the cloth with thumb and forefinger to reveal a finely carved and painted wooden sculpture of a delicate white rose lying across a plump peach, which bears a single green leaf. Both Gisa and Laurent stare down at it.

'A peach and a leaf, the heart and the tongue,' Laurent whispers.

'Truth and silence,' Gisa finishes. 'And the white rose for secrecy.'

'Take that as a warning, girl,' Odo says. 'A warning to both of you.'

Chapter 43

Albedo: the Whitening — The unclean body must be burned in water and washed in fire . . . kill the living and resuscitate the dead.

Regulus lowers his head as close as he can to the table, glancing sideways at Father John from under his mop of red hair. The priest eats slowly, lifting the slivers of meat to his mouth, while all the time his gaze marches up and down the double row of boys. But they are all quiet today, subdued, minding their manners. For there is an empty place on the bench, a boy who is not eating his supper, a boy who is locked in the carcer, and no one wants to give Father John the slightest excuse for sending him to join the miscreant.

As it is, two boys stand at the end of the room taking it in turns to read. Usually the boy reading has his dinner or supper saved for him, but these boys gaze with hungry eyes and rumbling bellies at the food on the table and know they will go to bed hungry for their crimes, but at least they will go to bed. Felix will not. It is their fault. They neglected to sweep the room properly, left crumbs under the table, which attracted the mice. But Felix is held most to blame. It is he who should have made them do it.

Father John is in a worse humour than usual, has been ever since the morning the boys woke up and discovered that, like Mighel, little Peter was also missing from his

344

bed. But Peter's parents had not come for him, death had. An inflammation of the bowel, Father John told them, though Peter had not seemed sick when he lay down to sleep. But, like Father John, God strikes swiftly and without warning.

'*Noctem quietam et finem perfectum concedat nobis Dominus omnipotens*,' Father Arthmael had intoned into the dark shadows at Compline that night, as he did every night. *May Almighty God grant a peaceful night and a perfect death.* But Peter had not had a peaceful night. He'd been taken. He'd walked out of the door with Death's hand on his shoulder.

Father Madron had buried Peter's corpse in the far corner of the orchard before dawn, and after Prime the boys were made to march in solemn procession to the place, holding candles, and watch as Father Arthmael sprinkled the raw mound of soil with holy water. Regulus wondered if the dead crept close together under the earth, holding each other, afraid of the dark. Once there was a boy called Wilky who used to snuggle close to his brothers under the blankets, pressing into their bodies to get warm.

But Regulus is not thinking of Wilky or Peter now. He is listening hard to the reading, waiting for the reader to stumble. He will, sooner or later, he must. Regulus is willing him to falter. The boy's tongue trips over a word. Father John turns his head in irritation, slaps his birch rod down upon the table to bring the reader to a halt. He orders him to repeat the whole page again, pronouncing the Latin correctly, unless he wants the rod to fall on him.

Regulus is ready the moment Father John's attention is diverted. He flips his meat down onto a rag he has laid on his lap. The rag is not clean, indeed some might consider it only fit for an arse-wipe, but Regulus doesn't notice such things. Besides, it was all he could find. The reader's next mistakes sees first bread and then cheese join the meat in Regulus's lap, before he makes a clumsy knot and stuffs it inside his robe.

If the others notice, they say nothing. As long as Regulus takes only his own share, what does it matter to them? Besides, Father John is apt to punish both the talebearer and the sinner in equal measure. *Let him who is without sin . . .* he sternly reminds them. Father John himself must be entirely spotless for he casts many a stone.

Regulus wedges the parcel between his stomach and the edge of the table during grace, so he can fold his hands in the manner on which Father John insists.

They have an hour, the canon reminds them, an hour to walk quietly in the fresh air without disturbing the sleeping brothers. Then he expects to return and find them hard at work at their copy tablets by the last chime of the bell. He withdraws and the boys peer through the door until they see the skirts of his robe whisk round the corner. Heaving a collective sigh of relief, they run out into the sunshine with the ball they have woven out of willow sticks, but Regulus does not join them.

He waits until they are pushing and shoving to get posses-sion of the ball, then slips away, following the line of the building round the side. He jerks back as he almost trips over a canon who is kneeling on the flags, peering into one of the drainage holes. The canon pulls back his sleeve and thrusts his arm deep into the drain as if he is searching for something he has lost. As he straightens up, wiping his hand on the grass, Regulus sees it is Father Madron. But he does not pause to wonder what the young canon is searching for,

346

only silently begs him to move on, which, to Regulus's abject relief, he does, vanishing around the corner.

Swiftly, knowing Father Madron might return without warning, Regulus edges along the building until he finds the long narrow iron grille set near the base of the wall. He kneels down. Felix is sitting at the bottom of the hole, his arms wrapped around his legs, his face buried in his knees. He is naked. Even from the top, where Regulus kneels above the hole, the place feels damp and chill, for it lies in perpetual shadow. It will be colder tonight, much colder.

'Felix, Felix,' Regulus whispers. The older boy looks up, his face is smeared with dirt and what look like tears, but they cannot be. Felix never cries.

'Go away. Leave me alone,' Felix says fiercely. 'If they catch you speaking to me they'll put you down here too.'

'Don't care,' Regulus says, and he doesn't. He'd rather be with Felix than sleeping unprotected in that dorter.

'Well, I do,' Felix whispers. 'I'm squashed enough as it is. Don't want you in here too, pissing all over me. And they'll keep me down here even longer, 'cause if you talk to me that'll be my fault too.'

Regulus hadn't thought of that. 'I'll go, but I brought you some food,' he says hastily.

He pushes and squeezes the bulging rag through the bars and Felix catches it. He deftly unwraps it, as indifferent as Regulus to the state of the rag. His face breaks into a grin.

'How did you get this?' He frowns slightly. 'Not your dinner, is it? Don't want you going hungry for me.'

'Course it isn't,' Regulus says. 'I'm full to bursting.' But even as he says it, he hears his belly rumbling. 'I stole it,' he adds proudly.

'Ought to call you the fox, not the wren. Now get out

347

of here.' Felix crams a slice of meat into his mouth. 'And don't come back, you hear me?' he says thickly, through the mouthful. 'I don't want to see your daft face again.'

Crestfallen, Regulus flattens himself against the wall, and starts to edge back along it.

'You're a good 'un,' Felix whispers, and Regulus beams.

Chapter 44

Citrinitas: the Yellow Death – Here Sol is buried and ferments and is overflowed with mercurius philosophorum.

A fierce wind has sprung up, shaking and rattling every byre and tree, like a wilful child. Unfastened doors and shutters slam themselves to splinters. Branches, made rotten by frost and winter's rain, come crashing down. The few birds that venture from their roosts to battle through the grey skies are tossed about like leaves.

Gisa stares fearfully at the heavy grey sky. Will it rain? Will the water streaming from roofs and paving slabs come gushing out of that hole, sweeping a chill flood over that narrow ledge? Peter's strength is ebbing from him as each day and night passes. Gisa cannot coax him to move and, indeed, she can see he has barely the energy to lift his head. The syrup she made in her uncle's shop has eased the ache of his fever, but not broken it. There must be something that will heal him, make him strong enough to search for another way out, but though she read the herbals half the night until her eyes burned, nothing in her uncle's books told her what she needs to know.

Inside the manor grounds, the high walls give some shelter, but the apple and cherry blossom has been ripped from the trees and covers the grass in drifts of pink snow. Gisa pauses, as she always does, staring up at the forbidding tower. But today Father Arthmael is waiting for her. Better the devil you know, they say, and she knows not this priest.

As she struggles to close the heavy tower door against the wind, she cannot help glancing at the bottom of the stairs. The trapdoor to the cellar is closed and she can't even see where it opened, but that does not erase the memory of what's down there. The swollen, purple face of the hanged man floats before her. It's a face she knows, she is sure, but whose?

As her head emerges through the trapdoor into the store room, she sees a man in long white robes standing with his back to her. Though Odo warned her yesterday that the abbot would be instructing her, the sight still unnerves her. What had the White Canons done to little Peter to make the child so afraid? Had Father Arthmael inflicted those wounds? Did he know?

The abbot stares down at her head, which is level with his sandalled feet. His toes are long, twisted over each other, like gnarled tree roots. The joints of his big toes are swollen and shiny, the skin on the others rough and calloused, where the leather has rubbed them for years. He does not extend a hand to help her up, but watches her mount the steps, his expression a mixture of impatience and curiosity.

He's taller than Sylvain, much thinner. His eyes are sunk deep in the sockets and his skin is drawn tight over the bones, as if even as an infant his body lacked flesh. His glance when he meets her eyes is covert, sly, as if he believes that to look at a woman is a sin yet a sin he is compelled to commit. She makes a small obeisance and he seems to be waiting for this, for he finally speaks.

'Your master is spending the day in meditation and rest,

preparing himself. But there is something he needs you to make for him. This will be your task for today, after which you may leave. Somewhere in this room is the skull of a human child. You will find it.' He waves his hand carelessly around the shelves, as if he has asked her to fetch something as commonplace as dried yarrow or a candle.

'You will heat it in the crucible until it is brittle enough to be crushed into powder. When you have ground the skull to a fine powder, you will empty the powder into this bag, taking great care not to lose a single grain of it. Fold the top over three times and sew it shut, using the hair in that box for thread.'

He hands her a scrap of parchment on which a five-pointed star has been hastily drawn. 'You must also stitch this sign upon the bag. It need only be very small, each line just a single hair, just so long as the pattern is complete with not the smallest gap between the lines of it.'

He points to the things he has laid out on the table behind him – a white bag made of fine linen, two bone needles and a wooden box. He flicks open the top of the box. Inside is a clump of curly golden-brown hair. She wonders what animal it has been clipped from for it is too thick and coarse to have been taken from a human head. A dog, perhaps?

'The hairs are too short to sew with,' she protests.

'You will sew one stitch at a time, as when you stitch a wound.' He slams the box shut, before the wind, forcing its way through the slit window, can snatch the hair away. 'When the task is complete, you may leave the bag here next to the box and return as usual tomorrow. I have lit the fire in the chamber above in readiness for you to heat the crucible. Do you have all that you need?'

She nods. She wants him gone.

'Carry out the task with diligence. Add nothing more than I have instructed, take nothing away. Men's lives and, more importantly, their souls depend upon your work.' He stares out across the garden towards the manor, then murmurs softly, 'There is a book that your master consults. Perhaps you have seen it – emblazoned on the front is a golden sun.'

She can see from the tension in his frame that the question is far from casual.

'Lord Sylvain has many books,' she says, keeping her expression blank.

'There is some detail I wish to check. Is that book here, in this tower?'

'Perhaps if you asked Lord Sylvain . . .'

The abbot spins round furiously. 'Sylvain cannot be disturbed. Why else do you imagine I am wasting my valuable time instructing you?'

His gaze fastens on her swan brooch. 'Sylvain walks a dangerous road. But for the moment it is one we must all walk with him until we reach that place where the road will divide in two. He is willing to kill the soul to protect the body, but Christ teaches us to slay the body to save the soul. Do not trust your master, child. Obey him, for the work you begin here will be used for God's glory in the end. I will make certain of that. Obey, but do not trust. I will pray for you, child. I will pray that God will save your soul at least.' He makes the sign of the cross over her. '*Perfectum concedat nobis Dominus mortis.* God grant us the perfect death.'

Gisa shivers. She needs no warning not to trust Sylvain. But she does not trust Father Arthmael either. As soon as she sees him walking away across the grass towards the hall, she runs downs the stairs to check if he has locked her in.

To her relief, she finds the door unfastened. She regrets coming down for now she will have to remount the stairs, walking over the steps she knows to be hollow, walking over the dungeon in which the winged creature unfurls its bat-wings in the darkness.

She tries to focus only on the task as she lifts the little boy's skull from the box in which she found it on the day she arrived. It is so very small, so very white and new. The baby teeth are still in the mouth, but his adult teeth will never grow now. The skull itself holds no terrors for her, but the tender age of its owner distresses her, for it might have been little Peter's.

As soon as the skull is baking in the crucible, Gisa turns her attention to the room. She has been waiting for this chance and there may never be another. She must find the book. Sylvain said it contained the knowledge to heal any infirmity, even if that person was already in the arms of death. She can heal Peter, she knows it, and once he is strong they *will* find a way out.

She guesses that Father Arthmael has already searched the tower, but she convinces herself she can find what he has missed. She looks in and behind every box, lifts every covering, but there is no book. The vessels, which are normally bubbling away, are cold and empty. All the braziers, save the small furnace she is using, have been extinguished. Things are being made ready, but for what? She searches again, going over the places she has already examined, as if the book will suddenly appear because she wills it, but it does not.

Gisa crosses to the window that faces the main house and stares at the blank wall of the turret where she guesses the hidden chamber to be. What reason does Sylvain have for detaining Laurent here? And she has the uneasy feeling that

that is exactly what he is doing, even though he does not like strangers. Something slithers through the back of her mind, something Peter said, but it will not lie still long enough for her to name it.

She hugs herself against the cold wind blasting though the windows. She is desperate to escape, but the heating of the skull cannot be rushed. Years seem to pass as she watches the fire, but finally she judges the skull is ready. She slips her hands into thick sheepskin bags to protect them from the heat and lifts it out, setting the brittle skull in the wind from the slit window to cool it.

Then she carefully carries it down to her own workshop. She gently cracks the bone into pieces and begins to grind. The teeth lie like white pearls among the grey powder. She hesitates. If this was a suicide's skull she was preparing for her uncle, she would remove them, for the powder would be made into a potion to be swallowed against the falling sickness and the teeth would cause harm. But this bag, sewn up with hair, must be some kind of amulet and Father Arthmael said all must be collected, so she empties the tiny teeth into the bag with the ground bone.

Teasing out one of the golden-brown strands of hair from the wooden box, she stretches the curl to thread the bone needle. The hair is surprisingly strong and just long enough to pull through the lips of the fine-linen bag. But she has fashioned only a few stitches when she hears the wooden stairs below her creaking and soft footsteps ascending. Pushing the bag aside, she backs away from the trapdoor, her skin crawling with fear. Someone or something is rising from that dungeon. She fumbles behind her and seizes the first weapon she can find, raising the iron pestle high above her head.

Chapter 45

Rubedo: the Red Death – He who has dyed the poison of the sages with the sun and its shadow hath attained to the greatest secret.

As I poked my head cautiously through the open trapdoor, there was a piercing shriek. It startled me so much I almost knocked myself out on the edge of the frame. It took me a moment or two to realise the cry had come from Gisa.

'Gisa! It's only me . . . Laurent,' I whispered, as I waved a hand above the opening.

I was afraid to stick my head back through in case she cracked my skull open with the pestle she was brandishing like some deranged Viking. I heard her footsteps crossing the boards and I cautiously peered over the edge of the trapdoor again.

'I thought you were . . . You shouldn't creep up on people,' she whispered angrily. 'I might have had something hot in my hands.'

'Instead of a lethal weapon,' I said sarcastically, as I stepped up into the small chamber. 'Look, I didn't mean to startle you, but I thought I'd best tread quietly. Odo said yesterday that Sylvain wouldn't be coming to the tower, but Father Arthmael would.'

Once again, thanks to the lack of windows in my chamber, I had woken unsure if it was still night or midday. A meal had been left for me, but cold meat and bread were hardly much of a clue. It had been placed outside my door this time and I wondered if Odo had reported Pipkin to his master, and he'd been ordered not to speak to me again.

'The abbot has gone,' Gisa said. 'But you shouldn't be here – not even Odo comes in – and if you were seen by one of the servants, they'll tell Sylvain. He might even be watching the tower himself. He sees everything.'

She pointed up to a silver ball that hung over the trapdoor above our heads. As if that thought reminded her she should be working, she pulled a strand of something from a box, squinting as she tried to wiggle the thread through the eye of a needle.

'You'd do better with a longer thread,' I told her. 'And you want to try wetting that with your tongue.' I'd been forced to repair the stitching of a book a few times, not to mention my own holed hose, and that always worked for me.

'It isn't thread,' she said. 'It's some kind of hair. Father Arthmael gave it to me. I think it's intended as an amulet.'

Curiously, I peered more closely. Didn't look like any sheep I'd seen. Horse's mane? It was too short and curly for that. I prodded the mat of coarse hairs. I snatched my hand back. The hair felt familiar and it certainly looked it. A slow, hot blush spread up over my face. In disbelief I watched Gisa innocently stretching the springy hair with her fingers, pulling it into place before tying it off. God's arse, I'd just told her to lick it!

Too mortified even to look her in the eye, I ran up the steps to the chamber above, hoping that the cold air rushing through the slit windows would cool my skin. A furnace was burning in the chamber, which didn't help, but I was far too embarrassed to face her yet. What was Sylvain up to? I'd told him the townsfolk were muttering *sorcery*. I hadn't actually believed it, but now I wondered if was true after all.

Gisa was whispering agitatedly below me, urging me to come down and to leave the tower at once. But my embarrassment had turned to fury. How dare he steal my hair, *that* hair, while I slept and use it for a charm or whatever the girl was making? I would not go down. I would stay right there and find out exactly what use Sylvain intended to make of my body parts. I had a right to know.

It occurred to me that witches and sorcerers used their victim's hair to cast a spell on them, putting it in jars with urine and pins then boiling it until the victim was seized with violent cramps and searing pains. There were certainly enough glass flasks lying around to keep a whole coven of witches occupied in mischief for a year. I felt a sudden stabbing pain in my leg. It was a very sharp needle that Gisa was threading with my hair.

But did she know what she was sewing? I'd believed her to be an innocent, forced against her will to work for Sylvain. But suppose she was his apprentice in the dark arts, or even the sorceress herself. After all, he'd been dragged out of the tower half dead, while she had sauntered out after him unscathed. She might have enchanted him. It might have been her who'd shaved my hair and she was down there now, stitching a spell with it to kill me. No wonder she was so eager to have me leave the tower.

This time it was me who shrieked at the sound of footsteps on the stairs.

Gisa thrust her head through the trapdoor, beckoning urgently. 'Quickly, Laurent, the master is coming across the grass. Go down. Hide at the bottom behind the stacks of wood till he's come upstairs, then you can slip out of the door. Hurry. If you are caught . . .'

The fear in her voice was contagious. Any defiance I'd felt instantly evaporated. I bounded down the flights of stairs and I'd only just reached the bottom when I saw the iron ring begin to turn in the door. I vaulted over the barrels and threw myself to the floor behind them. The door opened and I heard the slow, measured steps creaking up the staircase. I'd no idea if Sylvain could see behind the barrels as he ascended, but I prayed he wouldn't look down. It was only as I heard his footfalls on the boards in the chamber above that I permitted myself to draw breath, and became aware that my face was pressed against a sack of fresh, steaming dung.

The summons to dine with Sylvain came that night. It was the very last thing I wanted to do. In fact, I'd spent the hours since I'd fled the tower wondering how best to make my excuses and go. With Odo guarding the gate, there wasn't much chance that I could slip out with Gisa. There was nothing for it. I'd have to tell Sylvain that I hadn't thought of a story, couldn't begin to think of one, so I'd trouble him no further and take my leave. If I admitted I couldn't do the work he couldn't force me to stay, could he? No purse, however fat, was worth getting mixed up in whatever Sylvain and the girl were plotting.

When I entered the hall that night, Sylvain was already seated in a great chair set on the raised dais. Before him a table was spread with a crisp white linen cloth and set with silver and pewter vessels. I'd expected to see some sign of illness in him, since only the day before he'd been dragged unconscious from the tower, but if anything he looked fitter than he had on the day I'd arrived and there was a wild energy in his eyes, as if something had greatly excited him.

Below the dais, logs blazed in the round hearth at the centre of the floor, and beyond that, running down the middle of the hall was the long table used for guests and servants, but that was bare. Even the dish of rotting fruit had at last been removed, but no cloth, bread or dishes had been laid in its stead. Clearly, the servants would not be eating with us.

The baron gestured at a chair placed to his right on the dais. On the very rare occasions I'd eaten in Philippe's hall I'd been languishing at the very bottom of the lower table, so far from the count and Amée that I could barely distinguish father from daughter. Here, I was seated as an honoured guest. Although, in truth, since I was the *only* guest, he could hardly have banished me to the other end of the hall.

Pipkin and Odo, between them, carried in the dishes and served the wine. They were assisted by a gangling, slack-jawed youth who shuffled behind them to collect the empty platters and gravy-sodden bread trenchers. He gazed curiously at me, but when I attempted to smile he looked alarmed and swiftly dropped his gaze. It appeared he couldn't speak, or had been instructed not to, for he made signs to Odo and Pipkin, such as monks use in their periods of silence when they wish to ask for salt or ale.

I'd expected Sylvain to ask me how the story was coming on, and that was going to be my cue to tell him I was leaving. But instead he spoke only of the dishes that were spread before us, asking my opinion, as if I was in the habit of employing cooks. *Was there enough saffron in the partridge in councy? Did I think the dish of songbirds sweet enough?* I could see that Pipkin had his large bat-like ears pricked for my answer, so I praised fulsomely every dish as *perfect, magnificent, never tasted better.*

When the last dishes had been cleared, and we had washed our hands in the rose-scented water in the laver, the servants finally withdrew. Sylvain's manner changed the instant the door closed behind them. He leaned towards me, his expression darkening.

'So, you entered my tower uninvited.' He held up a swift hand. 'No, don't trouble to deny it. And, no, it was not the girl who told me this time. She doubtless thought she was protecting you, as girls often do when they develop what they imagine is fondness for a young man. You look surprised, but don't flatter yourself. She's had little attention from men thus far in her life, so if a cross-eyed hunchback had given her flowers she would mistake her gratitude for affection.'

Had she told him about the cowslips? She plainly acted as his spy. One thing I was certain about: if she had a fondness for anyone, it certainly wasn't me.

'But, Master Laurent, since you are so curious about what I do here, tonight you will join me in my work and I will show you. I think you will find it most instructive.' His tone was cold enough to freeze the flames in his furnace.

I won't deny that I'm possessed of more curiosity than most men. Even as a child, I'd stick my head down badgers' dens or over privy walls, desperate to know what was down there or behind that or being whispered in dark corners, but for the first time in my life, I had not the slightest desire to find out what *work* he was engaged in, much less join him in it. That was one secret I was in no hurry to uncover.

I yawned. 'Most kind of you to invite me, my lord, but I'm so weary and stuffed with good food, I'd fall asleep before I'd begun. I've still not recovered my strength from the accident.'

'On the contrary, it would appear, from the way you so speedily descended those stairs in my tower, you have recovered most admirably. And I assure you that even if you are feeling drowsy now, what you are about to witness will banish sleep entirely from your mind.'

That was exactly what I was afraid of.

He strode to the door in the panelling that led to the garden. I thought he was making for the tower. If I followed him out into the dark I could slip away and hide. Maybe find a way to scramble over that wall. But Sylvain did not open the door. Before I fully realised what he was doing, he had locked it.

'We don't want the servants bursting in at the wrong moment, do we?'

We did – God's bones, we did! Wrong moment, right moment, I wasn't fussy, just so long as they didn't leave me alone with him.

I found myself edging away, but he gestured to the long table at the opposite end of the hall from the dais.

'Take that end and help me to drag it aside.'

It was every bit as heavy as it looked, but we scraped it over the yellow and brown tiled floor, then dragged the benches aside too. It was only once the table and benches had been moved that I saw they hid tiles of a different pattern in the floor. These tiles formed a black and white twin spiral, broad on the outer edge and narrowing in like the coils of a snail's shell towards the centre.

Sylvain crouched on the floor a little way from the spiral, muttering away to himself. Using red powder from a pot and a long white swan's feather, he drew three concentric circles and inside them a five-pointed star, its points touching the inner circle.

He lifted one of the bird cages from its hook on the beam. I dimly recalled seeing gaudily coloured songbirds in those cages on the afternoon I'd first entered the hall, but now they were empty. Placing the cage on the floor over the very heart of the spiral, he slid something out from the breast of his robe. It was the bag Gisa had been sewing with my intimate hair. I was sorely tempted to demand he hand it over. But suppose he stabbed the thing before I could reach it, like a witch's poppet, and the wound appeared on my body? Something told me now was not a good time to challenge him. He laid the bag inside the cage and placed on top a gold ring, surmounted by a square stone of yellow amber. Then he locked the cage door.

Finally, he set a clay pot on the tiles in front of it. He touched the burning wick of a candle to the pot and a mass of flames leaped up. As the flames died away, a dense, bitter-smelling smoke billowed out. It was as well the roof was so high else we would have been suffocated.

Rubbing his hands clean, Sylvain gave a grunt of satisfaction and moved into the centre of the pentacle he'd drawn on the floor. 'Come, Master Laurent, step in here, but be careful not to disturb the lines I've drawn.'

I shook my head. 'I can see very well from here. I wouldn't want to get in the way.'

'It is your choice. But I must warn you that you will have no protection from whatever enters this hall tonight if you are outside these rings. Demons always seek human bodies to inhabit. I would hate them to choose yours.'

'Demons!' I shrieked. 'Tell me, you're not planning to summon—'

362

'What did you imagine this is for?' He gestured towards the smoke billowing from the pot in front of him. 'A game of blind-man-catch?'

Have you ever found yourself standing at the top of a sheer cliff, staring down into a deep ravine strewn with razor-sharp rocks, while a pack of slavering wolves runs towards you? Probably not, and neither have I, but if you can imagine the abject fear and indecision you might experience in those circumstances, you will have some inkling of the terror that paralysed me at that moment. Should I stay where I was and face whatever Sylvain was about to conjure up, or step into the circle with him and risk being caught up in whatever dark magic he was using?

'I will begin,' Sylvain said quietly.

He lifted his hand and a great gust of wind swept across the hall. The candles guttered wildly and blew out. The hall was lit only by the glow of the fire in the hearth and the flames in the pot, which made the billowing smoke glow red, as if a fountain of blood was welling up from inside it.

Sylvain's voice rose to fill the hall as he called out an invocation, and I heard a whirring as if a great flock of birds was flying over our heads, their wings fanning the air, driving the glowing red smoke downwards till it filled the room. My nerve had held until then, but when I saw the ragged black shapes circling above my head, I crossed that room in three strides and leaped into the circle, crouching behind Sylvain.

I could hardly breathe for the acrid smoke, but Sylvain's voice was as sure and strong as he spat out the final words: 'I conjure thee, Astaroth, Gressil and Balberith, by the Father, the Son and the Holy Ghost, by the Virgin Mary and by all the saints to appear in our presence and carry out our wishes.'

There was a sound as if a great piece of cloth was being ripped apart. Sylvain was peering through the smoke towards the cage.

'Look,' he breathed, 'he comes.'

The smoke was curling up from the pot, undulating, twisting, turning from blood-red to yellow in the light from the flames. It was so dense I could barely make out the cage, which kept appearing and disappearing through it, but I could have sworn something was forming beside it. Although the figure was dark and indistinct, it was a man, a young man, my own height, my own shape . . . my own shadow. He raised his head and looked straight towards us. His eyes, if you can call them that, were twin blue-white flames, burning with an intensity so fierce it blinded me. I was forced to look away, but still I could see the blue flames dancing in front of my eyes as if the image had been seared onto my eyeballs. Tears streamed down my face. I was blinking hard, trying to recover my sight, and only dimly aware that the smoke was beginning to clear. I felt the flick of Sylvain's robe against me as he brushed past me and stepped out of the circle.

By the time my sight had cleared, the fire in the pot had burned away, and the remaining smoke was drifting leisurely around the roof beams. Sylvain was re-lighting a candle at the hearth.

'It is safe to leave the circle now. Come, let us see if the demons have indeed done our bidding.'

He crossed to the birdcage and I followed, keeping at a safe distance. The bag and the ring were still inside where Sylvain had placed them, except they had changed. The threads of hair – my hair – on the bag had turned from red-gold to black. The stitches still held. They were not

364

charred or shrivelled, but now they glistened like wet tar. The amber in the ring was no longer pale yellow. It, too, had turned a gleaming jet black and was cracked in two, the crack glowing red against the black stone, as if blood was oozing from its heart.

Sylvain clutched at the bars of the cage, rocking backwards and forwards in delight.

'The demon has heard me. He has accepted the sacrifice. He has given me what I need. Now we require only one thing more and then she will rise. She will rise from death at last.'

Chapter 46

Best of all is matter which comes from living creatures,
such as blood and egg and hairs, and especially human
parts . . . to these quicksilver is added after it has been
put through the death-process.

Father John has hung bunches of water mint, willowherb and fleabane in the windows, and below them set little dishes of milk laced with hare's gall to stop the flies and gnats entering: now that the weather is growing warmer, they are swarming above the ditches and moats around the abbey. But even such precautions don't deter the bluebottles, which have somehow found their way in through the herbs and are buzzing lazily around the dorter.

The boys are easily distracted by them, and even Father John's repeated threats cannot control their urge to swat at them. It is at such a moment of distraction when the door to the courtyard swings open. The boys raise their heads at the sudden flood of sunshine that washes into the room, all except one who is completely absorbed in stalking the fly that has alighted for the third time on his writing tablet, purely to taunt him. The instant the boys see who has entered, their gazes drop to the table as if not even the appearance of Beelzebub himself could tear them from their letters. Father John, frowning at the interruption, turns his head towards the door, then scrambles to his feet,

366

inclining his head respectfully and gesturing for the boys to rise.

'Father Arthmael!'

His superior returns the nod, but his deep-set eyes are fixed on the boy who was endeavouring to kill the fly and now he extends a bony finger and wordlessly beckons to him.

The child shuffles miserably towards him, his face pale with fear.

'The fly, boy, who created it?'

'G-God, Father Arthmael.'

'And who determined its nature, how it would move?'

The boy hesitates. 'God, Father Arthmael?'

'And do you wish to eat this fly, boy?'

He shakes his head, looking even more terrified. Will Father Arthmael make him eat flies?

'Then you are not killing for your sustenance. You are killing this fly because this dumb creature is doing what God ordered it to do. To kill a creature that is obeying the will of God is to set yourself against God. Is that what you wish to do, boy, set yourself against God?'

The child shakes his head so violently that it's a wonder he doesn't snap his own neck. Every boy in the room is muttering prayers of thanks that it was he who got caught and not them. The child stands there, helpless, his eyes brimming with tears of fear, but Father Arthmael flicks a finger to dismiss him and paces slowly behind the row of stupefied boys. He comes to a halt behind Regulus and lays a hand on his shoulder. Regulus starts violently.

'Father John, with your permission, I would speak with this boy. Will you excuse him?'

It is not a request and every boy senses that but, nevertheless, Father John nods curtly.

Still with his hand on Regulus's shoulder, Father Arthmael pushes him in the direction of the door, but the boy is so paralysed with fear that even this gentle pressure does not move him. He turns to look at Felix, beseeching him to intervene, but Felix shrugs helplessly. He can do nothing. He cannot help him. Regulus's head sinks. His shoulders hunched, he allows himself to be guided to the door and out into the blinding sunshine.

As soon as the door is shut behind them, Father Arthmael removes his hand.

'Come, Regulus, let us walk. The orchard, I think, would be pleasant on such a glorious day.'

Regulus isn't hearing the words. He tries to remember all the things he's done wrong, all his guilty secrets. There are too many of them to count. Is he going to be put in the carcer? Or is Father Arthmael going to tell him his parents are dead? Only last week one of the boys was called out to be told his mother was dead and made to spend the day alone in the chapel saying prayers for her soul. Regulus has long given up the hope that his parents will visit him. They've never come to see him. No one's parents ever come. He knows that now.

Father Arthmael opens a gate in the orchard wall and ushers the boy inside. Regulus glances across at the little scar of earth in the far corner on which weeds are already beginning to feed. Why has Father Arthmael brought him here alone, to the place he is not allowed to go? Is he going to be buried here like Peter? Father Arthmael's hands are folded inside his white sleeves, but he might pull anything from them.

'Do you remember, Regulus, the first night you arrived here? You were brought down to my laboratorium and saw the furnaces and the distillation flasks. You must have wondered what great work was being undertaken there.'

The boy stares at white daisies in the grass at his feet. He did not wonder. He was afraid, confused. He only knows he was desperate to go home. He still is, though he has given up praying for that. Now he only prays to the Blessed Virgin to get him through the day without being punished and through the night without being taken from his bed.

'I am engaged on a holy task, a sacred work of transmutation, transforming base and corrupt materials, the *prima materia* of chaos, into pure gold. The transforming stone is to be found hidden in the corruption of the grave, concealed in dung and filth. Do you understand?'

Of all the jumble of phrases only one makes any sense to the boy.

'Are you looking for gold, Father Arthmael?'

A slight smile twitches the priest's thin lips. 'Ah, yes, there are some who seek that, but my goal is higher, purer. I seek the elixir that will give eternal life. If a man who is dying should drink it, he will stay exactly as he is at that moment. The Angel of Death will not be able to advance one more inch towards him. But if he should drink it while he is still in full vigour . . .' Father Arthmael takes a deep breath, his chest swelling as he fills his lungs with the warm, scented air '. . . then he will remain in health and strength to the very end of time. Think what such a man might accomplish as his enemies grow feeble and wither with age. Time, Regulus, that is the gold that is far more precious than mere metal. For a man may be as rich as an emperor but what good is his wealth if he is separated from it by death?

'You are a very special boy, Regulus, my little king. You bear the mark of the ouroboros, the sign of eternal life. And

369

what is that circle, but the shadow of the sun itself.' He lifts the boy's hand and traces the red scar that entwines the small finger. 'God marked you with the sign, so I would know you.' He strokes the boy's curls, gleaming red as fire in the bright sunshine. 'Rubedo, the red death, from which comes forth the final resurrection, the precious elixir.'

Regulus stiffens. It is not just the priest's fingers caressing his hair that makes him shudder, but the word *death*. He remembers what Felix told him, that all the dead brothers are buried here somewhere beneath his feet, lying under the grass with all that heavy wet earth pressing down on them, and the tree roots slithering towards them under the soil, burrowing into their flesh, drinking their blood to make the apples red. Regulus turns to stare at Peter's grave in the far corner of the orchard. As the hungry trees sway in the wind, they seem to be sidling towards it, as if they can smell him.

Father Arthmael pats his shoulder as if he senses the boy's fear. 'No need to be alarmed, Regulus, it is a symbolic death . . . merely a way of describing a spiritual transformation.'

But the boy does not understand.

'I brought you here to explain, so that you will not be frightened, for there is nothing to fear.' He smiles, revealing crooked yellow teeth. He reminds Regulus of his father's hound, Pouk, when he snarls at a stranger.

'I am sworn to protect the souls of all my flock, including yours. You're not afraid of me, are you?'

The boy is afraid, terrified, but he shakes his head, because he knows that is what Father Arthmael expects and he does not want to anger him.

'Good, good. Now listen carefully. Soon we will be going on a short journey to another great house. There you will meet a man who is engaged upon the same work, but his purposes are not mine. Our sacred art purifies the soul, but only if that soul has the strength to resist the temptations it offers and this man could not. He has committed a terrible sin, one that he does not repent, and so has damned his soul. But never fear, I will be with you, Regulus, and I will protect you. You must trust me. I take you there because I cannot do what I must without him. But only one of us will succeed, only one of us survive. God will destroy him.'

Father Arthmael kneels on the grass and Regulus starts to kneel too, thinking that they are going to pray, but instead the abbot grasps the boy's shoulders in his bony fingers and pulls him close. Regulus can smell the sour breath, see the black stubble on the chin and the tiny flecks of blood that stain the whites of his eyes.

'When we are in this man's house, you must listen only to me, Regulus, not to him. He is the devil and you know that you must never heed the devil. You must do only as I command, whatever I command. You are only a child and there is much you do not understand. Therefore you must trust me to tell you what is God's will. You know that, don't you, Regulus? Don't you?' he repeats, giving the boy a little shake.

'Y-yes, Father Arthmael,' he says, though it is not trust but fear that makes him say it. He fears Father Arthmael as he fears God, and why wouldn't he? In his mind they are the same. He's seen the painting of God on his throne in the chapel and both have the same grim expressions, the same unblinking, all-seeing eyes.

Pressing down heavily on the boy's shoulder, the abbot levers himself to his feet and pats his head. 'Good, good,

Regulus. And if you do exactly what I ask, I shall send you to be with your brothers. You'd like that, wouldn't you?'

Regulus's little heart gives a tiny leap of hope. 'To stay with them?' he asks eagerly. 'To stay with them for ever?'

'For ever, little Regulus, just like Mighel.'

Chapter 47

. . . brought a jar containing the hands, the heart, the eyes and the blood of a child, gave them to him, and then Francesco made an invocation to offer them to the demon.

As soon as Sylvain released me from the Great Hall, I tottered back up to my chamber as fast as my trembling legs would allow. A flagon of strong wine stood on the table next to the writing box. I'd probably have to down it all before I could even begin to sleep. But I wasn't sure I wanted to. Each time I slept, I woke to find someone had been in my chamber, and the thought of Sylvain returning that night, as I lay helpless, was enough to keep me awake for a year.

What had I seen in the hall? I was certain I'd seen my own shadow or my own reflection, I no longer knew which. But surely it was nothing more than an artfully concealed mirror, a trick of the firelight – it had to be! That bitter smoke was enough to addle anyone's wits. The noise of the birds' wings – just a flock of swans passing over the house, or a clamour of rooks startled from their roost in the nearby trees. The blackening of the ring and the hair on the bag caused by soot from the fire-pot.

Now that I thought about it, I realised the whole play had simply been put on for my benefit to frighten me, a warning not to go wandering around. The girl had doubtless helped him do it, hiding somewhere to produce the noises or sending shadows capering across the room. They'd added henbane or dwale to the fire. Such herbs can make a man see goblins swimming in his ale or his wife turning into a goat.

Well, I wasn't some ignorant marsh-dweller to be fooled by such tricks. I'd seen travelling players use a dozen better devices. They could make the mouth of Hell belch smoke and flames or the devil appear from nowhere in a flash of lightning. Why, even the conjurors at the fairs could make frogs explode in glass pots and eggs turn into doves that instantly flew away. But the question was, why should Sylvain go to such lengths to scare me while seeming determined to keep me there? Was he merely a bored noble who enjoyed playing malicious tricks on his guests?

I swung round on the bed to pour myself another goblet of wine, which, trick or not, I badly needed, for I was still trembling. It was only as I shifted the candle aside to reach the flagon that I noticed the shadow on the wall had not moved. I leaned closer. It wasn't a shadow at all but black mould. It had spread. It was at least two feet higher up the wall than it had been that morning and it was now encircling the whole room, as if a pool of black liquid was being sucked up the walls. But mould couldn't spread that quickly, not in a few hours. Perhaps it was just the light.

I held the candle closer and gingerly ran my finger across the black surface. I examined it under the candle flame. My fingertip was coated with a black slimy substance, and a line of dirty grey lime wash on the wall showed where my finger had rubbed the mould away. But even as I stared at the pale streak, the black mould crept back over it, like winter ice re-freezing on the surface of a pond.

Demons who resembled my shadow, amber turning black, birds shrieking – all that I could convince myself was some elaborate hoax, but this? How could Sylvain be doing this? The sight of that oozing black slime would have been enough to persuade even the most sceptical of men that now was the time to depart – and quickly.

My own clothes had not been returned to me and my pack was also missing, along with my purse. No matter. I would travel light. If I was to scale that wall, which seemed my best and, indeed, my only option, a pack would weigh me down. The robes I'd been given weren't exactly suited to the task of climbing walls, but I could loop them up between my legs and in the darkness there'd be no one to see.

But if I was going to leave empty-handed, the one thing I could not afford to abandon was Lugh. It was the only thing I owned in the world. The raven's head still stood on the old altar. I snatched it up and promptly dropped it with a curse. The metal was hot. I must have placed the burning candle too close to it. I took the wooden box from the table and, using the wool wrappings that still lay inside, I flipped the head into the box. The leather pouch in which I'd carried it had vanished, along with my clothes, so I pushed the box down the front of my robe and, as silently as I could, lifted the latch on the door.

I crossed the painted chamber and edged down the outside of the stairs, keeping close to the wall to guide myself in the dark. To my great relief, the door at the bottom was unlocked. I edged out into the darkness of the garden. Thick swathes of cloud drifted across the sky, glowing from above as they crept across the marbled face of the moon. In two of the casements of the Great Hall, single candles burned, no doubt set ready in case a servant should be wanted in the night, but all else was hushed and still. I'd never heard a dog barking in the manor, so I hoped that Odo was not in the habit of letting any beast roam free within the grounds at night, as was the custom in many large houses.

My sandal squished into something wet and soggy that oozed over my bare toes. A stench burst in my nostrils making me gag. That dead rabbit! It had still not been cleared away. I jerked my foot trying to fling off the maggots I could feel crawling on my skin. But I daren't stop to wipe off the foul mess.

I edged along the side of the turret, hugging the wall as closely as I could, and as I rounded the corner I found myself in a section of garden that was not overlooked by any of the windows in the main house. Hidden from view, I could at last risk sprinting across the open stretch of grass towards the wall that surrounded the grounds. The cloud had glided away from the moon and a sheen of silver light gilded the top of the wall. It appeared to be only about a foot higher than my upstretched arm, but the stones were smooth and snugly fitted with no handholds.

I hurried down the length of the wall, searching for something I could stand on. At the far end of the garden was an old apple tree and over the years the branches had been cut low and spread wide to make the fruit easier to pick. Its branches weren't touching the wall, but from where I was standing, the gap didn't look too great. I clambered up onto one stout branch and, grasping the one above to steady myself, began to edge along the rough wood towards the wall. My plan, if you can call it that, was to lean across, grab the top of the wall, then swing up and onto it.

I had taken two or three more shuffling steps before I

both heard and felt an ominous cracking. The branch, though thick, was clearly rotten. I quickly began to shuffle back towards the safety of the trunk, gripping the branch above even more firmly in case the one I was standing on gave way.

I became aware of something hot against my chest. The heat was growing intense. My skin was burning and the pain was becoming agonising. I clutched at the front of my robe and my fingers touched the wooden box. It was so hot it was like grasping a log that had just been pulled from the heart of a fire. Gripping the box through my robe, I tried to drag it away from my skin, but as I touched it, it burst into flames.

I crashed to the ground, squirming frantically on the grass, trying to extinguish my burning robe. The silver head exploded from the box and rolled away. The raven began to scream so piercingly that the pain in my ears almost equalled the agony of my burned skin.

Just when I thought my ears would burst, the head fell silent. I lay sprawled on my back, gasping for breath. The skin on my chest and hand was smarting like that of a sinner in Hell. As soon as I could summon the breath to move, I rolled over onto my knees and tried to struggle up. But before I could raise myself up, a large boot descended on the small of my back, pushing me face down into the grass.

The man's other foot was planted on the ground, next to my cheek. Even from that position, there was no mistaking that the great trunk of a leg belonged to Odo. But when I lifted my head and squinted up into the light of the lantern above me, the face I saw peering down was Sylvain's.

'Such shockingly poor manners, Master Laurent, to leave us without thanking us for our hospitality. Besides, you had promised me a story. You were insistent enough that I should employ you to write one. Surely you don't intend to renege on our bargain.'

He bent and picked up the raven's head, which was lying on the grass. The flames had turned it black, but Sylvain seemed to have no trouble touching it, as if it was quite cold.

'Never trust your secrets to a raven, when you are not its true master, Laurent, or should I say *Vincent*? Lately, I believe, apprentice scribe and librarian in the employ of Philippe, Le Comte de Lingones. Philippe should have warned you that a raven will never serve a thief. And he should know for he stole it from me. It was an ancient creature, old long before it came to the Great Master and he in turn bequeathed it to his most able disciple, the true inheritor of the royal art and, believe me, that was not Philippe, never Philippe!'

Sylvain stroked the bird's blackened beak thoughtfully. 'A more fitting name for Lugh would have been Huginn or Muninn, *thought* and *memory*, for, like Odin's ravens, there is not a single thought or memory you have confided to this bird that he has not in turn whispered in my ear. Perhaps you fondly believed you had brought the raven's head to me, but surely you must have realised by now that it was the raven who brought *you* here. You are his prey, his gift of flesh for his true master.'

Chapter 48

For of this secret shall know none other creature, but only you, as I make faithful protestation for all the time I here in life endure.

Gisa crosses the courtyard of her uncle's apothecary's shop. The casement above the shop is open and the murmur of voices drifts down onto the stones below – her aunt's strident tone and another, one that is all too familiar. Gisa feels her stomach tighten and peers up at the window. Sylvain is sitting in the casement seat. He glances down at the sound of the gate closing and nods gravely to her, as if he is a king looking down on his subjects.

Her stomach lurches into her throat. Why is he here? Her footsteps falter. She doesn't want to enter the shop, not with him sitting above her, but he might be waiting for her return, and will go on waiting. A tiny bubble of hope rises in her. Perhaps he's come to say he does not need her tomorrow – better still, that he does not want her to return. 'Please let it be so,' she murmurs. 'Holy Virgin, please let that be why he's come.'

In the shop the shutters are fastened, and when she closes the door behind her, twilight crowds in, throwing a grey shroud over every bright thing. At first she thinks she is alone. Then, in the far corner, she catches a movement. Uncle Thomas is sitting on a low stool, as if he is in mourning.

He raises his head from his hands and gestures silently up at the ceiling.

He looks dejected, but Gisa does not ask what is troubling him. Her aunt and uncle are not in the habit of discussing their affairs with her. She is a mere girl, a niece, a servant. And they have never once asked her how she feels, enquired if she is happy or why she is sad. Emotions in a child, if one must have them at all, should be concealed, for they are of no consequence to anyone.

He pats the table. 'Come, child, sit. There is something I must tell you.'

The knot in her belly tightens still further. She knows any news will involve Sylvain. She slides onto a stool opposite him, her hands clenched in her lap, praying silently. *Let him say I am dismissed.*

'Lord Sylvain is most complimentary about the work you have done for him. That is good,' Uncle Thomas says doubtfully. 'It reflects well on this shop. But he tells me that the next phase of his work requires the distillations and sublimations to be tended regularly through the night as well as by day. A task he tells me that will be easier if two people keep watch alternately, one resting or eating while the other ensures that the decoctions are heated and cooled correctly at their various phases. He wishes you to remain at the manor tomorrow night until the work is completed. You will need to—'

'Uncle, no! You promised! You said you'd insisted I must return here each night. You said it wasn't seemly for a maid to sleep under a man's roof.'

Peter! If she is closed up in the manor there will be no one to bring him food or drink, and he is tortured by thirst from the fever. He is only a child, a little boy trapped and helpless beneath the earth. Without her he will die and die alone.

Uncle Thomas shifts his buttocks on the stool. He does not meet Gisa's eyes, but addresses her mouth as if it has its own mind.

'I . . . have changed my mind. Now that we can see how much Lord Sylvain values your skills, your aunt sees no reason why you should not stay. The baron has a large house. He assures us you will have your own chamber at some distance from the male servants. Many widowers have serving maids and housekeepers who sleep in their house. Why, every priest—'

Gisa springs to her feet. 'And even I know what night duties most housekeepers perform for the priest. Is that what I am to become, Sylvain's mistress?'

'Never, I assure you, Gisa,' a voice murmurs behind her.

She spins round. Sylvain is standing on the stairs. Her uncle clambers to his feet, as Sylvain descends the last few steps, ducking his head to avoid the bunches of herbs and dried bones swinging from the beams.

Sylvain takes a pace towards Gisa and reaches out to caress the swan brooch, but she pulls away before he can touch it.

'I told you before, my little swan, my work requires a *virgin*'s hand. Do you imagine I would destroy the very virtue I require most in my assistant?' He smiles, but the smile does not reach his eyes and his tone is as cold and harsh as the east wind.

'There are learned men in this land who would give all they owned, and indeed their very souls, to be permitted to assist in this great work, and I am entrusting it to you, a mere girl.' He spits this last word at her, as if his tongue

381

cannot bear the taste of it. 'I believe it is time, Master Thomas, for your *niece* to understand fully the debt of gratitude she owes me.'

Uncle Thomas's brow furrows in alarm and bewilderment. 'But, my lord, all these years you have instructed us . . . We have done all that we can to shield her, as you asked.' A guilty spasm crosses his face and his gaze darts to the ceiling above. 'My poor wife may have mentioned that Gisa's father was not a good man, but that is all, I swear. Surely there is no need—'

'There is every need,' Sylvain snaps. 'If she will not come to me willingly, for the love of the great art I have tried to instil in her, then perhaps knowledge of the truth of what she really is will bend her stiff neck.'

Without warning, he grasps her throat with his long, cold fingers, pulling her towards him. 'Will it, Gisa? Will the truth soften you?'

For the second time, Gisa wrenches herself away from him but, hemmed in by the table, she cannot retreat. Her chin jerks up defiantly. 'I am no child. I do not need to be shielded from anything. So, what is it I must be told?' She flings the words at him with as much venom in her tone as there had been in his own. But the malicious smile on Sylvain's face makes her afraid she has said exactly what he wanted.

'Where to begin? Your father – how did Mistress Ebba describe him? Ah, yes, *not a good man*. An unusually benign judgement from your wife's lips, as I think you will own, Master Thomas. If she had called him *wicked, cruel and deceitful*, I think even that description might have been too kind. Your father spent his miserable life as little better than a leech. His chief amusement was to seduce wealthy women, luring them away from those who loved them, ruining their lives and reputations and, when he had extracted all the money he could from them, abandoning them, leaving them soiled and broken. But he did not confine his attentions to women. He charmed his way round their husbands as well, tricking them into investing in schemes that naturally lined no one's purse but his own, not caring when he left them penniless.'

'No!' Gisa's face is burning, her fists clenched. She wants to pound his mouth bloody to stop him uttering these cruel lies. 'My father was a good, kind man. I remember him. I remember how he played with me and soothed me to sleep at night if I woke with a bad dream. He was nothing like the man you say he was.'

'He was everything I describe and worse,' Sylvain growls savagely. 'If he had only conned a few gullible men or seduced silly women, you would not be here in this shop now, but you are, because his evil ran much deeper. In his greed he stopped at nothing. He set out to discover all he could about the king's plans to defend this realm, then attempted to sell that knowledge to France for a heavy purse. Had he succeeded, England would have been helpless to defend herself against a French invasion. But, fortunately, he was discovered in time. He stood trial for high treason and he was hanged—'

'It's not true!' Gisa shouts. But even as she denies it, some memory that has long lain sleeping in her mind is beginning to wake. She is chilled to her bones by the image that rears in her head, but still she cannot accept it. 'Tell him, Uncle Thomas, tell him my father would never . . . He was innocent! They hanged the wrong man.'

Thomas does not look at her. He sits, hunched, his

forehead resting on his hands and she sees he has become a withered, old man without her noticing.

'They hanged the right man, Gisa,' Sylvain says. His words burn like acid. 'Many said that such a death showed him greater mercy than he deserved and he should have burned for his treachery. But there was another punishment imposed. All your father owned was naturally forfeit to the Crown, but he was also declared *attainted.* It is a sentence rarely passed for there are mercifully few men who have betrayed their sovereign king as foully as your father did. Do you understand what that means? Your father and all his offspring have tainted blood and have thus forfeited all the rights of a free man or woman. As his child, you may never own land or property or enter into any contract or indenture. And should any man be foolish enough to take you as his mate, any child that is born of your tainted womb will also be attainted, as will all their children, in perpetuity.'

He pauses, allowing the full weight of his pronouncement to bear down on her, but she can't take it in. She knows that who she is, her whole life, has somehow been changed by that single word, but she cannot grasp what it will do to her.

'No.' She glares at him with cold fury. 'This is a lie. It is you who are evil and cruel. I will never work for you again, never! I'd rather pay my uncle by treading dog-dung in a tanner's yard.' She tries to push past her uncle, flee the room, but Thomas pulls her back. His face is etched with misery and pain.

'I know it is hard to hear, child, which is why you have been protected from the truth of it, but it *is* the truth Lord Sylvain speaks. And you owe him more than you can possibly understand. You were so young when your father . . . *left* you. You had no kin to care for you.'

'But I did have family – you and Aunt Ebba,' Gisa says, in bewilderment.

Thomas shakes his head. 'I am not your uncle, I wish that I were, for I have grown fond of you over the years, but though it wounds me to say it, you were a stranger's child, a friendless orphan. Alone, you would have starved to death in a week or been dragged into one of the town stews and used by men until it killed you. Lord Sylvain himself rescued you from the street and brought you here. He asked us to raise you as if you were our kin.'

'In return for my patronage and a more than generous allowance,' Sylvain says. 'I thought it unjust that an innocent child should suffer for the sins of her father, however grave.'

He steps towards her, his poison-green eyes staring down into hers. His hands glide, soft as snakes, over the skin of her neck. She smells again the stench of urine and myrrh on his black robe. His finger caresses her lips. Then, as she opens her mouth to protest, he presses his hand hard against it, silencing her. 'I saved you and I have cared for you better than any father. You owe me your life, little swan. And I always collect my debts.'

Chapter 49

The body is the form, and the ferment, and the tincture of which the sages search. It is white actually and red potentially; while it is white it is still imperfect, but perfected when it becomes red.

This time I *was* locked in. Sylvain was taking no chances that I would escape again. He did not do anything as crude as lock the chamber, merely the door of the turret at the bottom. But I was under no illusions that the chamber itself could and would be locked if I made any further trouble, for Odo made a great play of trying one of his keys for size in the door while he waited for Sylvain to return.

Sylvain came into my chamber bearing an earthenware jar and bandages. 'I cannot have your performance impeded.'

Performance? Did he mean my story or was he laying on another of his little conjuring tricks?

'This will cool the burns and help them heal. Gisa prepared it herself. She is a skilled apothecary.'

'Is Gisa here?'

Sylvain permitted a smile to twitch the corner of his lips. 'Impatient to see her? You shall. She returns in the morning, and after that you will not be dining alone. She will be living at the manor. Perhaps that will make you want to stay longer, which would enable all of us to enjoy a full night's sleep, wouldn't it, Odo?'

The great ogre grinned broadly, revealing a mouthful of broken and blackened teeth.

I was afraid that whatever was in the jar would bewitch my mind or send me back into a deep sleep, for I was sure now I had been drugged when I'd lain there with my broken arm. Had Gisa prepared those draughts too? But with Odo clearly willing to strap me down, if need be, I dared not refuse Sylvain's ministrations. Being kept prisoner was bad enough. Being kept bound would be even worse. But whatever was in the stinking green unguent certainly soothed the stinging. Sylvain placed soft linen cloths over the burns and bound them in place with bandages. Then he and Odo departed.

I lay on my back in the light of the single candle, cursing. Why hadn't I left the raven's head in the chamber? I knew well enough by now that it was far more than a lump of silver. Hadn't I seen for myself on my travels what it could do, the tricks it had employed to stop others buying it? Why hadn't I questioned what it was? The truth was, it had happened so gradually that I had simply grown to accept its powers, and since it had seemed to be protecting me, I'd assumed that it had been enchanted to serve whoever possessed it.

I'd read often of such things, pieces of stone that spin on a thread always to point north, mirrors that show you places that lie many miles away, rings that glow if an enemy is close by. But now I realised Lugh was far less innocent than any of those. Was a spirit or demon imprisoned inside that head? And the more I thought of it, the more I became convinced that every decision I had made, every turn I had taken, had been manipulated by the raven to drive me into Sylvain's clutches. As a sheepdog circles a sheep, slowly but surely herding it into the waiting arms of the shearer, so Lugh had guided me here.

I tried to recall all the things I had foolishly prattled about to that bird, which he could have revealed to Sylvain – the lies, the stupid fantasies, the girl who'd dragged me into her father's barn. My face burned as hot as my chest. It was worse than being caught fondling yourself by your own priest. God's arse, that bird probably knew how often I'd done that as well! I ground my teeth and tried to think of something else.

I wriggled into a more comfortable position and, as I did, I caught sight of the dark stain on the wall. I was sure it had not been higher than the bed when I left the chamber, but it was now and, what was more, the black mould was beginning to ooze out from the walls and spread across the floor. It was only by a foot or so, but even so, mould shouldn't spread across dry dusty wooden boards, should it?

I lay awake until the candle burned low, watching the wall, but, of course, I didn't see the stain spread. It was only mould, after all. And I had much more to worry about than whether the chamber needed a fresh coat of lime wash. Sylvain was plainly determined to keep me there by force, but for what purpose? Not even I could convince myself that all he wanted was to hear a good story. *You are his prey, his gift of flesh for his master.* A trap had been set, but this time it was the bird who had caught the man.

I knew someone had been into my chamber again as soon as I woke. I distinctly remembered watching the candle burn down to the last inch, but now a much longer one burned in its place. I sat up and swung my legs out of bed and immediately found myself anxiously glancing at the black stain on the wall. I didn't know why it troubled me so much. I'd slept in far worse lodgings on the road – wattle and daub huts with rotting thatch and whole forests of moss and fungi lurking in the dank corners. Mould was nothing. But all the same I was relieved to see it had climbed no higher up the walls.

But my relief lasted only for a moment, for when I glanced down at the floor I could see it had crept further over the dusty boards and was now even closer to the bed. One slender black line stretched out from the rest, like a tendril of ivy, as if it was trying to twine itself around the bed's leg. I shook my head impatiently. It was *not* creeping closer. It couldn't be. It had been like that for days and in the dim light I just hadn't noticed it.

But I wasn't imagining that someone had entered the room while I slept, for the scarlet robe I'd worn yesterday had been replaced with a fresh one, identical except that it was undamaged by any scorch marks or holes. Had I dreamed it? My hand and chest were bandaged and the wounds beneath were sore. I'd certainly been burned. That much, at least, was real.

The door at the bottom of the turret slammed. Someone was mounting the stairs, but it wasn't Sylvain. I could never hear him coming until he was in the room. If danger was approaching, I didn't want to face it naked. I dragged the robe over my head, wincing as my muscles twisted the burned skin beneath the bandages. The door to my chamber was flung open to reveal the gangling youth who had helped to serve supper in Sylvain's hall. He regarded me curiously for a few moments, before gesturing that I should follow him.

'Where are you taking me?'

I was beginning to fear any kind of summons from Sylvain.

389

The youth drew his finger across his forehead from eyebrow to eyebrow, which I was fairly sure was the monk's sign for either a trout or a woman. Either Sylvain was inviting me to go fishing, which did not seem likely, or the lad was taking me to Gisa. I wasn't sure whether or not to feel relieved. Gisa was less likely to feed me to demons than Sylvain, but then again, if she was working with him . . .

The lad beckoned again, more urgently, and stared at me as if he was trying to decide whether he should drag me out. Sylvain must be with Gisa. The thought of what they might be planning together made my stomach lurch. But I knew enough about my host to realise that refusal was not an option. I followed the lad down the stone stairs, while he bounded ahead, like a boisterous goat. If I'd been back in old Gaspard's turret, I'd have done the same, but the fear of what I was about to walk into had a remarkably sobering effect on my pace.

He led me across the grass, past the dead rabbit, which in daylight was no more than white bones and slimy fur. I thought we were making for the tower, but as I approached the door, the young man grabbed my sleeve and shook his head, grinning at me inanely as if he was privy to some hilarious joke. There was something strange about his open mouth. I peered at him, unable to place it at first. Behind his broken teeth there was nothing but a black cavern where . . . where there should have been a tongue! The lad's tongue had been torn out! God's arse! Odo said Sylvain would rip out Pipkin's tongue if he heard him gossiping to me, but I'd thought it was just an idle threat. Surely he hadn't really done that to the boy.

I was still trying to take in what I'd seen when the lad, gripping my sleeve, led me round the side of the tower towards a wall of yew trees. Loosening his grip, he forced himself between two, which were growing so close together that their branches interlaced. After some hesitation, I followed, cursing as the fronds rasped across my burned chest. Which idiot had not had the foresight to plant the trees far enough apart for a man to walk through?

They had been planted in a hollow square, perfectly concealing a low, circular stone building in the centre. It was not unlike a wayside chapel, except this had no windows and the domed roof was made not of thatch but of stone slabs. Strands of ivy had snaked over the roof, and the stone walls were clad in thick cushions of moss, which was hardly surprising since, even though the day was warm, the square inside the tall trees was dank and cold enough to make anyone shiver. The building must have remained perpetually wrapped in shadow, even during the hottest part of a summer's day.

The small door, which appeared to be the only entrance, was slightly ajar. The lad pointed and again made the same sign, drawing his finger between his eyebrows, but before I could react, the door opened wider and Sylvain emerged, ducking out under the lintel. The boy gave his cavernous grin and vanished back through the trees.

'I know you have been perplexed by the nature of my work, Laurent, and even frightened, judging by your attempt to leave us so precipitously last night. That is natural. Men always fear what they do not understand.'

Sylvain's tone was quite different from the menacing voice he had employed the night before. He sounded almost soothing, as if he was trying to calm a delicate elderly lady who'd been startled by a mouse.

'Perhaps if you understood what I am trying to achieve

you might be more willing to assist me. For I do want you to assist me, Laurent, I want that very much.'

He stepped aside, his hand sweeping towards the open door as if he was a gracious host inviting a man into his banqueting hall. 'Go in. Look, but I beg you to take the greatest care not to touch her. The slightest brush of a hand or even the sleeve of a robe could fatally damage her.'

I stumbled backwards, crashing against the branches behind me. If Sylvain thought I could be tricked into step-ping into that prison willingly either he was an idiot or he thought I was. I'd no doubt he could call on Odo and Pipkin, even the lad, to bundle me inside, but I'd no inten-tion of making it easy for them.

Sylvain looked amused. 'You fear a trap? That is, perhaps, not surprising, but I assure you I have no intention of leaving you in here. In fact, you are one of the few who have ever been privileged enough to see what I am about to show you . . . No? You still don't trust me? Very well, I shall go first, then, and you may stand between me and the door.'

He ducked under the lintel and vanished inside. I was telling myself simply to walk away – better still, run! Odo was probably concealed inside, ready to brain me as I bent to enter. But on the other hand, if that *was* the plan, they could have bludgeoned me as I lay sleeping in the tower and Odo could have carried me here like a trussed chicken. I hesitated. Curiosity was always my weakness and, once more, it got the better of me. I edged cautiously towards the door, trying to peer in without actually entering.

The inside of the building was higher than it first appeared, for the floor had been constructed below ground level, with three stone steps leading down, so that even a tall man could easily stand upright. A long stone slab, raised four feet above the ground, took up most of the space inside the circular chamber and Sylvain was standing at the far end, holding up a lantern, though the candlelight glowing dimly through the horn panels did little to illuminate the scene.

'If you came in, you would not be blocking the light from the door and you could see more clearly.'

Something was lying on the stone slab, but I couldn't make out what it was. I edged down the three steps and stood at the bottom, pressed against the stone wall. The chamber had been lime-washed and decorated with many of the same symbols I'd seen elsewhere in Sylvain's manor. In the highest point of the dome, a pair of ouroboros, snakes swallowing their tails, had been painted in green with golden fangs and scarlet tongues. They seemed to twist in dizzying spirals. I staggered sideways and grabbed at the edge of the slab to balance myself.

'Careful!' Sylvain snapped. 'Don't touch her.'

I glanced down. Now that my eyes had adjusted to the twilight, I found myself staring down at the life-sized effigy of a girl. The paint on the face and hands had a curious wet gleam under the lantern light, as if it had only just been completed. The statue was dressed like a saint in a white linen gown, with a linen coif over the hair. She'd been carved with her arms stretched down either side of her and her eyes were closed, as if the sculptor had intended her to appear asleep.

I guessed the stone slab covered a tomb and the statue on top represented the person who lay buried beneath. I had to admit, it was one of the most realistic effigies I'd ever seen, and if it bore any resemblance to the woman when she lived, she must have been beautiful. She vaguely reminded me of someone I'd met, but for the life of me, I couldn't think who.

As if he could read my thoughts, Sylvain said quietly from the shadows, 'You find her attractive? You would not be the first. My daughter was admired by many men.'

'Your daughter? Then . . .'

'Then, as you can see, she is not, as your rumours suggest, locked up in my tower, any more than her suitors are languishing in my dungeons. My daughter is dead . . . long dead.'

I tried hastily to think of something appropriate to say. It seemed a little late for condolences. 'The effigy must be a great comfort to you . . . to be able to remember her in all her beauty, as she was . . . The sculptor did a fine job.'

'That is no effigy, Master Laurent. That *is* my daughter.'

Sylvain gestured to a niche in the wall next to him in which stood several sealed jars, half hidden in the gloom. 'These vessels contain her organs, her heart, liver, guts and so on. All I have removed and carefully preserved. The cavities left in her body I filled with honey, precious oils and herbs, and she herself has been completely encased in wax. She is perfect. Just as she was on the day she died. She lies there waiting to be brought to life again.'

I stared at the figure on the slab in horror, my eyes now seeing for the first time what my brain was struggling to accept. I was looking at a corpse. The tones of her skin were not painted, but real flesh. The eyelashes and brows were not stuck on but had once burrowed out of her body and been frozen there in that moment of her death.

'This is my work, Master Laurent. To bring my daughter to life again, and I will.' Sylvain's voice reverberated in the small chamber, like a priest's before an altar.

'I have the bag that has been sewn with human hair to hide inside her belly. I have the ring your shadow transformed to place in her mouth. I have the blood of the boy to cleanse her. I need one thing more, Master Laurent, the most important object of them all. With that my daughter will rise again and live just as she was before. I will resurrect her. I will raise her from death to life, a new life. She will be reborn and this time she will never die.'

Chapter 50

Kill the lion in his blood.

Father Arthmael is taking such broad strides across the grass towards the great tower that Regulus has to trot to keep pace with him. The boy cranes his head around, trying to snatch glimpses of the unfamiliar garden – the manor house with its many windows, the lavender bushes, the apple trees and the high wall. He is looking for a way out, an open gate that he could run to, but with a tightening in his throat he sees that this place is as firmly sealed as the abbey. Several times he stumbles in his haste, but the canon's fingers burrow into his shoulder and he cannot fall.

As they reach the door of the tower, Regulus cranes his head back as far as he can to try to see the top, but they are so close it appears the tower is falling towards them. He tries to back away, but Father Arthmael only grips him harder. The boy can sense the priest's excitement, but his fear too. Regulus has felt this tension before in adults, like the time his father was pacing outside the cottage while inside his mother screamed in labour.

A man comes lumbering across the grass towards them, a covered basket held in the crook of his arm. He is brawny and broad, like Regulus's father. He is the first man the boy has seen since he was brought to the abbey who is not dressed in the white robes of the canons or the brown robes of the lay brothers. Though his expression is far from friendly, the sight of the green breeches and russet tunic eases Regulus's anxiety. He resembles the people the boy used to see in the forest and marketplace, people who were once his whole world. He might have come to take him home.

Regulus offers him a shy smile, but the man barely glances at him. 'Is this the boy the master sent for?'

'It is. This is Regulus. Is your master inside, Odo?'

Odo grunts. 'He's not to be disturbed. Says you're to settle the boy in the tower. He'll come soon as it's dark.' He squints up at the afternoon sky, as if to judge exactly when that might be.

'Here, you can carry this up,' Odo says, thrusting the basket at Regulus.

The boy obediently grasps it in both hands, staggering slightly. It is heavier than it looks.

'You'll find what the boy is to wear in the basket. There's a bite to eat and drink in it too. Master's orders, case he gets fretful.' Odo eyes Father Arthmael doubtfully. 'Master said you'd not be eating yourself.'

'I must prepare with fasting and prayer, as Lord Sylvain is also doing, is he not?'

Odo shrugs and, selecting the key from the great iron ring hanging at his belt, unlocks the door, standing aside for them to enter. Father Arthmael sweeps in. Regulus hesitates.

'What are you waiting for, lad? Shift yourself.' Odo's hand shoots out, as if he means to shove the boy through the door. Then he jerks back as if Regulus is indeed a consecrated little king, who must not be touched by baser men.

Taking a deep breath, Regulus edges inside and is relieved to see nothing alarming, just kegs and piles of wood. He smells the familiar odour of animal dung. He watches Father Arthmael mounting the wooden steps that run up the side of the wall. The door slams behind him, making him jump. The small chamber is plunged into semi-darkness and the kegs and timber take on new and menacing shapes. Regulus scurries after Father Arthmael, but it is not easy mounting the steep steps dragging the heavy basket.

He passes through the first room, which he barely has time to notice, and finally staggers, sweating, through the second trapdoor into the chamber at the top of the tower. A ladder ascends to a closed trapdoor above him, but with profound relief he sees that Father Arthmael is not climbing that but is standing by one of the slit windows, staring out.

For a moment, the boy looks around, puzzled. He can hear the forest, but he is inside a room. The sound is coming from a dozen or so tiny cages hanging from the beams above. In each one a single bird flutters and chirrups. Linnets and blackbirds, skylarks and robins, thrushes and magpies, all regard him with their bright eyes. He remembers what Felix told him about a black wizard who turns boys into birds. Is one of the birds Mighel? Felix never found a grave, but he found Mighel's amulet, the one he always wore, the one that slipped from his neck as feathers burrowed out through his skin and Mighel shrank down and down until he was no bigger than his own hand.

Father Arthmael called Regulus a wren. Will they turn him into one and lock him in a cage? Will boys batter him to death with sticks on St Stephen's Day, breaking his tiny wings so that he cannot escape them, crushing his fragile skull until the blood drips from his beak?

A wail of misery and fear erupts from Regulus. He lets go of the basket and tries to scramble back down the stairs.

398

But before his head has disappeared beneath the edge of the trapdoor, Father Arthmael has crossed the chamber, seized the back of his robe and is hauling him bodily up into the room. Regulus struggles, but his arms are pinned firmly by his sides. The abbot kneels before him, so that he can stare directly into the boy's eyes.

'You are Regulus, the little king. Kings are not afraid. They never show fear and you have nothing to be afraid of.'

'Don't . . . want to be . . . bird.' His small chest heaves in sobs.

He has to repeat it several times before Father Arthmael catches the words. He laughs. It is a strange laugh, like the excited bark of a fox.

'You are not to be a bird, Regulus. You are a lion. The young lion. The king-slayer.'

He reaches down and lifts the cover from the basket. Inside is a small flagon, a beaker and several small packages wrapped in sacking. Father Arthmael lifts them out, and sets them down beside an unlit brazier. Finally, from the bottom of the basket, he pulls out a length of woollen cloth, dyed to the colour of a poppy petal.

He smiles and, folding it carefully, returns it to the basket. Then he removes a small flask from a leather sheath that dangles from his belt. Ignoring the flagon, he pours liquid from his own flask into the beaker and hands it to the hiccuping boy. 'Drink.'

Walking in the hot sun, struggling up those steps with the basket and crying have all conspired to make Regulus extremely thirsty. He takes a sip from the beaker before he has even sniffed it. The liquid is thick, like mead or cream. It is sweet, herby and bitter all at the same time. He doesn't much like the taste, but he needs to drink. He gulps it down.

Father Arthmael unwraps a jar. The smell of honey rolls across the chamber. He holds out the jar, inviting the boy to dig his fist in and break off a piece of honeycomb. Regulus stuffs the comb into his mouth, chewing it happily. His father brought home honeycomb whenever he found a wild bees' nest and Regulus and his brothers would chew it just like this, squabbling over who had the biggest piece. Except that he hadn't been Regulus then. He had been another boy, with another name.

Father Arthmael, still kneeling, leans towards him. 'Listen to me, Regulus. What you will be asked to do tonight will be far beyond your understanding, but you must trust me. Tonight, two great powers will come together in this tower – Albedo, the white ablution, the rebirth born of fire, and Nigredo, the black death of putrefaction. Black and white, do you understand, Regulus? Only one of them may emerge from the tower. The other must descend into the tomb. He must die so that from his death the elixir of eternal life may be created. And he must die at the hands of the young king. You must slay him. But the old king will not want to die. He will tell you that it is I who must be killed, but you must not listen to him. Remember what I told you in the orchard – he is a wicked man. He is all the foulness and corruption that is the Nigredo. He is the black death and it is he who must enter that dark tomb.'

Regulus is not listening. He's sleepy and there are too many words, all jumbled together. All he can think about is whether he will be allowed to have more of the honey-comb.

'Have you watched your father kill a deer or a goat by

400

cutting its throat? Remember how he pulls the head back to expose the throat then makes one deep slash. It is so easy, isn't it? So quick. Over in the single flash of a knife. That is what you will do, just like your father. I will bind the black king for you, so that he cannot resist. I will pull back his head and you will slice his throat, here.'

Father Arthmael seizes the boy's hand and presses it to his own throat, so that he may feel and see exactly where he is to cut.

'The blade I have brought for you to use is new. It is sharpened so keenly that even a baby could kill with it. It will be all over in the beat of an angel's wing. Then I will send you home, just like Mighel. You'd like that, wouldn't you?' Regulus can feel a buzzing in Father Arthmael's throat as he speaks. It tickles his fingertips making him giggle.

But he can hardly stand now. The floorboards are undulating as if they have been turned to water. His legs have vanished. He crumples slowly into the abbot's arms. Father Arthmael catches him and gently cradles him, staring down into the boy's half-closed, unseeing eyes.

'Sleep now, little king, and when you wake it will be night and you will obey my every command. You will listen to my voice, only to my voice, and do exactly as I tell you. You will kill the old king and you will both enter the fire together. In the flames, youth and age, the living and the dead will melt into one and the fire shall consume them.'

Chapter 51

There are two fountains springing with great power. The one water is hot and belongs to the boy. The other water is cold and is called the virgin's fountain. Unite the one with the other that the two waters may be one.

Odo is standing on the other side of the gate as she enters, his great fingers grasping the ring of keys. Today he seems more like a gaoler than ever, for Gisa knows that when the Vesper bells sound he will not be waiting to unlock it again. She will not be returning to the other world tonight. She will not be able to reach the child.

She can still feel the grasp of Peter's tiny hot fingers as he clung to her hand through the hole. She tried to explain, warned him to make the food and ale last as long as he could, but thirst is driving him mad. As she walked away, the boy pleaded with her to come soon and the ache of his cries echo in her ears even in here.

She has to fight hard to stop herself trying to wrench the gate open again. But it is already too late. The gate is locked and barred. Odo usually looks somewhere over her head when he addresses her, but today his gaze flicks towards her face. There is an embarrassed curiosity in the glance, as if he is looking at someone for the last time. He grudgingly informs her that Sylvain is not in the tower, but Father Arthmael is up there in the laboratorium.

402

She is almost relieved. She fears both men, but she cannot face Sylvain today, knowing what she owes him, what *he* says she owes him. The knowledge has left her numb, dead. But once Father Arthmael has delivered his instructions, he will leave, as he did before. Then she will have the chance to search again for the book.

That book is the hope, the talisman she has used to ward off the despair that has been wrapping itself about her since the moment Sylvain revealed the vile truth. But she will not accept it is the truth. She will never believe it. She drives the knowledge from her mind with that one fragile hope – if she can read the book, if she can heal little Peter, release him from that stone prison, then somehow her own past will shatter too, like some evil spell.

She drags her feet up the two flights of stairs and finds Father Arthmael seated on a stool in the upper chamber in his immaculate white robes. Her heart thuds as she sees his fingers tracing symbols on a page of a book, his mouth working silently as he chants beneath his breath. She glimpses the gold leaf of the sun emblazoned on the cover, impressed into the human skin. She knows it is *the* book. But Sylvain would not have left it here by accident.

Sylvain's laboratorium is transformed. The flasks and glass tubes, the griffin's-egg vessels and the many bottles have been cleared away. In their place, cages of birds swing from the rafters. They flap their wings as she takes the final step up into the chamber, flinging themselves at the bars, screeching their calls of fear. They are wild creatures. They cannot comprehend doors and locks. They are breaking their wings in their desperation to be free.

She is so distracted by the piteous birds that it takes her a few moments to realise that Father Arthmael is not alone.

A small boy lies asleep on the floor at his feet, naked save for a length of scarlet cloth draped over one bare shoulder, the other end twisted about his waist as a loincloth. A narrow band of gold cloth, like a coronet, circles his red curls. His face rests on his arm, and tiny beads of perspiration spangle his upper lip. He looks even younger than Peter. But this boy seems peaceful, unhurt. Will he be safe here? If what Sylvain told her is true, he would not allow a child to be harmed, but if that part is true then . . .

Gisa makes an uncertain curtsy towards Father Arthmael. But he continues to read as if she is of no more substance than the air, though she knows he's seen her, for his gaze darted towards her as she emerged through the hole in the floor. She stares hungrily at the book, as if her will can dissect away the skin and reveal the words that lie like bones beneath.

'You are to fill the brazier and prepare the candles as you've been shown before,' he says, without lifting his gaze or hand from the page.

'The boy . . .' she says uncertainly. 'Perhaps I should return later so as not to disturb him.'

'He will not wake, I assure you.'

She arranges the kindling, placing the charcoal in the brazier fragment by fragment, and finally standing a pot of fumigant beside it, with which to colour and perfume the smoke once it is burning. Though she works softly, every new movement causes the little caged birds to cry alarm and dash themselves against the hard iron bars, till she is almost in tears knowing the pain and fear she is causing them. But the task must be completed or Father Arthmael will not leave.

She circles the room, putting fresh candles on the spikes

404

on the walls and trimming the wicks with a pair of tiny iron shears. In front of each one she slips a sliver of dragon's blood. She shudders as she does so, thinking of that cellar far below, but there is no stone coffin up here, only the abbot, the boy and the birds. Father Arthmael drove the demons and the dead back into the earth. Surely he will not permit them to rise up again now. She glances around the chamber, searching for anything she might inadvertently have neglected to do.

'There is nothing more to be done. You may go,' Father Arthmael says softly, as if he understands the unspoken question.

She is torn between relief and desperation. Each time she passed behind Father Arthmael, she tried to peer over his shoulder at the pages of the book, but she could only glimpse part of a circle, or a crowned man. The words that twine about the drawings were too small to read and she dared not move closer. If only he would lay the book aside.

'I could watch the boy for you, Father Arthmael . . .' she offers, '. . . if you wished to visit Lord Sylvain . . . or return to the abbey.'

'You are not required here,' he says quietly. 'Lord Sylvain has another task for you.'

She can think of no excuse to remain, and though she longs to snatch the book from his hands and run away with it, where could she run to? It occurs to her that Father Arthmael cannot leave either unless Odo or Sylvain unlocks the gate.

Everything is still now, motionless. Even the birds have fallen silent. They crouch, hunched, on the floors of their cages, as if they have abandoned any hope of release and simply wait for death.

Odo, too, is waiting, waiting at the bottom of the tower for her to emerge. She trails after him across the lawn, past the lavender and rosemary, but instead of turning towards the hall, he leads her instead to the door at the base of the turret where Laurent sleeps. He unlocks the door and stands aside. It is plain he means her to enter.

'Am I . . . am I to go upstairs to where the young man . . .?'

'Stay or go up. It makes no difference. Master will come when he's ready.'

He flaps his hand impatiently, and as soon as she steps over the threshold, he pulls the door shut behind her, with a bang that echoes from the walls. She hears the iron key grate in the lock on the other side of the door. Has Sylvain ordered her to be locked in, or is it mere malice on the servant's part?

A tiny part of her thrills at the thought that Laurent may be upstairs. She tells herself that it is because she fears to be locked in alone, but she knows it is more than that. She wants to be with him. She edges a few steps up the spiral staircase, softly calling Laurent's name. There is no answer. She climbs higher until she reaches the door of the painted chamber. She tries not to look at the nightmare images on the wall, but a flash of red catches her eye, and she sees a figure she does not recall noticing before – a young boy, dressed in a scarlet loincloth, a strip of the red material trailing across his shoulder. But the child in the painting is not asleep. He is in the grip of an old man who is falling backwards into a tomb, and dragging the boy down on top of him.

She gives a little cry – the boy in the painting so much resembles the child in the tower. The door of the chamber beyond opens abruptly. Laurent is standing there, leaning against the door for support. He looks both frightened and relieved.

'I thought you were Sylvain.' He peers over her shoulder with such intensity that she turns, expecting to find someone behind her. 'You're alone?' he demands.

'Odo brought me here, but he's gone. We're locked in.'

'I know that!' he says. 'They've kept that door locked ever since I tried to escape. I keep trying it. But I think Odo and Sylvain have the only keys and there's not much likelihood of either of them forgetting to lock it.'

He turns back into the room, but only as far as a chair that has been placed just inside the doorway. 'I don't know which is worse – looking at those paintings or watching that black mould growing. Each time I turn my back or fall asleep that foul slime creeps closer. But I can't bear to be out there either. I can't stop staring at the girl on the wall. They're identical. Can't you see it? The girl in the painting is the one in the . . .'

He is gabbling incoherently. 'Sylvain says he needs one more thing . . . the most important of all.' Laurent's eyes frantically search her face. 'What else is he going to take from me? You made the bag for Sylvain. You must know what else he plans to do to me . . . Tell me! You have to tell me!'

His fingers pluck at his scarlet robe in agitation. It is the same shade of red that the sleeping child wears. Gisa finds herself turning back to the boy in the painting, the boy who is being dragged down into the grave.

'Have you come to take something from me?' Laurent persists. 'Was it you who came here while I slept and cut . . .? Did you steal my shadow? . . . Blood . . . he said something about a boy's blood.' He stares down at her hands, as if expecting to see a dagger grasped in her fingers.

407

'I've taken nothing from you,' she protests.

A boy's blood. Peter's blood-smeared limbs float in front of her eyes. *Man in the black robes . . . snake man.* But it was the White Canons who cut Peter, not Sylvain. He would never torture a child, not if what Thomas says about him is true. Yet Father Arthmael is sitting up in his tower with another little boy, reading the precious book, the one she knows Sylvain would entrust to no one – unless that person had something he badly needed.

She is suddenly aware that Laurent is cringing away from her as if she is an assassin come to murder him. She doesn't understand. Why should he be frightened of her? A few days ago he was giving her cowslips and trying to walk with her. What has happened to him?

'It was my hair you used to stitch the bag. I saw you! The bag Sylvain used to capture my shadow.'

'*Your* hair . . .' She gapes at him. 'I didn't know where it came from . . . *Your* hair?' she repeats, staring at the lock of straight, fine hair that flops across his sweating brow. 'No, it couldn't have been. It was far too coarse.'

Laurent is stammering something she cannot catch. His hands are clenched, his eyes wild. 'But what is he going to do now?' he yells. 'He said he needed something else before he could bring the girl back to life.'

'What girl?'

Laurent stares at her. 'The one in the charnel house . . . chapel . . . I don't know what the place is. You've seen it . . . thought it was a carved effigy, but it's a real body . . . a corpse preserved in wax. He says he means to resurrect her.'

Gisa shudders. 'Call up the spirit of a dead woman?'

'He can summon spirits at any time he pleases,' Laurent

says savagely. 'I've watched him. But he thinks he can do more than that. He believes he can actually make this girl live again in the flesh. But why does he need me?' He grabs Gisa by her arms. 'You're helping him in his enchantments. You're working together. Tell me what he wants!'

'I don't know!' Frightened by the desperation in his eyes, Gisa jerks from Laurent's grip and backs away. 'I am as much a prisoner as you. He orders me to grind and distil, but he doesn't tell me the uses of anything I prepare for him, not really, not in a way that I can explain. There's a book. I've only glimpsed a page or two of it, but it is not like any herbal I've ever seen. Whatever Lord Sylvain prepares comes from that. I've tried to look at it, but he keeps—'

She's interrupted by a harsh cry and the sound of flapping wings. She thinks a bird must have found its way into the turret and is trapped somewhere. Laurent rushes to the top of the stairs, staring down, then up at the beams above the staircase, but there is no sign of any creature. They both stand tense, listening, but only silence floods back.

She wants to explain, to reassure Laurent that she is not his enemy, not in collusion with Sylvain. She cannot bear the fear she sees in his face when he looks at her.

'Yesterday, Lord Sylvain came to the shop. Uncle Thomas had always refused to allow me to stay here, but then he changed his mind. Lord Sylvain said he needed me to work through the night. I refused, but—'

'So you say,' Laurent spits at her. 'But you're here anyway. This uncle of yours drag you by force, did he?'

'I shouldn't call him "Uncle",' she says miserably. 'He's no kin to me. I'm here because . . . because Lord Sylvain says I owe him a debt.'

'Money?' Laurent says. 'Well, that debt should be easy

to work off. He pays handsomely for obedience and silence, so I'm told.'

Fury boils up in Gisa. 'You want the truth? You can have it. I have no mother and my father was hanged when I was little more than an infant. I was left alone to starve, but Lord Sylvain *says* he took pity on me. He *says* he paid the apothecary generously to raise me as his niece. I don't remember him bringing me to Langley. But my unc– Master Thomas tells me I owe Sylvain my life and my living, because I am attainted. Now do you understand, you numbskull? I am attainted!'

It is only as she says the words aloud that she begins to comprehend the full misery of the sentence that was passed on her. Ever since last night her mind has lurched from one revelation to another. *Thomas and Ebba are not my kin. I have no family, no one in the world. The father I loved was a wicked man, a traitor. Sylvain, the man I fear, the man I shrink from, has been my saviour, my protector all these years.*

All this she understood last night. All this is her past, but only now does the realisation explode in her head that it is *not* past and never will be. It is her future. *I shall never be other than a servant in someone else's employ. I shall never marry, never have children, because the blood that runs hot through my veins is tainted, poisoned, corrupt.*

Her throat grows tight with tears that she learned long ago never to shed so they do not reach her eyes. She wants to run from the turret, run from Laurent and those ridiculous feelings for him that even now surge up in her. What right does she have to yearn for him, for anyone, to touch her, kiss her? She is filthy, leprous. She can never be loved. She shrinks away, suddenly afraid she will infect him too.

But there is no escaping. She and Laurent are trapped

together until it pleases Sylvain to release them, and what will he do then? What will happen tonight in that tower, to Laurent, to the sleeping boy dressed in scarlet? Her gaze darts to the tomb in the painting. Will Sylvain really try to raise a corpse?

'The body that Sylvain showed you?' Gisa whispers. 'Who was she? His wife?'

But Laurent isn't listening to anything she is saying. He doesn't even turn in her direction. He's staring wildly into the windowless chamber. 'The mould – look at the black mould. It's reached the ceiling and it's still spreading. I can see it growing. The slime is moving!'

Chapter 52

So here is Sol turned black, becoming with mercurius philosophorum one heart.

Another sharp caw made me spin round. Instinctively I looked to the place on the altar where Lugh always stood. Then I remembered he was gone. Sylvain had taken him.

'You are observant, Laurent.' The voice was as harsh as a raven's croak. 'The mould spreads rapidly, as I intend it should.'

I heard a sharp gasp from Gisa and turned to see the figure of Sylvain filling the doorway at the top of the stairs. For a moment I thought I saw two great ragged wings folding themselves against his sides. It must have been nothing more than the folds of his black cloak stirring. But all the same, with both chamber doors open, how the devil had he got up there without us hearing him?

Sylvain extended his hand towards the windowless bedchamber. 'The mould creeps over every surface. Nothing can escape it. It smothers, it consumes, it reduces all things to earth, to dirt, to the filth from which all life springs. It is the nigredo, the black death of putrefaction. But buried in the filth is the precious stone of life.'

He took a step towards Gisa, who was closest to him, his gaze fixed on her face. She retreated back towards me. The expression in her eyes was not one of gratitude, much less affection. She was terrified. If she was knowingly assisting Sylvain in his black arts, it was far from willingly, not that that did anything to reassure me. She could just as easily kill me out of fear of Sylvain as out of loyalty to him, probably more so. Even that wretched bird, Lugh, had betrayed me to him. And women are far more treacherous than any man or bird. I wouldn't trust Gisa further than a flea could spit.

The girl and I were both now standing in the old chapel in the flickering light of the single candle, Sylvain blocking the doorway. Had he deliberately herded us in there? I stepped sideways, hoping I could slip behind him and out of the door. But, as if he knew exactly what I planned, he pulled the door closed with a great echoing thump.

The damp musty odour of the mould was stronger than before. In the restless shadows cast by the candle flame it seemed to be oozing across the ceiling towards the image of the raven's head painted in the centre. The bird's beak was open, as if it was summoning the slime to it.

Sylvain dragged the chair against the closed door and lowered himself onto it. 'Sit, both of you. Let's make ourselves comfortable,' he said, waving his hand like a genial host.

But we were not guests. We were prisoners in a turret, at least I was, and one that was rotting around us even as we stood. There being no other chairs in the room, Gisa sat down gingerly on the edge of the bed. I certainly had no intention of meekly obeying orders. I had only one thought and that was to get out of there, any way I could.

'Do sit, Laurent. I know you have many questions and I am here to answer them.' Sylvain's tone was that of some kindly old physician. 'You have still not fully recovered your strength. You must conserve what little energy you have.'

That made an odd kind of sense, and now that he mentioned it, I discovered I was feeling shaky – my legs would hardly hold me up. Breathing in the damp mould was making my chest hurt, too. I found myself sinking down onto the bed. It couldn't hurt to get the old man off his guard. Let him believe I was docile, and when he least expected it, I'd spring across the room, knock him from the chair and be out of that door before he had time to say 'raven'.

'Gisa, you were curious about the body I showed Laurent this morning.'

I jerked. Just how long had he been standing there listening?

'And it is right that you should be curious, for her life touches yours in ways you cannot yet imagine.' Sylvain gave me an icy smile. 'Laurent wanted to write a story for me, didn't you, Laurent? But he was having trouble knowing where to begin. So why don't I begin it for you?'

I glanced at Gisa. But I couldn't make out her expression in the flickering mustard light. Had they dreamed up this little entertainment between them?

'The corpse that lies preserved in the charnel house is that of my poor daughter, Isolda. I wish you'd known her as a child, for she was beautiful both in body and mind.' He wagged a long finger at us. 'Ah, I know what you're thinking – all fathers claim their daughters are jewels, even the ugly and stupid ones – but Isolda really was exquisite and the most precious thing I possessed after her mother left us. She and I were the whole world to each other. We needed no one else.

'After the treachery of her mother, I was determined I would never allow another woman to betray me. Neither did I ever want another child to spring from my loins, for no man who has created perfection will risk producing something that might be flawed. Yet, in spite of my hostility, women continued to offer themselves to me.'

Sylvain laughed bitterly. 'I'm under no illusion that it was my face which attracted them. It was purely my wealth they lusted after. Yet I confess that at times the temptation to lie with them was overwhelming and on several occasions I almost succumbed. I could not endure my own weakness. I had to ensure that my body would not also betray me.'

Sylvain rose, seized the front of his black robe and lifted it. Gisa turned her head away. Moments later, I was profoundly wishing I'd looked away too. For between Sylvain's legs where his prick and cods should have been there was nothing but a puckered scarlet scar, shaped like a rose.

'You did that to yourself?' I gasped. 'You cut off your own . . .'

Sylvain dropped his robe and sank back onto the chair. 'The pain of a cut to the flesh is brief and quickly forgotten, unlike the pain of treachery,' he said quietly.

'But you wished to know about my daughter. Isolda was a joy to teach and she devoured knowledge. I instructed her in astrology and mathematics, the properties of metals and plants, and before long her skill was so great that she was able to assist me in every aspect of my work, but . . .'

I was barely able to take in what he was saying. That livid scar was seared on my eyeballs. It certainly accounted for why there was always a faint odour of urine lingering about Sylvain. But what kind of madman would do such a thing to himself? If I'd been afraid before, I was doubly so now. Anyone who is capable of taking a knife and slicing

415

off his own member wouldn't hesitate to hack another man into small pieces.

I tried to make myself concentrate on what Sylvain was saying. Better I listened to his ravings, however deranged, than dwell on what lay between his legs or, rather, what didn't.

'. . . I was foolish enough to permit Isolda to accompany me on journeys to buy rare ingredients from the merchants. I thought it would please her to see new sights. And I reasoned that I could teach her how to appraise the quality of what she was buying, and to bargain so that she was not cheated. I knew the time would come, as it does to us all, when I would grow too old and infirm to travel with her.'

The muscle in Sylvain's jaw suddenly tightened. 'But there was one thing I neglected to teach her, that men will use many guises to cheat a woman out of something that is far more valuable than gold. On one of our travels, Isolda encountered a young man, by the name of Hamon, who lusted after her. I saw at once the base and depraved character of the man that lay beneath the charming surface, a man, in fact, who bore uncanny resemblance to you, Master Laurent.'

I spluttered indignantly, but Sylvain silenced me with a wave of his hand and continued. 'Naturally I removed Isolda from his company at once. But, unknown to me, he continued to pursue her. Hamon persuaded her to deceive me, to write to him without my knowledge, to send messages, even to meet him. I discovered their perfidy, of course, and forbade her to see him, but by then she was already in his thrall and he convinced her to elope.

'I spent months hunting for her and when I did finally track her down, it was too late. She was heavy with child.

I tried to persuade her to come home, telling her that I would forgive her everything and all would be as before. But she refused to come with me, foolishly declaring she loved him. Hamon returned as I was trying to convince her to abandon him and we fought. Our quarrel so distressed my daughter that the pangs of labour came upon her and the midwife was summoned. But the birth was long and hard, and the child became wedged. The midwife feared she was losing both mother and baby. Do you know what the Church teaches these women? Do you know what they swear before the priests and abbots they will do?'

Sylvain rose and began to pace furiously around the chamber. Gisa shrank further back onto the bed.

'The priests tell them that the child must be brought forth alive and kept alive just long enough for the midwife to baptise it, so that its soul may be saved for Christ, even if that should cost the life of the mother. I was not in the chamber with my poor daughter. Had I known what that ignorant old hag had determined to do, I would have cut her hands off. But I knew nothing of it until she had committed her foul deed. That midwife sliced open the belly of my daughter and pulled the living baby from her, then left her bleeding while she baptised the infant, just as the priest had instructed her to do. She murdered my daughter.'

Sylvain slammed his fist down onto the table. 'She should have killed the baby! She should have cut it up inside Isolda's womb as midwives do with a dead infant, so that it might be expelled without harm to the mother. If she had done that, my daughter would have lived.

'The midwife hurried the baby away and gave it into its father's arms. I didn't care. I couldn't bear to look at the mewling creature that had so selfishly taken the life of my beloved child. To me it was nothing more than a bloated tapeworm, feeding on her, sucking her strength, so that it could live. Hamon could do as he pleased with his brat.

'But I would not let him have the body of my daughter. I preserved her carefully, as I showed you, and brought her home. I had her laid in the charnel house so that I could continue to gaze on her lovely face, for I could not bear to bury her in the cold earth to rot and be consumed by worms.

'I returned to my studies alone, but as I pored over the books and charts we had once read together, I could still see her sometimes, sitting in the half-shadow, hear her soft breathing, smell the rosemary water on her hair. Then gradually, as if Isolda's spirit was guiding my hand to the pages, the idea took shape that I possessed the knowledge to bring her to life again. I could resurrect her, if I could but make the stone of life. I have devoted my soul and my strength in every waking hour to the pursuit of this priceless treasure and tonight it lies within my grasp.'

Sylvain was no longer looking at us, but staring upwards at the raven's head in the centre of the ceiling, his lips parted, his frame taut as a strung bow. There was a glazed expression in his eyes as of a man approaching the moment of ejaculation. He reminded me of the statues of saints I'd seen depicted at their moment of martyrdom. But I had the uneasy feeling that if Sylvain was contemplating death he didn't intend it to be his own.

I glanced towards the door, aware that Gisa was doing the same. I guessed the same thought was racing through both of our heads. If we rushed it, could we get out, while Sylvain was distracted? The girl was closest to the door, but I couldn't be sure she wasn't on his side. Would she attempt to block me? Cry out a warning? I leaned forward, tensing myself, trying to judge the right moment. But just as I was about to spring at him, I heard footsteps on the stairs beyond, and not just one set. Several people were climbing up the spiral staircase towards us.

Sylvain must have heard them too, for he half turned his head towards the sound, then looked back at us with one of his chilling smiles. 'Lie down on the bed, both of you, side by side.'

We sprang off it. Gisa ran towards the door, and Sylvain, instead of trying to catch her, stepped obligingly aside. I raced through the door after her, expecting any moment to feel Sylvain's hands grabbing at me, but he made no move to stop me. Gisa reached the far door of the painted chamber first, but she was pushed back into the room as, first, Odo, then the youth without a tongue and finally Pipkin crowded through the door and stood there, blocking any hope of escape. Odo's expression was as impassive as ever, but the youth was grinning broadly, the dark cavern of his tongue-less mouth more unnerving than before.

'I repeat – lie down on the bed, both of you,' Sylvain said, behind us. 'I wish to spare you as much pain as possible. The more willingly you submit, the easier you will find it. Death is but a gentle sleep if you surrender yourselves and do not fight it.' His tone was as soothing as poppy syrup, but however softly a man pronounces the word *death*, it is a word that thuds into your brain as sharply as an arrow.

I caught Gisa's arm and flung her as hard as I could at Odo, at the same time hurling myself between Pipkin and the lad, catching them off-guard. I tore down the spiral stairs, bouncing off the walls in my headlong dash, while the cries of rage from Odo echoed above me. But the steps

419

were uneven in height and the stone worn smooth and slippery. It was almost inevitable that before long my foot should miss the step. I found myself crashing down onto the hard stone, tumbling over and over as I rolled down the stairs. First my shoulder then my knee banged painfully against the walls. I barely escaped dashing my brains out as I tumbled off the final step and smashed onto the hard flagstones in front of the door.

But I couldn't afford to lie there nursing my bruises. I dragged myself to my feet and limped to the door, twisting the handle. I was certain that at any moment I'd hear Odo's footsteps pounding down the steps behind me. But all I could hear were the shrieks and yells of the girl. She sounded terrified. I ought to go back and help her. But what would be the point? It would be four against one. Better to get out and run to the town to fetch a crowd of armed men.

I turned the handle again, first one way then the other, frantically shaking it as the truth sank in. It was locked. Of course, it was locked! Odo wouldn't have been so stupid as to leave it open. Even as I searched around, trying to find a trapdoor or any kind of hiding place, I knew it was useless. That was why they hadn't bothered to chase after me. They knew I couldn't get out. They could come for me at their leisure. And they did.

I might have been trapped, but I had no intention of making it easy for them. It took Pipkin to kneel on me and pin me to the floor, while Odo and the youth bound my hands behind my back, then my ankles, before they could half drag, half carry me up the stairs. I wriggled like an eel, until Odo threatened to pull me up by my feet, so that my head bounced on every step all the way up. Even in my fear and panic, I had enough sense to realise that my chances of surviving whatever Sylvain had planned would be worse than a lobster dropped in boiling water if I was battered half unconscious before he'd begun.

Gisa was already pinioned to the bed when I was finally tossed down beside her. She was trussed up like me, except that her arms had been crossed over her chest in the manner of a corpse. Her eyes were wide with fear, but there wasn't a trace of a tear in them and her lips were pressed tight, as if she was determined not to let so much as a squeak of terror escape her.

Odo and the youth threw a rope over our shoulders and another across our legs to ensure that we could not wriggle off the bed. Even as I felt them pulling the ropes tight, then tighter still, I couldn't help noticing that the creeping fingers of black mould on the ceiling above my head had now joined together, so that only a slim circle of white remained around the raven head's, like a halo around the moon on a frosty night.

When we were firmly trussed up, ready for the slaughter-terer's knife, Sylvain nodded curtly to his three henchmen. They sidled from the chamber, the youth grinning and Odo expressionless, as if he was completely indifferent to whatever our fate might be. Only Pipkin, panting and sweating from his labours, darted an anxious but helpless glance towards us, as if he pitied us, though any fears he had for our future were nothing compared to my own.

When we heard the hollow echo of the door at the bottom of the tower slamming shut, Sylvain approached the bed. Gisa stiffened beside me. I glanced at his hands, searching for a weapon – a knife, axe, garrotte – but they were empty.

'Just what are you intending to do with me?' I tried to sound defiant. After all, when there's a woman beside him, no man wants to sound as if he is about to start sobbing in abject terror, which I confess I might very well have done had Gisa not been there.

'I am going to do nothing,' Sylvain murmured. 'Your death was set in motion the day you came here.' He gestured to the walls. 'As you observed, the mould is already closing in. I have been holding it back, but once I have left this chamber, its spread will accelerate. It will cover you, feed on you. Your skin, flesh and bones will putrefy into the black slime from which all life is generated. Your two bodies will melt into one, the ultimate union of male and female. And from the filth and decay of your marriage bed I will pluck the stone of life.'

'You intend to leave us here to starve to death!' I yelled.

'Of course not,' Sylvain said soothingly. 'That would be cruel. You will not have time to starve. See, the mould is already oozing up the bed towards you. By the first ray of dawn, nothing will remain of either of you but a single pool of slime.'

As if to demonstrate, a chunk of rotten plaster from the ceiling suddenly crashed to the floor, and burst into a mass of stinking, sodden dust. I heard a gasp of horror from Gisa. The room was being eaten away even as we watched.

'But when I was a child, you saved me,' Gisa said.

'I saved you for this moment, for this union, this consummation of the nigredo.'

Sylvain leaned down. Tenderly he unbound her dark hair and, carefully as any maid preparing a girl for the bridal bed, he arranged the locks so that they tumbled down her shoulders. He caressed them between his thumb and forefinger. Gisa, recoiling at his touch, turned her face away.

'So like your mother's hair,' Sylvain murmured to himself.

Even when you're terrified, or because fear sharpens the mind, you get flashes of blinding comprehension. Perhaps it was something in Sylvain's expression as he looked at Gisa, just as he had looked at the woman preserved in wax, or maybe it was seeing Gisa lying flat beside me, like Isolda on that slab, but suddenly I understood why the dead woman looked so familiar. God's arse, how could I have been so dull-witted not to see it straight away?

'Gisa's your granddaughter, Sylvain! Your own blood. I can see that she is.'

He nodded.

'But if you know that . . .' I stammered incredulously. 'I realise you don't care a pig's fart about my life, but this is your daughter's child. You surely don't intend to kill her.'

'She is her mother's daughter, Isolda's blood, *my blood*, as you so succinctly put it. That is precisely why it must be Gisa who dies. My daughter gave her life for her child. Now that same child must give her life for her mother. Can't you see how just that is, how right? And she will gladly sacrifice herself for her mother, won't you, little swan? She knows it is her duty. Her mother conceived her, succoured her in the womb, poured her blood into Gisa's veins that she might live and she has lived. All these years she has been alive, while her mother lay dead. Now she will return that love, that sacrifice. She will die, so that her mother can live for eternity. She was born for this moment. You want to do this, don't you, my little swan? You long for this.'

Beside me, I heard a breath drawn in on a sob. Gisa's hands were clenched into little fists, her body rigid.

'Tell him, Gisa. Tell him you won't do it.'

'But she will. She has no choice.'

'Listen,' I begged. 'Your daughter is already alive. She

423

lives in Gisa. Look at her. You said yourself her hair is just like her mother's, and not only her hair, her face, hands, everything. I would wager my own life that she even sounds like her.'

'But she is *not* my daughter. She is tainted with his blood, with the foul blood of the man who corrupted my child and took her away from me.'

I felt Gisa wince beside me.

'Girls take after their mothers, everyone knows that,' I said. 'Besides, you can't make your daughter's body live. I know the Church says Christ was resurrected, but he was only dead three days. Your daughter's been dead for years. If you kill Gisa you will have lost anything of her mother that is in her. Every trace of your daughter will be gone for good. If Gisa lives, your daughter, your beautiful Isolda, will go on living, through your granddaughter and great-grandchildren.'

'Each generation will be corrupted with his blood and the blood of all the men like you who take them to their beds, each drop of my daughter's blood growing more diluted and more polluted. Only in this way can my daughter fully live again, whole and pure. Did not Ezekiel raise a valley of dry bones into living flesh again?'

He smoothed Gisa's forehead tenderly. 'But you must have no fear, little swan. Simply surrender to death. You killed your mother. You killed my daughter. You should be grateful to me that I have given you this opportunity to atone. Those who kill can never be forgiven, for their victims cannot forgive them. And they go, drenched in guilt, to their graves. But your mother will rise and she will forgive you. You will be absolved by your own death.'

'You can't blame a baby for its mother's death,' I shouted.

424

Sylvain ignored me and I realised that he had said nothing about using the stone to bring us back from the dead . . . What was I thinking? I was starting to believe his tales now. No one was going to be raised from the dead. This was nothing but the twisted fantasy of a mad tyrant.

'The boy,' Gisa said. 'The little boy in the tower. What will you do to him?'

Sylvain smiled as if he was delighted by her question. 'The son must be swallowed by the father, and the son must slay the father, that is the magistery. The ashes of father and son, the old king and the prince, will be added to the earth of your putrefaction. As the sun rises tomorrow your earth and their ashes will be transformed in the furnace into the one stone that is beyond price. Four deaths to bring forth the final glorious and perfect resurrection. You see, all I require for the greatest work of all is come together in this place. All of you have been brought here for one purpose, to create the philosopher's stone.'

'You can't kill four people and hope to escape,' I yelled. 'They will come looking for us. You'll hang, if the towns-people don't tear you apart first.'

'But they will not come, Master Laurent. You see, the rumours you have so kindly spread have already done their work. They really do believe that I am the master of the dark arts. They are too afraid to attack me. Your rumours have been far more useful to me than any story you might have dreamed up to counter them. Do you really think after the tales you have spread about me that they will risk their own lives to save a serf's child, a wandering storyteller or the daughter of the traitor?

'You lie in your bridal bed, which is your tomb. You are the sacred consummation of the sun and the shadow and you will become the poison of death. Be grateful to me that I grant you such a role in this great and holy work. For you will become the essence of the stone that transmutes all things. There can be no greater destiny.'

Sylvain was already striding to the door. 'I will leave you the candle, so that you may watch your death approach.'

'Wait! I yelled, struggling frantically against the ropes. But even as I yelled out, I heard the door to the outer room close, the footfalls retreating, and finally the echo of the great wooden door closing at the bottom of the tower.

Chapter 53

For in the blood of this stone is hidden its soul.

A toad crawls across Peter's bare leg. Even its cold, soft belly rasps like a stone on the boy's burning skin. He kicks feebly and the toad drops into the foul water below. The boy whimpers as the movement drags him out of a fitful sleep. His mouth is so dry that it hurts to move his tongue. He fumbles for the skin of ale, desperate for even a sip, but though he sucks and sucks, there is not a drop left. Sobbing in frustration, he knocks the empty ale skin into the channel below, where it floats on the thick, stagnant water like a dead rat.

He shivers violently, cannot stop his teeth chattering. He threw off his shirt and blanket a while back for he was so hot he couldn't bear their touch, now he tries feebly to wrap them round himself, but even that small effort defeats him. He scratches at the gnat bites on his arms and ankles, but that only makes them itch the more. One of his eyelids is so swollen from the bites, he cannot open it more than a crack.

He turns his face towards the small gap between the stones. It is dark outside. Why hasn't she come? She always comes when the reeds on the other side of the ditch melt from green to grey in the fading light. Now he cannot see them at all. What if she cannot find the hole?

'I'm here . . . here,' he whimpers.

Then he remembers. She said she could not come tonight. 'I'll come tomorrow,' she said, 'or the next night . . .' She promised she would come. Come with something to make him well, something from a book that would make all the pain and burning go away. She promised . . . But is this night *tomorrow*? He doesn't know how many hours or nights have passed.

He must drink. Clinging to the ledge, terrified of falling in, he reaches down and pulls up the floating skin, scooping some of the foul green water into it. He falls back panting, exhausted by the effort, then drags the skin to his lips and sucks. There is a moment of relief as the liquid wets his mouth, but it doesn't quench the raging thirst. His small frame screams for more. He drinks again, but as he swallows the water rises in his throat and he vomits. He sobs, loudly, uncontrollably. He wants Gisa. He wants her to come. Why won't she come?

Stones rattle beneath iron shoes, but Peter is crying too hard to notice anything but his own pain, until the flame from a lantern lights up the hole. He recoils, squinting against brightness. He shields his eyes and glimpses movement behind it.

'Gisa! I . . . I thought you weren't coming.' He drags himself closer to the hole. Pushing his arm through, he feels a hand grasping his. Relief wells up in him.

'So this is where you've been hiding, Peter.'

Fingers tighten about his wrist, so that he cannot pull it away. Part of a face looms in next to the lantern. Only one eye, half a mouth, but it is enough for Peter to cry out, as he sees it is Father Madron.

'Father Arthmael and Father John think you are dead.

Do you know that? Even said Mass for your soul. Couldn't let them think I lost you, could I? I guessed you'd crawled into the tunnels under the vat, but I thought you'd be dead by now. I had to keep searching for your body, though. If it had blocked one of the channels or been washed beneath one of the drainage holes, Father Arthmael would have discovered he sprinkled holy water over the grave of a dog. He mustn't know I failed him. He trusts me, you see, Peter. He knows I am the only one who understands his work, not like Father John and the rest of them. They will never understand the mysteries. The abbot is a great man, a holy saint, and after tonight everyone will know it.'

Peter knows only the pain in his arm where the White Canon is grinding it against the stones. He knows only the terror, that Father Madron will drag him through that tiny hole, ripping the skin from his body. The great bell of the abbey tolls.

Father Madron's head jerks up, then he lowers his face to the hole again. 'It is time! I must go to Father Arthmael. He will need me. But when it is over, I will come for you, Peter. Don't think of trying to hide from me again. If you do, I will find you and you will suffer for it. I want you to stay exactly where you are and keep very quiet. If you're a good boy, I'll release you when I return. I'll make sure you vanish properly this time and Father Arthmael never need know you were not already in that grave when he blessed it.'

The lantern is snatched away and the tunnel plunges into blackness. Peter hears the creaking of a saddle, then the crunch of horseshoes as Father Madron turns his mount onto the track and is gone.

The child wants to run from the hole, hide, but he is too weak, too cowed to move. He lies curled on his side, trembling violently, his mutilated back pressed to the rough stones, his throbbing head buried in his arm.

'Gisa . . . please come . . . please come,' he whispers over and over again. But the only answer is a long, low rumble of distant thunder and a shivering of trees.

Chapter 54

And he is the whole elixir of the albedo and the rubedo,
the water of life and death.

It is dark when Regulus awakes. For a moment he thinks he is sleeping in the dorter with the other boys. Once, on waking, he would have imagined himself back in the cottage with his brothers and sisters. That memory now seems to him but a fading dream. He feels at once the unaccustomed softness of the red woollen cloth tied across his buttocks and over his shoulder. He feels another unfamiliar sensation too – in spite of the skimpiness of his garment, he is warm.

The source of the heat is a brazier that has been newly lit. The yellow and orange flames from the kindling leap upwards around the charcoal, which is already beginning to glow ruby red. Regulus gazes sleepily at it. His body feels unnaturally heavy. He has no will to move his limbs.

'Awake, little king? Good.'

Regulus quickly closes his eyes. He doesn't want to be awake, but Father Arthmael isn't fooled. He kneels beside the boy, dragging him to his feet. Regulus's legs feel shaky, as if he has been ill for a long time.

'You will sleep again very soon, Regulus. You will sleep till the stars fall from the heavens and the seas turn to dust. But before you can rest, you have one simple task to perform, just one. Remember what I told you.'

He turns the boy and shows him an elaborately carved chair, like the one Christ the king sits on in heaven in the painting on the abbey wall. 'This is where the old king will sit, and this is where you will kill him, because you are the new king.'

Father Arthmael pulls a package wrapped in an embroidered cloth towards him. The flames glint on the gold thread. The boy moves closer, intrigued by the pictures woven into the cloth. A flock of every different kind of bird he knows is gathered on the ground and above them flies a golden eagle, but sitting on its head is a tiny wren wearing a golden crown.

'That is you, Regulus – us,' Father Arthmael says. 'Do you know why the wren is the king of all the birds? The eagle is the strongest. But the wren is the most cunning. For once, long ago, the birds of the air decided that whichever among them could fly the highest should become their king. The eagle was certain he would be proclaimed king for he was stronger than any of the other birds. All the birds flew into the sky, but the eagle's great strength meant that it could climb higher than any of them. Then, just as the eagle's strength was exhausted and he began to sink down towards the earth, a tiny wren, which had been hiding in the eagle's feathers, flew up from his back. It was so light the eagle had not even felt the bird riding on him. Since the little wren had been carried all the way up, in just a few beats of its tiny wings it was able to rise higher even than the exhausted eagle, and so the wren was proclaimed the king of all the birds.'

Slowly, reverently, as if he unwraps the Holy Grail, Father Arthmael folds back the cloth with its eagle and wren. Regulus sees a flash of gold turn blood red in the firelight from the brazier. He is dazzled by the lights glinting from the object, which seems to his fogged mind the brightest thing he has ever seen, save for the sun. He stares transfixed as the tiny reflected flames undulate across the golden metal. Then Father Arthmael lifts it up in both hands and slowly Regulus comprehends what he is seeing. It is a sickle, though not nearly as big as the iron one his father uses. It is as long as the boy's own forearm, the blade curved and razor-sharp.

Father Arthmael takes the boy's hand and closes it about the handle. Holding the boy's arm he makes small jabbing movements, as if he is slicing at ears of invisible corn.

'When I tell you, you will strike his throat, like this. This blade is so keen, it will take little effort. Do you—'

'He is coming, Father Arthmael.' The voice is soft, urgent. Regulus cannot see the speaker, though he recognises his voice.

The birds in cages start to cry out in alarm and fly against the iron bars as if they, too, are warning – *he is coming, he is coming!*

Laying the golden sickle on the table, Father Arthmael seizes the boy, pushing him back against the wall. 'Stay there. You must not utter a word. Even if he should address you, say nothing. Do you understand?'

Regulus nods. In truth, he is not certain he could speak, even if he wanted to. Words float in his head, like dead fish, and he cannot make them swim to his tongue.

Father Arthmael seems to take his silence as obedience. He straightens the plain gold band of cloth encircling the boy's brow, and steps back just as a man's head emerges through the floor.

The man climbs up into the room, glancing first at Father Arthmael, then at the boy and finally at the chair that is set before the brazier. He is clad in black robes with silver thread-work at the neck and round the sleeves. His hands are encased in fine black leather gloves, with silver snakes encircling the wrists.

'The marriage bed has been entered. The nigredo embraces the couple even as we speak. It will not be long before they are united in the ecstasy of death and putrefaction. Their union will be complete by dawn.' He nods approvingly. 'I see you have prepared the boy.'

Father Arthmael, his hands folded across his hollow belly, inclines his head. 'If you would be seated, Sylvain, I will lay the boy across your knees and hold him as his blood is spilled. The vessel is ready.'

Something flutters in Regulus's head, a fragile memory that this is not what Father Arthmael said before. The words are wrong. He wants to tell them. But when he forces his mouth open, no sound comes out.

The black-robed man shakes his head. 'No, take him to the roof. It must be done where the wood is laid ready for burning, in the white light of the moon.'

He seizes the boy's arm, urging him towards the bottom of the ladder that leads to the closed trapdoor above. 'Up there, boy.'

Regulus turns his head, searching Father Arthmael's face. Both men frighten him, but he knows he has most to fear from the man who rules the abbey.

'Regulus,' Father Arthmael warns, 'remember what I said.'

The boy does not remember, not properly. He remembers a jumble of words, but they swirl round his head and he cannot make them stand still. Felix said if a man in black robes . . . What . . . what did Felix say to do then?

'On the throne, Sylvain, that is where the blood must be

spilled,' Father Arthmael insists. 'Come here to me, Regulus.'

The boy tries to pull away from the gloved hand holding his arm and return to the voice he recognises.

The man tightens his grip. Regulus jerks his head up to look at him, feeling a sudden tension in Sylvain's body. He is staring at Father Arthmael.

'The throne . . . You called it the throne. That is where the old king dies.'

He takes a step forward. With both hands grasping the boy's shoulders, he pushes him in front of himself like a shield. 'And which of us is the old king, Arthmael? Black or white, which do you intend will fall into the grave with the boy? No, don't bother to answer that. I can see it in your face. I seek resurrection for one who is dead. You . . . you seek eternal life for yourself. But what you fail to grasp, after all those years of study, what you failed to learn from the Great Master is that to gain the eternal life you seek there must be death, and the death must be your own. You cannot escape the grave, Arthmael.'

Without warning he shoves Regulus forward hard against the abbot. Regulus's head smashes into Father Arthmael's stomach, knocking the breath from him. Regulus crashes down onto the wood boards and Father Arthmael doubles up, crumpling down against the wall, trying desperately to pull the air back into his lungs. In one fluid movement, Sylvain snatches the golden sickle from the table. Regulus sees only the flash in the light of the brazier, which seems to leave a long golden-red trail in the air, as if a flame hangs there suspended.

Sylvain springs towards the crouching abbot. He raises the sickle in his right hand and with his left tries to grab Father Arthmael's hair to drag his head back. But the priest

435

is tonsured and the short fringe around his head is slippery with grease. The hair slides from Sylvain's fingers. With a shriek of frustration, he lifts the sickle higher as if he means to cleave the man's skull in two. Father Arthmael, still struggling for breath, raises his arm to shield his head, his face distorted in fear. But just as the murderous blade descends, Sylvain shrieks again, this time in pain, as a thick staff knocks the sickle from his hand and sends it spinning across the floor.

Father Madron shoves Sylvain aside and hauls his superior to his feet.

'Forgive me, Father. I know you gave instructions I was to keep watch outside, but when I heard the commotion I—'

'Stop him! Stop him, you idiot!' Father Arthmael cries.

But it is too late. Sylvain is dragging Regulus across the floor. The young canon and Father Arthmael try to lunge for him together, but succeed only in falling over each other in their haste. Sylvain releases his grip on the boy only long enough to grasp him around the waist and, with the small child tucked under his arm, he mounts the ladder, using his own head as a battering ram to push open the trapdoor above him. Regulus's shoulder is rammed against the frame, and he yelps in pain as Sylvain drags him through the small opening. The trapdoor falls back into place with a hollow thud, and Father Madron, scrambling up behind them, puts his hand to the trapdoor just moments too late to prevent the bolt being kicked into place above him.

Chapter 55

They must be extracted, conjoined, buried and mortified and turned into ashes. Thus it comes to pass that the nest of the birds becomes their grave.

Gisa turned her head to me. It might have been the shadows cast by the single trembling flame, but her face suddenly looked as gaunt as a skull, her eye sockets hollow, as if all the flesh had been sucked from her.

'I am sorry,' she said, 'sorry that I drew you into this, that it is my grandfather who is responsible.'

Not as sorry as I am, I thought. Why on earth had I persuaded her to ask Sylvain to see me? I should have taken it as an omen when Odo first refused me at the door. I should have walked as far away from this accursed place as I could. I should never have crossed the river. I should never have crossed the sea to England. I should never have mentioned the forgery to Philippe in the first place. Why had I ever left my life with old Gaspard?

'Not your fault,' I said gruffly, though I wasn't sure I believed that.

Come to think of it, it was entirely her fault. I had come merely to offer my services in telling stories. If she hadn't gone around sewing bags with my intimate hair or helped Sylvain brew his potions, things would never have got this far.

Gisa gave a startled cry as another lump of blackened

437

plaster crashed to the floor. The stench of rotting wood was growing stronger. Was it just a shadow thrown by the candle flame, or was the mould now creeping up over the end of the bed towards our feet?

My hands were still tied firmly behind my back and the full weight of my body was pressing down on them. Pains were shooting up my arms and shoulders. My hands had already gone completely dead. I twisted, trying to turn onto my side to ease the blood flow.

'Stop! You're just tightening the ropes,' Gisa said. 'We have to try to undo the knots.'

'And how exactly do we do that?' I snapped.

We tried, but with her wrists crossed in front of her and tied to the bed posts and mine pinioned behind my back, not to mention the ropes lashed across our chests, neither of us could reach a single knot, not even with our teeth. Odo had made quite sure that even an acrobat couldn't have freed himself from those bonds. Sweating from the effort, we sank back exhausted again.

'We're in no danger,' I said, trying to sound as if I believed it. 'This is just some insane fantasy of Sylvain's. All we have to do is wait till morning, and when he finds we're still alive, he'll realise whatever spell he thinks he's cast isn't working and give up. Whenever have you heard of mould killing anyone? It can't. It just can't!'

But it was already covering the toes of my leather shoes.

'Look, up there,' Gisa breathed.

The mould covering the ceiling was swelling out in fat black cushions. But there was something else up there too. Spiders! Dozens of them, swinging on threads across the chamber on currents of warm air from the candle flame. They were spinning webs, great thick swathes of them.

Even as I stared up, a movement on the walls caught the edge of my vision. The stones appeared to be trembling. For a moment, I feared the tower was collapsing, but there was no sound. Then I saw that what was moving were worms, thousands of them, wriggling out between the cracks, burrowing through the crumbling stone and falling in thick slimy handfuls into the carpet of mould on the floor.

I clenched my jaw, trying to suppress a scream. The spiders swung lower on their threads, dropping down towards our faces. I started to struggle frantically again. But even as I did I heard a murmur of voices, snatches of words, as if there were people close by.

'In here!' I yelled. 'Up in the turret. We can't get out. Help us. For God's sake, come quickly.'

The mutterings grew louder, though I could not distinguish anything that made sense, but somewhere close by was a whole crowd of people. They really had stormed the manor, after all, and come to rescue us. Relief surged through me.

'Up here,' I yelled. 'Hurry, for God's sake, hurry. Break the door down!'

But the words were turning to shrieks, moans and wails. Then came a rhythmic thumping, like the sound children make with bone-clappers on All Hallows Night, as if a crowd of people was trying to smash through the walls of the tower.

I called out again, but was cut short by Gisa, who had gone rigid.

'No! No! Don't call to them. For pity's sake, don't.'

'But we need their help,' I protested.

'They won't help us,' Gisa whispered. 'I've heard them before. Those are the dead. And they're coming for us.'

Chapter 56

The wingless bird that is below holds the winged bird that is above and will not let it escape the nest.

A cloud passes across the moon and a tide of darkness floods over trees and buildings alike. On the road outside the manor house a weasel-thin boy grins to himself. He has already moved the broken cartwheel into position against the wall and he's been watching the cloud creeping towards the moon, waiting for it to obliterate the light. He won't have long, though. The wind is gathering strength. The clouds are moving more swiftly. Far off there is a growl of thunder. A storm is coming, but it will not break yet.

He balances precariously on the wheel's rim, stretching up to a stone near the top of the wall where he is sure he can get a finger-hold. He grabs the stone with one hand and, as the cartwheel topples away beneath him, gropes wildly for the top of the wall with his free hand. For a moment, he hangs there limply, like the hanged felon he may very well become if they catch him breaking in. Then, as his bare toes scrabble against the rough stones, he gains the purchase he needs to haul his belly onto the top of the wall and tip himself over it. He lands on the grass, jarred and smarting from a dozen grazes, but he doesn't care. He's suffered worse, far worse, and his elation at having got inside dulls any pain.

But his triumph does not last long. His plan, if such it can be called, extended no further than getting over the wall, and now that he has done it, he swiftly realises he has not even the wisp of an idea of how to find Regulus.

When Regulus did not return to the dorter for supper, or appear among the boys at Compline, Felix knew at once that, like Mighel and Peter, he would never come back. In the morning, Father John would provide some explanation for the boy's absence – Regulus's family had come for him or he had been sent out to become an apprentice to some great man. The little boys would believe it, because they wanted to believe it, in the way a dying man wants to believe that the figure he sees sitting in the corner of his chamber really is an angel, not a huddle of discarded clothes. But Felix never would. They'd never convince him that Regulus was back in his mother's arms, not even if they swore on a thousand virgins.

They had not taken Regulus down into the cellars, Felix was certain of that. No lights burned through the slits of the chamber that led to the staircase, and as they filed out of Compline, he'd seen Father Madron heading towards the main abbey gate. Felix was certain they'd given Regulus to the black-robed wizard who changed boys into birds. He'd wagered his dinner for a month on that.

In the dark, it had not been difficult for Felix to slip away from the others just before they reached the dorter. He'd scurried along beneath the walls, keeping to the pools of shadow, well away from the candlelight spilling from the casements. Father Madron was deep in conversation with the gatekeeper, as his horse was led snorting into the yard. The beast's breath spurted in white plumes from its nostrils and its iron shoes struck blue sparks against the cobbles.

Felix's stomach gave an excited lurch. The gatekeeper would have to open the main wooden door to let Father Madron out. No one could ride or even lead a horse through the narrow wicket gate.

The gatekeeper began opening the heavy door before Father Madron had even walked across to his horse. Felix crept closer, sidling round behind the White Canon as he was occupied with mounting his beast. The boy ran for the shelter of a cart that stood in the corner of the yard, close to the gate. Two chickens roosting on the cart opened their blackcurrant eyes and watched him, fluffing their feathers in annoyance at being disturbed. He prayed they would not start squawking.

Felix waited, crouching low. The flaming torch on the wall flooded the whole archway with yellow light. If he ran through the gate now, he would be lit up like a heretic on a pyre. But if he didn't move soon, the canon would have ridden through and the gates have been locked behind him.

Felix leaped up and, seizing one of the roosting chickens, tossed it into the middle of the courtyard. The indignant bird fluttered to the ground, screeching and flapping its wings. Startled and disoriented, it fled across the yard, directly in front of the horse, which reared and whinnied at the sudden appearance of this demented creature. Father Madron fought to bring his mount under control, swearing and cursing at the stupid bird, while the gatekeeper and groom rushed forward to help.

Felix didn't hesitate. Keeping low to the ground, he dashed through the archway and threw himself into the shelter of some reeds beyond the moat bridge. Panting and sweating, he knelt there until Father Madron, having calmed his horse, finally passed through the archway and trotted past his hiding place. The great wooden gate closed behind him with a thud that echoed off the stones.

Two thoughts struck Felix at the same instant. The first was that any punishment he had thus far suffered at the hands of Father John was mere play compared to what he could expect when he returned after having sneaked out. The second was that he was free. He need never return and nor would he.

His absence would surely be discovered as soon as Father John came to lock them up for the night; probably it already had been. But they would search the abbey first, all the usual places a boy might go – the necessarium, where he might have gone to relieve himself, and the kitchens or store rooms he might have raided to steal food. Everyone knew it was impossible to leave the abbey save through the main gate and the gatekeeper knew better than to let any boy go out unescorted. So, if Felix was lucky it would be some hours before they thought the unthinkable and began to search for him outside the abbey grounds. By which time he would be long gone.

A thrill of excitement rippled through him. He could go anywhere in the world, do anything he pleased. But excitement turned swiftly to anxiety. Where could he go? He'd been brought to the abbey when he was even younger than Regulus. They'd told him his family was dead. He didn't know if that was true, but even if they still lived, he'd no idea where they might be or what they were called. He couldn't even remember what he'd been called before he became Felix. The name was there, submerged somewhere beneath his nightmares, but he couldn't reach it.

And how would he live? Food, clothing and shelter might have been meagre, but they had appeared in his life day after day, as the sunlight and the rain fall on grass. He had little idea how to obtain such necessities for himself. A great chasm of fear and loneliness opened beneath him. He wanted to run back to the gate and pound on it, demand to be let back into the safety of those cloisters. He didn't care that he'd be punished. Punishments always came to an end eventually. He wanted to be safe in there with the other boys.

He shook himself angrily. Regulus wasn't safe, not if he was with the man in the black robes. That was why he'd escaped, Felix reminded himself sternly, to save Regulus, and when he had rescued him, he'd take him back to his family. Regulus's mother would be so glad to see him that she'd hug them both till they couldn't breathe. Maybe she'd ask Felix to stay with them – for ever. He clutched at the thought. He and Regulus would be brothers. He'd have his own family then and they'd live in their own cottage deep in the forest. He'd help his new father cut wood and tend traps. He'd mind the little ones – he'd had plenty of practice at doing that – and in time . . . He shook himself again. Time was running out. Before he could return Regulus to his family, he first had to find him.

Felix had never visited the manor, but from what he'd overheard the lay brothers saying, it wasn't far along this track. That was what they'd said, anyway. But when he was creeping along the ink-black path, tripping over unfamiliar ruts and holes, it had seemed a very long way to Felix and several times he almost turned back, fearing he was walking in the wrong direction. His heart had been thumping most of the way too, as he bolted past the rustling bushes, or started at the sudden screech of an owl. Once, he thought he heard the sound of sobbing coming from a ditch. Maybe it was the ghost of a drowned child. Felix ran.

But now that he is finally inside the manor walls, his escape and the journey seem a mere stroll across a sunny courtyard compared with the task of finding Regulus, never mind rescuing him. As the cloud slides away from the moon, Felix sees that he is standing in a garden, not unlike the cloisters at the abbey. To his left is an imposing house. All the stout wooden doors are firmly shut, probably locked too.

As the silver lake of moonlight spreads out across the grass it reveals another building to the right of him, a gaunt square tower. Candlelight flickers in the upper window slits, and the deep red glow of a burning fire in the topmost chamber. But where are they keeping Regulus? Is he in the great manor building or up in the tower? Maybe he's somewhere underground, like the vaulted cellar beneath the abbey. Felix can hardly march up to one of the doors and demand to know where his friend is, and in truth, he suddenly loses all confidence that Regulus is here at all.

He's a toadwit, a clodplate, a muttonhead! Regulus will be safely back in the dorter by now. He returned while they were all at Compline and right now he's curled up under his blanket asleep. He hasn't even troubled to imagine what's happened to Felix, much less care. Why on earth has Felix risked everything to rescue a stupid little maggot who isn't even in any danger?

Felix turns back, searching along the wall, trying to find a foothold or a thick stem of ivy he can use to scramble back over the top. He grows frantic, expecting at any moment to hear a pack of savage guard dogs running towards him or a watchman yelling. The man who lives here is a wizard. He turns boys into birds and keeps them prisoners for ever, caged in his dungeons. What will he do to a boy he finds prowling in his grounds at night? As he runs down the length of the wall, Felix tries desperately to think of any excuse he can for being here. He hears a cry above the gusting wind. Is that the scream of one of the enchanted boys? Is it the shout of a guard who's spotted him?

Even as Felix turns his head, a flash of light catches his eye. A beacon has been set ablaze on top of the tower. It's a warning that there is an intruder in the grounds. It will bring the guards running. Felix wills the blaze to die away, but the red and orange flames leap higher into the black sky as if they mean to set the stars ablaze. Thick smoke, hell-red in the glow of the fires, twists and turns in the wind, one moment spinning skywards, the next licking down over the side of the building.

Felix stares frantically around him for some hiding place, but before he can move, his gaze is arrested by something else on the roof of the tower. Two figures are silhouetted by the flames, a man in long billowing robes and another, much smaller. Even though they are at some distance, Felix's young eyes are sharp. He cannot see the boy's features, nor does he recognise the strange red costume, but he has seen his friend day and night these past months. He can recognise his shape, his movement, his stance. That is Regulus up there. Felix is certain of it.

Even as he watches, two more figures smash their way up through the floor of the tower, like demons rising from Hell. The white-robed Father Arthmael and Father Madron stand side by side in the light cast by the twisting flames. The man in black robes grabs Regulus, dragging him away from the two canons, pulling him towards the very edge of the battlements as if he means to hurl him from the top of the tower.

Felix does not hesitate, does not think, does not plan. He just runs, runs as if the devil himself is roaring at his back.

Chapter 57

Et moriendo docebo – I will teach you how to die.

I don't know which is worse, to be left in darkness so that you can't see the horror that's crawling towards you, or to be left with just enough light to see death edging ever closer as you lie, trussed up, awaiting it. But even if we hadn't been able to see death coming, we would have smelt the wet, decayed reek of it and heard it scuttling towards us on spiders' legs. Worse still were the whispers and shrieks of the phantasms echoing inside those walls. For I had little doubt that Gisa was right: the living could not have scaled that turret – only the dead could climb those stones.

The stench of decay was by then so strong it blistered my nostrils, as if the mould was already eating its way inside me, its slimy black threads burrowing into my heart, liver and brain. I could smell dead flesh. Was it my own? My shoes were encased in thick cushions of mould. It was creeping up my hose. I couldn't feel my feet any more. Had they already rotted away?

I turned my head to look at the girl. Her jaw was clenched, as if she was trying to bite back a scream. Her breath was coming in sharp snorts. She was staring up at the spiders as they circled above us, weaving their webs, which turned black and glistening even as they were spun. The webs were spreading wider and wider above us, running into one

447

another, as if we were giant flies to be wrapped. I could feel Gisa shrinking down on the pallet as if she was trying to push her way through the bottom of it.

'Something's touching me!' she burst out. 'It's moving. I can feel it. My neck! What is it? What's on my neck?'

I craned my head to look at her. A tendril of black mould had slithered up over the side of the bed and was twining itself about her throat.

'Worm, just an ordinary worm,' I lied.

Even if she hated the creatures, it was better she believe that than know the truth.

'I . . . I can't breathe. It's choking me.' Her breath was coming in dry sobs now.

I wriggled my shoulder, trying to reach her neck and rub it off, but though I strained against the ropes until I thought I would sever my own hands, I couldn't reach her.

A stone crashed to the floor, narrowly missing the bed. I stared up to where it had fallen, expecting to see a glimpse of sky, but instead small clods of earth trickled down as if we were buried deep underground.

'God's arse! Where are we?' I yelled. 'It's a turret! There can't be anything above us. I know there can't.'

There was another crash and more stones fell, handfuls of earth pattering down behind them. Was that a jaw bone? I could see it lying yellow in the rubble.

'We have to get out. We'll be buried alive.'

Something was crawling over my forehead, wet and slimy, yet my skin was stinging beneath it, as if it was slowly being peeled back from my bones. It was edging down my face towards my eye. It was a worm. I tried to convince myself it had to be a worm. Yet I knew from the horrified expression on Gisa's face that it was not. Cringing, I screwed my eyes shut. I turned my face as far as I could into my shoulder, nearly snapping my neck in the effort to scrub the mould away. There was another rumble and crash. Gisa shrieked, or maybe it was me.

'Here, hold still,' a voice said.

Gingerly, I opened one eye. A dark figure was standing beside the bed, leaning over us. For a moment I thought the mould had gathered itself into the terrible aspect of a man, until I saw the whites of two eyes and the flash of steel in the candlelight.

I felt a blade sawing at the rope across my chest.

'Lie still, you codwit. Got to get you out afore Odo comes back, or this bloody tower falls in on us.'

It was only when I heard his voice that I recognised Pipkin.

'What happened to your face?' I said, staring up at the blackened skin. God's bones, had the mould infected him?

The rope gave way and Pipkin chuckled, jerking me up into a sitting position, so that he could reach the rope that tied my arms. 'Blacked it, didn't I? Learned that trick long ago. Only way to sneak in and out of this place of a night time without Odo sticking his great beak in. There was one time—'

He broke off as another piece of masonry crashed behind him and, with a frightened glance at the ceiling, he hastily resumed sawing at the rope binding my arms. With enormous relief, I felt my bonds burst open.

'Leave me. Untie the girl – you must get her out!'

I surprised even myself. I hadn't realised until that moment how badly I wanted her to live.

'You make haste to free your feet, then,' Pipkin urged, glancing nervously up at the roof again. 'That'll not hold long.'

449

Frantically, I flexed my numb fingers, trying to get enough feeling back into them to tackle the knots. Desperate though I was to escape the crumbling chamber, I hesitated, staring down at my mould-encrusted shoes, fearing to touch them. I couldn't move my feet. Were they just numb like my hands or had they been eaten away? Were my shoes nothing more than slime-filled bags?

Pipkin dragged Gisa off the bed moments before another lump of stone crashed down, straight onto the place where her head had been. I threw myself off the bed. Gisa's legs were buckling beneath her, as if she couldn't feel her feet either. Pipkin grabbed her waist and with his other hand hauled her arm across his neck, heaving her upright until she dangled beside him. He twisted his head to look at me.

'Shift your fecking arse,' he roared, tossing the knife down to where I lay on the floor. 'Cut yourself free, else you'll be wearing that roof on your pate.'

He staggered towards the door, hauling Gisa with him as she made feeble kicking motions with her legs in a futile attempt to walk.

I grabbed the knife and hacked at the rope, thanking every saint in Paradise that Pipkin was a cook and kept his knives sharp. As the rope snapped, there was another rumble, and stone, earth and bones crashed onto the floor, inches from my face. For a moment, I found myself staring straight into the empty eye-sockets of an ancient skull. More earth rained down and the candle was snuffed out.

I said I wondered if it was worse to face death in the dark or by candlelight. Now I knew that the dark is worse, much worse. I couldn't stand. If my feet still existed, they certainly wouldn't bear me up. I crawled forward over the rubble, choking in the cloud of dust, my lungs burning from the mould. My fingers squelched through heaps of soft, sticky worms, and my skin crawled as if a thousand insects were running across it. I wanted to tear at my body, slap them away, but I dared not stop. All around me I could hear stones falling, but I couldn't see a damn thing. Nothing. Not even the smallest glimmer to tell me if I was crawling towards the door or straight into a wall. The darkness was so complete I thought for one terrifying moment the mould had reached my eyes and eaten them away.

'Pipkin! Gisa!' I yelled, between coughs. I shrieked as a falling lump of stone bounced painfully off my shoulder. I jerked away and immediately banged my other shoulder into something hard.

'Pipkin!' I shrieked again. 'In God's mercy tell me where you are. I can't see!'

''Ere, over 'ere,' he called. 'Lass is on her way down. But you'd best hurry.'

He kept calling to me as I crawled towards the sound and a hand reached down and grasped my upper arm, trying to drag me to my feet.

'Stand up,' he urged. 'You'll break your neck if you try to crawl down those stairs.'

There was a great rumbling sound behind me as he hauled me upright. The violent pains stabbing through my feet at least reassured me I still had a pair. I staggered to the top of the staircase, following Pipkin, who was already lumbering down. I was vaguely aware of a red glow coming from somewhere, but thought little of it, save that at least I could dimly make out the top step.

But as the stairs twisted away, I found myself back in darkness again, pressing my sore shoulder and arm against the rough wall and trying to feel for the next uneven step.

451

But I dared not pick my way too carefully. The sounds of falling stone reverberated through the turret, driving me on until I finally tumbled out of the door and onto the flags outside.

I crouched there on all fours, gulping the cool fresh air. But Pipkin did not let me rest there for long. Once again he was dragging at my arm. 'Come away – if the tower falls . . .'

I scrambled to my feet and stumbled forward across the grass until I tripped and lay face down, panting and moaning.

'Look!' It was Gisa's voice.

I raised my head. She was sitting on the grass a few yards ahead of me, evidently trying to regain her breath, too. She was safe, thank God, she was safe! But she was trying to scramble to her feet, pointing towards Sylvain's tower.

A great red glow spread over the sky above it. Some kind of beacon had been lit on top of the tower and I could see figures moving about on the roof. As if plugs of wax had suddenly been pulled from my ears, an explosion of sound hit them. Screams and shouts from the figures on the tower mingled with the roar and crackle of flames.

A great rumble, like a violent thunderclap, made us jerk round. The turret, in which minutes before we'd lain imprisoned, had finally collapsed in on itself, sending up a cloud of dust that glowed as red as the mouth of Hell in the light of its twin. The ruins stood jagged as a broken tooth, the staircase still rising into the dark sky, but leading nowhere, save to death.

Chapter 58

Whoever takes the blood of the lion and then does him justice by burning to ashes, with heat and violence, the body of his father . . . he will obtain a remedy healing all sickness.

By the time Felix barges through the door at the bottom of the tower he is trembling with a fury that has driven out all fear. He feels again every punishment he has ever received at the canons' hands, as if he is covered with a hundred stinging welts. And it's not just the beatings that make him smart, but the humiliation, the way they stare at his naked body with the slack-mouthed expression that he does not fully comprehend. He shudders with shame. But, above all, it's the lies that anger him most, treating him as if he is stupid. Do they really think he believes their stories? Do they laugh together at how gullible he is, how easily fooled? Well, he isn't. He never has been.

He races up those two flights of stairs, scrambles up the ladder like a squirrel. Through the open, splintered trapdoor above he can see a little square of night sky. He has almost reached the roof. He edges cautiously up the last rungs, feeling the wind tugging the top of his hair as he peers over the rim. He still hasn't the slightest idea of what he is going to do, except that he wants so badly to hurt them that he can almost feel his fist smashing into their faces.

None of the men notice the top of Felix's head in the shadows. On the far side of the roof, a man clad in billowing black robes holds Regulus in front of him. One hand grips the boy's shoulder, the other arm is locked tight about his throat. Regulus, his eyes bulging, is clawing desperately at the arm that is choking him, but he might as well try to bend an iron bar. Father Arthmael stands facing them, with Father Madron close behind, their white robes flapping in the wind. The golden sickle is once more in Father Arthmael's hand and he is inching ever closer to Sylvain and the boy, while behind them the flames and smoke from the beacon twist up into the dark sky.

'Sylvain,' Father Arthmael is saying, 'do you want your daughter to live again? Then the death must be yours. You are the father, the father who is slain. Let the boy do his work. It will be over in a moment. Unlike him, you will be dead before the flames touch you. Your corpse will drag his living body into the flames. Isolda will live. Your souls will be reunited in God.'

Sylvain is shuffling backwards. His legs touch the low parapet. He can go no further.

'It is you whom the boy must kill, Arthmael. The old king, the white king. Don't you have faith in your Saviour that He will raise you to life again? *Et exspecto resurrectionem mortuorum. I expect the resurrection of the dead.* Isn't that what you recite daily? Isn't that what you teach those grieving widows and bereft parents? *Your husband, your daughter will live again.* But you don't really believe that. You see nothing beyond the grave, so you are determined never to enter it. You want eternal life for yourself now, here in the flesh. You want to remain just as you are now, while all around you wither and die. Ruling an abbey is not enough. You crave the power that will come only when you can outlive them all.'

'How dare you accuse such a holy man of base ambition?' Father Madron yells. 'His only desire—'

'The raven has returned!' Sylvain holds Regulus out in front of himself, brandishing the boy as if he is a trophy of war. Regulus squeals in fear, but he, too, is ignored. 'The raven's head came to me, to my hand. It knows I am the true inheritor of the mysteries.'

Father Arthmael reels back. 'You . . . have the raven? I don't believe you. Count Philippe has—'

'Had,' Sylvain corrects. There is no disguising the satisfaction in his tone. 'Philippe believed the bird would do his bidding, but the raven serves only the true master. It kept the youth alive and brought him to me, the perfect partner for the marriage of death.'

'The raven would never serve the man who betrayed the Great Master,' Arthmael says savagely. 'I *know* it was you who betrayed him to King Philip of France for that is where your allegiance has always lain. Our master died in agony at the hands of the torturers because he would not reveal the secrets of our art. How much did Philip Augustus pay you for your treachery, or was it only the Great Master's book you coveted?'

'The Great Master was the traitor, not I,' Sylvain says. 'He betrayed *us*. He became obsessed with transforming his soul, purifying it for God. In the end he was spending more time in the chapel on his knees than in his laboratorium. And that was your doing, Arthmael. You poisoned his reasoning.'

The abbot's hand strays to the wooden cross he wears round his neck. 'I convinced him that God and God alone can open our eyes to the true meaning of the symbols and mysteries, if we ask Him.'

Sylvain gives a mirthless laugh. 'Tell me, Arthmael, do you honestly think that your God will hear you over the screams of all those children who died at your hands?'

The boy standing unseen in the shadow of the trapdoor feels a strange mixture of terror and elation. So Father Arthmael did kill Mighel, Peter, too. He wants to shout out – *I told you!* But his glee at being right is instantly drowned beneath a flood of fear.

Father Arthmael lifts his stubbled chin as if challenging any to dare to condemn him. 'He blesses me for sending those boys straight to the arms of the Holy Virgin. Those children in Heaven pray for me in gratitude that I spared them the horrors of this world. Half those boys would have grown up to end their days on the gallows and spend eternity in the fires of Hell, if I hadn't saved them. And you . . . you didn't hesitate to make use of them too. As soon as you believed you could raise your daughter from the dead, you came to me begging for a share of their water and their blood. The book was useless to you without those. But what you fail to understand is that if you raise Isolda you will do no more than raise a revenant, the walking dead. Her body will be saved, but her soul destroyed for ever. You must surrender your body, Sylvain, sacrifice yourself, and I swear on the Blood of Christ, I will use the stone to send both your souls to the eternal flame.'

Sylvain gives a slow, mirthless smile. '*Sacrifice* – you Christians are so devoted to that word.' He fixes his gaze on Father Madron. 'You said that Father Arthmael was a holy man. I've heard you call him a saint. Very well, then. Take the sickle, give it to the boy, and let Father Arthmael

456

prove to you and all those he leads that he has faith enough to die, as Christ and all His saints have done.'

Arthmael does not take his gaze from Sylvain, but with his free hand he gropes behind him until he has caught hold of his young canon's voluminous sleeve, dragging him forward.

'Seize the boy, Father Madron! You are sworn in obedience to me.'

Felix holds his breath as the young priest takes a pace forward, but before he can touch Regulus, Sylvain shifts his arm from the boy's throat to his waist. He swings him out over the parapet, so that the child is dangling high above the flagstones far below.

Regulus screams, arching rigid over the sickening drop. Felix has no hope of grabbing him. If he launches himself at Sylvain, he will let Regulus fall. Felix stares around, looking for something, anything, he can use to distract the men. He ducks back down into the chamber below, and seizes the first thing he can find, a leather-bound book, gilded with a great golden sun. It looks valuable. If he threatens to throw it on the beacon fire, maybe . . . maybe they will give him Regulus to save the book.

He jerks, staring upwards as another scream rings out above his head. The edge of the book knocks against the brass brazier in the chamber, tipping it over. It rolls across the wooden boards, spilling a trail of glowing charcoal across the floor, but Felix barely registers this as he clambers back up the ladder, clasping the book to his chest, and scrambles across to the blazing beacon. He holds the book as close to the flames as his fingers can stand.

'Let him go!' he demands fiercely. 'Let Regulus go or I'll drop this in the fire.'

Father Arthmael gapes at him. 'Felix! What are you . . . How dare you come . . .' he splutters, almost speechless with shock and indignation. He struggles to regain control. 'Give the book to me and return to the abbey. I will speak with you in the morning.'

'Not leaving without Regulus. Let him go, else I'll burn this, I swear!'

'Stop him!' Sylvain shouts.

'Felix!' Father Arthmael bellows. 'Do as I order! These are matters you cannot begin to understand.'

The cold rage in Father Arthmael's tone would make any man or boy in the abbey blanch in fear, but Felix suddenly realises he no longer cares. Arthmael can't threaten him because he's never going back to the abbey. Arthmael is not his master any more. The realisation almost brings a grin to his face, but they could still hurt Regulus. He braces himself against the heat and edges the book closer to the flames.

'I'll do it. I'll burn it unless you let Regulus go.'

Sylvain, his arms growing weary from holding the struggling boy, is forced to set him back on the roof, but holds him tighter than ever. Regulus is sobbing, but is too frightened and weak to resist.

'I will count to ten,' Sylvain says quietly, 'and if you do not take the book away from the fire, I will throw the boy over the edge.'

'You pick him up again and I'll throw the book straight on the fire,' Felix says, holding it higher, so that the light glints on the gilded sun, making its halo of flames dance as if the book is already ablaze.

Father Arthmael seems to make up his mind and suddenly lunges at Felix, trying to catch the back of his robe and haul him back from the beacon. Felix twists and dodges away. Father Arthmael raises the sickle, swinging his arm back to strike, but stumbles sideways as a huge bang shakes the flags beneath them. Blue and scarlet flames leap up through the trapdoor.

Father Madron rushes to the hole, trying to peer down, but is forced back by the heat. Sylvain has let go of Regulus. The men scatter, running to the parapets, but on every side smoke and flames are licking upwards through the slit windows below. From beneath comes the crash of objects falling from burning shelves and small explosions as glass vessels shatter in the heat.

Regulus runs to Felix, clinging to him. 'Down! Want to go down!'

He rubs his tear-stained face against the flap of red cloth on his shoulder, leaving a trail of silver snot and soot. Felix grips the boy's hand, staring at the smoke and flames roaring up out of the trapdoor. They can't go down, not that way, and what other way is there? It's all his fault. He knocked over the brazier. He didn't mean to. He should have stamped the charcoal out. Why hadn't he? Why?

He stares down at the pale face of the boy looking fearfully up at him. Those blue eyes are brimming with fear, but also trust. Felix knows Regulus expects him to find a way out, expects him to make everything all right. He believes Felix can do anything. But he can't. He couldn't save Mighel and he can't save Regulus. He is useless. He can't help anyone.

Felix pulls the boy over to the parapet. Maybe there is a ladder, a rope, a twist of ivy which they can climb down, but there is nothing. Not even a cat could climb these walls. Below he sees three figures lit by the glow of the fire, shouting and waving their arms. They vanish and reappear as the smoke and flames from the room billow up from below.

Felix's eyes are stinging. He rubs the tears away with the back of his hand, but that only makes them hurt more. He thinks the people below are urging them to jump. But they can't. It's too far down.

The heat from the beacon and from the flames below is suffocating. The flagstones beneath his bare feet are growing unbearably hot. They are going to roast alive. Regulus is shrinking into him, shrieking and trying to lift one foot at a time, and Felix sees his feet are also bare. The boy is crying in pain.

Felix bends down and heaves the child into his arms, as best he can, to raise his feet from the hot stones. He turns back, trying to find someone to help them. A figure is lumbering towards them through the smoke, his arms outstretched. For one joyous moment, Felix believes they are going to be rescued. He staggers forward, but stumbles back as he recognises Sylvain. His face blackened with smoke, the golden sickle swinging menacingly in his hand. Red drops like rubies glisten wetly on the blade and Felix cannot understand why.

Then as the wind gusts away a billow of smoke he sees something white lying on the flags – a blanket. His stomach lurches. He will be punished because a boy has dropped his blanket and not tidied it away. There is a scarlet stain on the cloth and it is spreading wider and wider. Then he realises it is not a blanket at all, but a man, a man in white robes.

Father Arthmael lies in a crumpled heap, his hands clutching his throat as blood spurts in a fountain between his fingers. His eyes are bulging, his mouth is open wide, but nothing emerges except a strangled gurgling. Father Madron blunders out of the smoke, his face contorted in horror. He kneels, cradling Father Arthmael's head, pressing his fingers to the wound as if he can push the blood back into the veins. But he can stutter out no more than a single word of the Absolution before his abbot's head falls back, and the gash in his throat gapes as wide as a scream.

Felix is so shocked that Sylvain is upon him before he can move. Sylvain makes a grab for Regulus lying across Felix's arms. He seizes a handful of the little boy's red hair and jerks his head backwards. He sweeps the sickle upwards and a shower of scarlet droplets falls on the child's face. Twin flames burn in Sylvain's green eyes, as he thunders his triumph into the wind.

'Astaroth, Gressil and Balberith, I give to you the living stone of the boy-king that Isolda may live!'

The glittering sickle arcs through the darkness down towards Regulus's bare throat. Felix whips round, twisting the boy sharply away from the blow, trying to shield him. The blade catches Felix on his back, slicing deep into his flesh, but it is so sharp, he scarcely registers the pain of the wound. As Sylvain tries to regain his balance, Felix lunges towards the parapet. Choking from the smoke, his eyes streaming, his lungs searing with pain, he heaves the boy up in his arms.

'Catch him! Catch him!' he bellows at the figures below.

With all his remaining strength, he tosses the boy out as far as he can, away from the flames leaping through the window below. He cannot tell if the people below have heard him. The smoke is too thick: he cannot see Regulus fall. But he can hear the boy screaming as he plummets down. As Felix falls to his knees on the burning stones, the blood streaming from his back, Regulus's scream is almost the last sound he ever hears. The timbers holding up the roof finally give way, and the floor vanishes beneath them, plunging boy and men alike down, down into the blazing furnace below.

461

Chapter 59

*Take the old black spirit and destroy and torture with
it the bodies until they are changed.*

'Which way now, Regulus?' I asked, swivelling round in the
cart. 'Does any of this look familiar?'

The boy winced, as he levered himself up to peer over
the edge of the cart. Gisa had done her best for his leg,
setting it in a comfrey cast. It was a clean break, and she
thought it would heal without the leg shortening so he
would not have a limp. Provided, of course, he could be
persuaded to let it heal properly and not test it too soon. I
wasn't convinced even his mother would be able to keep
him still. The brat was already trying to crawl and shuffle
to reach what he wanted, too impatient to wait for help.

I'd caught the boy as he plummeted downwards from the
burning tower, but he'd fallen a long way and we'd both
ended up on the ground. He could easily have smashed
every bone in his body and, as Gisa said, at least he survived,
which is more than can be said for the other poor lad. There
was no hope of rescuing any of the men or the boy from
that inferno. I only hoped the lad had been killed as the
floor gave way. Burning is a horrible death. I wasn't sure I
even wished it on Sylvain.

None of the servants attempted to fight the blaze. As
soon as Odo realised his master had perished in the flames,

he drove off with a wagonload of spoils from the house. But I think even before the fire started he believed that Sylvain would not survive the night, for judging by the carefully wrapped boxes and bundles, he must have started packing well before the blaze broke out.

Pipkin, too, was busily collecting his own plunder. He was only loading a pack horse, but he was determined to get as much onto it as the poor beast could carry. 'Owes me that in wages,' he said, 'after all the years I've put in for him. 'Sides, the carrion crows from the town'll be flocking out here to pick over this place long before the sheriff's men arrive to secure it. Suppose it'll be up to the king to decide which of his men is to be favoured with the manor, seeing as the master had no son.' One of his eyes was peering at Gisa. 'And you'll be given to the lucky bastard along with it, I reckon, seeing as you were his kin.'

A spasm of revulsion crossed her face and I knew she, too, would be leaving long before the sheriff's men arrived.

'Wait,' I said. 'You knew Gisa was Sylvain's granddaughter. Did he tell you as much?'

Pipkin grinned. 'Told me nothing, but I've ears and eyes and I'm not as thick as pottage, whatever some may think. Master sent Odo to hide the letters to the French in her father's house. There were suspicions someone in these parts was sending information to the French king. I reckoned it were the master himself, but if it was, he knew it would only be a matter of time afore sheriff came a-calling on him. So, the master told sheriff where to look, to shift suspicion from himself and settle a score with Master Hamon into the bargain. Had him arrested and tried for a traitor. Hanged him, they did, in the market square, gibbeted him after. There was a plague of mice that year, and they swarmed all

463

over the corpse, ate the flesh right off the bones almost afore he was cold.'

He turned to Gisa, who was standing rigid, her eyes wide with horror and pain. 'Made you watch the hanging, they did, poor little mite. I reckon you was too young to remember it, which is a mercy, but they put you right in front, so as your tears'd be the last thing your father saw and he'd die knowing that he'd left you to starve or worse. Sylvain was cock of the dung-heap that day. Got his revenge on your father for running off with his daughter and proved his loyalty to the king in one stroke.'

Pipkin nodded to himself in satisfaction. 'If you was to ask me, I reckon the master got just what he deserved up in that tower.' He patted one of the well-stuffed saddle packs, as if every looted item was another blow against Sylvain.

I watched Pipkin lead the packhorse out across the draw-bridge and down the track, vanishing into the darkness. I noticed he'd set out in the opposite direction to Odo. He was clearly anxious not to find himself in the same town as his fellow servant again, and I didn't blame him for that.

The wind was stronger than ever and blue flashes of lightning forked across the heavy clouds, between great rumbles of thunder. I glanced anxiously at the tower where flames were still blazing into the sky. In the darkness it seemed far too close to the house. If the wind carried the fragments of burning wood, the whole manor could go up. Maybe it would be wise to leave now, but I didn't fancy spending the night out in the open if the storm broke.

I returned to the Great Hall, where I found the boy wrapped in skins, fast asleep, his head cradled in Gisa's lap. Her face was pale and she was so exhausted, she could barely sit up.

'Your father . . . what Pipkin told you . . . I'm sorry,' I said awkwardly.

'I'm not,' she murmured. 'At least I know he was the good man I'd always believed. But Pipkin was wrong about one thing. I do remember seeing him hang and I remember the mice too. Down there, beneath the tower, I didn't understand what I was seeing. I thought it was demons or ghosts, but I think now I was seeing the memories and nightmares that haunted Sylvain. Maybe that is what Hell is, being trapped for ever in your own nightmares and never being able to wake.'

I shuddered and tried to cast round for something to divert her. A red glow flickered through the shutters and from time to time came a distant crash or rumble as more stones and timbers fell from the tower. I could hardly forget that inside lay the remains of four bodies still burning and guessed Gisa couldn't either.

'Where will you go?' I asked her. 'Back to the shop?'

'Never,' she said emphatically. 'Better if my uncle . . . better if Master Thomas believes I died in the fire. Then I can go somewhere no one has ever heard of Sylvain or my father. But I have to do something first. I'm too tired even to think now, but if I can sleep just for an hour . . . I *will* get him out . . . Now the abbot is dead . . . must let me take him . . .'

She was falling asleep even as she spoke. I'd no idea what she was babbling about, but I'd heard someone else say *I will* in the same vehement tone as he looked down at the dead body of his daughter. I wasn't about to tell Gisa so, but at that moment I saw Sylvain's eyes burning through hers, and her mouth set in the same expression of determination and obsession as his when he'd announced we were going to die. Whatever he believed, Gisa had Sylvain's blood throbbing in her veins. For the world's sake, I hoped she had a little of her father's blood, too.

I don't know how long I dozed, but a violent clap of thunder jerked me from sleep. I lay there for a few moments, unable to think where I was, and was suddenly aware of a roaring, rushing sound above me. My stomach lurched. Fire! Was the roof of the manor ablaze? I stumbled to the casement, dragged open one of the shutters and peered out into the darkness. I gave a great sigh of relief. It wasn't fire at all, but torrential rain. The storm, which had been threatening all evening, had finally broken. A few wisps of smoke rose from the smouldering ruins of the tower and at the bottom I could still see a faint red glow, but the rain had extinguished the worst of the blaze. At least we could sleep soundly for the remainder of the night without fear of the manor catching fire.

Gisa groaned, and sat up, rubbing her neck. 'What is it?' she mumbled. 'Someone out there?'

'No, it's raining – coming down like a waterfall. It's almost extinguished the fire in the tower, so at least we needn't worry about it spreading to this place.'

It seemed an innocent enough remark to me and I was quite unprepared for the effect it had on Gisa.

'Raining! How long? How LONG? Why didn't you wake me?' She scrambled to her feet and fled to the door.

'Gisa, wait . . . It's only rain. The roof is sound enough and the manor is hardly likely to . . .' I was about to say *flood*. But the door was already banging behind her.

Chapter 60

Two fishes swim in our sea, with neither flesh nor bones.
Cook them in their own water and they will become a
vast sea, which no man will be able to describe.

Gisa is soaked to the marrow before she has run even a few yards. Icy water streams from her hair, blinding her. A flash of lightning hangs for a moment in the black sky, lighting up the trees that bend over the track, their branches flailing inches from her face. She holds her wet skirts up about her waist to keep them from twisting round her legs. She slips in the mud, sending a spasm of pain jolting through her back, but she does not slow her pace. She daren't. Her heart is racing faster than her legs. *Hold on, Peter, I'm coming. I'm coming!*

Great puddles fill every rut and hollow. She can hear the water rushing in the ditches on either side. Another lightning flash, and she sees silvery water running down the trunks of the trees, bright rivulets bubbling along the edge of the grass, the tiny streams merging into torrents of water that soak her feet as she wades through.

Let him be alive, Blessed Virgin, let him be alive. She will hammer on the door of the abbey. She will demand they bring pickaxes, hammers, iron crows, smash the stone, stop the water flowing, drag him out. *Let me get him out. I can heal him. I can heal him if I can only get him out.*

Neither Laurent nor Pipkin had seen the book fall from

467

the tower – they were too intent on the boy – but Gisa was watching, waiting. She had known Sylvain would sooner throw himself into the flames than let that book burn. She had watched him hurl it to safety, had seen the glitter of the golden sun as it arced through the smoke, stretched out her arms as it fell to the blackened earth. She had caught it. It is safe, hidden. *Though a man be already crossing from this life to the next, what is written here will restore him to such perfect life and health as even the angels have never known.*

Her foot slides from under her and she crashes to the ground, banging her elbow on a stone. The pain makes her vomit. It is several moments before the numbness in her arm wears off and she can clamber up. She must not fall again. If she breaks her leg and cannot walk . . . If she breaks her leg she will drag herself to the boy on her arms.

She realises she has no idea how far she has come. Suppose she has already run past the place. She peers up and down the track. Are the abbey walls behind her or ahead? It's as dark as the grave, and the rain falls in curtains, obliterating everything. She begs for another lightning flash, just one, and it comes as an answer to a prayer. The wall is ahead of her. A few more yards is all.

She counts the paces from the corner, she learned the number days ago, in case she was delayed coming to Peter and it was too dark to see. She counts and she calls.

'I'm coming, Peter . . . Peter!'

She no longer cares that the canons might hear her now. She wants them to hear. But in truth no one inside those high walls would hear even a whole army marching down the road, over this rain and wind.

She stops. She has reached the place, though she cannot see it.

'Peter! Peter! Talk to me!'

She can hear the water surging along the ditch, but it would be useless to search for the plank she has hidden to bridge it. She crawls over the sodden grass until she can feel the edge of the ditch, then gingerly lowers herself into the torrent of icy water. Her feet sink deep into the mud and filth. The current buffets her sideways, threatening to knock her over and drag her under. For a terrifying moment she can't move her feet.

She lunges at the grass and plants that cling to the bank on the other side of the ditch, and drags herself free. Planting her legs wide apart and clinging to a thin cleft, she slides her free hand along the streaming stones towards where she thinks the hole must be. A torrent of water gushes out of the wall, pushing her hand away. She edges closer, forcing her hand into the hole. There is still a gap, a narrow gap above the cascade. The water has not yet filled the tunnel.

'Peter,' she screams above the roar, 'take my hand.'

She pushes her numb fingers into the hole and now she understands why the water rushing out has not filled the drain. Something is wedged against the roof of the tunnel, the force of the water pressing it against the stone. She feels hair rippling in the current. She feels the hard skull, the soft cheek, the limp arm. Still she goes on praying. *Let him be alive. Please let him be alive.*

Only when the final lightning bolt of the storm flashes across the black sky, only when she glimpses the blue lips, the unseeing eyes fixed wide in terror and despair, only then does she finally stop praying, for she knows her prayer will never be answered. She has come too late.

Epilogue

**Under the Astrological House of Gemini, the Twins,
in the year of Our Lord, 1225**

*Our Stone is the leaven of all other metals and changes
them into its own nature. As leaven, though of the same
nature with dough, cannot raise it, until from dough
it has received a new quality it did not possess before,
so our Stone cannot change metals until it itself is
changed.*

Gisa returned before dawn. She was soaked and shivering
uncontrollably, but she said not one word about where she'd
been. She huddled, steaming, in front of the hearth fire,
staring into the flames. Whether she slept or not, I don't
know. I certainly did, but when I woke again, I found her
still lying in same place, gazing into the embers, though
young Regulus had somehow wriggled across to her in spite
of his cast and lay clinging to her leg as if he feared she
might vanish if he let go.

After we had raided the kitchens for breakfast, I searched
the stables until I found a small cart on which I could carry
the boy, though it was Gisa who finally had to show me
how to hitch it up to one of the horses. She insisted she
would take nothing from the house, save some food for the

470

journey. She certainly wouldn't survive on the road if she thought pride would fill her stomach or warm her bones.

I knew only too well that a handful of dried meat doesn't last long, or buy you a dry bed in an inn, so I purloined a few things I knew I could sell to keep both of us in comfort. I ignored the goblets and boxes with their strange engravings, anything that might be traced back to the manor, and took only what no one could identify, plain pieces of silver and pewter, which I hid in sacks and kegs beneath the smoked meat and flour. Gisa would be grateful to me when she was sitting by the roaring fire in a tavern instead of huddled at the roadside in the rain.

The first and only time I saw Gisa cry in the whole of that nightmare was when she realised the birds in the tower had also died in the flames, trapped in their cages. She started to sob as if the birds had been her own pets. I think if she'd thought even one of them might have survived I'd have been hard pushed to stop her going back into the smouldering ruins to release it.

Instead, she went round every room in the manor and collected up all the caged birds she could find, taking the cages outside and opening the doors one by one. Some birds flew free at once, making for the safety of the tallest trees they could see. A few scuttled across the ground, running to hide under bushes, as if they had forgotten how to fly, but some just sat in their prisons staring at the open door, and even when we shook the cages they clung to the sides chirruping piteously as if they were afraid to leave.

'We'd better get on the road,' I urged. 'The flames must have been seen from the town last night. I don't want to be here when the sheriff arrives. Even I'd find it hard to think of a tale to explain this.'

She nodded and, with a last sorrowful look at the birds still clinging to their open cages, she walked back across the grass towards the house.

She suddenly stopped. 'Where's my mother?'

I gestured towards the back of the tower.

'Show me.'

'No, believe me. You don't want to see her. Besides, we daren't delay any longer. If the bailiff or one of the White Canons finds us here, they might take it into their heads that we started the fire. And with both of us stinking like kippers, we'd have as much chance of proving our innocence as a fox caught in a chicken coop with a mouthful of feathers.' I gestured towards the smoking ruins. 'There are bodies in there, remember?'

But Gisa could be a stubborn little vixen when she wanted, and I found myself pressing my sleeve to my mouth as I led her past the smouldering tower, reeking of wood smoke, burned dung and charred flesh. I held the branches of the yew trees aside so that Gisa could squeeze through and jerked my chin towards the door of the chapel. Though the sun had risen, flooding the garden beyond with light, not a single shaft penetrated the yew grove. Twilight never departed there.

Taking a deep breath, Gisa turned the iron ring and pushed the door open. I watched her vanish down the steps. But a few moments later, she was back.

'She's not there.'

'I thought it was a carved effigy at first, lying on the marble slab, but look at it more closely.'

She frowned. 'There *is* no effigy.'

I sighed impatiently. Couldn't she see what was right in front of her? I'd no wish to go into that place again, but I

472

could tell I was not going to get her to leave until her curiosity had been satisfied.

I pushed past her and took a couple of steps down. 'Look, there . . .'

But Gisa was right. The slab was bare.

'But . . . I don't understand . . . The body was stretched out on that. It was right there.'

I peered around in the gloom, wondering if for some reason she had been moved to the floor, but the charnel house was so small, there was nowhere to conceal a body.

Gisa gazed up at me, her eyes shining in the gloom. 'Do you think . . . Do you think Sylvain succeeded . . . that she really has come back to life?'

She, too, gazed round the tiny chamber, as if she thought her mother might be standing somewhere in the shadows, waiting to speak to her.

'I imagine Sylvain moved her body to the tower in preparation for whatever alchemy he intended and it burned in the fire. It was covered with wax, so it was probably one of the first things to catch. We won't find any of it now.'

I saw her shrink into herself, as if she'd been slapped, and I cursed myself. Why had I said that? I could have let her go on hoping. Where would be the harm?

Awkwardly, I turned away, to give her time to recover herself.

At the far end of the slab of marble, something caught my eye. I hadn't noticed it when I first came in – it had been too dark to see clearly – but now as I moved my head I saw the faint ghost of light from the open doorway glinting on something.

I moved closer, stretching out my hand curiously and instantly drawing it back with a cry. The raven's head! It was as shiny and bright as the day Philippe first showed it to me.

Gisa gestured towards it. 'I saw that in your chamber when you were lying sick. Is it yours?'

She moved closer, but I caught her arm and pulled her back. 'Don't touch it!'

Startled, she stared at me. 'But it's valuable. You could sell it.'

'A king's ransom couldn't buy that.'

I charged out of the chapel as rapidly as I could, half fearing the accursed thing would come bouncing after me. In truth, to this day, I don't know if the *pruk-pruk-pruk* I heard as we left that yew grove came from the head or from the three ravens that sat upon the roof of the charnel house, watching us depart.

Gisa hid under some sacks in the back as I led the horse and cart out across the little drawbridge, for she was determined the apothecary and his wife should believe her dead and she didn't want to be seen by anyone from the town. It was as well she did, for the road was already crowded with townsfolk. They were milling around outside the manor walls, muttering and pointing at the smoking ruins of the tower. Even though we left the gate to the stableyard wide open, it seemed none dared to cross the forbidden threshold. But finally a bored child slipped from his mother and ran in, ignoring her commands to come back. She had no choice but to hurry after him. Seeing that she hadn't been turned to stone or struck by a thunderbolt, the rest of the townsfolk crept inside, still talking in whispers as if afraid to disturb the ghosts that dwelled there. I wondered how long it would be before they plucked up the courage to start looting. I guessed it would take only one person to snatch something up and the rest would quickly follow.

No one tried to stop us leaving. Apart from a few curious glances in our direction, they were far more interested in what treasures or horrors they might discover in the manor than in a dirty, dishevelled youth and a scrap of a boy. I led the horse up the track away from the town, in the direction Regulus seemed to think went to his parents' cottage, though in truth the brat was decidedly vague about where that might be found.

We passed a few latecomers hurrying towards the manor, and then I saw someone in the distance standing by the side of the road, gesturing for us to stop. He beamed, a wide grin that showed the empty cavern of his mouth. But almost at the same moment he seemed to recognise me and his expression turned to fear. He flung his arm across his face, as if I might give him the evil eye, and fled into the nearest grove of trees. Pity – I would have enjoyed giving him a good kicking for helping Sylvain tie us up.

We searched the whole day for Regulus's family. Several times he was certain he recognised turnings off the road, but before long he'd shake his head and declare this wasn't the right path, or this wasn't his forest, and we'd have to retrace our steps. I don't know how he knew they weren't the right trees – the whole damn forest looked the same to me. Towards dusk, by which time I was ready to throttle the little runt, I called a halt.

'I'm famished and we need to find a safe place to build a fire and hide the cart for the night. I don't want outlaws stumbling into us. We'll search for your family again tomorrow, Regulus. But try to think this time. You must remember something about the place other than trees.'

The boy glanced anxiously at Gisa, gnawing on his finger.

'Well,' I demand in exasperation, 'can't you remember anything about the route you took to the abbey that night?'

'I . . .' he squirmed '. . . don't want to.'

'What do you mean you don't want to?'

'Don't want to go back to the forest. I'm not Wilky any more. They won't want me.' He touched the cast on his broken leg.

'Course they'll want you.' I tried to sound convincing. But would they? He'd told us his parents had given him to the canons. Perhaps they wouldn't welcome another mouth to feed, especially if that leg didn't heal straight. No one had wanted me as a brat until I'd learned to make myself useful. But we couldn't very well leave him here.

'Look,' I said firmly, 'it's either your family or back to the abbey. You can't fend for yourself. I had to at your age and I wouldn't recommend it even with two sound legs. Who's going to feed you or build a fire to keep you warm until your leg mends? Have you thought of that?'

'Gisa could,' he said sullenly.

I snorted. 'We can't take care of you on the road.'

If he thought I was going to saddle myself with a crippled brat, he was gravely mistaken. He wasn't my responsibility. Besides, I suddenly realised that, for some strange reason, I wanted to be alone with Gisa.

'*We*,' Gisa said coldly. 'What makes you think I'll be travelling with you? I only came this far with you to see the boy home. Tomorrow I go my own way.'

I was crushed and not a little hurt. I'd assumed Gisa would beg me to take her along. Of course I wasn't in love with the girl. I'd resolved never to fall in love with any woman after the treacherous Amée, but I'd thought Gisa had taken a fancy to me and regarded me as her protector.

'You've never lived on the road,' I told her. 'You haven't the faintest notion how hard it is, especially for a woman. You'll starve within a week, if you don't get murdered first. You've no idea how many rogues and cut-throats there are out there – and don't imagine they'll spare you because of your sex. They'll see you as easy prey.'

'I've hardly lived my life so far without danger,' she said coolly. 'Given what my own grandfather tried to do to me, I rather think I'd be safer taking care of myself. I have skills enough to earn my bread and I must get used to being alone. My blood is tainted, remember. Whether the traitor was my father or grandfather scarcely matters, I am still attainted.'

She jerked her chin up as if the thought pleased her and she could spit her defiance in the face of the whole world.

'I'll take care of myself, too,' Regulus said fiercely. 'Not going back to the forest and I'm not going to the abbey! If Felix was here we'd take care of each other. We wouldn't need no one. We swore . . .' Tears as fat as slugs began to slide down his face. 'Why didn't Felix jump with me? Even if he got broken too, I would have looked after him. I would have fetched him food.'

Regulus gazed up at Gisa as if he thought she could set a cast around his grief and mend it. 'Father Arthmael said if I killed the man in the black robe he could make the people who are dead alive again. My – my brothers in the forest and Mighel and Peter, they'd all have come alive again if I'd killed the wizard. I should have killed him. I should have . . . It's my fault Felix is dead! I'll kill every man in the world to make him alive again. I will. I will!'

He covered his head with his hands and howled. Gisa, folding him in her arms, cradled his face to her chest, rocking him back and forward. 'It isn't your fault,' she murmured. 'Killing Sylvain wouldn't have made the dead live. Sylvain has been killed, and the dead have not come to life. But we will find a way one day. The answer is in there, I know it. We will make the dead live again.'

Regulus raised his tear-stained face. 'Together?'

Gisa nodded gravely.

'*We?*' I asked, a trifle sarcastically.

She shrugged. 'If I'm to take the boy, I'll need the cart, so I suppose all three of us will have to travel together.' Then, seeing my grin, she added, 'But just until he's fit enough to walk. Not a day longer.'

My grin only deepened. I was certain I would have persuaded her long before then that she needed me.

A sudden *pruk-pruk-pruk* reverberated through the trees above us. The boy glanced up, as if he expected to see a living raven perched in the branches above us. I knew that cry came from no bird of flesh and feathers. But it was not coming from my pack.

Gisa was staring at her own sack. The cry came again, insistent, triumphant. Her brow creased in puzzlement. She dragged the bundle towards her and began to empty it, pulling out a blanket, flint and steel for making fire and some of the meagre supplies of food she had taken from the manor. She half drew out an object wrapped in cloth that looked as if it might have been a book. I should know: I'd seen more of those in my short life than most men see in a dozen generations. She flushed, hastily thrusting it back into the sack as if she didn't want me to see it. But before I had time to ask her what it was, something rolled out into

478

her lap. The setting sun caught the shining metal, turning it blood red.

I stared at it, aghast. 'You swore to me you would take nothing from your grandfather's house, save food. And that . . . that is the most dangerous thing you could have chosen. I told you to leave it in the charnel house. It's cursed, possessed. Don't you realise that this is what led me to your grandfather's house and nearly got us both killed?'

She stared. 'But I didn't touch it. Don't you remember? You dragged me out of there with you. How could I have picked it up?'

'Then I don't know how it got there, but I do know one thing. You have to throw it away. Now! Hurl it as far into those trees as you can and then we're getting out of here.'

Gisa lifted her head and gazed straight at me. When I'd first met her I'd thought her eyes were grey, almost colourless, but now in this witch-light I suddenly saw that they were the same vivid green as her grandfather's. She lifted the silver head high into the last glittering rays of the setting sun. For one brief moment I stupidly thought she was going to do as I had told her and toss the thing into the dark mass of trees. Then I caught the expression on her face.

'"Though a man be already crossing from this life to the next, though he lies buried in his grave . . ."' she murmured. She threw back her head and laughed. 'We shall succeed, Regulus. I know it. My grandfather failed, but we shall not!'

And as Gisa caressed the smooth, curved beak of the raven's head, I swear it winked at me.

Historical Notes

In 1215, the English barons rebelled against the unpopular King John and invited Crown Prince Louis (later Louis VIII) of France, son of King Philip II, known as Philip Augustus, to seize the English throne with their support. Philip and Louis had frequently fought the Angevins, and two years previously had defeated King John when he had attempted to retake Normandy.

On 21 May 1216 Louis, known as the Lion, landed on the Isle of Thanet, entered London and was proclaimed king by the English barons, though he was never actually crowned. A few weeks later, he took Winchester and soon had half of England under his rule. But in October 1216, before Louis could secure the throne, King John died and many of the English barons abandoned the Lion's cause to support the claim of John's nine-year-old son, Henry III. The regent, William Marshal, rallied support for the boy-king, beating the French army at Lincoln on 20 May 1217. Louis's ships were then defeated in battle off Sandwich on 24 August 1217, by the British fleet, led by Eustace the Monk. Louis was forced to renounce his claim to the English throne in exchange for ten thousand marks.

Louis finally acceded to the French throne on 14 June 1223, but reigned only for three years. He continued to wage war on the Angevins and wrested Poitou and Saintonge from them. He constantly quarrelled with his own nobles, such as the powerful Count of Champagne, over issues such as prohibiting Jews from moneylending, which had provided a good income to the count through the imposition of taxes. Louis, like King John, always feared treachery among his nobles and with good reason. But in the end, he died from dysentery on 8 November 1226.

Supernatural Tales – Some readers may find it hard to believe that people would invent or believe a supernatural story that explained a family's history, but it was not uncommon in the Middle Ages. In the twelfth and thirteenth centuries, rumours circulated from time to time that several of the noble houses of Europe, including that of Godfrey of Bouillon, Knight Commander of Jerusalem, were of rather dubious lineage. Godfrey was extremely wealthy: he had gained many spoils from his conquest of the Holy Land and had been lavishly rewarded with lands and riches by the Pope and other crowned heads of Europe for having recovered the Holy City for Christendom. He was held up as a shining example of all knightly virtues, for only a man of noble birth could exhibit such valour and courage. The only trouble was, it was rumoured that Godfrey was not, in fact, of noble birth.

If these rumours had taken hold, they would have undermined the whole of the feudal system, since feudalism was based on the idea that only those of noble birth could become rulers and leaders. At the pinnacle of the nobility was the king, who was divinely appointed and ruled by virtue of his royal bloodline. Serf or noble, God Himself had ordained your place in society. If the common people had grasped the idea that anyone could rise up through the ranks, they might have started to rebel. These wealthy families realised that the social consequences would be disastrous for them if it was proved they were not of noble birth. They stood to lose their power, wealth and, not least, their positions in the royal courts, so several such families, including Godfrey's, whose ancestry was in doubt, employed troubadours or scribes to invent a story that told of a mysterious event or supernatural ancestor to explain why their noble line could not be traced through the heraldic records.

In Godfrey's case, the story was invented that he was the grandson of the mysterious Swan Knight. It proved so successful that several other families claimed this tale as a means of explaining away their lack of lineage. Another supernatural ancestor who appears in several noble family histories is Melusina, the beautiful bride, who in secret would change into a terrifying mermaid or water sprite with a serpent's tail, and whose image appears in their heraldic devices.

A glance at some of today's tabloid newspapers, 'true life' or gossip magazines may remind us that even in the twenty-first century we are still willing to believe the most far-fetched and outrageous things about people, especially celebrities, who are, after all, our modern nobility.

Alchemy – Alchemy, known as the *royal art*, dates back at least as far as the fourth century BCE when it was developed in Egypt by the ancient Greeks. The European alchemists of the Middle Ages inherited their traditions from the writings of the ancient Greeks, which had been translated into Arabic, then brought into Spain and southern Italy.

During the twelfth and thirteenth centuries the practice and teaching of alchemy spread throughout Europe as Christians learned more about Muslim science, which was far more advanced than that of the West. Christian and Islamic students studied together at universities such as

Pamplona, Palermo, Toledo, Barcelona and Segovia; great influential works of philosophy and alchemy were translated for the Church in the 1100s by scholars such as Adelard of Bath, Robert of Chester and Gerard of Cremona.

This brought about the first major flourishing of Western medieval alchemy, led by scholars such as Albertus Magnus (1193–1280), Roger Bacon (1214–92) and Raymond Lully (1235–1316), who were all devout Catholics. A number of the prominent alchemists were also highly skilled hypnotists, among them Michael Scot, a court astrologer for the Holy Roman Emperor, Frederick II. He is believed to have learned the art of hypnotism from the Sufis.

Later, famous alchemists include Sir Walter Raleigh, Queen Christina of Sweden, King Charles II of England and Sir Isaac Newton.

The Western medieval alchemists combined Christian theology and the philosophy of Aristotle, who believed in *prima materia*, the chaos or primal material from which everything was created and to which everything ultimately returned when it decayed.

They also believed that the four elements, *earth, fire, air* and *water*, each possessed two of the four qualities: *hot* or *cold* and *fluid* or *dry. Fire* is *hot* and *dry*, while *air* is *hot* and *fluid*. One quality predominates in each element, so in *fire* it is *heat*, while in *air* it is *fluidity*. One element can be transmuted into the other through the medium of the quality they both share. So *fire* can become *air* through the medium of *heat*, but *fire* can also become *earth* through the medium of *dryness*, because *earth* is *cold* and *dry*. Also, by taking the quality of *heat* from the element *fire* and *fluidity* from the element *water*, you can combine these two elements to produce a third element, which is *air* – *hot* and *fluid*.

Since the alchemists believed that everything in the world, animate and inanimate, was composed of the four elements, they thought that if the proportions of the elements in a substance could be changed through the various processes of *burning, calcination, solution, evaporation, distillation, sublimation* and *crystallisation*, it would be possible to produce a different substance. Thus lead could be transmuted into gold.

Alchemy has two sides, the physical and the mystical. The physical goal was the search for the *stone, elixir* or *tincture*, which could transmute base metals into precious metals, prolong life and restore health by changing the balance of the body. But this quest became symbolic of the mystical side of alchemy, which meant transforming the base soul of man, his nature and corrupt body into the pure, incorruptible spirit that could not die.

Alchemy was a dangerous practice. Many of the chemical experiments its proponents attempted could go horribly wrong, leading to explosions or fires, and neighbours, fearing their own properties would be set ablaze, especially when houses were made of wood or thatch, often attacked those they suspected of practising it. Another hazard was that thieves, and indeed kings and even bishops, believing the alchemists had succeeded in producing gold, would murder them in order to steal it or torture them into revealing their secrets.

The opportunities for fraud in alchemy were great. Many wealthy investors were duped into financing experiments in the hope of obtaining a limitless supply of gold or the elixir that would give them eternal life. So from time to time, the art was banned by kings or popes in order to stamp out fraud and often because alchemists were suspected of using the dark arts or were guilty of the capital crime of heresy.

For all these reasons, medieval alchemists were advised to

carry out their experiments in secret in isolated locations and the methods and formulations were often couched in an elaborate symbolic code, while the pieces of apparatus, such as the glass flask known as the griffin's egg, also acquired mystical symbolism of their own.

The various stages of the chemical processes of alchemy and the mystical quest were also depicted symbolically. *Nigredo*, the black death, in which alchemists reduced matter to its original earth-like state, was symbolised by the raven's head. *Albedo*, the whitening, which involved cleansing, is depicted by a king drowning or sweating in a bath of blood or by a pelican tearing at its breast, or by a white rose. *Citrinitas*, yellow death, is symbolised by a sower casting golden grain into the earth. The climax, *rubedo*, which produces the philosopher's stone through chemical union, is represented by the marriage of king and queen, often shown as the wedding of the sun and moon, or by the starry lion or by the ouroboros.

Langley and the White Canons – The Order of Regular Canons, known as Premonstratensian or White Canons, was founded in 1120 by St Norbert at Prémontré, near Laon, France. White Canons, sometimes called Norbertines, are not monks but ordained priests who carry out priestly duties of celebrating Mass, administering the sacraments, preaching, teaching, hearing confessions and ministering to the laity, while living together in a religious community under the rule of an abbot. They follow the rule of St Augustine, but with more austere disciplines than many other Augustinian orders. Their habit – a long white robe and hood with a tall white cap – gave rise to the name White Canons.

The order came to England around 1143, establishing its

first abbey at Newsham, near Brocklesby in Lincolnshire, and by the time of the dissolution of the monasteries under Henry VIII, they had thirty-five abbeys in England.

The Premonstratensian abbey at Langley in Norfolk was founded in 1195 and was dedicated to the Honour of the Blessed Virgin. It flourished until its dissolution in 1536. The land for the abbey was given by Sir Robert FitzRoger Helke, who was lord of Langley through his marriage to Margaret, daughter of William de Cheyney. Sir Robert was sheriff of Norfolk and Suffolk, in 1192–3. The abbey acquired a great many properties, including the manor of Langley and eighteen others. Its wealth continued to grow, and by 1291, it had property and lands in sixty-two Norfolk and thirteen Suffolk parishes, with an annual income of £178 5s. ¾d. But in 1334, the abbot complained to the pope that the income from the abbey's market was being badly affected by river and sea floods. And though their fortunes rose and fell through the centuries, by the time they were dissolved in 1536, the house was reported by the commissioners to be in debt to the amount of £120 16s. 8d.

Langley Abbey was surrounded by a wet ditch, or moat, the remains of which are still clearly visible today. The moat was probably built less for defence and more to drain the water from the low-lying land, irrigate the gardens and protect against flooding from the nearby river and marshland. Excavations of the ruins have revealed a cruciform-aisled church, sacristy, chapter house, dorter, vault, warming house, frater and cellarium, with a vaulted undercroft, stables and gatehouse. The remains of a furnace were also found. The stable and cellarium are still in use today, though at the time of writing the site is in private ownership and not generally open to the public, except for functions.

In the 1920s, Norwich Museum housed two medieval lead jars with lids, which were discovered in the ruins of Langley Abbey in 1816. They were believed to have contained human viscera.

Throughout its history, the abbey was beset by scandal, and abbots were repeatedly replaced only for their successors to find themselves accused of serious offences. We shall never know if the abbey itself exercised some kind of malevolent and corrupting influence on those who became abbots there or if the canons invented tales of their superiors' misconduct out of revenge against abbots who tried to discipline them.

On several occasions a group of canons and lay brothers had to be removed from the abbey for 'evil living' and 'incontinence'. In 1306, the abbot and one canon were charged with falsely claiming that some men owed money to the abbey when in fact they knew it had already been paid. In 1478, discipline had become so bad that the canons were punished with bread and water for forty days, forbidden to lock their cell doors or take recreation outside the grounds. In 1482, the abbot had to be removed for undisclosed grave offences and the canons were forbidden to frequent the town taverns. While their behaviour improved slightly under the new abbot, there were still complaints that the canons were out all night hunting and fishing, and ignored the periods of silence. Even the abbot himself had to be sternly warned not to associate with women.

One of the most bizarre incidents took place in 1491, when one of the White Canons, Thomas Ludham, whose behaviour was described as *instigante diabolo*, 'instigated by the devil', got into an argument with a Carmelite friar and hacked off the friar's hand, for which Ludham was sentenced to life imprisonment in a carcer in Sudbury.

Glossary

Aqua regia – King's water or nitro-hydrochloric acid is a highly corrosive red or yellow acid solution. It was given the name *aqua regia* because it can dissolve the 'royal' metals, gold and platinum. The mixture is formed by freshly mixing concentrated nitric acid and hydrochloric acid. It was used to etch gold.

It was once believed that *aqua regia* was invented by the alchemist Maria Prophetissa or Maria the Jewess who lived around the first century BCE, and whose name lives on in the *bain marie*, which we now use for cooking, but which she invented for chemical experiments in her laboratory. Most people now believe *aqua regia* was in use earlier.

In the Middle Ages, gold was often contaminated with copper, and this would have turned the acid green; in alchemy the process was symbolised by the image of the sun being devoured by the green dragon.

Averer – a beggar who was fit and healthy, but pretended to be sick or maimed to gain sympathy from passers-by or to obtain alms from the Church. Common tricks included sticking on fake boils made from wax or foul tumours fashioned from animal offal, or pretending to be blind or lame.

Cletch – a dialect word that comes from old Norse, meaning a family of young children or chickens, from which the word *clutch* is derived.

488

Coffin of lampreys – a *coffin* was a popular baking method in which the meat was cooked inside a round pastry case, which was designed to set hard as a container in which food was served, but the pastry itself was not eaten. The method was to cut living lampreys and let them bleed, then die in their own blood. The blood was added to cinnamon, pepper, salt, wine and bread soaked in vinegar and cooked until it was a thick gravy. The cleaned lampreys were laid in the coffin in the gravy and covered with pastry. A hole was made in the top, down which the cook blew to raise the lid to a dome. The lampreys were baked in the coffin. The gravy was then removed and recooked with ginger and more wine and the whole thing returned to the coffin to be served hot as 'meat for a lord'.

Comfrey cast – broken limbs were set with casts in Europe from at least the time of the ancient Greeks onwards. To make a cast, a linen or woollen cloth was wrapped round the limb, then soaked in one of several different pastes so that it would set hard. These pastes often included grated comfrey root, which was known to aid healing, but would also include egg white, flour and fat or clay. Since the casts could not bear weight and broke easily, patients were usually confined to bed for many weeks until the bone had healed.

Cooper – a person who makes round casks and barrels of various sizes, shaped with a *bouge*, *bilge*, or *bulge* in the middle. The casks are made from wooden staves bound with hoops or bands. *Barrel* refers to a particular size of cask. The term 'cooper' may come from the Dutch *kūpe*, meaning a basket, wood or tub, or from the Latin *cupa* meaning a vat.

Corrodies – the pension scheme of the Middle Ages. A lay-person would pay a lump sum of money or sign over a parcel of land to a religious house. In return, the monks or nuns would undertake to care for that person when they became aged or infirm, either by housing them in special lodgings within the monastery, or by delivering meals, fuel, clothing and medical treatment to them in their own homes.

Employers would often reward a faithful servant by buying a corrody for them or even promising a corrody in lieu of proper wages. Better-off individuals, such as merchants, would buy one for themselves and their spouses when they were in their prime, as an insurance against their old age. Of course, the corrodian would gamble on living long enough to get back far more than the sum they had originally paid, while the religious houses prayed the corrodians would die quickly, so they could make a profit. Religious houses often used corrodies to raise easy money, only to find themselves crippled by the cost of providing for dozens of elderly people some years later.

Councy – birds such as chickens, partridge and duck were often served *in councy*, which was a spicy egg sauce. It was an easier dish to prepare than stuffing, tinting and dressing the bird in its feathers, therefore recommended for the less artistic cooks. The bird was roasted, then cut into pieces and put into stock, which had been thickened with egg yolks and breadcrumbs and flavoured with cloves, saffron, pepper, cinnamon and ginger. The dish was edged with the chopped whites of hardboiled eggs and crowned with the whole egg yolks.

Dorter – otherwise known as a dormitorium. It was the communal sleeping place of the monks in an abbey or monastery or of the boys being taught in the religious house. In the early Middle Ages, the dorter was a long room in which the monks slept in individual beds, with candles burning constantly through the night to prevent any impropriety and to help them to rise quickly for the midnight offices. Later, the monks' dorter became separated into open cubicles with a walkway down the middle.

Dragon's blood – the name was given to various substances, including gold chloride, but in the Middle Ages it most commonly referred to the red resin that can be obtained from one of several different trees – *Dracaena cinnabari* found in Socotra, *Dracaena draco* from the Canary Islands and the palm *Daemonorops* from Malaysia.

The name *Dracaena* comes from the Greek *drakainia* meaning female dragon. In the first century AD, a Greek sailor records an island called Dioscorida, probably the island of Socotra in Yemen, where dragons lived and trees shed drops of cinnabar. Pliny recounts a legend from India about Brahma and Shiva, in which a dragon bites an elephant and drinks its blood. As the elephant dies, it falls on the dragon, crushing it, and from the intermingling blood springs the dragon's blood tree.

In the Middle Ages, this very costly resin was brought by merchants to the Mediterranean and sold right across Europe. It was believed to have all kinds of healing properties and was considered to have particular potency in alchemy. In later centuries, it was used most commonly as a dye, particularly to stain the wood used to make violins.

There are three grades of dragon's blood resin. The best and most expensive is *Edah amsellah* – meaning tears. The medium grade is *Edah dukkah* – fragments of tears. *Edah mukdebah* – resin-dust and bark melted together into blocks – is the most inferior grade.

Firkin – a wooden barrel or a measure of liquid such as ale. A firkin was nine gallons.

Galbanum – is an aromatic gum resin collected mainly from a Persian plant species, *Ferula gummosa*, which grows in the mountain ranges of northern Iran. The resin is translucent and brown, yellow or greenish-yellow. It has a bitter taste and an intense musky scent. It is mentioned in the Book of Exodus as an ingredient in *Ketoret*, the consecrated incense used in the Temple. Both Hippocrates and Pliny used it medicinally, claiming that a single touch from it could kill a serpent.

Goat-leaf – *Lonicera caprifolium*, otherwise known as goat-leaf honeysuckle, Italian honeysuckle or perfoliate woodbine, not to be confused with English honeysuckle, *Lonicera periclymenum*. Goat-leaf is native to Europe. Since ancient Roman times the seeds have been ground to make ink, and the leaves, which have antibiotic properties, were used to treat sore throats and abscesses. The leaves, fruits and seeds were also employed as a strong laxative or emetic, but since the fruits are poisonous, goat-leaf is rarely used today in Western herbal medicine though it is found as an ingredient in some traditional Chinese medicine.

Limier (French), limer or lymer (English) – were hounds used to locate quarry for the hunt. A good limier is not distracted by other scents and can track silently to avoid alerting the quarry. They would track on a long leash, usually in pairs, with the handler, known as the *valet de limier*, following on foot. When they had harboured (found) the quarry, the huntsmen would release the *running hounds*, or *raches*, to bring it to bay. A limier was a more valuable hound than a rache, so it did not take part in the kill for fear it might get injured, but it would be rewarded with some of the raw meat to keep it keen. Bloodhounds, or their forerunners, were favourites for use as limiers, but other breeds were also used.

Lugh – also written as *Lugus*, was the semi-divine Celtic warrior 'of all skills'. He gave his name to the city of Lugodunum (Lyon) in Gaul. His name is often translated as 'raven' because of the bird's association with battlefields, and Lugh's animal symbols are the raven and the lynx. The raven would bring him warnings of danger and of enemies approaching. In Celtic mythology, Lugh's raven is also associated with power, prophecy and retribution.

Lugh was celebrated at the summer feast of Lughnasad, meaning the Assembly of Lugh, to ensure good harvests. In order to reign, Lugh had first to kill his grandfather Baal, whose feast, Beltane, is in May. Lugh traditionally kills Baal with a stone hurled from a sling, which knocks his only eye out through the back of his head. Lughnasad later became the Christian festival of Lammas, or loaf-mass, the day harvesting began, and the loaf baked from the first sheaf of grain to be cut was brought to the church. Even today, bread shaped like a wheat-sheaf is still often used as the centrepiece in harvest festivals in churches.

Metheglin – an alcoholic beverage that was popular in Anglo-Saxon times. Like mead, it was made by fermenting honey and water, but metheglin was flavoured with herbs. In winter it was often served warm, which made a soothing drink against the cold. It gradually went out of fashion in the Middle Ages, though was still drunk in country areas, especially in households that kept their own beehives.

Moon plants – in the Middle Ages it was believed that dew was the sap from the moon that fell on the earth. Several plants were linked to the moon and were used in magic to aid lucid-dreaming and for divination. These included the *moon poppy*, which was pale pink, or the *white marsh poppy*, which had hallucinogenic properties. Another moon plant is *lunarie*, or *Lunaria biennis*, better known these days as honesty. The generic name *Lunaria* comes from *luna* meaning moon, because of the papery, silver-white discs that form its seedpods. The third moon plant mentioned in the novel is *moonwort*, a fern credited with having great magical powers, including the ability to open locks, draw out nails and pull the iron shoes off horses' hoofs if they accidentally stood on the fern. It was also thought to have the power to change mercury into silver.

None – during the course of the monastic day, a series of offices were sung at specific times and people labouring in the fields or workshops would have marked the passing of the hours by hearing the bells ring out, summoning monks and nuns to the prayers. The times of the services varied between different orders of monks and between winter (mid-September to Easter) and summer.

The typical monastic day began at midnight with the Nocturns, that is Matins and Lauds, followed by Prime at daybreak. Terce succeeded the morning Mass, which was conducted after breakfast, with Sext at noon. None took place about three o'clock, then Vespers at six, and finally Compline, after which the monks would be sprinkled with holy water as they processed out to go to their dorter to sleep, which would be around seven thirty p.m. in winter and eight thirty in summer.

Many laws governing the laity were linked to these offices. For example, it was illegal for the poor to go out gleaning in the fields before the Prime bell had rung.

Pipkin – a small earthenware pot used for cooking, which in poorer households could be transferred straight to the table for everyone to dig their spoons into.

Prepositus – means *leading man*. These men were employed by a lord or bishop to oversee and manage their properties, which might include lands, manors, castles, villages or towns. They also presided over the local courts. In Anglo-Saxon times they were known as reeves, but after the Norman Conquest they were given the Latin title *prepositus*. The term *ballivus* was also used in towns, suggesting they had authority over an area or bailiwick. In English *ballivus* became *bailiff*, which was the title most ordinary townsfolk would have used for them. Eventually the bailiff was replaced with an elected mayor.

Raven's head – otherwise known as *caput mortuum,* was the alchemical symbol of nigredo, the black death and putre-faction. The bird's head is often depicted either floating inside a glass flask or as the stopper to the flask. It symbol-ises the human terror of death, utter despair and the process of putrefaction whereby the body is reduced to a black slime.

495

Ravens have long been associated with death and destruction as they were frequently seen feeding on the corpses of the slain on battlefields. But the Norse god Odin had two ravens – Huginn, Thought, and Muninn, Memory – who flew across the world to bring him news. It is said he believed that one day the birds would not return to him, and of the two birds, the one he feared losing most was Memory.

Sea-swine – now known as the porpoise, it was considered a 'dainty blubber' in the Middle Ages and much preferred to seal or whale. The clergy in the Middle Ages called it *porco-marino*. It was often served as a savoury pudding in which the blood and fat of the porpoise were mixed with oatmeal, salt, pepper and ginger, then boiled in the beast's intestine. Seal, whale, porpoise and beaver tails were all deemed 'fish' by the ecclesiastical authorities so, with ordinary fish and shellfish, could be eaten on fast days and during Lent, when meat was forbidden.

Seven Whistlers – a superstition found in all parts of Britain. The seven birds are believed to be lost or wandering human souls whose piercing cries warn of death and disaster. In some parts of the country, the superstition is that they are six birds seeking a seventh, and when they find it, the world will end. Several different birds with a plaintive, eerie cry are thought to be the Seven Whistlers, especially the curlew, but also plovers, whimbrels and widgeon.

Sailors believed the Seven Whistlers were the souls of drowned men warning of a storm that would wreck the ship. Soldiers thought they predicted a battle in which many would die, and as late as 1855 a newspaper carried a report that miners on their way to work turned back, because they had heard the Seven Whistlers. All the miners in that colliery flatly refused to go down the mine that day, even though it meant losing a day's pay, saying the birds were warning of a mining disaster and they knew of men who had ignored such warnings and been killed.

Shuck – or black shuck, was a shape-shifting beast or demon, which would appear as a large shaggy black dog, with enormous, glowing, fiery eyes. The creature most frequently took the form of a spectral dog, but could also appear as a black goat or calf. The name *shuck* comes from the old English *scucca* meaning *devil* or *fiend*. In latter centuries the black shuck has come to be regarded as an omen of death. But in earlier centuries it more often appeared as a warning or as a guardian. In some accounts it was said to have saved the person's life by blocking their way on a road, causing them to turn back and preventing them walking into unseen danger.

Soap – soft soap, made from mutton or goat fat, soda and potash or wood ash, was in use in Britain from the ninth or tenth centuries onwards. It quickly went rancid and was quite caustic. The Arabs perfected hard soap made from olive oil, soda, lime juice and sweet-smelling herbs. It was made mainly in the olive-growing countries such as Spain; hence it was known as Castile soap. It was imported into Britain from the twelfth century, though it was obviously a luxury item found only in the wealthier households.

Still room – most great medieval manors and castles in Europe had a still room or separate building where herbs were prepared for use in medicines, perfumes or cosmetics.

The still room functioned as the pharmacy for the household and all those employed in the manor. In the still room they also made distillations of roses, mint, lavender or bergamot to perfume candles, furniture polish and the water in the lavers used by all to rinse their hands before and after every meal. The still room was managed by the lady of the house, assisted by her daughters and trained still-room maids. It was vital that the mistress of the house should have the means to treat the sick and injured, both in war and peacetime, especially when the nearest physician or monastic infirmary might be several days' ride away.

Tantine – meaning 'Auntie'. The girls in the Ricey-Bas inn address the tavern owner as *Tantine*. They might have been her real nieces, as Vincent innocently presumes, but equally it was common for female brothel-keepers to claim that the girls in their houses were their nieces and to be addressed as 'auntie' by them, in an attempt to avoid being charged with keeping a disorderly house.

Tatterfoal – many tracks and roads in the east of England, particularly in the fenlands, were said to be haunted after dark by the tatterfoal, a rough-coated horse with glowing eyes, from which an eerie blue light emanated. It was said to make the sound of rattling chains or a coffin lid opening and was believed to be a malicious goblin, able to change its shape at will. It terrified anyone foolish enough to venture along the road at night, driving travellers into bogs, drowning children and causing horses carrying riders to bolt. In other areas, it was known as the Shag, Shagfoal, Brash or Hedley Kow.

Unguentum basilicon – an unguent or ointment that heats the skin and is used to draw out pus and infected material from wounds. It was made by melting beeswax, pine resin, suet and Greek pitch in oil. The more expensive version also contained turpentine, frankincense and myrrh and was known as greater basilicon, while the basic version was known as lesser basilicon.

Wren – many of the names given to the wren in European languages make reference to the bird as king. In Latin it was called *regulus*, in French *reytelet* or *roi des oiseaux* meaning 'king of the birds', and in Swedish *kungs fogel* or 'the king's bird'. In German it was known as *Zaunkönig* (hedge king) and *Schneekönig* (snow king), and in Dutch, *Konije* meaning 'little king'.

The ritual of the hunting of the wren in midwinter culminated in the bird being beaten to death, then processed from house to house on a decorated bier or hanging from a wheel on the end of a long pole, before being solemnly buried. There are a dozen different legends to explain this custom, many involving the idea that the wren's shrill cry betrayed a hunted man to his enemies. For example, one legend says the wren's call warned St Stephen's captors that he was escaping, and another version tells how the wren led the Roman soldiers to Christ in the Garden of Gethsemane. These legends may have arisen from the Christian belief that the wren was the messenger to the pagan druids, whom the early Christians in northern Europe regarded as enemies of the Church.

But the origins of the wren hunt are almost certainly pre-Christian, dating back at least to the ancient Celts, if not earlier, when the wren, as the scientific name, *Troglodytes*

troglodytes, suggests, was thought to be a cave-dweller, a bird of the underworld, as it often nests in tombs and holes. The wren represented the god of the underworld and of winter and darkness, and the king of winter had to be ritually killed in order to allow spring and light to return to the land.